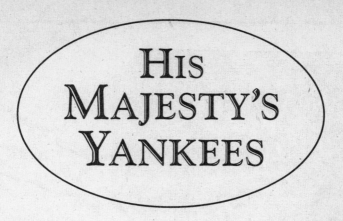

His Majesty's Yankees

Thomas H. Raddall

NIMBUS
PUBLISHING LTD

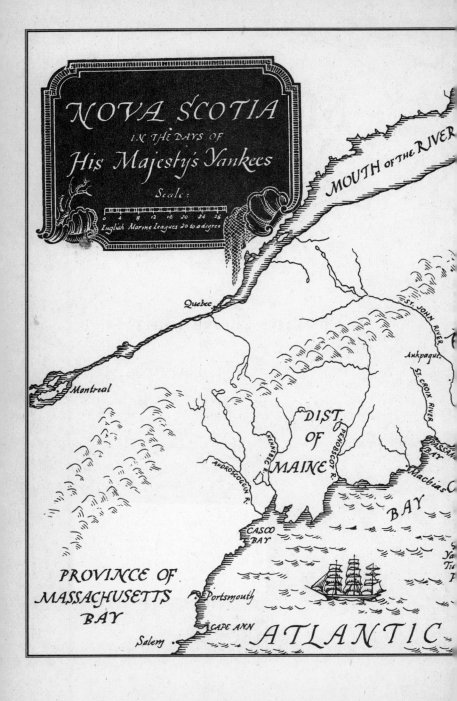

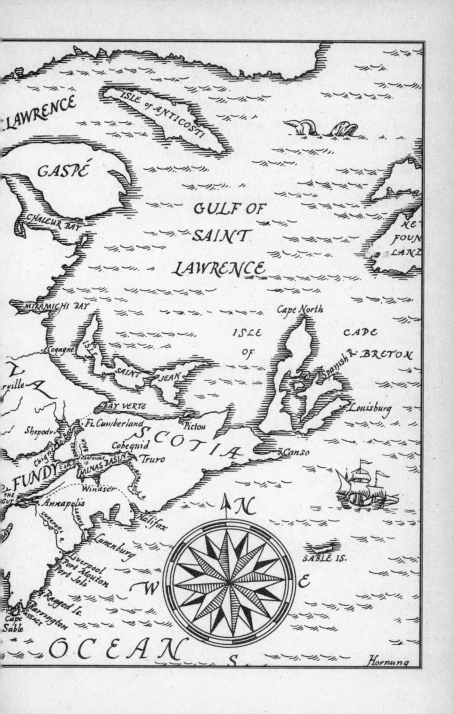

Nimbus Publishing Limited
PO Box 9301, Station A
Halifax, NS B3K 5N5
(902) 455-4286

Cover design: Arthur B. Carter, Halifax
Printed and bound in Canada

Canadian Cataloguing in Publication Data
Raddall, Thomas H., 1903-1994.
His Majesty's Yankees
(Nimbus classics)
ISBN 1-55109-195-X
I. Title.   II. Series.
PS8535.A27H5 1997   C813'.54   C96-950207-9
PR9199.3.R23H5 1997

This book is
for my son.

AUTHOR'S NOTE

The author's thanks are due to all those friends in Nova Scotia, New Brunswick, and Maine who assisted in gathering the historical material for this book, with especial gratitude to Dr. D.C. Harvey, who granted the full facilities of the Public Archives of Nova Scotia, and to Dr. James Martell and Miss Margaret Ells of the Archives staff, who offered valuable suggestions and read the manuscript in addition to their generous help in the collection of material.

CONTENTS

CHAPTER 1

In Which I Go Ahunting

I SAT with young François, Peter Dekatha's son, in the huckleberry
bushes, peering into the morning mist. There had been a sharp frost in
the night, and the wild grass and cranberry vines of the old beaver
meadow were white as if snow had fallen. We had rolled out of our
blankets and crept, wordless and foodless, to our posts at the fringe of
the little pine knoll. Peter Dekatha, the cunning old hunter, would
permit no sound—indeed no movement beyond the cautious reprim-
ing of our muskets. Our small fire of twigs had died in the night; there
was no reek of smoke to betray us, and our human scent was killed by
the frosty air. We could hear the big bull coming to Peter's call. He
was striking his horns against trees, smashing his way through under-
brush, uttering a deep coughing "*Waugh!*" at almost every step, and
the sounds rang enormous in the silence of the ridges. He sounded like
all the bull moose in the world. I felt my flesh creep and told myself
it was the cold that made me shiver so. But it was what our hunters
call buck fever, and I knew it, and young François knew it, watching
me from the corner of one black, shining eye. Peter Dekatha knew it,
too, though his back was turned. He stood in the shadow of a big pine
trunk, twenty feet away, staring into the mist.

The knoll was a small island in the soggy meadow. Fifty yards away
flowed the brook, deep and black and silent, which drained the
meadow and a chain of others like it in the trough of the hardwood
ridges, going back for miles. We could not see the brook, for its water
smoked after the night's frost, and thick rolls of white vapor hung over
the open, thinning and gathering mysteriously in the still air. My
father's gun, the gun of Louisburg, lay heavy across my cramped knees,
its brown metal gleaming with dew; his great gift to me for my seventeenth birthday and my first moose hunt with the Indians. I wondered
how François felt. He was about my own age, the son of Peter Dekatha
by a Micmac woman. In François's veins mingled the blood of deadly
enemies, for Peter Dekatha was part white and mostly Mohawk—one
of the half-breeds who formed the rank and file of my father's old
corps, Gorham's Rangers. Between Mohawk and Micmac there had

been no love in the time gone by. Peter had the thin high beak of the
Mohawks and was tall, but François took after his Micmac mother in
looks and speech, with a round Micmac face and the broad Micmac
nose and a fall of lank black hair about his shoulders. Peter was proud
of his drop of white blood and kept his hair in a queue and in the
settlement wore shoes and homespun. But here in the woods we all
were dressed in soft caribou-hide hunting shirts and breeches, with
leather fringes dangling along the seams, and moccasins of moose hide
—the tough hide of the foreknee—and caps of raccoon fur with glossy
tails behind. Molly, Peter's squaw, who was one of our house servants
and lived in a hut by the mill brook in Liverpool, had made these
hunting garments.

The big bull smashed his way toward us for an age that was probably
ten minutes. But when he came to the edge of the open he hesitated
warily and whined. He wanted the cow to come to him, to risk the
open herself; there is no chivalry in an old bull. But the cow, who was
Peter Dekatha, made neither move nor sound. There is no silence like
the death quiet of our Nova Scotia woods on a frosty fall morning.
Southward where the brook trickled over a ledge in a neck of woods
we could hear its water, a good mile. Somewhere in the mist a chicka-
dee wakened, then another, and another, and their small bird voices
pierced the silence like sharp little knives. A pair of meat jays came to
us, flitting like small gray ghosts from branch to branch, inspecting us
with bright, inquisitive eyes. Peter frowned up at them, but I thought
how much worse a pair of blue jays would have been. Blue jays would
have set up a screeching to warn the woods for miles.

Daylight was growing. Soon the sun must break over the pine tops
to the east and burn off the mist. That would give us a clear view, but
it would make the big bull more wary than ever. I could make out
two or three of the sickly hackmatacks that stood in the meadow, like
shadows at first, then clearly. Peter put the birch-bark horn to his
mouth. I have done much moose hunting since and heard many cunning callers—have called moose myself, come to that; but I have never
heard a man imitate a cow moose as Peter Dekatha could.

He began with a high, faint, nasal whine, the whine that most human ears miss in the call of the cow, and then came down the scale,
pouring forth sound as the note deepened until the hollow bark was
roaring and vibrating in his hand, and ending with a long, windy sigh
that was half cough and half grunt. He began all this with the horn
pointed upward and toward the invisible bull, swaying his head gently
and turning slowly as his voice deepened, and swaying the horn wider

and wider, and lower and lower, until his stooping body was moving
violently from side to side. When he uttered the great final sigh his
back was toward the bull across the meadow, and the horn's mouth
barely cleared the gnarled pine roots at his feet. The sound went echoing from ridge to ridge—*eeee-OOOOoooo-awwrrr!*—like a far-scat-
tered procession of lonely cows, and died in the silence of distant
Bewtagook Woods.

Again silence, but not for long. There was a tremendous splash from
the mist over the brook. My heart thumped the breath out of me. It
amazed me to realize how quietly the moose, that great, ungainly
creature, can move when he so chooses. The big bull had crossed two
hundred yards of wild meadow without a squelch, without a whisper
of grass stalks, until the brook crossed his path, too deep to wade and
too wide to jump. He must have hesitated a moment before making
the plunge but now he was across, and we could hear every splattering
step. The buck fever rattled my young teeth. I looked down at the
gun of Louisburg to reassure myself. Cautious Peter had forbidden me
to cock it until he gave me leave. Seen from above like this, the brown
gun hammer looked exactly what the Micmacs called it, *ab-oog-wo-ku-
jeech,* "the little thigh," and it seemed to cry out for a leap. The bull's
footsteps came on in the mist, cautiously, halting from time to time,
but nearer always. I looked at Peter and François, rigid as rock, Peter
against the pine trunk, François crouched in the huckleberries, staring
into the vapor. Their own guns leaned against trees. I was to kill my
first moose alone.

Now the mist seemed to roll like a wave of the sea, and out of that
wave loomed a mighty figure, black and shapeless. The bull's long legs
were swathed in the ground vapor; his great body seemed to swim
toward me, high and enormous to my startled eyes, for I sat on the
ground. I jumped up, with cramp pains twanging every cord in my
legs. I do not remember cocking the gun; I heard it click, and then I
was squinting wildly along a barrel that seemed to reach out and touch
the great dark object in the mist. I squeezed the trigger and saw the
pan guard jump as the hammer came down, and the sparks of the
flint and then the quick light flare of the priming. Then that awful
two seconds of waiting and holding which was to come to me many
times afterward. At last the leap in my hands, the blow at the shoulder,
the spurt of red fire from the long muzzle, and the black smoke rolling
out into the mist, and the shot echoing far and far and dying at last
amongst the ridges like distant thunder. The discharge seemed to blow

away the mist for a space. It blew off my buck fever, too, and I was glad. I do not like buck fever.

The big bull stood in the open, at not more than twelve paces, staring at me with fierce and enormous eyes. His head was up and carried a mighty tree of horns. The palms of those horns were brown and hard and dew-wet, shining in a shaft of sunshine through the upper mist, and under his chin dangled the queer hairy ornament we call the bell, a good twelve inches, maybe more. A mighty moose, a king of moose —and mine.

All this, which takes so long to write, so many scratches of my poor quill, passed in a count of twelve. Dimly I heard Peter Dekatha crying out and François's movement in the bushes. They could not see the great beast. The miraculous opening had appeared for me, and me alone; and I stood there with the gun half lowered, the muzzle smoking still, waiting for the bull to spread his feet and drop, as moose drop always in the hunters' tales. In my great glow of fatuous pride I stood there and did nothing. Peter and François came crashing toward me like bears in the huckleberries, and the big moose turned his head to the sound. Then, amazingly, he wheeled and was off, running like a horse. The vapor swallowed him. I listened for the returning splash in the brook, but no splash came. He followed the brook until he reached the woods below, and there was no more sound, not even the crack of a twig.

Peter Dekatha came to me, swearing in Mohawk, Micmac, and English. I knew no Mohawk, and in moments of excitement Peter's English was too broken for quick understanding. But Micmac was my second tongue, and in that you can say much in a few words.

"By God-the-maker," he screeched, "thou art no son of Pe-poog-wess. Thy mother has played him false with fools. There was a fool at thy begetting!"

The corners of his yelling mouth frothed, and his face and eyes were cruel. He had thrown aside the calling horn and his lean hands were half raised, the fingers hooked like claws, as if to tear me to pieces. I was afraid, but his words touched an unsuspected spring in me as savage as his own. At seventeen I stood nearly six feet and had my father's hands if nothing else. I dropped the gun and struck that dark contorted face a violent buffet of my fist and followed forward, hurling my whole body, clutching at his lean, stringy throat and crying out strange foul things I had learned in boyhood from the drunken Indians who came to town with furs. Peter clawed at me, nothing loath, screeching and spitting like a trapped lynx, and we fell together and rolled through the bushes and into the open, crushing the wet marsh grass. His claws raked my cheek, and I tasted the salt of my own blood; but I kept my hold on his throat and whenever in our squirming I came on top I tried to batter his head against the grass humps. He attempted to sink his teeth in my wrist—his bared fangs that were long and yellowed as the chisel teeth of a porcupine; but now François stood over us, kicking us ineffectually with his moccasined toes, and finally he drew his ramrod and belabored us both, cruelly, giving the rod the full swing of his arm. We hung on for a time, but under that rain of strokes our flesh ached and screamed, and at last we crawled apart, gasping abuse at him and at each other. Peter would have leaped at his own son then, but François flung the rod aside and drew the hatchet from his belt, swinging it suggestively. So Peter sat on his heels and plucked viciously at the grass. I had come to my knees a few feet away, breathing hard and astonished at myself and them. We were like three savages of hostile tribes, chance-met in the woods. We remained in those queer attitudes a long time, like wary dogs, each unwilling to make the first move. Peter kept plucking at the grass. At last he looked up at me.

"I spoke with a forked tongue," he said in Micmac. "Thou art a true son of Pe-poog-wess."

"And my mother?"

"The true mate of Pe-poog-wess. Thou knowest I meant not what I said."

"*Weltaak*," I grunted. ["It sounds well."]

"We are fools together," Peter went on. "To shoot without aiming, to speak without thinking, that is one foolishness."

"The fault was mine."

"It was mine, Pe-poog-wess-a-jeech."

My heart glowed then—when Peter Dekatha called me Young Hawk. The Micmacs had called my father Hawk—Pe-poog-wess— since the days when he and his rangers fought them up and down the length of Nova Scotia. So I had come to manhood and had a name. I had fought with Peter Dekatha, hand to throat, and held my own. It was no playful wrestle, there in the wild grass. In that quick flare of passion the savage old hunter would have killed me if he could. I knew it, and so did he. He was quiet now, muttering as if to himself—but in Micmac so François and I would understand. "Youth . . . youth . . . the young man comes into strength . . . the strength runs out of the old . . . the young man is proud . . . the old ashamed. But whose is the shame? Surely the young man's. Him I have taught the wisdom of the forest, which is not to be learned in houses, yet he has forgotten. Hawk was a chief among men; he was proud; he was wise. Young Hawk is still downy-winged; he is vain; he screams at the eagle. That is the way of the young."

"The young man is ashamed," I said angrily, "not for his blows, nor his words. He is ashamed that he failed with his father's gift. That is a great shame. Why dost thou sit and talk, Old One? Let us find the moose. I must quench my shame in his blood."

"*We-la-boog-we*," grunted François. ["These are good words."]

Peter Dekatha's lip curled, like a leaf with a worm in it gone twisted and brown. "There has been ill fortune . . . not a calm morning for calling until this day . . . and what befalls? . . . Besides, there is no food since yesterday."

"Now," I cried, "I know thou art truly old. It is for young men to hunt on empty bellies."

He leaped up at that, and I thought he would strike me; but he uttered a torrent of Mohawk and Micmac, crying that he could out-suffer either of us, and we should see. He ran to the pine where his musket leaned and ran off along a path that the wandering moose had worn deep in the edge of the meadow. The open was full of sunshine now, and the mist gone. Already an air stirred the green-gray moss beards on the small swamp spruces; soon the day wind would be blow-ing from the west, and then we must hunt upwind. Peter was heading straight east. I wanted to yell my objections. I was sure I had hit the big bull. There would be a blood trail and certainly tracks in the frost of the meadow. But an angry Indian is past reason, so I said nothing; we must run at his heels till the frenzy went.

So we ran in file, swift and silent in our moccasins. The meadow was fringed by thin clumps of hackmatack and mop-headed black spruce—nothing else would grow in the soggy soil—and soon we came to a black-spruce swamp which thrust its narrow length a mile back into the upland. Moose love that sort of cover, and our path followed it, firm and dry after the summer heat. It was good going and soon it was perfect, for the path swung up into the pine woods, a brown rib-bon, beaten bare, with a scatter of moose dung like grapeshot every few yards. It climbed out of the shadow and silence of the pines to the sunny green-and-gold of a hardwood ridge, where Peter Dekatha halted and leaned, panting, against a tree. He stared up at a tall poplar whose upper leaves stirred faintly, marking the wind, and reasoned aloud in a harsh whisper thus: "The big bull is wise, but the call is too much for his wisdom. He is saved when young man fires too soon. Big

Bull is scared and runs without thinking, but in the trees at the foot of the meadow his wisdom returns. He feels the sun on his horns, and soon comes the morning wind, which blows his scent into the sun. To get back—to get back to the cow in the sun, she whom he left for the strange new call. But there is the brook, wide and deep to the river, and there is the long meadow. That is the danger path. Better to seek the west ridge and follow it north across the wind, like a shadow under the bright leaves, until the meadow is passed, and the brook small. *Ayah!* This way he must come."

"He has come and gone. He is passed," grunted François testily.

"There is an ill fortune upon our hunting, and it may be that he has passed. Still, we shall wait."

I began to grumble that we should have sought a blood trail in the meadow, but Peter snarled, "*Ankodum* [Look out]!" So we separated, each taking post where he could see well to the front and to right and left. The hardwood ridge was quite broad, and several game trails followed it. I stood beside one in the shade of a sugar maple, where my musket leaned, and stared to the south. I was angry and sore in flesh besides. I expected nothing and saw nothing. The sun climbed. The morning wind rustled the leaves softly. The maples had begun to turn, but the leaves would not be at full color till the October moon. I thought how that brightness in the hardwoods every fall gave the Indians their love for such colors in dress. Then I saw the big bull. As quick as that. Like a shadow under the stirring leaves he came slowly along the game path, pausing from time to time to swing his great nostrils to the cross wind. I aimed the gun of Louisburg carefully, steadying the long barrel against the maple trunk. The head shot? Too uncertain. This time I must be sure. The breast shot? That would send the ball plowing the length of his body cavity, splattering the meat with the contents of his guts. The Indians would not mind that, but I did. I waited. Suddenly he threw up his head toward my right, scenting François on the young wind. He turned cautiously for a run back the way he had come—and gave me the sure shot behind the fore-shoulder. The gun jumped in my hands, and in the gust and eddy of black smoke I saw him give a mighty leap and fall in the bushes. I ran to him whooping, first in the shrill yip-yapping dog fashion of the Micmacs, and then in the harsh scream of Gorham's Rangers, the old Mohawk yell my father had taught me. When the others ran up I was down on my knees with my hunting knife, stabbing the big throat vein to bleed the meat and laughing like the pleased child I was. One of the shining brown palms of his mighty horns bore the fresh groove of a bullet, the mark of my wild shot in the meadow, but I cared nothing for that now. He was mine, this great bull, and I had killed him with my father's gift.

We butchered him at once, slitting down the belly first and pulling out the steaming mass of guts in a heap about our moccasins. We breathed the strong reek of it as we worked, and I had to turn and spit frequently. Soon we were blood to the elbows, with dark clots spattered all over our long leggings and shirts. We junked the carcass into its four quarters with the hide on, for better carrying, and when that was done the Indians made a fire and roasted the big dark liver on a stick and ate it like gluttons. I could eat none, for all my hunger. I wanted to retch but fought it down for the sake of my pride. Peter and François lay in the warm September sunshine with closed eyes, belching comfortably.

A full belly improved Peter's temper, for he said a little grudgingly, "Now I know thee were born lucky, Pe-poog-wess-a-jeech. It was ordained that this bull should die at thy hands."

"To be a son of The Hawk is to be born lucky," I snapped, for the insult rankled.

"True, Young Hawk." Peter Dekatha opened an eye in the seamed brown face and regarded me. "And thou hast his spirit, which made him terrible to the Meeg-a-mahg people and the Wenjoo [the French]. *Heugh!* Verily he was The Hawk in those days. But the young one has much to learn. The young one must learn to keep hold on that spirit."

"That will come," I returned boldly, squatting on my gory moccasin heels and staring at him across the fire. He rose to hands and knees and spat in the scuffled earth, and stirred the spittle to a thin mud with his forefinger.

"Oh, Young One," he said softly, "I see trouble for thee in the time to come, and pain. Thou shalt have need of thy father's spirit then."

I was amused—Peter Dekatha poking into my future with his dirty finger!

"What else dost thou see, Old One?"

"War."

I looked up at him, surprised. "War, Old One? How can that be? The Wenjoo have gone from this country forever." How often I had heard my father say that—peace, peace forever in our America, now that the bloody-minded French were gone. My father hated the French as he hated the Indians who fought for them, a powerful and abiding hate. But all that was past, and best forgotten.

Peter wiped his finger on his greasy leggings, absently. "War. Blood. I smell it."

I arose, laughing. "You smell the blood and guts of my bull, Old One. Come! We have a long carry to the canoe with this meat."

He grumbled, "If Young Hawk had been wise at the meadow this meat would lie forty steps from the canoe. Let us rest awhile, for the day is hot already, and we shall sweat greatly."

They slept by the faint wisp of the fire, snoring together, and to pass the time I walked to the tall sugar maple and cut a blaze to mark the killing of my big bull. And with the point of my knife I carved into the live wood:

DAVID STRANG
SEPT. 30, 1774

CHAPTER 2

Home-coming

WE CAME DOWN the river in Peter's big canoe, made for hunting about the windy lakes at the head of our river. It was more than twenty feet long and nearly four feet in the beam, with a strong spruce frame and ribs, and covered with bark of the canoe birch, sewn into place with tough spruce roots. Peter had made one concession to the white man's way of doing things; he had tarred the seams instead of using balsam. Balsam must be renewed often on a rough journey—and on our Nova Scotia rivers all journeys are rough. The black seams made a queer patchwork of the white bark, but this canoe was better than anything the Micmacs made. It held easily all three of us, and the meat of the big bull, and our guns and blankets.

We had to portage around the long rapids which white hunters call Big Falls. The Indians hated carrying and would rather take any water risk; but the river was so low after the summer's drought that the V-shaped piles of stones at the foot of the rapids showed clear and dry. The Micmacs had caught eels here in their fall migration ever since the time of Gluskap, the kindly god of the Micmacs who pro-

vided them with all things and then went away to the Land of the
Sunset. They called these rapids Mes-ne-sa-wa-nook (big-fish-weir-
place). In a week or two they would come to set up a fence of brushwood in the stone Vs, ready for the rains and the seaward rush of
eels which happened always in the dark of the October moon. One
family already had a wigwam pitched on the ancient camp ground at
the foot of the rapids, and we gave them meat for the pot and lay on
the grass while our sweat cooled.

Peter Dekatha had the Mohawk's contempt for Algonquins of any
sort, and the old wars in Nova Scotia had given him a special dislike
of the Micmacs, though he had married a Micmac woman and bred a
Micmac son. As we sprawled on the grass and drew forth our little
black clays and tobacco, and François brought a coal from the fire,
nipped between a couple of chips, Peter grumbled to me, "See these
shiftless people! The French spoiled them with gifts in wartime and
now they would rather beg than hunt. The brass pot on the fire—
how many furs did that cost, suppose thou? In the old time the woman
dug clay from the riverbank and mixed it with fine gravel, so that the
pot might not crack in the firing, and molded the thing in her hands
and put the magic marks on it with a sharp stick and cords and baked
it in the fire. It broke at a blow—*these* never made strong pots like
the Mohawk people—and thee can mark a Micmac camping place by
the litter of broken shards; but it was easy to make another and it cost
nothing but a woman's time, which is worth nothing. Now they must
have a brass pot, which must be paid for by a man's hunting. That
makes a woman of a man, seest thou? Heugh!" He spat.

I smiled and smoked. I had been smoking for a year now, to my
mother's disgust, and my clay bowl shone black and beautiful. I was
happy. My one regret was that the head of my bull with its mighty
horns had been left behind as worthless. François had sliced off the
muffle for supper, that was all. But we had the big carcass anyhow,
and I would make gifts of meat to my father's friends and boast a
little of my prowess.

The sky was high and the dark blue of fall, and the west wind
hustled woolly fine-weather clouds across it and rustled the leaves of
the oaks about the camping place. Fall is the best time in our Nova
Scotia. Spring is long and dreary; summer is fine but gone too soon,
and winter is winter; but fall is the good time, the long, fine time
between August and December, with clear sunshine, and cool winds
to stir the blood, and just enough rain to fill the millstreams for the
work before winter.

The Micmac woman called us to the pot, and we squatted about it and scalded our fingers plucking out the steaming chunks of meat. Satisfied, we lay back on the grass, wiping mouths on sleeves and hands on our buckskins, and the woman brought water which we drank one after another. Then, timidly, she went to the pot and ate our leavings.

The Micmac man wanted powder. Peter and François lied easily, saying how they had run short in their hunting, but I was feeling generous on my full belly and emptied my powder horn into his. It was my father's, a big ox horn polished and carved with his totem, the hawk, and the Micmac regarded it respectfully, though I knew he thought me a fool for my charity. We left without words, except that as Peter Dekatha carefully pushed off the canoe, the Micmac man called after me, "*Ah-de-o-ne-dup* [Good-by, comrade]"—in the bastard French-Micmac patois that all his people spoke.

Peter growled to me, "Since when is a son of Hawk comrade to these sons of dogs?"

"Thee mated with a bitch then?" I taunted, and François, at the bow paddle, giggled over his shoulder.

"A man must have a woman and must take what he finds. That is a truth which shall come to thee one day, Pe-poog-wess-a-jeech. Thy tongue is sharp. It were better for thee to keep it sheathed until thy claws are grown."

'Twas a temptation to remind him that my claws had been a match for his, back there in the meadow, but I held my peace for a wonder.

At sunset we came to the place we call The Falls, at the head of tidewater, two miles above Liverpool. There was a low wooden dam, a sawmill on each bank, and a few small houses in clearings. The mills were silent for lack of water. We carried around the end of the dam and found the tide high, reaching almost to the dam's footing. Below The Falls our river runs wide for a mile and then narrows with a tall and gloomy pine wood on one hand and a point of birch trees on the other. The Micmacs call that place Kebek, a name they give to any narrows where a river joins the tide. Beyond it lies our town of Liverpool.

We paddled through the narrows into the broad tidal pool and found the town and the masts of its ships ashine in the sunset. Wood smoke rose blue from the chimneys, the smoke of supper fires, peaceful and inviting, all around the southern shore of the pool, a straggling procession of one-and-a-half-story houses with clapboard sides or shingled sides, and steep shingled roofs with little dormers jutting out, and big central chimneys, in the New England fashion. Some houses were whitewashed, and the homes of the well to do were painted—but these were few, and mostly merchants like James Bingay; and there were many log huts in the outskirts, the homes of fishermen and other poor folk. But there was a notable exception in the northern outskirt, where our laden canoe now approached a good-sized two-story house with brown painted clapboards and a gambrel roof, which overlooked a small stone wharf and wooden warehouse from a grassy knoll above the water. This was my home, and the schooner at the wharf was my father's *Jolly Nan*.

So my brothers were home again, and it would be a family gathering; Mark, who was master of the *Nan*, Luke, who was his mate, John, who had no taste for the sea and was my father's clerk, and I—who had no taste for anything but roaming in the woods. A house of men, now that I was seventeen and a man.

We ran the canoe alongside the *Nan* and carried our meat across her deck to the wharf.

I pointed to a hindquarter. "Thine, Old One."

"That is too large a gift, Pe-poog-wess-a-jeech," said Peter Dekatha meekly. "If thee must give, let it be a forequarter."

I wanted to laugh. The shadow of our house was for Peter the shadow of my father. He had for my father a queer mixture of fear and respect and idolatry, rooted in the wild past, when they served together in Gorham's Rangers.

"A hindquarter!" I snapped as harshly as my young voice would allow.

Peter shrugged and padded off toward his small hut by the mill brook, François behind with the guns and paddles; and after a time Molly came down, a little brown ghost, and began to tug at the great hairy shank of my gift.

I had managed to shoulder a hindquarter but I dropped it now and came back. "Let me, little mother." I was fond of Molly.

She looked at the ground. "It is not good that a man should carry meat."

I tell you I swelled when she said that. I had killed and was a man and a lord before women. It is no easy trick to swing upon your back the hindquarter of a bull moose, nor to carry it up a steep, grassy field in the uncertain dusk of a September evening; but I managed it and forced myself to breathe evenly, though it nigh burst my lungs. I set the meat down where the alders screened Peter's hut—I could not let him and François see me toting meat for a woman—and turned to go. Molly caught my buckskin sleeve—the sleeve she herself had made.

"O, Young One, thou hast thy father's eye and his bones, but in thy body is the soft heart of thy mother. *Welaalin* [I give thee thanks]."

I snatched my arm away and stalked off, displeased at that word "soft," but feeling magnificent, and I went whistling to the wharf and shouldered the other hindquarter and staggered with it to my mother's kitchen. She was there, the quiet dark-haired mother, shorter than any of her great-boned sons, just lighting the evening candles, and at sight of me she flung the spill into the hearth and ran to me crying, "Davy, Davy boy!" I dropped the meat on her clean floor and hugged her, laughing; her eyes were bright, and she took my face in her hands and kissed me hard on the mouth as a girl might kiss a sweetheart and said, "Oh, Davy, I'm so proud." That was music.

The kitchen was the heart and belly of our house. We had a parlor to be sure, as became the house of the town's founder, a long room full of stiff, uncomfortable furniture surrounded by a fancy landscape wallpaper, a great extravagance in our poor town, that Mark had brought from France on one of his trading voyages. But we never used the parlor except when the preacher called or some of the merchants and their ladies came for talk and a dish of tea. And just so, we never used the maple-wainscoted chamber which my mother fondly called her sitting room. We ate and lived in the kitchen, the scene of my earliest memories, and no other part of the house ever seemed home to me barring my small bedchamber under the eaves. Our Liverpool was still a new and struggling settlement then, with little time and less money for social graces; even the merchants lived simply. God knows I am not one to cant about the homely virtues of poverty now that I am no longer poor and young, but it seems to me our town was a good place to live in, then. All that came after, while it gave some ease to the hard life, and some gaiety and polish, brought first and foremost bloodshed and suffering and bitterness.

We sat about the long board, my father at the head, my mother at the foot, Mark and Luke on one side, John and I on the other. It was the first time since spring that we had all sat down together, for Mark and Luke had spent the summer fishing on the Banks, and Father had made voyages to Halifax and to Boston about his affairs. Fish chowder is a dish I love, and the smell of it, all through the house, had watered my mouth while I put off my filthy hunting dress and got into small-clothes and shirt and waistcoat after washing away the grime of ten days' hunting and hovering over fires.

Joanna, the young Dutch bound-girl, ladled chowder into our dishes in great juicy heaps; and while the steam rose like veils about the candles my father said a long grace. He was a pious man, though high in temper.

That scene was to come back to me many times. We were all tall except John, who had the middle size of my mother's people and the pale skin that goes with ink and books and countinghouses. My father's face was gaunt and set in hard lines, with the uncompromising nose and chin of the Cape Cod folk. He was well named by the Micmacs; the eyes that looked straight at you from under his shaggy brows were the all-seeing, all-challenging eyes of the hawk. His straight black hair, graying about the temples, was gathered into a queue with a narrow green ribbon, and a linen shirt and white stock showed in the gape of his flowered yellow waistcoat. John, eighteen, wore a waistcoat of broadcloth like his smallclothes and tied his neat hair with a broad red band. Luke, twenty, six feet in his stockings, wore a gray flannel shirt and a pair of loose sailors' trousers and kept his pigtail tarred. He and Mark had been seafaring together in Father's vessels since they were boys. Mark was the great man among us, the oldest—twenty-four —and biggest, for he stood a good two inches over the fathom in his bare feet and was thickly built. His hair was black, but he had my mother's lively brown eyes and the rather swarthy skin of her folk. He had a great ringing voice, fine for hailing the masthead in western ocean gales. As for me, I have said I was tall like the others; let me add that my eyes were gray-blue and my hair as black and straight as a horse's tail, that I was gawky and all legs and hands and still growing out of my clothes—and you have me as I sat at the table that night.

Between Mark and me was the affection of first-born for last-born, a grinning rib-poking but protective brotherhood on the one side and sheer hero worship on the other. Luke worried himself over my aimless manner of growing up—roaming the woods with the Indians and absorbed in hunting and fishing. He had gone cabin boy in the old *Breeze* before my age and thought it high time I learned some navigation and got the feel of a deck under my feet. John considered me hopeless, spoiled, and willful and the makings of a rogue. And Mark and Luke and I were together in our scorn of John, the quill driver, the pale bookworm. Father disregarded our quarrels. I think he rather approved them as a sign of spirit, which I suppose they were; but our gentle mother took them to heart, and if we had known all that was to follow that meal we would have prayed God to pity her, instead of bowing our wooden heads to Father's slow, sonorous grace.

Chapter 3

A Council

IT WAS a rather silent meal, though we seldom talked at food. Mark made some small talk with Mother, and Father asked one or two questions about the hunting, and Luke and John stared at each other and said nothing. I had a queer feeling that something was afoot, something that made them all uneasy; and I knew at the meal's end, the time when we usually sat about and smoked and talked, for Mark jumped up abruptly and took a candle to the garret and came down with pieces of an old thin-worn topsail and began to cover the kitchen windows. That was astonishing. Nobody in our town covered windows at night—a few timid old women, perhaps. My father watched him for a moment and then struck the table with his fist. The girl Joanna dropped a plate and it broke.

"Damme, I'll have no shrouds over the windows, as if we were up to some hole-and-corner business!"

Mark shrugged his big shoulders and went on draping the canvas.

"I tell ye, Mark," my father roared, "I'll have no shrouding the windows!"

We were all watching Mark, and I suppose that is why none of us saw the Reverend Israel Cheever come in and why his harsh voice startled us so. "Let your light so shine before men that they may see your good works!" Silence, and then Luke's gibing voice, "And glorify the Great White Father which is in London?"

"Blasphemy!" said the preacher. He was a small gaunt man with blue eyes that were always a little bloodshot. He drank too much, and from time to time there were meetings to decide on his dismissal, but they never came to anything. He was a godly man, a graduate of Harvard College, and I dare say our poor Nova Scotia settlement was lucky to have a preacher of such learning, drunk or dry. The women enjoyed feeling sorry for his wife and family.

"Blasphemy!" he repeated, standing just inside the door and glaring at Luke across the candles.

"Treason's the word!" snapped John, and his face, always pale, seemed white as a virgin page in his ledger in Father's countinghouse.

Mark went on covering the windows. The sounds of dishwashing ceased in the corner, and my mother took a candlestick from the sideboard for bed. She lit it from one of the table candles, and in the momentary flare of the two wicks her face looked drawn and sad. At the door she paused and looked over our faces, and her eyes held mine.

"Davy, you must be tired. Go to bed, there's a good boy."

I didn't want to go; I was eager to learn what this mystery was about; and my father said gruffly, "David's a man grown now, Nance. It's time he learned a thing or two." Mother nodded slowly and gave me a sad, pale smile, moving out toward the stairs like a small resigned saint in the halo of her candle's light. That picture haunted me for years—it haunts me still.

Soon after came knockings at our kitchen door and hands at the latch and men entering with an odd furtiveness, the leading men of our town, in little groups. With them came a stranger whom I recognized from hearsay, shrewd William Smith of Halifax, one of Queens County's representatives in the provincial assembly. Queens County in those days included the whole southwest of Nova Scotia from the Lahave River around to St. Marys Bay, and our Liverpool was the county town. The inhabitants were almost entirely settlers from New England and regarded the Halifax assembly with indifference, partly because they were poor and few men could afford the time or expense of attending the legislature, but mostly because they were Yankees of the Yankees and considered Boston still the center of their world. Smith had been chosen a member for our county because he lived in the capital and our merchants had done business with him and liked him. The other county member was Simeon Perkins, a Liverpool merchant, one of us; and there was a member for the town itself, Seth Harding, a Liverpool sea captain.

I looked about the room as it filled. Sturdy Seth Harding was there. But where was Simeon? Someone put that question aloud.

"Scared to come!" snapped Luke. "Pious old hypocrite! Calls himself an American and shivers in his shoes every time someone in Halifax says Boo!"

"A Conne'ticut man," observed Mr. Cheever, as if that explained everything, and forgetting that Seth was a Connecticut man. Most of our folk were from Massachusetts—Plymouth and round about Cape Cod.

At a sign from Father I went with Mark outside to the cellar hatch with a candle in a tin lantern and lighted him while he selected a keg of rum and carried it up to the kitchen. He stood the keg on the table's end and fitted a spigot, and Luke fetched from the pantry shelves every mug, cup, and glass our house could muster. We were silent while the spigot trickled and the stuff was passed. Rum was the wine of our country, an essential part of the West India trade; our folk drank it like water—it was part of every workman's daily wage. Mr. Cheever's hand shook as he reached for a mug of it, and I knew his wife and daughters would be sorry for this meeting. I noticed my father drinking a great gulp, and that brought sorrow nearer home. I understood a little of my mother's look as she left the room. Time and affairs had made a sober merchant of Matthew Strang, the onetime captain of Gorham's Rangers, but now and again some stress of emotion set him drinking, and then the old violence flared.

Somebody put a glass in my hand. I had tasted rum before, of course; it was part of growing up—smoking old rope and dried weeds in clay pipes behind Father's barn and sneaking down to the West India wharves and making little bung dippers and lowering them through the bungholes of rum casks for a mouthful of the fiery brown stuff. I had never liked the taste of it but now I sipped carelessly—because I was a man—and fought down the shudders that followed and the queer, hot heave of my stomach.

The girl Joanna was busy at her candlemaking by the hearth: the big iron pot full of boiling water and tallow, the two poles bridging the backs of a pair of chairs, the slender withes—sixty in all—lying across the poles, each dangling half a dozen wicks. Patiently, one by one, Joanna lifted a rod from the poles, dipped its wicks quickly into the simmering tallow, and replaced the rod. The wicks dripped but grew in girth with each dip, and when she had come to the last of the rods it was time to begin again. It was one of the marks of fall—making candles for winter, a long chore that could not be stopped once begun. It would be late when the girl got to bed. So she remained, silent, her young face serious and absorbed, the firelight gleaming in her yellow hair.

Some of the men stood about the walls; some sat and some squatted, and all of them looked at Will Smith. There was something exciting in his tense attitude, the look in his eyes, the lines about his mouth.

"First," he began in a level voice, "I thank you, Captain Strang, for the chance of meeting my Liverpool friends in your house. I warned that it might bring upon you the displeasure of the governor, and you were the more determined. For that, sir, I admire and thank you."

My father blinked and shrugged. The men regarded Smith narrowly. Most of them had never seen him before. He talked like an orator, and they distrusted orators. But now he squared his shoulders and threw up his head and poured out a spate of words as if ridding himself of a burden.

"Gentlemen, I've been representing your county in the assembly since '65—the year of the Stamp Act. Remember that year? You people used little stamped paper in any case, but you opposed the principle of the Act like your brother Americans everywhere."

"But without violence," put in Parson Cheever a little thickly.

Mr. Smith made an impatient gesture. "Of course! You weren't the sort to rush about in mobs, calling yourselves Sons of Liberty and that kind of thing. But you opposed the Act—you burned some stamps in fact; and when the Act was repealed in '66 you people put torch to an old tumbledown house, for a bonfire, in celebration. There was some carousing, naturally, and it lasted into the next day, which happened to be the king's birthday. No insult intended—it happened to be the day after you got the news—but there 'twas. In Halifax they'd put up a gallows on the common and hung an old boot on it—meaning Lord Bute, of course. So it went, people openly rejoicing—and the governor making notes. As representatives for Queens County, Seth Harding and I came in for a special share of suspicion. Mr. Perkins"—there was a biting scorn in Smith's voice—"Mr. Perkins chose to stay home from the session. Why, I can't say."

(A voice, "'Twas safer," and some laughter.)

"In the following year," Smith went on, "the British government taxed a new list of things, including tea. That wasn't popular either here or in the other colonies. But again we Americans of Nova Scotia preserved law and order."

"And smuggled our tea!" cried the voice, and again everyone laughed.

"In '68 the Massachusetts house of representatives sent a letter to ours, setting forth common grievances and urging us to work together with them for improvement. Massachusetts sent that letter to all the colonies. Some say 'twas written by Sam Adams of Boston, but 'twas signed by the speaker of their house and addressed to the speaker of ours. It should have been brought before our house as a matter of courtesy, if nothing else; but Mr. Nesbitt, our speaker, concealed it from us and gave it to Lieutenant Governor Francklin—and Francklin sent it to England. We heard about it, of course, in roundabout fashion. If it had been brought before us in the proper way I think we'd have passed it to Francklin anyhow, to show him the feeling in America. But hiding the thing from us emphasized what we already knew—that Nova Scotia is ruled by Michael Francklin and his circle of merchant friends in Halifax, and our assembly is nothing but a whistling down the wind."

A low growl went round the room, like a mutter of stirring hounds. I looked at Mark. My emotions wanted a better leader than this dry man from Halifax. But Mark was watching the play of firelight in Joanna's hair with an interest I'd never seen before. It shocked me, for Joanna was only a bound-girl and Mark was my hero. I looked at Joanna resentfully, but she was intent on her candlemaking.

"Now in that year," the dry voice went on, "—in '68—the British government forbade any further digging of coals in this province, lest it interfere with home trade. Fuel's important in a cold country, and besides there's a chance of a great coal trade with Quebec and New England. All that came to an end—that wealth in our dooryard—by a stroke of pen in London. Of course, men used to go up to Cape Breton and dig coals on the sly—I bought coals myself in '69, right in Halifax, at thirty shillings a chaldron. So in '70 the governor sent troops to Cape Breton to stop it. Then we realized for the first time that the home government was prepared to use force in its efforts to restrict provincial trade. It opened our eyes—wide! Many of our settlements held town meetings, in the New England fashion to which they were accustomed, to discuss the laws and government of the province. The governor's answer was to forbid such meetings. Remember? 'Twas only four years ago—a direct blow at your order of life, which you brought with you when you came here from New England. A blow at every Yankee settler—at two out of every three people in Nova Scotia!"

Again that growl in the room. Mr. Smith's long upper lip was beaded with small drops of sweat, and he took out a handkerchief and wiped his mouth and dabbed at his temples.

"That," he cried sharply, "put the king's foot on our rights as Englishmen!"

The mutter leaped to a shout at that, voices crying "Good!" "That's true!" "Well said!" and "Go on, sir, go on!"

Smith lowered his voice again, but it shook. "I'll give it to you in plain English—in Halifax they call plain English 'treason' now, and that's why I'm here. I spoke my mind—and yours—and I am dismissed from my seat."

Up jumped Obediah Cannell, crying, "They can't do that!" and everyone looked his way. Obed was a small bony man with a long pointed nose, and his lank gray hair was gathered loosely on his neck with a bit of red tape.

"As one o' the original proprietors o' this settlement," he went on a little pompously, "I'd like to say a few words. The proprietors o' this town o' Liverpool came nearly all from Plymouth and around Chatham, Massachusetts Colony. Most o' you men in this room are sprung from the Pilgrim folk that set the first foot in Massachusetts. All New England began with them. They asked Old England for nothin'—an' got nothin'. They worked things out for 'emselves. When we come here in 1759—at the invitation o' Governor Lawrence, mark ye—we proposed to foller the New England custom. Promised that, we were. Inside a couple o' years Hal'fax begun meddlin'. They begun with our committee, appointin' men who'd do what Hal'fax wished. Well, we weren't the men to stand for that—not us—not men like Cap'n Strang here, who'd fought the French an' Injuns up an' down the province for years, makin' it safe for them gentlemen at Hal'fax. So we drew up a memorial to the Hal'fax council. Got a copy of it here"—he fumbled in his brown coattails and brought forth an old, much-folded paper—"and I'll get one o' you young men that's got good eyes—you, Davy boy—take an' read that there paper out loud."

I took the paper and hitched myself to let the candlelight fall on it and in a great silence began to read slowly and aloud:

"'Liverpool, Nova Scotia, July 8, 1762 . . .'"

Mr. Cannell broke in impatiently, "Ye can pass over all that fancy stuff—Greetings et cetera et cetera—an' begin where it says 'We look upon ourselves.'"

Obediently I read out, "'We look upon ourselves to be free men, under the same constitution as the rest of His Majesty's subjects, not only by His Majesty's proclamation but because we were born in a country of liberty, in a land which belongs to the Crown of England. Therefore we conceive that we have the right and authority vested in ourselves (or at least we pray we may) to nominate and appoint men amongst us to be our committee . . .'"

"There!" Mr. Cannell cried, taking the paper from my fingers and folding it reverently. "That's enough. That bit about 'we pray we may' was put in by the moderator's clerk; he said 'twould look better and wouldn't cost us anything, so we let it go. But there was our stand on liberty under the British flag as far back as '62—made on our own hook, afore there was any trouble in New England to speak of. I bring it to your attention now because it's still the same principle, and we're still the same men. We acknowledge the Crown but we're free men born in a free country. Now, sir, you go on from there."

Mr. Smith acknowledged this assistance with a stiff little bow.

"Things are bad over there"—giving his head a nod toward the west. "The port of Boston is closed; General Gage has an army encamped on Boston Common, and the citizens are gathering in thousands in Cambridge, armed with muskets, pitchforks—anything—and ready to use them. All the colonies but ours and Georgia have sent representatives to a meeting in Philadelphia which styles itself the First Continental Congress, and they've decided on non-importation of British goods, and non-exportation to Britain is to begin this time a twelvemonth. You see where it leads? All your trade is with America. Unless Nova Scotia throws in her lot with the others, well-nigh her whole trade is gone at a stroke."

The men in our kitchen looked very solemn, staring at each other's faces and back to Mr. Smith. My father said, "Ye came to tell us why you're no longer our representative in the assembly, sir. Let's have it, please."

Mr. Smith prepared himself with a pinch of snuff in each nostril, carefully flipping the yellow dust from his stock and waistcoat with the handkerchief afterward. "All you men know about the Boston Tea Party last winter—and other 'tea parties' elsewhere. Some Massachusetts merchants got frightened and began reshipping their tea to Halifax. That shifted the problem to us. A big shipment came to Mr. Monk at Halifax back in July. Many of the merchants refused to touch it, but 'twas landed amid the hissing and booing of a large crowd of people. This month came another consignment, and I told Governor Legge to his face that I'd have nothing to do with it if the tea belonged to the East India Company. It turned out that it didn't; but I wanted to make sure and called a meeting of the merchants at Rider's Tavern to discuss it. I was promptly brought before the governor and council, charged with sedition. So was my friend Mr. Fillis. Fillis got off with a wigging. But I was too dangerous, apparently, to leave in public offices; so I was stripped of them all in a swoop—Justice of the Peace, Judge of the Inferior Court for Halifax County, and—this is what I came to tell you—member of the assembly for the county of Queens."

"And the question is," Obed Cannell shouted, jumping up like a little gray cat, "what are Mr. Smith's freeborn electors goin' to do about it?"

CHAPTER 4

Some History and Some Kisses

OBED'S QUESTION, flung like a stone into their midst, seemed to stun all those serious men of our town. Then my brother Luke leaped up roaring, "We'll fight—that's what! By God, yes."

"What with?" my father said. He was a little flushed with the rum, but still the quiet, curt-spoken man.

"Muskets—pitchforks—ye heard about the men at Cambridge, Father—ready to fight with anything handy . . ."

"You mean they'll holler a lot aforehand, son. But when it comes to Gage's infantry, that Cambridge mob'll leave their riflemen to face the music. How many muskets have we?"

"Must be a couple o' hundred, anyhow. One over every mantelpiece."

"Two out o' three busted or weak in the spring. How about powder?"

"Why," Obed Cannell said, "every man that owns a gun has powder for't—a hornful, say. And there's a keg or two in each o' the stores."

"Enough for a day's fight. What then?"

"There's Halifax," Luke said boldly.

"I see. You and your two hundred old muskets and fowling pieces and your empty powder horns are going to drive the redcoats out o' Halifax Fortress."

Mr. Smith put in quickly, "Don't forget, Matthew, that we're not alone. A good two thirds of the people of Nova Scotia are Yankee-born."

"Umph! What o' the rest?"

"There's the Scotch-Irish around Truro and Onslow—levelers all. There's the remnant of the Acadians, who hate the British for the persecutions of '55. There's a handful of Scotch in Cape Breton, driven out of their Highlands by English oppression and sentimental still about Prince Charlie. And there's the Germans and Huguenots at Lunenburg, the people you call 'Dutch'; they were defrauded into settling in Nova Scotia, and if you'll remember there was a rebellion that had to be put down by troops from Halifax."

"Ah!" my father exclaimed. He turned painfully in his chair and addressed the girl at the fire. "Joanna, my dear, ye must have heard what's been said. Will your Dutch folk fight for a swig o' free tea?"

The girl flushed, and for an instant her eyes turned to Mark and then down to her wooden shoes. She was outlined by the fire glow, and I remember how her round breasts swelled and sank in the tight bodice with her agitated breathing. She said to her shoes, "Wars—that was why our people left the old country. I have heard the old people. Soldiers. Armies crawling over the country like ants, eating everything. Young men sold like sheep by their princes to fight in other people's wars. Yes. That is what they talk about. When they came over the sea they were promised many things by the English. They got nothing but a piece of this cold rocky country, covered with forest. They were told it was theirs. It belonged to the Indians, and the Indians came to the little lonely farms and killed and scalped the people. Our people had to fight for their lives for many years. *Ach*, yes. That is what our people talk about."

"What's she mean?" Robert Slocomb said. The girl spoke distinctly but in the rich Dutch accent of the Lunenburgers.

Mark said sharply, "She means her people won't fight except in self-defense. They just want to be let alone. That's plain enough."

"All this talk of troubles over there"—Joanna gave her head a little nod toward the west, and her hempen hair caught the firelight in bright gleams. "You English speak one language. You are all one people. We do not understand."

"Don't ye understand liberty?" snapped Luke.

Slowly she shook her head, regarding him with grave blue eyes. "When there is fighting, young men die and women suffer. That is all I understand."

She looked at Mark when she said that, and it was Mark's turn to flush.

Will Smith dragged his subject out of a silence. "Captain Strang, sir—Matthew, my good friend—you've had a vast experience in this country. It was you who saw the advantage of this place for the fishery and brought your old neighbors from Cape Cod to make a settlement. Let's have your mind."

"On what?" my father said.

"On the matter of rebellion!" my brother John spoke up hotly. "Go on—tell 'em, Father! Tell 'em it's treason they came here to plot!"

"What . . . liberty?" burst out Seth Harding, and his passion surprised me. He was quiet as a rule.

"Treason's the right name," John said defiantly, "and hanging's the right remedy."

I don't know where he had heard that phrase. We were to hear it many times in the next eight or nine years, but it was new and shocking that night in our kitchen.

"Experience," my father said in his deep voice. His head was bowed. He sat in his place at the table's head and might have been saying a grace before meat but for the absence of food and the presence of the little squat keg. "Ay, I've had experience, if that's what ye want. I was fighting the French and Injuns on the Maine frontier afore some o' ye were born."

We looked at each other swiftly, my brothers and I. The rum was working in him, casting the old black memories loose and lifting the curb from his tongue. Mother always hushed him when he got in this mood and put the rum away; but she was now at her bedside prayers, out of sight and mind.

"I came to Nova Scotia first as a young man, with the army o' raw provincials that took Louisburg. Came again in '49, when Cornwallis and his English settlers built Halifax town in a summer. His redcoats were useless outside the palisades, so he'd called in John Gorham and his Mohawks and half-breeds and adventurers—Gorham's Rangers, egad!—to harass the Micmacs and keep 'em off his woodcutters. One or two o' Gorham's officers were Plymouth men, and they sent for me. Gorham was no soldier—too easygoing. But we were a hard crew. Lord! Lord!"

He stared about the kitchen from face to face. His eyeballs were bloodshot, but his gaze was hard as the gray whin rock of our hillside pastures, and some sort of devil mixed of rum and recollection leered from the small black pupils. "Injun fighting was our business. Our business, mind! See this house, my friends? One o' the best in town. I brought it from Massachusetts in my vessel in '59—frame, boards, shingles, clapboards ready-sawn—ay, and the bricks for the chimneys and the furniture and the tiles for the parlor hearth, all ready to put up. 'Spensive, that. Guess where the money came from! Eh? From scalps! Ay, scalps! Governor Cornwallis paid up to fifty guineas for a prime bit o' Micmac hair in the old days. The price depended on the state o' his settlers' nerves. When things got quiet the value went down—and us rangers loafed on the king's rations in a log barrack at the end o' the Basin. Then the Injuns 'ud raid a sawmill on the Dartmouth side or cut up a party o' redcoats out for fuel or a townsman fowling outside the palisades. Up went the price o' hair—and off we went! Days, weeks on the trail, by foot and canoe, dogging 'em, watching a chance. Then a swift rush in a clearing somewhere, about daylight for choice, yelling our Mohawk yell, and their women screeching, and our hatchets whistling down and down. Then the scramble for hair, and the quick, wet slit-slit-slit o' the knives . . ."

"Enough!" cried Parson Cheever in a high, cracked voice.

My father chuckled, a fearsome sound. "Not half enough. Listen!" His gaunt features broke into a wide, terrible smile which he turned upon us all, leaning forward over the table, as a boy on Guy Fawkes Night turns the grin of a pumpkin lantern. "D'ye know how to take a scalp? Ye begin at the hairline o' the forehead and slit back over the ears and round the back, and ye run your knife atween scalp and skull at the front to give it a start, and ye set your foot on the neck and grab the front lock and give it a wrench; and there 'tis, a fine bloody wig for the Halifax trade. Then ye jump to the next corpse, or someone's got it afore ye. Snarl and worry, snarl and worry—that was the way, like dogs over a sheep's head in the butcher's yard. But that's not all. There's tricks to all trades, and ours was no exception. The English officers' notion o' scalps is a wisp o' dried hair and skin, three or four inches across. That's what the governor put in his proclamation— 'scalps after the custom of America.' He and his officers never saw a Micmac on the warpath, and they reckoned the Nova Scotia savages shaved their heads to a scalp lock like the continental tribes. Which they don't. The Micmac kept his hair long and full, tied up with a thong on the top o' his head, 'stead o' the nape like a gentleman. So there ye were—each o' those sodden wigs at your belt 'ud make three for the Halifax trade—four with skill and a sharp knife. Ah, 'twas a fine game, I tell ye, if ye knew your peltry and the price was right.

"Now, about the women and kids. Our lads didn't kill women as a rule—they'd other use for 'em, aha! And the squaws didn't mind, I guess, so long as 'twasn't a knife in their flesh. But sometimes in the flurry of a fight a woman or two got killed. And when ye shoot into a cluster o' wigwams at day-dawn there's youngsters inside, as often as not. There they were, dead as salt herrings—and scalps worth half a fortune. Those white-wigged officers at Halifax never knew the difference and seldom asked questions when matters were hot. All they could think about was their own dead outside the palisades and the bare bloody skulls and the flies. Besides, the French started the scalp buying, didn't they? The fault was theirs. Five . . . ten . . . twenty . . . the guineas jingling on the council table . . ."

"Stop it, Matthew!" Obed Cannell shouted.

"In God's name," added Mr. Cheever. Sweat shone in beads on his bald top and trickled down the thin pepper-and-salt locks that hung over his ears.

"God?" my father said. "There wasn't any god in Nova Scotia in '49. Only the Injun god Muntoo—him the French priests called the devil. We gave 'em Muntoo, from '49 to '61, when they buried the hatchet at last. Put the fear o' Muntoo into 'em, we did—and into the French, come to that. The English wouldn't buy French scalps—'twasn't gentlemanly, 'less ye could pass off a black-haired 'un for an Injun's. Ah, but we weren't gentlemen, us Yankees—we'd done too much o' the marching and fighting and seen too many of our own settlements ravaged and burned in time past. We wanted to settle in Nova Scotia—fought for it, hadn't we?—and there wasn't room for us and the French and the Injuns together. A dead Injun's a good 'un, and the Micmacs were getting almighty good by '55. But ye couldn't rub out the French like the sum from a slate. A pity, too. The French were heathens, weren't they? Bowed down to graven images, didn't they? Worshiped a woman and set God—our God—back somewhere about the head o' the saints, didn't they? Murdered all the Protestants in France onetime, hadn't they? All that ought to count for something now—now that we'd captured Beausejour and made the peninsula ours. Yes, by God—by the Protestant God! We put the matter strong, and Governor Lawrence at Halifax put it strong, and the governors o' New England put it strong. And the gentlemen in London didn't know what to say, didn't like to be bothered with bloody details, and hummed and hawed and finally washed their hands."

"Like Pilate," our preacher put in.

"Umph! Well, we Americans knew what to do. We'd pluck the French off their farms—off the fat red 'Cajun lands around Fundy Bay that we wanted for our own folk—and we'd send their villages up in smoke to show 'em the change o' wind. And we'd ship 'em off to the other colonies, a few here and a few there, where they'd always be under suspicion and couldn't do harm. By God, yes. And that's what we did. Ay, we scattered the 'Cajuns over the face o' the continent from Boston to the mouth o' Mississippi. We don't do things by halves, us Americans! Ah! That was nigh twenty years ago, but it comes back like yesterday. The soldiers got the easy part—the 'Cajuns o' the Annapolis Valley and Minas Basin; they went to the ships fairly quiet, though some o' the kids got apart in the scurry, and the women caterwauled. But the isthmus, aha! There was another matter. Around Chignecto and the Petitcodiac the 'Cajuns had taken up arms and roused the Injuns and got Boishebert down from Quebec for a leader. So the governor sent us rangers up there with the pick o' the light troops. Give the devil his due—that Boishebert was a woods fighter good as ourselves, maybe better, for he gave us a mauling at Petitcodiac we didn't forget very quick—me with a ball in my thigh! But we liked the work up there, for all. 'Twas more satisfaction somehow, putting torch to houses and barns—ay, and their mass houses, images and all—knowing the owners were handy, waiting to send a volley into our backs as we returned to the boats. That put a spice in it ye didn't get at Grand Pré or Minas. By God, yes. And 'twas fun to catch one o' their dogs and fasten birch bark to his tail and put fire to the bark and head him into the standing grain. I tell ye 'twas comical—the cur ki-yi-ing and the red fire running through the crops. The French had turned some o' their cattle into the woods; the rest we shot, a sinful waste, for our settlers needed 'em when they came to farm. But ye can't think of everything—not in war. It *was* war ye wanted to hear about, wasn't it?"

"Not that kind!" shouted several men together.

Will Smith spoke quickly. "You talk of the past, Captain Strang. It's the present we've come to consider—that, and the future."

"Ah!" my father said. "Now that's a tarnation pity, for there was a lot more I wanted to tell ye about the 'Cajuns and the way we used 'em after we'd won the war. Ye're dry, that's the trouble. Mark! John! Fill the mugs and glasses, damme, for I see drought in all these faces. Fill mine too. It's dry work, talking. Must be some mortal dry throats in Boston now, the way they're hollering for liberty or death—and no tea. Liberty's thirsty business. Pass the cups, boys. You, too, Mr. Cheever, sir—drink up. It's right Jamaiky, the *Spray's* last voyage, and I'll warrant every drop. Drink up! Drink up!"

Mugs, cups, glasses, jacks clattered and thumped and jingled down the long kitchen board, and nobody said very much while the spigot sang its little brown song.

"What we want to know," Seth Harding said at last, "is our prospects if it comes to fightin' here, Cap'n Strang. I don't count on the Dutch folk, myself. I don't count on any but ourselves, come to the fine point. We're not only two thirds o' the population, us Yankees, but we own most o' the shippin' and the sawmills, do most o' the tradin', and, what's more important, raise most o' the provisions. The Yankee farms along the Valley and about the end o' the Bay are the breadbasket o' Nova Scotia. And there's the rub. When General Gage finds he can't get provisions from Massachusetts nor any o' the colonies that sent a delegate to the Congress, he'll turn to Nova Scotia—to us—us Yankees of Nova Scotia."

He paused. Seth was a townsman, one of us, an able shipmaster, and the elected representative of our town in the assembly. All through the room you could feel the respect our people had for him, a different respect from the kind they had for my father, the old ranger, crippled by a musket ball in the thigh, a figure lame and in a few years doomed to impotence in a chair.

"I was in Boston a fortnight since," Seth said quietly, "and I can tell ye Gage won't back down. Nor'll the Americans. That means war, this year or next. Come to open warfare, the other colonies'll back Massachusetts. I reckon Georgia'll stand with the rest when it comes to actual bloodshed. That leaves only one colony in doubt—which is ours."

"What about Canada?" demanded my father.

"Canada's French, always has been, always will be. Conquered a scant fifteen years, held by an English garrison in Quebec town. The people have little love for the English and less for Americans—what with Congress denouncin' the Quebec Act—which secured the French their religion—and old scores to pay. They'll sit on the fence and hope to God that France'll find opportunity in the squabble between England and America. But I want to hear Cap'n Strang on our fighting chances here. No man in Nova Scotia can tell us better."

The men joined a chorus of "Ay!" "Matthew!" "Matt!" "Speak up, Cap'n."

My father hunched himself in his high-backed chair, brooding over the table's end like the old tired hawk he was and twisting a black leather drinking jack in his strong fingers. When he spoke his tongue was rough—rough as a farrier's rasp.

"Told ye something o' war. Not enough, I see—but enough to show ye war's a nasty beast, once ye've turned it loose. Now there's a big difference atween talking a war and fighting it, and it's been my experience that those who talk war ain't the ones that fight. D'ye think those fine gentlemen in London'll risk their heads and bellies toting a musket in the wilds of America? Not they! They'll scour the streets and the village greens and gather the 'prentices and plowboys of England; they'll empty the jails and hire the scum o' Europe and put 'em all in red jackets for the honor o' the king. That's what they'll do.

"And d'ye think that Boston rabble will fight when it comes to powder and ball? They'd rather snowball a sentry from the cover of an alley or bust some gentleman's windows with stones. Will Sam Adams fight, think you? Will John Hancock—Smuggler John? Bah! They'll holler a lot about liberty and such but they'll leave the fighting to men with guts for it—they'll wheedle the farmers and woodsmen into it, and the clerks and mechanics, the fishermen and seamen; all the men that are good for something besides talk. That's what they'll do. That's what their kind always do. And the war'll be fought and finished by men on both sides that scarcely know how it started or what it's about, except they've got to fight it out and get it over with before they can go back to their homes and their work.

"Now, those fine gentlemen in England are talking o' the Americans as a sort o' half-savage tribe that they can put to rout with a volley, white man's fashion. They'll find out different, and the poor damned redcoats'll pay the cost. Ye can't rout three million people with a volley nor a battle nor a single campaign—not people that's fought for their lives, generation after generation, like us. On t'other hand, Sam Adams and his friends talk as if the English were just a lot o' drunken boobies in red coats. They'll find out different too. A man's a man in any jacket, and six months' marching and fighting in America'll make him a tough 'un. I found that out years ago, watching Cornwallis' men and Monckton's and Wolfe's. Never forget that our own folk were Englishmen that didn't know a pine tree from a pincushion when they came to America. A man can learn a lot and learn it awful quick when his life depends on't.

"But apart from all that, there's a lot of us Americans that don't like Sam Adams and his Sons o' Liberty any more'n we like the king and parliament."

"Tories!" Luke snapped.

"No, not by half, son. That's the point. Sooner or later they'll have to take sides. They're the people that'll have to finish the war Sam's brewing. Set the redcoats aside; they'll fight a few battles for the history books, no doubt. But the real war'll be between Americans, our own people up and down the continent, and it'll go on till one side's dead or drove out—like the 'Cajuns were. A civil war, that's what we're faced with, a savage struggle between neighbor and neighbor, like the war between King Charles and Cromwell that the old folk from England used to talk about."

Again his eyes roved the room, challenging each face in turn; and some men blinked, and some glanced aside, and some gave him stare for stare.

"Ye want military advice. I'm not sure I'm qualified, for my fighting was done against French and Injuns, a mighty different sort o' war from the one ye're heading into. As I see it, the king has got a fleet and the Americans ain't. That means the king can land troops anywhere he pleases—and of all the fourteen colonies, Nova Scotia's the nearest to England. Consider that well. Nova Scotia's a big piece o' country; it stretches up to Canada on the north, and west to a line somewhere atween the St. John River and the Penobscot—which line's never been run out. But all that country north and west o' Fundy Bay is just a hunting ground for Injuns. It's the peninsula we've settled, and the isthmus is only a jump across; so we're living on an island, ye might say, and scattered around the coast at that. We're open to attack from the sea at every point."

"The other colonies are exposed to the sea," objected Seth.

"Not like us, they ain't, Seth. They've a settled interior, where there's shelter and supplies at their hand. Come to the worst, they can shift upcountry and make war till Kingdom Come. But we've no retreat but into the woods, where's only a living for hunters and a northern winter to face."

"Matthew Strang, speak reverent of Judgment Day!" cried Mr. Cheever in his high voice. He was tipsy now, and nobody paid him attention. They were all staring at Father with various emotions—anger, fear, contempt, agreement, curiosity—set on their faces like masks.

"Now," my father said austerely, "I come to the thing that clinches all the rest. T'other colonies have three million people to draw an army from. How many has Nova Scotia? Barring Injuns, something between fifteen and twenty thousand in the whole province. Ye keep saying 'two out o' three Yankee-born' as if that made a whole lot. It makes ten or twelve thousand by my arithmetic, scattered around the entire coast from Cape North to Machias, with no roads worth mention, no connection but by sea. Say two thousand men and boys able to bear arms. But what arms? And where'd they get powder and shot?"

"From the Congress," Benajah Collins said promptly.

"The Congress is going to have its hands full keeping its own armies in the field, without risking good ammunition by sea to Nova Scotia. Bah! I've talked enough. I could ha' said it all in a breath. Listen! A wise little dog keeps out of a big dogs' fight."

The whole room leaped up in an uproar, every man shouting his opinion. And in the first lull, Obed Cannell pointed an accusing finger and cried, "And the Injuns called ye The Hawk! Why, ye're nothin' but a little old he-hen like Simeon Perkins—beggin' all hands .

to keep quiet and mebbe the war'll pass over their heads! Faugh!" He spat on our clean kitchen floor.

Mark reached him first—I fell over a stool, and John had to come all the way around the table—and shook him by the collar of his brown cloth coat till a seam went and the horn buttons flew, and the little gray man, all teeth and claws, fell into a corner. Young Ab Cannell sprang at Mark then, with more courage than sense; but Seth Harding and Benajah Collins and some others thrust in and stopped the affair. Everyone was shouting, this one for Obed, that for Mark, and some condemned them both for a pair of fools that couldn't hold good liquor.

Joanna was crying, "The candles . . . mind my candles . . . oh, please!"

We had come pretty nigh knocking a winter's lighting into the fire and we all looked a bit foolish. Joanna's task was at an end. She took a flat candlestick from the sideboard and lit its wrinkled stub at one of the table candles and passed into the hall toward the stairs, moving quietly in her wooden shoes—a knack Dutch women have. My father began to speak again, and only I noticed Mark slipping into the hall behind her.

"That was the first proof o' my words," he rasped to those muttering men. "In another six months ye'll be burning each other's fish sheds. Then ye'll be shooting. It's excitement ye want, not liberty. Notice I didn't say much about liberty tonight—nor patriotism nor loyalty nor any o' the catchwords that come so cheap in America nowadays. Take loyalty, now. I fought for the king in my time and took his pay but I don't care a tinker's damn for him or his parliament. Tell ye why. Nine-and-twenty years ago we took Louisburg, us provincials —most of us from Massachusetts. Louisburg! The biggest fortress in America, that the French called their Dunkirk o' the West. To take it we had to land in small boats on a rocky shore, climb a cliff, haul our cannon and supplies through hills and bogs and woods. We froze in the cold Cape Breton nights and suffered the heat and the flies o' the day. We fought six weeks on end, day in, day out, half starved and dizzy with the bloody flux, and buried our dead by hundreds, outside the ramparts afore the surrender and in the town afterward. And reckoned it worth the price. Inside three years His Majesty's government kindly paid our cash expenses and handed the town back to the French—without so much as a by-your-leave. That stuck in our crop— hard. Sometimes I think it's at the bottom of all the trouble in America since. Anyhow, I'd no love for those fatheads in London; and nothing that's happened since—writs of assistance, navigation laws, sugar, stamps, tea—all the rest of it—none o' that improved my temper. That's one side. T'other side is Sam Adams and his Patriots and Sons o' Liberty and whatever else they call themselves. I don't like them either. I'm not sure but what, if it came to a choice, I'd rather be ruled by the king. The king's across the sea in England, but Sam's just the other side o' Fundy. That's too close for comfort. I know Sam—had dealings with him in the old days, and every deal I had with Sam cost me money. A great one to look out for Sam Adams, was Sam. There'd be no comfort living with *him*; so, come to a hard choice, I'll take the king, thank'ee—him and his taxes. Ask anyone in Boston about Sam and *his* tax collecting—for Sam collects taxes or used to. Aha, Sam! Sam's a rogue if ye want to know. And as for his Sons o' . . ."

"Matthew!" Mr. Cheever hiccuped.

"Sons o' Liberty . . . they've started something and got every colony into it clear down to Florida; now they're after us Nova Scotians. For *our* liberty? Hell! Sam knows we haven't a chance. But every shot we fire'll take that much o' His Majesty's attention off Sam and his Sons. That's what Sam wants of us. They figger to get their liberty, and we'll pay the royal piper for our own little dance. Get that into your thick skulls and go home. Mr. Smith, sir, if ye take my advice ye'll go back to Halifax and sit tighter'n an owl in the daylight. And that goes for the rest o' ye. Let Simeon Perkins alone. Simeon's a pious old woman in smallclothes—just what we need for our figgerhead in times like these. He'll keep us out o' trouble, I lay. If the 'Cajuns'd had someone like Simeon at their head in '55, 'stead o' that wild man Le Loutre, they'd be on their Nova Scotia farms today. Keep that in your minds always—what happened to the 'Cajuns. They got crushed atween the English and the French. We're atween the king and the rebels—never forget it! Now go home, all o' ye! I'm tired and want bed. I hereby declare this seditious meeting dissolved!"

He took a last pull at his jack and drained it and sat back chuckling to see how they went. There was some hesitation. Bold ones like Seth Harding and the Cannells and Benajah Collins and Ephraim Dean went out the front door to the road, Seth whistling "A Stout Heart and a Thin Pair o' Breeches" at the top of his pipe. The timid and cautious clustered by our kitchen door and looked toward the river and the wharves.

"Moon's up," said one dismally.

"King George ain't the man in it," Luke said.

"What o' James Bingay and the other Tories in town?"

"Take the shore for it," Father said.

They slipped away in small, furtive groups, as they had come, and vanished into the blue moon shadows of the fish sheds, supporting Mr. Cheever amongst them. William Smith, our representative in assembly, went with them, and I felt my lip curling at the smell of a coward. But I was wrong in that judgment. Back in Halifax, Will Smith played his cards cautiously, but they were American cards, and he played them out to the end.

Luke and John carried the keg below, a light-enough burden now, while I helped Father out of his chair. He caught up the maple staff with which he mended his gait and shook off my hand. He was steady, and the staff was leather-shod, and we walked softly for the peace of my sleeping mother and so came soundless into the hall. There we saw Mark and Joanna framed in her candle's glow at the end of the long hall. He stood at the foot of the stairs and she on the first step, which brought her face level with his. I think he had overtaken her there, and she had turned and found herself in his arms. She was trying to hold the candle clear and making a poor job of it with a hand over the baluster rail. Suddenly she gave up her flushed face to Mark's kisses, and her soul, too, I reckon, for the hand over the rail drooped, and the candlestick with it, and the dip shed hot tallow on the floor of the hall in a rain of pattering drops.

Father nipped my arm cruelly, and we shrank back into the kitchen.

"So!" uttered my father, with his shaggy brows upraised and a comical look on his face. "He's wenching at last—our Mark. And time! It's a sign o' health in a young man."

I knew then that my father was indeed drunk on his own Jamaica, for he knew that Mother would suffer no hanky-panky with maids in her house. (Luke had found that out with a brown-faced slut from Port Medway the previous winter. That was how Joanna came to us.) We gave them some time and then clumped into the hall and found Mark groping alone in the dark on the stairs and looking mighty put out and heard the girl's soft-footed rush, shoes in hand, to her small bed in the garret and the shut of her door and the drop of the bar.

Luke and John were coming out of the cellar by that time, and we five Strangs crept up the stairs together in a silence that somehow seemed guilty.

CHAPTER 5

Strawberry Lips

OUR TOWN was peaceful enough in that September of '74, and people
went their ways busily, as if there were nothing in the offing but winter,
as if nothing ever would change but the seasons. The Bank schooners
were home, and the vessels from Labrador, with good fares of codfish.
The town had been built about the crook of the river's elbow, where it
mingled with salt water, and the mile between it and the point which
guarded the harbor bar was laid out in fish lots, one to each proprietor.
There stood the fish flakes, crude platforms of poles and brushwood
spread with split codfish for drying; row on row of fish flakes, with
alleys between for the hand barrows to pass along; a mile of flakes
marching between the wooded ridge and the shore, like tables spread
for a multitude, for a fish feast out of the Scriptures.

At the foot of each lot was the owner's shed, for storing his fish
and his gear, and each man had his boat slip of spruce poles smeared
with gurry, and some had wharves of cribbed logs and rock, where a
West India schooner could load. In the mouth of the harbor sat Peleg
Coffin's Island, like a watchful beast whose back bristled with wind-
bitten spruce trees and whose tail was a long stony flat where the Labrador men dried their catch.

There were a few small sawmills like those at the Falls, and there
was a tannery and a grist mill and a shipyard or two; but fish was the
life of our town, and whenever the wind came east in summer and
fall we smelled its breath from the flakes.

Cash was hard to come by in the West India trade—in any for that
matter—and our trading brigs exchanged their fish for what was offered
there, salt from Turk's Island, molasses and rum from Jamaica or some
other of the Indies, with a few seroons of indigo and some log wood
now and again. But there were always a few Spanish dollars in the
captain's chest on his return, and these were our currency from the
earliest times. Our merchants kept accounts in pounds, shillings, and
pence, but there were no English coins in the province but the guinea,
too big a piece for our poor needs. On the way home, too, our vessels
put in to New England ports and sold what West India stuff they could

in exchange for dry goods and grain and cider and potatoes and apples and turnips and other garden sauce.

For you must understand that Halifax, with a full garrison and the fleet, sucks all the farm produce of the province into its maw, and we on our rocky southwest shore must buy where we can. To be sure, we raise a few cattle in our small salt meadows and cut wild hay from the muskegs for our work oxen, and our sheep find grazing amongst the stones of the pastures (and get mighty short commons in winter) and we have small patches of garden sauce, which we fertilize with seaweed and fish compost; but none of this is sufficient.

This you must keep in mind if you are to understand how necessity bound us to the old home in New England, and not merely ties of the heart, which God knows were strong enough.

It had been a full summer in many ways. It began with a day of abstinence, as a full time should. That was a day in May, which our people set aside every year for fasting and prayer, an offset to the feast of Thanksgiving which we celebrate every fall. And it seemed that our prayers were well heard.

I remember how the alewives came thronging out of the sea and into our river, just when the Indian pear began to bloom like a living snow on the hillsides and so proved the Micmac saying that alewives must come to the wild pear's flowering lest their own spawn be unfruitful.

Peter Dekatha and François and I sailed upstream to the Falls in my father's gondola, an unwieldy thing which Dutch folk call a scow and is useful for freighting within the harbor and goes well enough with a stiff wind and a rag of old sail.

At low tide the river runs all the way down to Salmon Island, so we anchored below in a fleet of boats and other gondolas and carried our barrels ashore in the small boat and rolled them through the woods to the Alewife Brook. The sawmill dam bars the river just above tidewater, so the fish must go up the brook to spawn, braving our dip nets all the way to the lake and its sandy bars. We posted ourselves on the brook bank, just above the river, each with a dip net on a ten-foot pole and our barrels arranged behind. The fish came in schools, so thick that you felt you could walk their backs from bank to bank, and the nets rose and fell both sides of the stream, and fish glittered silver in the sunshine as we tossed them into the barrels. In our haste we cared little whether they went into the barrels or not, and they flapped in the grass and the bushes and slithered about our feet and often gained the water again. Between each rush of fish was a pause, when we rested our poles and watched the men waiting downstream. Then the poles began to fly once more, with the air raining fish and the laughter and shouting passed up the banks like the running crackle of fire in the woods.

We dipped as long as the fish ran, though the barrels were full and the grass a silver sea and our shoes and stockings aglitter with wet scales. The fish ran while the tide flowed. The first of the ebb brought an end to our fishing. The Indian men and boys shouldered their dip nets and went home to their camp at Potanoc, leaving the patient squaws to string the catch on cords and bend their backs homeward under the weight of many loads.

And we townsmen poled our gondolas up over the now tide-flooded rapids and headed our barrels and rolled them aboard and dropped down to Liverpool on the ebb. There was less pleasure in the splitting and gutting, the preparation of salt vats, the selection of fat fish for smoking, and the hanging in the smokehouse and the fetching and carrying of green maple-wood for the fires.

But the alewife time was a good time, for all that, and I loved it.

Close on the tails of the alewives came the shad; and the night run of salmon weighted our nets in the mornings. And sometimes—since a man must play, even at fishing—Peter and François and I walked up the mill brook and cut long birch poles and rigged lines and "flies" which were nought but hooks dressed in deer hair and small partridge feathers and swindled the fat trout into our baskets. The birch leaves crept into the sun, and the maple and beech and the others, like a green mist at first on the hillsides, and then a green sea. And the dull green pines and spruces and firs were suddenly shabby by contrast. The red maples stood by the streams and scattered their bright blossoms into the water, like girls strewing flowers for the path of a king. And in field and pasture, at the roadside and along the riverbanks, by the well path and the wharf lane, ay, and under the fish flakes themselves, green sprang the grass, with the fresh, moist green that you see nowhere but in our Nova Scotia. We pay for that green. It comes of the rain and the fogs of our long, dreary spring and the sudden hot sunshine that comes and is gone and the wet wind from the east that brings dye from the green of the sea.

I remember the heat of that summer of '74 and the thunderstorms which our people call "tempests," rumbling up and down the wooded valley; and the white wall of sea fog, just offshore, that threw the sun's heat back on the land. But chiefly I remember how thick and sweet the wild strawberries grew on the harbor slopes in that summer, and how the young folk (and some not so young) went in sailboats astrawberrying; ay, and love-making, for there is something about the moist red of strawberry lips that brings 'em together, willy-nilly, in the shade of a bush in July.

On one of those days I went with three or four youngsters to a cove down the eastern side of the harbor. We had refreshments of a simple sort—mine were bread and cheese and a small jug of cider—and I remember that I had picked a whole pailful of berries before I was hungry and found myself in the cool green of a thicket with young Fear Bingay and nobody else. I had never spoken a dozen words with a girl till then, and none with her. James Bingay was a merchant in a prosperous way in our town, in favor with the ruling clique at Halifax, and a stout and bigoted Tory in consequence. My father despised him for his fat self-importance and his lickspittle manner with visiting bigwigs. He and Fear's mother had grand plans for their daughter—a school for young ladies at Halifax, beginning next fall—and I'll never know why she was allowed to go on our strawberry frolic, except that Arthur Carper was along. But Arthur was nowhere in sight when Fear and I sat down together to eat our refreshments.

She was about my age but seemed very much older and self-assured and wore a dress of some light stuff sprigged with flowers, with black shoes and a peep of white stockings, and her eyes were the color of new apple cider and her hair was the color of old. The cider in my jug was old—a mistake of my mother's—and perhaps that is why I noticed Fear Bingay so particularly. It made my skin prickle all over, in a hot uncomfortable way, when she came over beside me and took and nibbled a piece of my cheese. She gave me a piece of her cake for fair exchange, and we talked about strawberrying and suchlike simple things, and all the time I could think of nothing but the white of her teeth and the red of her lips. And when I looked in her eyes—which was often—'twas like gazing down a well at night for a wish on the moon. The gleam at the bottom, I mean, and the queer, silly wanting to dive.

Her hand plucked at the grass between us, and it seemed the most natural thing in the world to take it in my bony brown fist, where it lay like a slim white bird, ready to fly at a moment. But the hand did not fly. It lay cool and alive and somehow expectant in mine. I stared down at it stupidly, like the mooncalf I was, and Fear Bingay leaned back and laughed softly and mocked me with her clear-cider eyes, and I wished to God I had let it alone. Then in her warm liquid voice that was like the smooth gurgling pour of brook water, she said, "Well, Davy Strang, d'ye like me?"

I went clean out of my head. I lifted the white hand to my lips and fell to kissing it thirstily, then the wrist, and the smooth white forearm that invited somehow under the fall of lace from her short sleeve. And all this bussing and tugging brought her curly brown head to my shoulder, with her face upturned like a flower to rain and the mocking eyes closed. So awkward was I that I kissed her closed eyes first, and her brow and her cheeks, and even the tilt of her nose, before I discovered her waiting red mouth in a mixture of fear and delight.

But in the midst of that charming discovery came a voice from another world, and we sprang up and apart and saw Parson Cheever in his snuff-colored waistcoat and dark smallclothes and his broad-rimmed round hat, regarding us balefully. In one hand was a quart pot nigh full of wild strawberries, in the other a red handkerchief which I suppose contained his lunch.

"I thank God," he announced very loudly through his nose, "that my innocent daughters were spared this disgraceful spectacle."

"Eh?" stammered I.

"In all innocence I brought my family aberrying in Squire Perkins' shallop and landed yonder. What's this mean, Miss Bingay?"

The mischief was gone from Fear's eyes. They were cloudy, as cider will cloud when the cask is jolted, and gazed between Mr. Cheever and me to the blue July sky and the white, wheeling gulls.

"I think you had better ask David," she said in a cool voice. "I was sitting here eating my cake—like Miss Muffet, you know—when David sat down beside me and caught my hand and went to kissing. I didn't know what to do, for such a thing never happened to me before. I don't think he meant harm, did you, David?"

"No," spluttered I.

She turned her wide gaze to Mr. Cheever, and eyes were never so round and innocent.

"What harm could David do me, Mr. Cheever?"

"Hem!" Mr. Cheever said and favored me with a suspicious blue stare.

"Speak up, Davy," Fear said calmly.

"It's true, sir," I blurted. "She sat there, eating her cake, when something came upon me and set me akissing her hand."

"Why didn't she cry out then?"

"He put his mouth on mine," she said plaintively.

"Hem! Well, Master Strang, I shan't take this before the deacons, for the sake of this innocent gel and her God-fearing parents, though I'd like to see you in the penitent seat as a warning to others. Better there, sir, than munching an apple in the back of the meeting, as I've seen you before this. But I'll speak to your father. I reckon a lick with the rough side of his tongue'll do more for your morals."

Perhaps it was the glint of mockery shining again in Fear's eyes, perhaps only the "Master Strang" which made me feel childish and guilty and urged me to assert my years and manhood—anyhow, something put spark to the Strang powder in my breast, and it flared.

"Take care," said I, "that ye don't get a lick o' his tongue for yourself, sir. I doubt I'm the first boy that ever kissed girl on a berrying frolic. If I am, 'tis a happy invention. Besides, there's frolics—and frolics, as my father well knows. The kind they hold at Port Mutton, say!"

I was sorry as soon as I said it for the shadow that came into his eyes. He was a good man and a scholar, and our physician when home simples failed. Our congregation paid him barely enough to support life and excused itself with his failings. Mr. Cheever's weakness for cordials was well known, and there had been a fine scandal a year ago when a party of respectables—captains and merchants—sailed around the Western Head to Port Mouton, where, on the shore of a lonely island safe from prying eyes, they drank strong liquors and frolicked a day and a night. 'Twas said that our preacher had danced a hornpipe on the beach with the others and sang songs not to be found in the psalter.

He said no more. Fear picked up her kettle of berries and walked past him, nose in air, and I went off in the other direction, glad to turn my back on an uncomfortable business. When we sailed home at the day's end she devoted her conversation to Arthur Carper, while I sat glum at the tiller. The day's affair sickened me. I had made a fool of myself on an impulse that must have come from Old Scratch— it was certainly none of my own—and I wanted to forget the whole thing as quick as I could. But a man once bedeviled is seldom set free, especially when there's a woman in it. From that time on, though I avoided Fear Bingay, she haunted my thoughts and filled me with longing to be near her. 'Twas like a fever or a gnawing aching hunger that cannot be satisfied and so brings on delirium. I was angry, for till that time I'd been master of myself in all ways, waking or sleeping, and now with a queer sense of doom I knew I would never be wholly master again. My life was changed, and I did not like the change. So I was savagely glad when September came and I could go hunting with

Peter Dekatha and François and give myself body and soul to an emotion I could understand.

CHAPTER 6

The Man in the Moon

SOON AFTER that memorable moose hunt, which marked for me the high point of the year 1774, Simeon Perkins called together the officers of the Queens County Militia. He was their colonel—surely the most unheroic, uneasy, un-everything military colonel that ever wore sword on a drill day. In his hand was a new regulation from Halifax, calling upon all militia officers to take the oath of allegiance, a thing which in ordinary times would have passed without quibble. But these were no ordinary times. It was well known in Nova Scotia that the province was nearly naked of regular troops. The stripping had begun as far back as the time of the Stamp Act troubles, when General Gage called in all the troops from the outposts to Halifax. By that stroke every post in the province, outside the capital, was abandoned or left to a corporal's guard; places with famous names—Fort Cumberland (that was Beausejour under the French) and Annapolis, Louisburg, Fort Frederick on the St. John, and Fort Amherst in lonely Isle St. Jean. And now these troops had gone from Halifax itself, to strengthen Gage's hand in Boston, and the preservation of law and order in the province depended on the militia, neglected for years and none too pleased with its duties now. The oath of allegiance now thrust under their noses, bound our militiamen to fight "the king's enemies"—and the king was making no bones about enemies in New England. The notion of shooting our own folk outraged all of us.

So when Simeon in his nasal deacon's voice read the oath aloud to the gathering in his house they shrank away as if his breath suddenly stank. Luke, who was a lieutenant in the town company, told me later how they searched their minds for a way out of it. The new commissions called for a fee, payable as usual to some blood-sucking secretary at Halifax, and they seized on that. They would pay no fee. Simeon (prompted, Luke thought, by James Bingay) then offered to see the fee paid, and one or two weak ones accepted the oath and the commission. The rest refused, fee or none.

"This is open defiance of His Majesty!" snorted Bingay.

"Call it what ye like," they said, and walked out.

The whole county wondered how Colonel Perkins would explain that to Halifax; but explain it he did, in some way we never knew, and the matter did not come up again for a year.

In October, when the hardwood leaves were at their loveliest on the flank of Great Hill and the southwest wind was warm and soft as a woman's breath, Fear Bingay went to Halifax to school. I told myself 'twas none of my concern—but I was there on the packet wharf, lurking amongst the molasses puncheons, and she saw me. She wore a red cloak that shone in the sunshine like a slender red maple by a river meadow and a bonnet that framed her eager face and shaded the cider-brown eyes. Her parents and friends had come down to see her off, and they stood about her little leather-bound trunk chatting lightly while the crew of the packet schooner bustled with freight. Her eyes were everywhere, and her tongue rattled merrily to this one and that, as if she were bound for high adventure rather than a dull dame's school in Halifax, and presently she espied me between the puncheon tiers and came over at once.

Her eyes danced under the bonnet's brim. "Why, David, you've come to see me off. How nice!"

I went hot and dumb and shifted my feet uncomfortably, and my shoes made little tacky sounds in the sweet leakage from the puncheons.

"Cat got your tongue, David?"

A girl has no right to bewitch a fellow against his will and then taunt him with his condition. I burst out angrily, "I just came down to watch the schooner."

She made a little mouth. "I see. Well, good-by, David."

Penitently, cravenly, I muttered humbly, "I was lying. I came to see you. I've got to see you again too. I don't know why. I'm not much good at talking—not to girls."

She burst out laughing. "So I see."

I saw her father approaching, with a cold blue eye on me, and the group about Fear's trunk was regarding us curiously.

"You must write me a letter from Halifax," I said urgently. "Promise!"

"La!" she pouted. "You sound just like Papa and Mama. Goodness me, I'll have writing enough to do at Ma'am Mawdsley's, without writing letters to half Liverpool!" She was watching her father's approach with a sidelong eye under the long lashes and edging away from me. "Good-by, David."

"But you'll think of me sometimes?" I entreated, unconsciously putting out a hand as if for alms. The log jam in my mouth had given way under stress of emotion, and the words came tumbling off my tongue. "Because I'll think of you . . . all the time. . . . I dream about you at night and hear your voice when I'm doing my chores. . . . I feel about you the way I feel about my mother . . . only it's different . . . it's like music that makes you feel hungry . . . or lying on your back looking up at the stars and getting all dizzy thinking how far away they are. . . ."

She was moving toward her father, walking backward with her eyes on me, and they looked round and surprised. "Yes, David. That's very nice, David. Good-by, David. Good-by . . . good-by!"

Mr. Bingay was saying, "Come, my dear, your friends . . ." with a parting blue stare at me. I couldn't bear to see her go. I turned and fled—to a pine top on the ridge above the town, whence I watched the stained old sails of the packet go down the harbor and vanish around Coffin's Island—and I climbed down and flung myself on the pungent brown needles and wept. Calf love! And what's sadder than calf love bereft—discharged after ninety days' sight like one of Mr. Bingay's own bills of exchange? I was crushed. But I rose again in time for supper. And as a first step toward seeing her again I resolved to acquire a trade.

I began to learn navigation from easygoing Mark; but on my father's insistence in November I commenced going to Mr. Cheever three evenings a week for instruction in mathematics, especially those dealing with the measurement of planes, angles, and suchlike. 'Twas a painful affair in all ways. I had no hankering for the sea; my thoughts were all of the land—and Fear Bingay. In the second place I hated mathematics as the devil hates psalm tunes. In the third place the affair of the strawberry frolic was still fresh in my mind—and Mr. Cheever's—and made for no ease between us. And finally Mr. Cheever could not afford a fire in a separate room for such ill-paying business (sixpence a lesson) and I had to sit over a candle in a corner of the kitchen, in the presence of the family.

Mr. Cheever watched me constantly, and especially when my eye strayed from the bleak sums on the slate toward the bright fire where the girls sat sewing with Mrs. Cheever. The kitchen table was pushed back against the far wall, and I sat at its coldest, uttermost corner with my slate (a thin slab from the ledge above the Falls, set in a pine-wood frame) and Mark's rule and brass compasses and Mr. Cheever's old cherished globe, whose oceans and continents were faded and worn to mere shadows and looked like the man on the moon.

My head ached with definitions—Plane Sailing, Traverse Sailing, Middle Latitude Sailing, Mercator Sailing—and with problems and examples which never came right on the slate. I can see Mr. Cheever now, delighted with his role of schoolmaster and pleased with himself, for navigation was a fad of his, and he had read a good deal on the subject. He would honk his long nose in a big blue-and-white handkerchief and peer through his small spectacles at an old chart spread out on the table and held down at the corners by knives and spoons and he would bark at me something like this: "A ship sails southeast from a position in latitude fifty degrees ten minutes south, longitude ten degrees sixteen minutes east, until her departure from the meridian is nine hundred and fifty-seven miles. I demand her distance sailed and the latitude and longitude she is in."

Down would go my head, with a shriek of pencil on slate and a thumb in the table book and a great invisible spoon in my skull stirring a whirligig of figures that never fell quite into place. I love ships. They are beautiful things, I truly believe, the only handiwork of mankind that approaches the beauty of God's. But I could not see ships in this thrice-weekly nightmare. The kitchen was lined with pine boards, nailed on green when the house was built and now shrunk dry, leaving long black cracks between one and another. On bitter January and February evenings the wind down the frozen river whistled through the walls, the draft past my shoulders kept the candle aflutter, and my feet turned to stone in my shoes. Mr. Cheever had chosen this spot for my labors because it was farthest from the fireside chatter and the less distraction; but I think, too, he considered a cold corner best for hot blood like mine and seemed to get a good deal of satisfaction from the wriggle of my shoulders and the rattle of my young teeth and the sight of my bold Strang nose as blue as a bluenose potato.

Between excursions into the cold for a peep at my slate he stood back to the fire, teetering comfortably on the heels and toes of his house moccasins, with his hands behind hoisting his coattails for the better warming of his bony behind. And from time to time he came and looked over my shoulder, said, "Humph!" through his rum-blossomed nose, and walked away, giving the old globe a twirl in passing. The globe shrieked on its worn metal axis; my pencil shrieked on the slate, and my soul shrieked within me.

There was much political talk in our town that winter. Seth Harding was gone many weeks on a West India voyage, and Halifax was quick to declare his seat vacant for non-attendance. With the same ready excuse, Halifax was emptying country seats right and left—all those held by men of Whig views. Few of the country members could make a regular attendance on account of the cost and the distance. At one time they had introduced a measure of payment for members, but in '72 that was repealed. In short, Halifax, which dominated the assembly as Citadel Hill dominates Halifax town, made true representation as difficult as possible and then tempted the countryfolk with candidates from the ruling Halifax coterie, who stood well with the governor and council and would save the people all this trouble and expense.

In this fashion now they urged our town, by letter and messenger, to appoint a Halifax merchant in the room of Seth Harding, dismissed. That met no favor in Liverpool. Our people felt their importance—the second town in the province after Halifax. Even Mr. Cheever declared we must cease selling our Yankee birthright for a mess of Halifax pottage.

In the face of the governor's ban no town meeting could be called. But in kitchen and parlor, in the stores, in the porch of the meetinghouse of a Sabbath afternoon, on the sunny side of the wharf sheds —wherever men gathered for a word or a whiff of tobacco—the talk was all for sending a man of our own. But what man of ability would go? If he missed a session he was dismissed the seat. If he attended faithfully and spoke the mind of his electors faithfully, and that mind ran contrary to the governor's (as ours surely must) he was dismissed the seat, as William Smith had been. So where was the point in his going?

The matter was argued and argued and finally put over till spring.

In late February, with its clear skies and increasing sun, which put a good crust on the winter's snow, Peter Dekatha and François and their dogs went moose hunting day after day in the woods up the river. I longed to go with them and was forever sneaking to the kitchen mantel and taking down the long musket of Louisburg, throwing it to my shoulder and sighting on something outside the window. But hunting was forbidden by my father as a distraction from lessons, and barring Sundays the only fresh air I got was in the bright noons, when I stood in the hard-beaten snow of our dooryard with Mark's old quadrant in my hands, taking the sun under Mark's quizzical eye.

Once or twice Luke and Mark went off to hunt, waddling awkwardly on snowshoes, as Mark said, "Like a youngster short-taken in green-apple time!" and came back exhausted and sore in the ankles, with empty hands and eyes red-swollen and weeping with snow blindness. 'Twas my turn to laugh then, and laugh I did, maliciously. For I was a native son, born in a hut on the shores of Liverpool Bay two years before the settlement, whereas these older brothers of mine were Massachusetts-born. They were typical of all our Yankee settlers on the Nova Scotia shore—sailors and fishermen, knowing little and caring less for the woods at their backs. They could talk of Halifax and Quebec and ports in Newfoundland and Labrador and New England and were full of sly tales of girls in the Western Isles and the Caribbean and down the Spanish Main as far as Demerara. They could tell a ship's nation by the cut of her jib or the set of a topsail, dim-seen in the dusk on the broad western ocean. But I could count on my two hands the men in our town who had seen the first lake on our river, not more than twenty miles inland. The sea was their countryside, and like gulls they looked upon the shore as a place for nesting and drowsing a bit in the sun—no more. I think that is why, when war came to them, they were pinned to the coast like a pelt to a barn door. For them there was no retreat into the woods.

So passed our winter, as dull a winter as I ever spent. We heard that folk in New England had sworn to drink no tea while the tax remained. A vain gesture it seemed to us, for most of the tea—theirs and ours—was smuggled in any case. And what was a neighborly call of a winter evening without a dish of tea? On the other hand, in our town James Bingay and his small circle of Tory friends made a rite of drinking tax-paid tea to show their loyalty and even pledged the king in it, which seemed silly to us. Rum was so much better. But the taste of tea at these winter parties kept American troubles in mind. Every captain home from a New England voyage was questioned eagerly, and newspapers and broadsides from Boston and other New England towns were passed from hand to hand and house to house, till the very print was past reading and the paper reduced pretty much to its original rags. Things seemed quiet over Fundy Bay, and some folk said all would blow over. But my father declared it was merely the quiet of winter, which kept folk housed and shut up the talk like the steam in a pot, which would blow off the lid, come spring. The port of Boston remained closed, sealed by the king's ships, and that was how we saw it—as a pot simmering over a winter fire.

In March, Simeon Perkins astonished our whole town by announcing a visit to see his family in Norwich, Connecticut. He was the busiest man in Liverpool, a small, round-faced, frugal man who turned his hand to everything from fishing to the manufacture of leather breeches and was not above swinging a scythe in the salt meadows at Pudding Pan yet somehow never quite caught up with prosperity. In six years he had never set foot outside the township except to make an appearance in the Halifax assembly—which he said he couldn't afford. Now he spoke of a two months' holiday, at the busiest time of the year, with the fishing fleet to make ready, as if 'twere a step up the street.

He was to sail on a Monday, and the previous Sabbath I watched him in the meetinghouse, very earnest about his prayers as always, yet somehow absent-minded. 'Twas a full meeting, and Parson Cheever gave us a long sermon on the wickedness of the world and the wrath to come. Simeon sat in his lonely pew near the front, chirping "Amen!" now and again. There had been a fine row about pews in time past. Our stern Cape Codders had been content to stand in the presence of God except when they dropped on their knees; but Simeon, a Connecticut man—a gentile, you might say—and some others had put in pews for their comfort. A storm in a teacup, not yet forgotten, though most families of any substance had pews now, and only the very poor stood. Simeon looked a little forlorn there in his prominent pew; our leader by the town's insistence—or rather the insistence of the men of force amongst us—yet never quite one of us, wearing his ill-fitting leadership like a purser's shirt on a handspike and accepting it humbly as if 'twere a burden from God.

On the Monday—the 20th of March, 1775, if you want it exact—my father took staff and cloak, and my mother put on his oiled boots, and I gave him my arm to the wharf, for the spring thaw had set in, and the street was a river of slush. Captain Benajah Collins' schooner lay at his wharf ready for sea, all but some last-minute stores which a negro hand was putting aboard in a wheelbarrow, and presently Seth Harding came down the lane with two seamen behind carrying his stout oak sea chest by its rope beckets. Then came Simeon in an old boat cloak, with a red woolen muffler tied over his little old three-cornered hat and knotted under his chin and followed like Seth by two men and a chest.

They drew together by a mooring post, Benajah and Simeon and Seth and my father, talking in low tones and thrusting hands out of their cloaks from time to time to emphasize some point or other.

There was a raw air from the southeast, growing in strength, a bad wind for our harbor, bending the town's chimney smoke low over the housetops and ruffling the water in little gray chops. They would have to give over their jawing, thought I, or be wind-bound another two days.

The thought struck them all at one time, apparently, for the group opened, and my father shook hands with the other three and watched them aboard. As the lines were cast off, Seth and Benajah took a hand with the halyards, like the ready-fisted seamen they were, and the sails went up to a chuckle of well-greased blocks and the black sailor's chanting of "Haul the bowline." Simeon stood at the stern with his solemn gaze fixed on my father's face, and as the schooner dropped down the river the gilt name on her counter flashed in the sun. It was "Liberty."

It meant little to me then. Liberty had been a popular name for vessels since '68. An old silly cradle rhyme was jingling through my head:

> *The man in the moon got up too soon*
> *To ask the way to Norwich.*
> *He went by the south and burnt his mouth*
> *With supping cold pease-porridge.*

CHAPTER 7

Love Makes a Mystery

ACCORDING to the almanac, spring began the day after Colonel Perkins left for Norwich; but there's precious little spring about a foot or more of snow, even when the sun has begun to shine both sides of the pasture fence. The streets were full of slush, which a sharp night frost turned to ice, the gray, rugged ice which defies next day's sun and makes walking an adventure.

The river, which had opened as far up as the Narrows, now froze again right down to Dean's Point, across from the old jail. Then came a week's sunshine and a week of rain. The snow shrank to a mere crust in the fields, and between the sled tracks where the dung of horses and oxen lay thick and caught the sun, the ice began to decay and finally broke into clods, exposing the dark road which we had not seen since Thanksgiving. The road turned to mud, like a black stream between banks of gray ice and slush, and the mud spread as the ice shrank, till the whole town stood in a sea of it. Men wore their sea boots abroad, and women their clinking iron-shod pattens, and children tracked mud indoors, and housewives scolded and plied their birch brooms.

The first robin whistled in the fields, and song sparrows came and chanted "Pres-pres-presbyterian!" in the birch clump east of our house, and a flock of juncos worked over the dead weeds in last year's garden patch.

The sap began to run in the sugar maples, and Peter Dekatha and François went up the ridge with our buckets to tap them. They brought back their first tapping at sundown when the sap ceased to run and stood the buckets in our dooryard, and we all ran out with mugs and dipped up the sweet, clear liquid for a toast to Spring.

But our Nova Scotia spring is a cat-and-mouse affair. That night the wind shifted east and howled in the chimneys and brought in a storm of snow from the sea. It snowed all the next day and the following night, the wet heavy snow of spring. Followed an iron frost that drove all the town within doors. Then rain, then sunshine, and away went the snow and back came the mud. So went the round. On clear nights the northern lights spread their pale flames in the sky, like a beacon to the fox sparrows on their way from the south. Those strange fires seemed to melt the river ice—there was precious small sun to account for it—so that it broke up and went to sea one wild westerly night. When the ice went out the salmon came in, and codfish and pollock appeared on the inshore grounds, and our fishermen took up their trade.

The saws at the Falls began to scream down the river when the wind was right, and shipwrights laid a new keel or went on with a hull half-built before winter drove them off. Vessels fitted out for the Banks, and some for Labrador.

The graveyard grew, for it is spring in our country that kills the sick and the old with its rains and fogs and scraps of sunshine. Mr. Cheever wrestled with such an epidemic of rheumatisms and pleurisies and pneumonias as our town had never known in its history and exhausted his medicines and himself to a point where he scarce could preach more than two hours a Sunday.

By some chance there were no trading voyages to New England during April and May and therefore no news from the one place that filled our minds. There was hearsay from Halifax that fighting had begun over there, and my father hobbled up the street day after day and down the lanes to the wharves, asking news "from the west'ard."

Now and again a man slipped over to him whispering, "Where's Simeon? What's become o' Seth? What did they find?"

And always my father shook his head, growling, "They'll come—soon. We must know—soon."

It was now settled that I should go afishing to the Labrador in the *Nan* with Mark and Luke, to learn the practical side of seafaring and to make myself useful as a foremast hand. My mother insisted I must berth and eat in the cabin. My father refused, snorting that I must work my way aft from the hawse the same as Mark and Luke had done; but Mark joined his voice to Mother's, and Luke grinned, and in the end I took my sea bag, quilt, and straw sack to a small spare berth under the cabin stairs. We dropped the *Nan* down the river on a warm May evening and moored her at one of the fish-lot wharves, ready to go over the bar on the early-morning tide.

Said Mark, "We'll sleep aboard, Davy. So we'd better walk up home now and make our farewells."

He and Luke set off at once, but I had some small labors to perform, stowing sea stores, and it was dark when I set off, with candle-light yellow in all the town's windows as I walked up the long winding street. I came in the kitchen door whistling—and my whistle went dead.

The girl Joanna was sitting at the table, weeping into her folded, bare arms. My mother stood beside her, with her hands clasped and white at the knuckles, with such an air of anger about her as I'd not seen since Luke and I stole a winter's apple jelly. Mark and Luke were side by side in the midst of the room, hands clasped behind and pig-tailed heads bent to avoid Mother's eye, and instinctively I ranged myself alongside them—a hangdog trio in loose canvas trousers and red shirts, Mark in a coarse blue pea jacket. Our sea boots, water-proofed with fish oil, stank the whole room. Thank heaven there was no sign of Father—off on one of his mysterious conferences, no doubt. John was away at his books in the countinghouse.

"I can get nothing out of Joanna," said my mother in a voice that sent my heart into my boots. I stole a side glance at my brothers, but their faces were stiff and intent on the floor. Like me, I suppose, they were going over past household crimes and wondering which had brought down the wrath.

"The girl has never been outside the dooryard," the accusing voice went on, "and I thought—God forgive me—she was safe in my house. But it seems she was not. I shall say nothing of that wanton creature from Port Medway"—this was for Luke—"that one was no better than she should have been, and a good riddance. This is a different matter. Your father and I brought you up to be God-fearing young men, as we thought. But more than that I tried to teach you gentleness, kindliness toward others, especially those that were in any way weak or helpless, as this girl was helpless. An orphan, a bound-girl, with no friends nor kinfolk to give her affection. I'm very fond of Joanna"— she put out her fingers and touched the girl's bright, smooth hair— "but there's a kind of affection that a girl craves and a woman can't give—and that a young man withholds if he's truly kind. She was a good girl and deserved that kindness from all of you, and I had thought that none of you would touch her except in the way of kindness, as a brother might. It seems I was wrong. Now here is a matter to be put right. This poor girl's undone, and one of you is responsible, for she broke down when the *Nan* went down the river, knowing you'd be gone the whole summer. Luke, is it you?"

Luke did not lift his head but glanced under his thick brows at Mark and me. His lips were set stubbornly.

"Luke!"

No answer.

"Mark!" my mother cried. Her voice broke a little, and the sound filled me with misery. I was angry with Joanna. Why didn't she speak up and save us all this? Why was she making such a fuss anyhow? As if a girl had no liability in such a matter! According to my father, Mother Eve swore to the end of her days that Adam crammed the apple down her throat. Besides, I had learned a vast amount about man and woman from the idlers on the wharves these past few years and knew that no man could take a maiden unwilling—and she in good health and strong in the knees—without beating her senseless first.

"Mark!" said my mother again.

No answer. I could see the girl's rigid shoulders, her part-raised head; she was tense as a spring. I looked curiously toward Mother then and found her staring at me with a flush spreading over her face and her eyes full of unbelief and a queer dark pleading that made me feel like a wretch.

I twisted my mouth firmly and looked down and so made myself one with the others.

There was a terrible silence. Then Mother said briskly, "Very well! Since it was none of you, go back to your vessel, my sons; you'll need sleep if you're to make the morning tide." A pause. "As for this guilty girl"—our eyes all turned together to the bent golden head of Joanna—

"I'll not have her in my house another night. No! She shall pack up her traps this very hour!"

We saw Joanna's head sink on her arms again and the great shudder that came from inside her somewhere and ran up her slim back and neck and head like the flick of a whip.

"Ye can't do that, Mother!" Luke jerked out, astonished.

Her eyes blazed. "Why not?"

Luke gave his head a stubborn shake and looked down at his feet. Mark spoke slowly, in a voice unusually deep. "Because 'twas me."

Joanna's head came up. She turned her face to him, with the childish blue eyes all glassy with tears and something else—love, maybe, or hope or gratitude—I don't know. In a long and stormy life I have learned one thing about women. When a man meets the eyes of his one true love he can read what is there like a message in print. The eyes of all others are riddles, which may mean one thing or another—none worth his solving.

Mother said, "Do you love him, Joanna?"

The girl nodded her head wildly and clasped Mother's hand to her own breast, wetting the sleeve with her passionate kisses and tears.

There was a sound at the front of the house—my father's stick and shuffling step and his hand fumbling for the latch.

"Quick, girl!" Mother cried. "Pull yourself together and stand over there with Mark. Mark—put your arm about her; it'll look better. Luke, go and light your father along the hall. And you, Davy, go out the back way and fetch Mr. Cheever."

"No," Mark said calmly, with his big arm about Joanna's shoulders. The girl had performed a miracle with Mark's handkerchief, as women do; a dab at the eyes, a small but vigorous nose blow, a lick of dry lips and a hand patting the hair. She looked a different creature, a little sad still, but smiling and liking the weight of Mark's arm on her shoulders, you could see.

"Why not?" Mother said sharply.

"Not him," Mark said abruptly. "I couldn't stand Cheever. Get one o' the justices, Davy boy. Mr. Hunt, if ye can."

I ran out the kitchen door just as Father came tapping and roaring along the hall; he could never quite get his voice down to house size after an argument out of doors. It was a night of stars, with a few smudges of cloud drawn across them in untidy fashion like rope ends. The street mud had dried and was crumbling, the beginning of summer's dust. Our town went to bed soon after candlelighting as a rule, but tonight a number of people were abroad, mostly young men and women enjoying the soft spring dark. I passed Mr. Johnston, the elderly deputy registrar, before I remembered that he was also a justice of the peace. I hurried back and caught his arm. He was a Scotsman and more than a little deaf. I had to scream my errand thrice before he understood and I wished I had gone on to Hunt's, for one or two pairs of the shadowy strollers halted and tittered, and I heard an interested window opening somewhere above our heads.

When we entered the kitchen Father had thrown off his cloak and stood at his habitual post at the table's head. God knows what explanation had been given him. He scented mischief, I could see, and Mother was watching him anxiously. So were Mark and Joanna. I wondered how much he remembered of that scene at the foot of the stairs last fall. The trouble with Father's drinking bouts was that you never knew how much he would call to mind afterward.

"This girl is doubtless a good girl," he said loudly, like a man getting his mind clear on a point, "though she's of another people. Dutch! Dutch! Well, they're all right, I suppose, but I'd hoped different. Damme, Mark, how many times have I told ye to steer clear o' marriage afore thirty? A man don't know his own mind till then, and some woman's always ready to make it up for him. No reflection on you, my dear. Thrown together in the one house . . . long winter . . . and spring . . . only natural. You're a pretty thing. And a good worker. Come o' good honest people. Well! Maytime and the sap rising—trees or young men, it's the same. . . ."

"Matthew!" chided my mother with a glint in her eye.

"Don't Matthew me, Nancy," protested Father jovially. "A man's entitled to a bam or two at a wedding, ain't he? Aha, Mark, ye scamp! Courting all winter, I'll warrant. And now ye must have her tonight, on the eve of a Labrador voyage! Don't make sense, that. Not like us Strangs, that. Strang men always knew what they wanted as soon as they saw it and wanted it quick. One night with a new wife and then off to Labrador, well I'm damned!"

All this was wasted on Mark, who looked grim, and Joanna, whose face rested pale against his blue sea coat, and Mother, who looked indignant, and old Mr. Johnston, who heard only half and understood none of it.

"If ye don't mind I'll get on wi' it," said Mr. Johnston in the roar of the deaf, "for I'm expectit hame the past hoor."

"Get on with it then," Father said and winked at Luke and me.

It did not take long. The justices never took as long as Mr. Cheever. They did most of the marrying in our town, as the custom was.

"That'll be one shillin'!" Mr. Johnston roared at the end of it.

Mark rummaged in his canvas trousers and paid him two pistareens out of a handful of small coins, and the justice departed thankfully.

"There should be a second-day wedding tomorrow after the fashion of our people," Father grumbled, "and here's the bridegroom sailing on the morning tide. I'll not have it! The Labrador cod can wait another couple o' days, Mark. We'll have a proper feast at Ma'am Dexter's Tavern for the quality and a keg o' Demerara in the street for the poor folk."

"No!" said Mark quickly.

"What, kiss and run? What'll the girl think?"

"She'll think of her husband's business first, like a sensible girl," Mother put in swiftly.

Mark said, "The *Nan's* below and ready to sail. My men are shipped, and *they're* ready to sail. And since they're to fish on a lay of half-the-hand they won't like idling here another two days. No more would I."

The girl still held her face against his coat. Her eyes were closed, and she looked calm as death, but her breasts rose and sank with her unquiet breathing.

"Besides," added Mark, "you know how chancy the winds are, Father, and the lie of our harbor. A slant east and you're wind-bound —maybe for days. I tell you I sail in the morning."

There was a knocking at our front door, slow and cautious, as of someone weak in the wrist.

"Here's old Johnston back for a kiss o' the bride," Father said. "Let him in, Davy."

But it was Colonel Perkins who stood in the flicker of my candle as I threw open the door. He whisked inside and shut the door himself, his eyes wide as an owl's, and trotted at my heels to the kitchen and stood there blinking.

That ended the argument. Father hobbled over in a fever of excitement and caught Simeon's hands, drawing him into the far corner by the pantry. They pulled up chairs knee to knee and put their heads together like a pair of gossipy women. Simeon's high, hurried whispering reached us in a jerky, unintelligible hiss, like a kettle just coming to the boil.

"Go on down to the vessel," Mark said to Luke and me. "I'll be right along."

"You can't, Mark," Mother said primly, with a little spot of color coming and going in her cheek. "Don't you understand that a child will be born to Joanna while you're away? What will your father think? Take Joanna to your room."

Joanna shrank away from Mark then, gasping, "Ah no! Please, ma'am!"

Mother set her mouth firmly. "Take a candle, Mark, and go upstairs. Joanna, you go with your husband, and let's have no more of this nonsense."

They went, like a pair of sleepwalkers, and we heard Simeon's rising voice clearly above their slow feet on the stairs.

". . . all America in an uproar. Fighting at Concord and Lexington and the king's troops driven back into Boston. Crown Point and Ticonderogy's taken by the rebels, with all their guns and stores, and the way's open to Canada. The Congress is meeting at Philadelphia to raise a reg'lar army and appoint a commander in chief and arrange supplies and suchlike. It's war, I tell you. And every colony south o' Fundy's back of it! Embargo . . . they told me plump and plain there's to be no more trade with Nova Scotia till we come out for liberty with the rest. No ships sailing . . . I waited and waited and at last had to charter a small schooner to get home. I'd no money to pay the charter and must now satisfy the captain with a lading of timber from my mill at the Falls . . . and what'll Halifax think of that, I wonder? Dear, dear, dear! This is all very terrible to me, Cap'n Strang; my family in Norwich . . ."

"Bah!" snapped Father, and his voice rose. "Is it easy for any of us? What are the rebels' chances, think you? What are their chances o' beating the king?"

Simeon pursed his little prim mouth. His queue had come untied, and his hair was wild; he looked as if he had rushed straight out of a seasick berth and doubtless had. "That's very hard to say. You talk to one of the Committees of Safety and you think the British will be driven into the sea in a month. You talk to one of the Tory gentlemen —and they're a great many—and you decide the rebels will all be hung in a month."

"What did ye see? That's what we sent ye for."

Simeon shrugged his small shoulders. "Cap'n Collins landed us at Salem. Seth and me went on to Norwich ahorseback, a tiresome journey. We gave Boston a wide berth but had to pass through the American lines—they appeared to stretch from Boston town to the Mystic River. Mr. Ward and Mr. Putnam seem to be the generals, but there was very little order anywhere—a Committee of Safety at every crossroads, and Sons of Liberty and Patriots and minutemen rushing out of the bushes to our horses' heads every few miles."

"Did ye say ye were from Nova Scotia?" There was a sneer on my father's lips.

Simeon avoided his hard eyes. "No, Cap'n. I begged Seth to let me do the talking and told 'em we were Conne'ticut men. 'Twas the truth, after all."

"What does Seth think?"

"The same as you—that it'd be suicide for us in Nova Scotia to hoist the rebel flag, what with Halifax at our backs, and a British army just across Fundy Bay, and men-o'-war arriving constantly on our coast from England. But he believes firmly in the rebel cause and says they'll win in the end."

"Well?"

Simeon hesitated. His fingers stroked his small beak of a nose. "Seth says we must have liberty, same as the rest. Says we must earn it, same as the rest. And there's only one way to do it. We must pick up, lock, stock, and barrel, and remove our families to safety in New England. Then join the rebels and fight."

"What! Leave everything we've built up all these hard years? Where'll that get us—or Nova Scotia?"

"He says when the rebels have won we'll put in our voice for Nova Scotia's rights, same as the rest. Then we can come back."

Father was thunderstruck. "Damme, Seth must be mad."

"He says the Tories over there are doing it, on the king's side."

I heard a little crack and saw the stem of Father's long clay snapped in his fingers and the bowl spilling burning tobacco on the floor. Out of a long silence he said, "The Tories over there have no choice. They're being driven out o' their homes by the mobs. But nobody's driving us—yet. And by God, sir, we'll not go till we're driven! Seth—will Seth practice what he preaches?"

"Yes. He plans to sit tight in Nova Scotia for a time, as you advised, but he'll go when the test comes."

"Test? What test, sir?"

"When the governor orders the oath of allegiance throughout the province and calls upon the militia to do what the oath binds 'em to do—fight the king's enemies."

"Aha! And you, Simeon—you're a magistrate and member o' the assembly . . . and colonel o' the militia . . . what'll you do?"

I thought Simeon Perkins was going to weep. He kept passing a hand over his small round face, so like a sad little saw-whet owl that I wanted to laugh.

"What d'ye think I ought to do, Cap'n Strang?" he asked meekly.

Father put his chin up and pointed the broken pipe at Simeon's breast like a pistol. "'Tain't me alone, Simeon. Mind that. Rule out Seth and James Bingay—rule out all the hot Whigs and Tories amongst us. There's cool heads here, and mine's one. We've got to sit tight, like I told ye last fall. What ye saw over there makes me all the more sure. Sit tight—sit tight. That's our policy."

Luke thrust in suddenly, crying, "Father, what coward's talk is that?"

"It's mine," said Father loudly. "And hold your tongue, son. Any thief can cry Liberty when there's plunder to be had by it. Any leech can cry Loyalty while there's fat blood to suck. By God, sir, it takes a sound man to keep his mouth shut in times like these."

"That's what the 'Cajuns did!" Luke taunted.

Father turned and stared him down. "I'm thinking of the 'Cajuns, son. Trouble with them was, they didn't sit tight enough. We'll not make that mistake."

Simeon picked up his hat and departed, with a grave little nod to my silent mother, and Father hobbled to the door with a hand on his shoulder. The door closed, and Father drew the latch for the night.

"Go down to the vessel now and get some sleep. Thank God you're going to Labrador," Mother said to Luke and me. She kissed us fondly, as if we were going to the end of the earth.

"Good-by, boys," my father said. We had his own horror of emotion and uttered our good-bys casually as we slipped out the back way. Halfway down the lane I looked back and saw the candle still lit in Mark's bedchamber.

Chapter 8

"Halifax"

THE *Nan* was a sweet little schooner of a hundred tons, setting a square topsail on her foremast. Father had her built six years before, at Shipyard Point, in the shadow of the meetinghouse, and all her timber had come from our own lands, sawn in the mill at the Falls. Ten men slept forward, and in the cabin aft were berths for Mark, Luke, and Bradford, the old Labrador fisherman who carried a chart of that wild coast in his head, and there was my small berth under the stairs. A small stove stood on the cabin floor, with a pipe to carry its smoke through the deck. It blackened the mainsail infamously. The deck was a clutter of boats, firmly lashed for sea. The *Nan* was ballasted for the voyage with beach stones from Coffin's Island, which would be thrown out on the shores of Labrador, as if that barren country had not stones enough; and in the hold was a summer's provision and stores, some trumpery for the Eskimo trade, and some hogsheads of Turk's Island salt for our fish.

The night was chill, and old Bradford had a wood fire crackling in the stove and lay in his berth smoking a stubby black clay by the light of a lantern. Luke and I set about stowing our chests, and I turned in soon after. Luke sat on the edge of his berth whetting his sheath knife on a bit of stone from Whetstone Hill, and as I drifted into sleep I heard him spitting on the stone from time to time and the soft slip-slip-slip of the steel. I was wakened by heavy steps on the deck overhead and opened an eye to see Mark's boots coming down the ladder past my head. I thought 'twas morning and was marveling how fast the night had gone, when Luke exclaimed, "What! Only an hour? What kind o' bridegroom . . ." That was as far as he got, for Mark struck him a buffet that sent him sprawling.

I was up on my elbows peering between the stairs at them, astounded. Mark's face was a thunderstorm. He stood with his boots planted apart and his big fists doubled, while Luke slowly picked himself up.

"What was that for?" Luke said thickly.

"I reckon ye know," Mark said. "Put up your fists and drop that knife, while I beat the skunk out o' ye."

"Ah! That's easy said. I'll give ye a fight if that's what ye want. But first tell me why? Not that I care a damn."

Mark paused. Then, through his teeth, "Ye don't know? Ye swear to that?"

"On a stack o' Bibles if ye like. What's the matter, Mark?"

Mark said nothing. He slumped suddenly on his berth and put his face in his hands. Luke watched him for a time and looked at Bradford and through the stairs at me. I think in all Nova Scotia there were not three more astonished creatures. Finally Luke crawled into his own berth, in his clothes, and lay still. I knew the blow must have hurt, for the sound of it was the sound of an ax on a block. I could see old Bradford half raised in his berth, across from me, with his eyes like saucers. Like me he had expected a terrible brawl, for Luke was not the kind to take a blow meekly, not even from Mark the skipper, and both were able and young—and Strangs. But nothing more happened. Mark sat hunched in the same attitude of misery. When the candle guttered and died in the lantern he was sitting there still.

Our first port of call was Halifax, for a supply of fishhooks. This was our first consequence of the stoppage of trade with New England. Halifax prices were high, and we had never bought there in time past. There was a fresh breeze off the land, and the sun shone brightly on the little stone lighthouse of Sambro as I put down the *Nan's* helm for the long beat into the harbor. 'Twas the pride of Halifax, that lighthouse, the only one on the coast, built with the proceeds of a government lottery, and dark whenever the rascally Halifax contractor failed to send oil for its lantern. That, growled Bradford, was just like Halifax and its money-grubbing Tory merchants.

The harbor at Halifax is surely one of the best in the world, shaped like a thick-handled spade and shut in by steep wooded hills. There is deep water everywhere inside Cornwallis Island, which guards the mouth of it, and I reckon the whole of the king's navy could ride secure in the great basin at the end. We beat up the wide west passage past Maugher's Beach and its row of gibbets, where mutineers and pirates were hanged from time to time as a warning to all who passed in or out of the port, and the small green hump of George's Island showed a row of old log casemates like a grin of rotten teeth, and beyond them rose the masts of the shipping. Under the shoulder of Citadel Hill the town huddled in a haze of its own chimney smoke.

As we reached away from Maugher's Beach on the starboard tack, Mark decided to run into the Northwest Arm, whose narrow length now opened before us.

Luke protested, "Why, that'll give us a two-mile scramble through the woods to the town!"

"Good for the legs," answered Mark coolly; and to me at the tiller, "Keep her so, youngster. This is poor man's alley. On the harbor side there'll be wharfage or port fees or some damned thing or other to pay."

The Arm was an alley in truth, running up into the woods behind the town. We anchored about a mile inside, and it was beautiful, a trough of blue water between steep timbered ridges, with a few fishing huts along the shore. A favorite haven for small craft like ours, a quiet place at the town's back door, with clean brooks for the filling of water casks and plenty of wood for the cutting.

We went ashore in the jolly boat, Mark, Luke, Enos West, Dean Christopher, the two Freemans, Innoot the Eskimo man, and myself, and left Christopher to guard the boat against water thieves. The sun was nigh down and the wind with it, and a swarm of black flies plagued us as we climbed the plateau by a smugglers' path through the trees. We were hot and sticky when we emerged from the woods into a stretch of pastures south of the town, whose green was spotted with grazing cattle. Chimneys of scattered farmhouses smoked lazily in the evening air. We struck off through the fields toward the high hump of Citadel Hill and presently came to a dark swampy brook fringed with alder thickets.

"In case ye lose your way coming back," Mark observed, "fix this brook in your minds, for it's the southerly boundary o' the town more or less—flows out of a pond in the common, up there to the no'thard, and goes on through these fields and across the Spring Garden Road, then takes a turn to the west'ard and flows into the harbor by what's called Black Rock, near Point Pleasant."

"Let's go down the Spring Garden Road," urged Luke. "It's easier."

"Nunno! The English general's headquarters is there, t'other side o' those pastures, with a guard hailin' strangers and damnin' their eyes. If ye want to keep out o' trouble in Halifax, lads, steer clear o' His Majesty's army and navy. Mind that!"

So we leaped the brook—fat Innoot the Eskimo fell in and made a fine splash that set us in a roar—and crossed more pastures and stone walls to the south foot of Citadel Hill, where we found a cart track which proved to be the head of Sackville Street. The green tip of the hill caught the last of the sunset, and we could make out a straggle of grass-grown entrenchments made there in the town's first days. I was disillusioned. I had expected a fortress with towers and battlements, but there was precious little fortress about a sugar-loaf hill still covered largely with stumps and boulders and blueberry bushes, with a crumbling ditch or two at the top.

There were houses now, and to our right was an enclosure with a gate, through which our frugal south-shore eyes gaped at winding walks and masses of shrubs and fruit trees, some in blossom already, and a fancy pavilion in the middle. "Adlam's Gardens," grunted Mark. "A great place for fops and petticoats a-Sundays. They're mighty fond o' nature in Halifax so long as it's dry-footed and got a good fence round it. The governor's got a garden, too, over on the Spring Garden

Road. A fine situation, next to St. Paul's burying ground and across the street from the workhouse. They can sit in the shade o' the governor's trees and see the poor devil at the whipping post over the road, ay, and watch the paupers buried on the one hand and the gentry on t'other. Only trouble is, the workhouse don't bury its dead deep enough, and the stink comes over the road in spring and spoils the smell o' the cherry blossoms."

From Sackville Street, just below Adlam's Gardens, a road branched off to the north, along the harbor slope of Citadel Hill, and we could see a huddle of frowsy huts and dwelling houses.

"Barrack Street," chuckled Luke. "Dram shops and whore houses, a fine place to get a bloody nose when the fleet's in. Knock-'em-down Street, the townfolk call it."

One or two of our party stopped, and fat Innoot said brightly, "Gal?"

Mark fetched him a kick behind. "Get along, ye graceless savage. There's cleaner in Labrador."

"A drink'd do no harm," suggested Enos West thirstily.

"There's other places, man. The business o' half Halifax is to sell rum, and t'other half to drink it."

Halifax was in darkness already, lying as it did in the gloomy shadow of the big hill; windows were yellow with candlelight, and below we could see a lamplighter going his rounds. There was no footpath. We took the middle of the street for it, dodging the bigger rocks and walking with a sharp rake to our spines, for the road fell down the slope like the pitch of a roof. I wonder now what Lord George Sackville would have thought of the street they had named after him, for grass grew amongst the old stumps at the roadside, with a beaten plat before each door, and the air was rich with garbage and slops which lay everywhere underfoot. The houses were small and stood on dry wall or a bank of sods, well clear of the spring floods, which once a year swept all this filth down to the water front.

We crossed several streets running across the slope parallel with the harbor. All had the look and smell of Sackville Street, although here and there was a fine stone house—stone from the ruins of Louisburg, most of it—and to the left above the fine willow trees of Argyle Street I saw the spire of St. Paul's very clear against the light evening sky and the first stars.

We turned off along Barrington Street, a long wooden valley of houses and shops with shutters up for the night. Upon each corner a lantern flickered on its post like a small, disheartened moon.

The capital was a disappointment. I had expected gay and jostling crowds. We met no one but a few seamen like ourselves tramping along in the mud and dark, watchmen making their first rounds, an old, furtive man with a bundle of rags under his arm, and one woman, who scurried along like a scared hen, face drawn well back into bonnet. There was less grass and more filth in the gutters of Barrington Street, and as we drew opposite St. Paul's, a noble bulk in a mass of willows, there was no grass at all. The street at this point, the heart of the town, was a river of mud and stones, with many bad holes; a proof of Halifax piety, gibed Luke—the road worn out by people going to church. I gazed at the shadowy wooden building with awe and a certain queer affection; like our own home in Liverpool, St. Paul's was a real portion of New England set down in the northern wilds. I'd heard Father tell how the oak frame and pine boards came from Boston in the town's first days and how the Reverend Tutty did his preaching in the open air, on the garrison parade ground opposite, while the church was abuilding.

Most Halifax folk belonged to the Established Church or went there, at any rate. The Roman folk had no church, and all Protestant dissenters worshiped in the meetinghouse down at the corner of Prince and Hollis streets, which was called Mather's Church after the great Cotton Mather.

"All the shops are shut," Luke declared, pulling up at the corner of George Street. "Ye'll get no hooks tonight. Let's have a drink."

"There's a Jew down by Market Square that'll open any time," Mark said. "But what's wrong with the town? I never knew it so quiet of a weekday night. Where's all the soldiers and men-o'-war's-men?"

Luke reached out and tapped the shoulder of a passer-by, a lean, yellowed fellow coming along at a great rate with a ledger under his arm and a pair of quills stuck in his hatband. The fellow gave a little startled cry and made off, but Luke's big fingers closed on his flying coattails and brought him up standing.

"Please, sir," whined Luke through his nose, in the manner of a bumpkin from the outports, "we be three poor sailormen up to town for a frolic, and where's everybody?"

"To bed—where I'm going," the fellow said, "if you'll be so kind."

Luke gathered the fellow's coat front into his fist gently and dragged him forward, body and bones, until you couldn't have put sixpence between their noses. We stood under a lamppost and the sickly light made the man look like a corpse.

"Listen, Inky Fingers! I ask a civil question and want a civil answer.

Where's everybody? Why's the town so silent? Is there a plague, or what?"

"Let his heels down," Mark said. "A man can't talk cozy-like on his tiptoes."

Luke eased his hold a little.

"I meant no harm," the fellow gasped. "It's the trouble in Boston—all the troops have gone there, the last company of the 65th left a few days ago, and there's not a regular left in town but the governor's guard. Every rogue's abroad these nights—saving your presence, sirs—and the constables are helpless without the military pickets."

"Where's your militia?" Mark said. "Or wouldn't they take the oath?"

"There—uh—there's a great amount of sickness. The militia couldn't turn out enough to make a guard. Colonel Butler's asked that the militia be excused duty, and the council's given its consent."

"And the fleet?"

"Gone to Boston with the troops. Except there's a number of tenders left here to pick up recruits—and now for God's sake, let me go!"

Luke opened his fingers and the man ran off.

"Now for a drink!" growled one of the Freeman men.

But at this moment there was a vague cry from one of the lower streets, and it was taken up by a surprising number of voices, a single word, short and explosive, uttered over and over. There came a sound of running feet and a knot of men in fishermen's dress came past in a great hurry, crying out to us, "Press! Press! Run, lads, run!"

And now we heard chamber windows going open and voices, male and female—mostly female—crying down to the street, "Press! Press! Press!" The sound sprang up everywhere, from scampering men and boys caught abroad like ourselves, from upper windows all over the town, in a swelling, screaming chant that had in it a note of malediction as well as warning.

A lantern came bobbing along Barrington Street from the south and behind it a purposeful group of men armed with cudgels of some sort. We started to run down George Street, but from a dark doorway a woman's voice cried out to us, "Hold up! There'll be another gang comin' up from Market Slip. Into the alley, lads!"

Into a dim alley we dived like hares, and a dark stinking place it was, where the shopfolk emptied their chamber pots. Crouching there we saw the men with the lantern go past, a dozen of them in short wide-legged sailors' slops, some in pea jackets, some in tarry waistcoats, some in shirt sleeves. His Majesty's lower deck wore no uniform like the army, but we knew them for men-o'-war's-men by the tight cock of the three-cornered hats amongst them, though one or two wore striped nightcaps like our own, and some had narrow-brimmed straws tarred black, that went by the name of tarpaulin hats. They were a tough and able lot, picked for the work, no doubt, and armed with oak foot stretchers out of their boats.

In their rear they hustled along the first fruits of the night's work, three or four seamen—Dutchmen from the Lunenburg coasters by their accents—with arms bound behind and heads bloody.

Their shoe patter died away toward Market Slip, where doubtless their boats waited, but Mark held us quiet in the reeking dark for a time.

"So that's why all the town's indoors!" he said at last. "Lucky we put into the Arm, or they ha' boarded the *Nan* afore this. Now listen, all. No drinkin' tonight. They search the taverns first and last. It's a case o' cut and run, boys, and devil take the hindmost. Slip upstreet and across the parade ground and make over Citadel Hill for the fields. Watch your chance to cross Barrack Street, mind—they'll be searchin' all the dolly shops."

"And you?" Luke growled.

"I'm goin' for my hooks, press or no press. We can't fish without 'em."

"Then here's with ye!" said I fiercely.

"Ay, ay!" whispered the others.

"Do what ye're told!" hissed Mark savagely. "Luke and Davy can come with me if they want to risk it. More's a crowd. Off wi' ye!"

They slipped out of the alley and nipped up George Street and across Barrington into the dark of the parade ground. We waited, listening anxiously, for a time. Down the hill came a steady uproar from Barrack Street, where His Majesty's press was battering at doors, and women leaned out of upper windows emptying slops and abuse on their heads and screaming "Press! Press! Press!" at the top of their pipes.

At last we slunk out of the alley, Mark ahead, and crept down George Street keeping close against the shop shutters. In a minute we were at the corner of Granville Street, in the shadow thrown by a very smoky lantern high on the corner post. I sucked in a great breath. Before us stood the great town pump; beyond, and extending far to the right, lay the grounds of the governor's residence, a fine two-story wooden mansion built in the time of Governor Lawrence. It stood on a green terrace enclosed by railings, and every window was bright with candlelight, thrusting broad beams into the outer darkness, and one glittered on the fixed bayonet of a sentry pacing before the Granville Street entrance. Governor Legge, that quarrelsome and suspicious man, had been seeing spies in every corner since his private desk in the mansion was robbed of its papers in '74, and he suspected the Yankee settlers more than any. 'Twould not do for us to be found skulking here.

But Mark was gazing at the far corner of George Street, where a wooden platform ran all the way from Granville Street to Hollis, with an old ship's cannon planted muzzle-down at each corner. This I knew from hearsay was the core of our capital. Upon that platform in the mornings the merchants of Halifax took coffee and made plans and bargains; and on fine afternoons it was the promenade of all the town's idle and fashionable. Beyond it, at the foot of George Street and appallingly close, it seemed to me, was Market Square with its slip where the press gangs kept their boats and the guardhouse where they flung their catch until 'twas time to take them off to the ships. The store of Hart the Jew, where Mark thought to buy his hooks at this hour, lay at the far end of the merchants' walk—within sight of the guardhouse, the press gangs' boatkeepers at the slip, and the sentries of Government House! I was scared and so, I think, was Luke; but Mark's big jaw was up.

"If we're hailed," he announced softly, "or if ye see any sign o' the press, take to your heels. All's clear just now. Come on!"

We slipped across the open of George Street, and it seemed ocean-wide. The town still rang with the cry of "Press!" rising and falling as the gangs moved in the hunt. We gained the upended cannon at the corner of the merchants' walk. Now we could see the sentry at the Hollis Street entrance to Government House and the small dark office of Captain Bulkeley, the provincial secretary, in the corner of the grounds nearest Market Square. Not a soul was in sight but the sentries, and it came to me with a little shock that these tall-capped grenadiers, this corporal's guard left behind for the governor's protection, were now the entire garrison of Nova Scotia.

Chapter 9

His Majesty's Press Gang

I SHALL NEVER FORGET the ominous quiet in the midst of all that tumult, as we stole crabwise down the merchants' walk with our backs to the countinghouse shutters. Government House blazed into the night like a great chandelier. I wondered at the governor's scorn of privacy, but it occurred to me that his windows shone forth for a reason—to light the lawns against intruders. A puffy-faced, violent, intolerant major of foot, thrust into this high office by the influence of his English relations, who were anxious to get him off their hands no doubt, Francis Legge was bewildered to find himself governing the one province on the whole seaboard which had not joined the Congress, and what he could not understand made him angry. Government House on this May night was a picture of his own frame of mind—a little blaze of loyalty surrounded by darkness.

'Twas a little thing that ruined our bold expedition into the lion's mouth—a knot sticking up from the worn plank walk. Mark tripped and fell heavily, and the hollow platform boomed like a cannon under the shock. The sentinel at the Hollis Street gate to Government House challenged loudly and sprang into the road, leveling his piece at the sound. We saw the flash of his pan and flung ourselves down, and the musket shot and the whack of the ball into the wooden wall beside us came almost together. We scrambled up for a run back the way we had come—and saw the Granville Street sentry with leveled piece and behind him the guard turning out. We swung then for a dart north along Hollis Street, away from all this, and ran straight into a party of His Majesty's seamen from the guardhouse at Market Slip. There were eight or nine of them, grinning in the light of their lantern and swinging their oak stretchers suggestively.

A big fellow in a striped shirt and pea jacket, a boatswain by the look and air of him, said to us, "Well, my hearties, what's here?"

"Three honest fishermen," Mark said quickly.

"Why d'ye creep about like thieves then?"

"Because the whole town's crying, 'Press!'" Mark confessed boldly.

"Ah! That's well spoken, friend. And why are ye afraid?"

"Because I'm skipper, and these are my mates, and the schooner can't sail in the morning without us."

When he said this the men nodded to each other and to the boatswain delightedly.

"What!" roared the boatswain in great humor. "Have we picked up three topmen so easy? Take 'em, lads."

"Hold on!" Mark cried, doubling his fists.

"Ay, we'll do that," said the boatswain. They closed in, swinging their stretchers and eying our fists and shoulders with a calculating air. We stood together and struck out fiercely. Mark felled one, and Luke another, and I'll wager their jaws were sore for a week; but the stretchers fell cruelly on our heads and wrists, and suddenly Mark went down in a heap. Luke lunged like a bull beset by dogs, with three of them clinging, and cried out to me, "Run, Davy, run!"

I ran off a little way obediently but thought better of it and came back.

Mark lay very still in the mud, and they had drawn Luke's arms behind him and thrust a stretcher between his arms and his back, lashing his wrists to it, at the same time beating him about the face with their fists and crying great oaths. I sprang in, striking hard at them, and fetched one fellow a fine thump square on the nose and felt it crunch under my knuckles. A stretcher whacked my wrists sorely. I caught it, wrenched it, and had it and fetched its owner a whack over the nightcap that dropped him out of the fight. The gang had split up now. Two men were dragging Mark's senseless body by the heels down Market Square, and two were hustling Luke off in the same direction, still beating him with their stretchers, for he was kicking and struggling in spite of bound arms. Three were down and would press no more men this night. The boatswain and another remained and came at me now. I got my back to a doorway and swung the stretcher viciously, but a smart blow from the boatswain's cudgel knocked it out of my hand. They sprang in and seized me expertly, twisting my arms behind my back and thrusting a stretcher into place. I cried out wildly, in sheer rage, and for the pain in my arms. It seemed all up with me then.

But now came another man into the fight, a tall fellow from nowhere, with a broad set of shoulders and a fist that fell on the boatswain's jaw with the sound of a maul on a fence post. Down went the boatswain, and his mate gave back a little, swinging his stretcher and yelling for the others. The two with Mark dropped him and came back on the run. I picked up the stretcher at my feet. The stranger and the boatswain's mate were at it hammer and tongs. I saw a chance and thumped the sailor's head with the good hard oak. Down he went.

"My sweet man!" cried the stranger, in a brogue as Irish as Paddy's pig.

The seamen approaching could not see us for the gloom of the doorway, but they could see the boatswain lying in the muck, in the small pale ring cast by the lantern, and their yells brought up reinforcements—the guard from Government House, or part of it anyhow. I could make out the approaching white crossbelts and the faint glitter of bayonets.

There was a shoot of bolts behind, and the door gave at our backs, and in we fell, the stranger and I. We leaped up and saw a handsome gray-bearded Jew holding a candle and a young woman fastening the bolts. A stick thumped on the door violently. The woman turned a pair of dark, frightened eyes to the old man, but he shook his gray locks and put a finger to his lips. 'Twas the stoutest door I ever saw, six inches of native oak on a pair of enormous H hinges and barred and studded with iron. There were four bolts, each as thick as a handspike. Several shoulders came against the door and must have been the worse for it. At last a voice said, "Ah, save your breath, lads. It's old Hart the Jew—they'd never get in there. They've made off somehow. What odds? We've a fine pair o' topmen. We'll get a double o' rum from the lieutenant for these, or I never served His Majesty!"

The voices faded away, and I turned to inspect my saviors.

The tall stranger was a young man, twenty or twenty-one, and stood a bit over six feet if my eye knew anything. His light eyes twinkled with humor and just then with something else—the love of a fight. His face was long and large like the rest of him, and the fresh-colored cheeks were marred a bit by the bruises and cuts of the tussle. 'Twas my first meeting with Richard John Uniacke and a fateful one for me. He was to become a great man in our Nova Scotia, though our people have not yet measured the full of his greatness. He and I were to have queer adventures together, but I remember him best as I saw him that night, a big young man gleaming with health and courage and humor, who looked and talked like a gentleman brought up to books and had the dress and the hard hands of a countryman.

The Jew urged us to an inner chamber, a comfortable place with a thick Turkey carpet underfoot and fine mahogany furniture, a mahogany table that gave back the gleam of two silver candelabra, and walls hung with prints and small paintings. On the tiled hearth, in an iron basket, burned a small fire of Spanish River coals against the chill of the spring night.

The young woman fetched a decanter of wine and glasses, and we drank, nothing loath, while old Mr. Hart got a basin of warm water and a soft cloth and washed our cut knuckles and faces.

The tall fellow and I swapped names and, after a glass or two of the wine, were telling our histories like cousins new-met. Uniacke said little, then or ever, of his home in Ireland—a mansion called Mount Uniacke—but I gained that he came of the Protestant gentry somewhere about Cork and had studied the law in Dublin. There had been a quarrel with his father, and a ship, first to Saint Kitts in the West Indies and then to Philadelphia.

"Faith," he laughed, "I was down to my uppers when I landed in Philadelphia. But"—he turned to Aaron Hart the flashing, handsome smile that all Nova Scotia knows now—"it seems there's always a quiet man with a beard somewhere by when I need him. On the quay was a Swiss named Moses Delesdernier, a merchant of Cumberland in the province of Nova Scotia. 'What can you do?' says he. 'Anything!' says I. And off to Nova Scotia I went with him. That was a year ago. He has a store and a farm up at the end of the Bay of Fundy. What did I do? Och, I made myself useful at everything from the plow to the account books, and I've lately married his daughter—ah, my sweet Martha Maria, if ye could ha' seen your quiet new husband five minutes back!—and, begob, I'm clark to the Proprietors' Committee there, for it's a Yankee settlement like nearly all others in Nova Scotia. In short, I'm a solid countryman up to town for a gift for my new wife and here I've been trading bloody noses with His Majesty's army and navy as if I was a student again in the merry streets o' Dublin!"

He grinned and fetched me a whack on my shoulder that rattled my teeth.

But there was no mirth in me. I could see nothing but Mark, senseless in the muck of Market Square, and Luke's bloody head and raging mouth, and the black future for both of them in the slavery of His Majesty's navy. And I thought of the *Nan* and our fishing voyage to Labrador, ruined at the start.

I burst out, "How can such things be? The press is against provincial law."

"The law, yes," Uniacke said contemptuously. "And who makes the laws? The assembly. And who makes the assembly? The Council, a cabal of Halifax gentlemen, with the connivance of the governor. What's their power? Money. Where do they get it? By bleeding the province in peacetime, and the king in time of war. What's their policy? To keep the one quiet and play up to the other for their own ends. Och, I could go on with the catechism half the night."

The old Jew spoke mildly. "The excuse under which the press is permitted is that the town is overrun with rogues and vagabonds. That is true. But the rogues and vagabonds know well how to keep out of the way, and it is the poor fishermen and merchant seamen and countrymen up for the market who are taken and dragged away. For a year past it has been the curse of Halifax. Heaven knows things are bad enough without that. Halifax was founded by the army in the first place and has been dependent on it ever since. There was some true commerce, but the other colonies killed most of that when they issued their non-intercourse decree. Then General Gage took the garrison off to Boston and left the town a corpse. That is Halifax today, my friends, a wooden corpse lying unburied on the side of Citadel Hill; and the press gangs are the worms in its rotten flesh. The fleet must have men—men—men. So the coasters are being frightened away, and the country people will not come to market, and God knows what we are to burn for fuel next winter."

"God knows what ye'll eat, for that matter," Uniacke said grimly. "All the supplies from our Bay of Fundy farms are under requisition, are being taken to Halifax for shipment to the army in Boston. Our Yankee farmers refused to sell at first, but three frigates arrived in the Bay and they had to give in. The province couldn't feed itself before. What'll it do now?"

"What'll the province do anyhow?" I cried. "This can't go on."

"No?" Uniacke said with a quick, fierce light in his eyes. "And what's to stop it, David Strang?"

"I don't know."

"Umph!" He turned his eyes to the fire. "David, when I left Ireland 'twas to seek my fortune in the colonies. That's the way every man in the British Isles regards the colonies—as a thing to be milked in some fashion, so that he may return home in due time and live on the fat he's skimmed. Half these Halifax money grubbers are of that sort. The rest have got so they like the country or can't leave off milking. If anyone questions their right they yap about loyalty. Anyone who sets down his stool on the other side of the cow is a rebel. That is the British colonial policy. Well, as I've said, I went to the West Indies, which they've always considered a pretty fine cow, at home. There for the first time I saw the policy in action and its effect on the milkers, not to mention the cow. No race in the world can equal the creole

English of the West Indies for laziness or pride or show. A creole lady won't even stoop for a pin but must have a black girl to reach it for her, while she reclines on a sofa the livelong day. And I came to see how ridiculous 'twas—a people whose ancestors knew so well the value of liberty as to maintain it with their last drop of blood, content there to live at ease on slavery. 'Twas revolting. I got out after a year."

I turned to Aaron Hart. "What of my brothers? Isn't there something I can do?"

"My son, there is nothing to be done—here. Take your vessel home and explain to your father. It may be that he has friends who can do something. There was a time twenty years ago when your father's name opened all doors in Halifax. I knew him then, a tall man in hunting shirt and leggings, usually with a Mohawk or two at his heels, faithful as dogs. He had a great contempt for the townsfolk, huddling inside the palisades; and the townsfolk, from the governor down, regarded him with awe—a legendary creature who covered the wilderness of Nova Scotia in some kind of seven-league boots, scattering the Micmacs like chaff. But those days are past, and government is in different hands, and a generation has grown up that never heard a war whoop. Old times—old men—best forgotten—that seems the motto."

Then Uniacke asked the question that every man in Nova Scotia was asking every other. "And what," said he, with a steady eye on the old man, "d'ye think of the troubles in America?"

Mr. Hart lifted and dropped his thin shoulders in the gesture which comes so naturally to his people. "In these times a man may be hanged for what he thinks. Nevertheless, I think the troubles in America will bring about, in one way or another, a great change in British colonial policy, which you have so well described. I am an Englishman—if a Jew can claim nationality in this world—and the colonists are fighting for their rights as Englishmen. I see nothing strange about that. In England itself Englishmen are crying for their rights. A man named Wilkes . . ."

"And Nova Scotia?" Uniacke interrupted eagerly. "What about Nova Scotia?"

Aaron Hart looked at him somberly. "Nova Scotia has neither the men nor the means to fight the Crown. She must get rid of the British colonial policy in some other way."

"What with—words?" Uniacke asked contemptuously.

"Why not? I come of a race which has long found words more effective than cudgels. Listen, my friend. You say Nova Scotia is controlled by a Halifax cabal. That is true. And it exists by favor of the king, as other cabals exist in other colonies. But one man in our cabal is very different from the others. His name is Francklin—spelled with a *c*. Michael Francklin is an Englishman who has spent the best years of his life here in this frontier town. He is clever; he has gathered great wealth from army contracts, and money no longer means much to him. His wife is an American—Susannah Boutineau of Boston, a granddaughter of Peter Faneuil. He has visited New England frequently. He has visited every part of Nova Scotia—the only member of the cabal who has ever really set foot outside Halifax. He has the ability to see with the eye of the common man—even the eye of an Indian; for he was captured by Indians once and in months of captivity learned the Micmac tongue and also the Malicite. He prefers the country to the town—lives most of the time on his stud farm at Windsor and maintains a manor in the meadows of Minudie, by Fundy Bay. Some say he aspires to the governorship. If so he has been disappointed, though he has been lieutenant governor of this province for the past nine years. But here is the point: Michael Francklin is the only man in Nova Scotia who has influence with the Council and at the same time with the people, and I know—no matter how—that he believes in reform in our colonial government and that it must come gradually and without bloodshed so that there will be no bitterness afterward. Well—all movements begin with a man. There is Nova Scotia's man."

"A Tory of the Tories!" snorted Uniacke.

"Governor Legge considers him a radical."

"Pooh, Legge!"

My head still sang with blows and was full of dismal pictures of Mark and Luke; and now there was a dull vibration, a sound from outside somewhere, and Mr. Hart jumped up quickly. "A gun!"

"A ship coming in," suggested Uniacke.

"At night?" snorted I. "Besides, there's no wind."

"A gun," repeated the Jew. "And from the northward. Fort Needham? But that is only a ruin of rotten logs and tumbled earth without even a watchman. It must be the dockyard."

He ran to the window and brailed up the heavy curtain with a tug on the cord and opened a lozenge-paned casement into the night. We stuck our heads out into the cool dark together. The window opened upon a small court, and overhead in a sky of stars the Dipper sparkled and pointed the Pole. There was a glow along the ridge of the opposite roof, and I thought 'twas the northern lights, which often give fine displays in late spring in our latitude. But now came another gun and a ringing of alarm bells, and we could hear windows going wide everywhere and a confused clack of voices as if the press were abroad again. But the word was different now. It was "Fire!"

"Your chance to escape!" cried the old man. "A fire at the dock-yard. All the king's ships will have to send their crews, for there's no fire company."

In our hurry we gave the good man small thanks for all he had done for us and ran up George Street toward Citadel Hill and the fields. But along Barrington Street we could see a great glare in the north and Uniacke said, "Och, what are we running for? His Majesty's seamen will have their hands too full of buckets and pump handles to bother the townsmen now. Come on! Let's have a look."

His legs were as long as mine, and we covered ground famously northward, past scuttling groups of townsfolk in all sorts of attire, swinging lanterns and screeching "Fire." There were no lantern posts past the Parade, and the houses were small for the most part and scattered, with fields between, and Barrington Street became nothing more than a cart track, rutted and cumbered with rocks and stumps. At the stone gateway of the dockyard we found a crowd gathered. The gate was closed, and a couple of seamen stood guard with drawn cutlasses. The sightseers had to content themselves with the flames now visible over the top of the wall. Uniacke plucked my sleeve, and we ran farther north, and at some distance came upon a small, stocky man sitting like Humpty Dumpty on the wall itself. A plank leaned against the mortared stones, and we got up beside him and saw what appeared to be a large yellow building, square and roofless, in flames at the waterside, perilously close to the store sheds and sail and rigging lofts. The ground about it was swarming with seamen, some at the handles of portable chain pumps, six men each side, bowing rigidly to each other like wooden German toys, and others ranged in long lines passing buckets of water from the harbor to the pump troughs.

The building was very odd, without doors or windows, and of a material that looked like blocks of yellow stone, yet burned like wood.

"There," chuckled Humpty Dumpty, "goes the forage for General Gage. All of it! All they've collected from the Fundy farms these three months."

I saw then 'twas a mountain of hay, bundled for shipment and piled in a great square stack. The pumps and buckets were useless. The fire had a firm hold in the heart of the stack and was putting a thick red tongue of flame into the sky that lit all the dockyard buildings and quays and the spars and yards and gaffs of His Majesty's brigs and schooners, which had been hauled out to safe moorings off the careening wharf. The man's amusement nettled me, for I knew the scarcity of hay along our frugal south shore, and the waste seemed terrible—all that fruit of good Fundy meadowland, all that sweat of reapers and tedders and carters going up like rubbish in a bonfire. I clucked my tongue in disgust, and the fellow gave me a quick look and slipped down in a most agile manner—not like Humpty Dumpty at all, though he ran off into the shadows on the far side as if all the king's horses and all the king's men were at his heels.

Uniacke and I remained watching the spectacle, and others found our plank and came to peer, until the wall had a topping of perched men and boys. We were seen, and a number of seamen broke away from the pumps at a command and came yelling up the slope toward us. There was a fine scramble to get down and away. Uniacke and I struck across the fields and their low piled-stone walls toward Dutchtown, whose little church caught the fire's light on its steeple and made a good mark in the darkness. The village was dark and abed, and we separated—Uniacke toward the Windsor Road and I toward distant Citadel Hill. Dutchtown lay between two country lanes which its German folk grandly called Brunswick Street and Gottingen Street. The church and most of the houses were ranged beside Brunswick Street, a muddy wagon track running north along the harbor slope. It was really an extension of bawdy Barrack Street; I wondered what the pious Germans thought of that. I was weary in body and mind and after a few steps toward the town I came to rest on a stone at the roadside, to sort myself out. I had planned a very different sort of adventure in Halifax. I had planned to slip away from Mark and the others and hunt up the dame's school, demand to see Miss Bingay on some pretext or other—anything for a sight of her charming face and teasing eyes again; for I would be in Labrador while she was home for summer holidays, and she would be gone when I returned. Man may propose, and God dispose, as the almanac declares; but the devil himself invented that arrangement.

I decided to spend the night here, in the safe darkness of Dutchtown, and wait for sunrise to light my way across country to the *Nan*. It was cold, sitting there. The dew sparkled like frost in the starlight. The little wooden church, cleanly in whitewash, seemed to beckon me inside. The door opened at a touch, and I crept in, fumbling amongst the simple pews, and at the far end found a small altar with a bit of carpet before it. I lay on the floor, pulled the carpet over me, and was asleep in a wink.

I wakened at cockcrow and found a gray light staining the small windows on the east. There was a patter of rain on the roof and a murmur of voices outside. I thought I had been discovered and crept to the door for a dash before the good burghers could hand me over to the watch as an impious vagabond. Outside, in the dull dawn light stood the stocky little man of the dockyard wall and another who stood back to me in a cloak with three capes and a wide-brimmed black hat cocked at one side. What were they muttering about, there in the pride-o'-morning? There was a clink of coins. Said Humpty Dumpty, with the chuckle that seemed part of him, "Thank'ee! Thank'ee, sir, and a good night's work, both for me and for Liberty. See old Gage now, I can, abitin' his nails in Boston. Fodder's hard to come by, this time o' year."

With that he gave a little tug at the tail of his greasy nightcap, in courtesy, I suppose, and scuttled off amongst the houses. The taller man turned to his horse, tied to a fence post near by. I caught only a side glimpse of his face as he swung a spurred boot over the saddle, and then he was off at a gallop toward town. But I could have sworn it was Will Smith the Halifax merchant and our late representative in the assembly.

CHAPTER 10

The Testament of Luke

OUR RETURN to Liverpool in the *Nan* was slow and melancholy. In addition to our skipper and mate, the Eskimo and one of the Freeman boys were missing—nabbed by the press gang as they ran across Barrack Street. Old Bradford and I had to stand watch-and-watch down the coast, and we had to warp in over the bar, the wind not serving. We had to warp up the river, too, and as we crept about the capstan (tuneless—no one had heart for a song), men came running down the wharf lanes shouting questions. The ill word sped up the town street ahead of us, and Father was waiting for us on the home wharf, with our anxious mother beside him, and Peter Dekatha and François and half a dozen neighbors. It did not take us long to tell how our voyage had been ruined. The press was nothing new, of course. Many a luckless Nova Scotiaman had been taken out of his fishing boat and off to the world's end in one of His Majesty's ships and his family left without word or support. Some managed to desert after months or years and make their way home; but a good half laid their bones in far places, and their wives and children never knew what became of them. 'Twas accepted as one of the sea's hazards, like storms or ship fever. But now, with a war at our doors and His Majesty's fleet hovering between Halifax and Boston like dark birds of prey, the press had become a pestilence that carried men off right and left. Father tried to get another captain and mate for the *Nan*, but none would go.

Then we had a visitor, Thomas Cochrane, a leading merchant of Halifax. He stepped ashore from a coasting sloop and, ignoring poor Simeon Perkins, our figurehead, came at once to my father. All Liverpool knew what he wanted—the assembly seat left vacant by Seth Harding's dismissal—and all Liverpool knew what Father's answer would be. But they were proved wrong.

There was a long discussion, held in our parlor, seeing the importance of the man, and Father stood his ground until Cochrane suavely brought up the matter of the press. He had heard, he said regretfully, that two of the Strang sons had been taken and a Labrador voyage ruined.

"Of course you realize, Captain Strang, there is no recourse through the law. The fleet is a law to itself, and the governor, rather than see his authority flouted, grants the admiral the right to press at certain periods. One thing alone can get your sons back to their trade, Captain—and that's influence. Need I say more?"

Father flared up at that. "Are ye suggesting, sir, that I get ye this seat for my own ends?"

"For ends affecting the whole town," Cochrane said smoothly. "Others of your townsmen have been pressed in the past and will be in the future. Halifax has been pretty well combed, and the fleet's tenders are already slipping along the coast to pick up men where they can. You know that. You may be assured, sir, that I have the town's best interest at heart."

I'll never forget the silence, and the final glum nod of my father's head, and how after Cochrane had gone he had up rum from the cellar and drank himself insensible.

Soon arrived a letter from alert Mr. Smith in Halifax, informing Colonel Perkins that he was to be "excused" from attending the assembly (thus leaving our town and county without representation at all) and adding that a writ would now be issued requiring Liverpool to choose a new member in place of Seth Harding. Thus was the way paved for Thomas Cochrane.

Soon after, Colonel Perkins had another shock. As chief magistrate in our town he had been issuing passes to New England. Now this power was cancelled and given to William Johnston, the doddering old Scot. So was revealed to us for the first time Governor Legge's distrust of us Yankees of Nova Scotia, deepening as time went on, and his determination to strip us of our last vestige of self-government.

We heard from Halifax that William Smith and his partner Fillis had been accused of the burning of the army forage at Halifax and that they had managed to clear themselves of it. But the most important news in the four weeks that followed our Halifax adventure came on June 27th with Captain Gideon White, a young shipmaster of Plymouth, Massachusetts, who arrived with a tale of a great battle outside Boston at a place called Bunker Hill, with the rebels driven off and great slaughter on both sides. Gideon was an ardent Tory, though he came of a good Whig family, and we wondered how much to believe. He had brought with him a sergeant recruiting men for Gage's army, and the redcoat threaded his way through the crowd on the wharf, cajoling the young men. He got only one recruit, but that one astounded us all—no less than our John, our pale, bookworm John of the countinghouse.

"Why, you're mad!" Father shouted.

"I'm a loyalist!" said John defiantly. He was always bringing out new words like that; God knows where he heard them—at James Bingay's, I suppose.

Our poor mother went down on her knees, there on the dirty wharf, and begged him to change his mind.

"He can't change it now," growled the sergeant, waving his ribboned staff. "He's took the king's shillin'."

And, faith, he had, a shilling and threepence, Halifax currency, to be exact.

Two days later he left for Boston in a tender, with half a dozen fellows from up the shore, absconding debtors by the look of them, and one or two old-country Irish. When I got home that night I found my mother and Joanna sitting with their arms about each other and weeping.

We were now in the summer heat, and the thunder along the wooded valley seemed like cannon echoes from New England. And like another dark cloud, Halifax showered our sweating magistrates with letters and admonitions and proclamations, ordered them to administer oaths of allegiance, abjuration, and supremacy "to all persons lately come to the province from New England," forbade all intercourse with the rebel provinces, required the justices to "take special care that there be no opposition to the government," and God knows what else.

Nevertheless, when our election was held in July, Captain Ephraim Dean, that advocate of open rebellion amongst us, offered himself as a candidate in opposition to Tory Thomas Cochrane. Only fifty men turned up at the poll, and the vote was 28 for Cochrane, 22 for Dean, a narrow squeak for the Halifax man despite my father's influence.

Men turned from these things to the raising of a new meetinghouse, fervently, as if for a refuge, floating the timber and boards downriver from the mills at the Falls and sawing, planing, and hammering the summer through. The old meetinghouse was crammed to the doors every Sabbath, and Parson Cheever scourged us triumphantly for the wickedness which had undoubtedly brought affliction upon us. But for all that there was a certain comfort within those walls, even for me, who had always considered Sundays damned dull; and my father took my arm going home, a thing he had never done before. The house was very lonely now, with my three brothers gone and Mother and Joanna moving about like ghosts.

From Halifax, Mr. Cochrane wrote that he was making endeavors in Father's behalf, but the boys had gone to the fleet, and release was not simple. He warned us also, in a pompous screed, that the Council considered us a lawless and rebellious people, and plans were afoot to annex our town to the Lunenburg seat (to offset our freethinking Yankees with the immovable Dutch) and to remove our courts to Yarmouth. We laughed at the last bit. The Yarmouth folk were Yankees like ourselves and did a busy smuggling trade with the rebels across Fundy Bay.

In August came the step that Seth Harding had prophesied. Throughout the province our inhabitants were ordered to appear at the next quarter sessions and take oaths of allegiance, abjuration, and supremacy. Magistrates were to send Halifax a list of those who complied and those who refused. And to put the thing to an immediate test, the militia were ordered to hold themselves in readiness to march at once.

I went with Father to bid farewell to Seth and his family, at Seth's wharf where his vessel lay. He left most of his furniture and effects in his house—where His Majesty confiscated them later on. Several others were going to New England with Seth. Old Johnston had granted them passes at Bingay's urging, I think, considering the town well rid of such able rebel partisans.

"What are your plans, Seth?" Father asked.

"A command o' some kind in the Congress's war vessels," Seth said quietly. "Failing that, in the service o' the province o' Connecticut. When all's won and done I'll come back here."

One of the men leaving our town with Seth cast some sneer at my father which I did not catch, but I heard Seth's rebuke. "Cap'n Strang has his notion o' what's right for this province; I have mine; you have yours. We're all working to the same end, but every man must pick his own star to steer by. No more o' that!"

Seth Harding was one of the ablest men in our town, and the most popular, and his departure filled us with gloom. Colonel Simeon Perkins up and married the widow Headley right after oat harvesting; an astonishing affair, for Simeon had been a satisfied widower since old days in Connecticut. A blister to cure other worry, the town decided, in a last flicker of humor.

Goldenrod began to bloom all along the roadsides, and the swallows left for the South, and the nighthawk was heard no more over the fields in the evening. Hardwood leaves began to turn color, the red swamp maples first, and the ferns were suddenly brown and crisp, rustling at every step. The west wind was cool, blowing white mares' tails over the blue fall sky, and the sea turned a hard fall blue, and the summer-run mackerel left the coast. Chokecherries were ripe, and bunches of berries hung like tiny grapes, green, pink, and blue, on the withe-rod bushes; corn tassels waved in the kitchen gardens, and we picked our few apples, and horses grazed happily in the sweet aftergrass of the hayfields.

At Michaelmas a shipmaster from Maine brought a wild tale of an American army on the Kennebec River for Quebec and another marching by way of Lake Champlain, and the fall of Canada a matter of weeks.

Father scoffed, but he added gravely, "If it's true they're trying to swallow a snake by the tail—all wrong! Nova Scotia's the place for them to strike; handy home, a friendly people that speak their own language, and itself the key to the St. Lawrence and all Canada. What in God's name are they doing up there in the Canadian wilderness—at this season?"

"Figgerin' to strike Quebec about the close o' navigation. The garrison can't get help by sea once the freeze-up starts. Got to reckon with the king's ships, y'know," observed the Maine man.

"Bah! There's a garrison in Quebec, and with any sort o' commander they'll hold off any attack, short of a siege with heavy batteries, anyhow. The way to take Canada is to cut its throat first, in Nova Scotia, as Wolfe did. Listen, in all Nova Scotia at this moment there's nought but a corporal's guard. A quick stroke with a properly armed force, and it's all over; and with Halifax in American hands, what could the fleet do?"

The Maine man shrugged, and we all shrugged and went back to digging potatoes.

There was no word from Mark or Luke. But a letter came from John, written in Boston and addressed to Father in his neat clerk's hand.

" 'I am well and happy and am now enlisted in the Royal American Regiment. You may remember this was Monckton's regiment at Louisburg and was first raised in Virginia twenty years ago. It has been off the rolls for some time but is now being raised here as the Royal Fencible Americans, Colonel Joseph Gorham. You will recall him as the younger brother of the Gorham who commanded your rangers years ago. Col. Gorham tells me he was a ranger himself and asks to be kindly remembered to you.' "

Father sat and stared at the sheet. "Umph! Joe Gorham! Remember him well. A good amiable feller, but too easygoing to make a soldier. Always was, anyhow. Colonel—Colonel Joe—well I'm damned! And the Royal Americans! Stiff Bob Monckton'll have a fit if he ever hears about this!"

"Read on, please," Mother exclaimed impatiently. Father grunted and took it up again.

" '. . . Recruits for the regiment come in slowly, and not all of a quality I could wish to see in His Majesty's uniform. There are some ardent loyalists among us; but many are actually deserters from the rebel militia, looking for better pay, and riffraff from the Boston streets, and General Gage is not proud of us.' "

"Pooh, Gage!" snorted my father.

"Will he—our John—be fighting very soon?" Mother asked with pale lips.

Father considered, with his left eye shut and squinting with the other along the folded letter as if 'twere a rifle barrel.

"I reckon not, ma'am. Gage is the kind that regards every colonial as a kind o' white Injun—not to be trusted in posts of importance. I met his kind in the army in Nova Scotia in the old days. Brave enough, but muttonheads, muttonheads. He's not proud o' Joe Gorham's Royal Americans—ye heard what John said. Well, that means the Royals'll keep their skins whole. When Gage is proud of a regiment he forms 'em in triple rank so the enemy can't miss and marches 'em up to the guns. There's a lot o' dead redcoats under the sod o' Bunker Hill that'd be living now if Gage hadn't been proud of 'em."

"Don't!" Mother begged and began to cry.

Father and his friends this fall persuaded Simeon Perkins to go up to Halifax and take his seat in the assembly session. Simeon protested that he couldn't afford the cost, so they subscribed twenty dollars Halifax currency, and off he went in a coaster. I cannot recall that he did or said anything there but sat in his seat, a shabby and uneasy figure amongst the town swells, while the assembly took sides in the quarrel between Governor Legge and his lieutenant governor, Michael Francklin. Few in our town had taken the oath of allegiance. The "king's enemies" in it stuck in our throats. There was no downright refusal. The people simply stayed away from the quarter sessions, and the magistrates grumbled or exulted or scratched their heads, according to their sentiments. As for the militia, Colonel Perkins made no attempt to muster them, fearing open mutiny. And soon we learned that the men of Lahave had refused to muster, and the men of Truro and Onslow and Cumberland and in fact pretty well the whole province. The next move was up to Halifax, and we wondered what it would be.

Late in October, Luke came home. It was a night of stars and the hunter's moon, with a cold wind blowing dead leaves along the street, and he opened the kitchen door in a gust that blew out half the candles. He was in rags and was brown and haggard and hard-eyed and stood for a moment looking slowly all round, mouth twisted, as if the sight of comfort turned his stomach. Father leaped up, and Mother ran and flung her arms about Luke's neck, and I looked past him, expecting Mark. But Luke closed the door with a backward kick and awkwardly patted Mother's shoulder.

Father sent me for beer while Mother brought cold beef and bread and cheese and a new pumpkin pie. Luke ate like a wolf, answering our torrent of questions jerkily, with his mouth full and eyes on the pie.

He had been in His Majesty's ships *Vulture* and *Centurion*—Lord Anson's old *Centurion*, the one that made the famous voyage around the world in Father's time and was still in service and would one day end her long service as a hulk in Halifax Harbor. Luke did not seem particularly proud of serving in so famous a ship. He had been at Boston. New York. Off the Jerseys a good deal. Mark? He hadn't seen Mark since the night they were caught. Where was Joanna?

"Abed," Father said curtly. There was a silence. Then Mother said quietly, "Joanna had a baby a week ago."

Luke paused in his eating and lifted his black brows. He took a great wedge of pie and began to devour it in enormous bites.

"They don't seem to feed very well in His Majesty's ships," observed Mother primly.

"No, they don't."

"Treat ye well?" Father asked.

Luke stared across at me with a queer expression in his eyes. "They treated me—the way they treat everybody, I guess."

"That's nice," Mother said.

"Yes, that's nice."

"Cochrane was a long time getting around to it," Father said.

"Cochrane?"

"Our new representative for the county. He got you released."

Luke sat back and stared at him openmouthed, showing a yellow mass of chewed pumpkin pie. "Release, hell! I jumped ship!"

"What!" we all cried together.

"What's strange about that? There's no release from His Majesty's service except what ye take for yourself. I had to wait for a chance. We were at sea for weeks on end, and in harbor they kept heavy nettings over the ports to prevent desertion—the ship was full o' pressed men. I got my chance in a prize. A small sloop out o' Boston that we picked up off the Isle o' Sable. Our captain put a midshipman and three English seamen into the sloop and sent me along to navigate her into Halifax, seein' I knew the coast. I knew the coast, all right! I ran the hooker ashore on a nice shelvin' beach at Lahave Islands, in the dark. There wasn't much sea; she was safe enough and easy got off, if the middy'd only known. But the breakers sounded bad and broke white in the dark like the middy's face, and I ran along the bowsprit and dropped on the beach, yellin' she was a goner. After that 'twas easy enough. Through the woods for a bit, then a house by the shore, a fishin' family, Dutchmen. Told 'em I was on the run from a man-o'-war, and they rowed me off to the mainland, ready enough. Made my way down the coast—daren't beg passage in a coaster for fear o' bein' overhauled by a king's ship—and I can tell ye it's time we had a road along the shore. That horse path from here to Halifax is mortal hard on the feet."

"It'll go hard if ye're caught," Father said grimly. "Better pull foot in the morning."

"No!" Mother cried.

"Yes," Luke said. "I'm off in the mornin'. Cal'late to slip across to Massachusetts in a smuggler out o' Yarmouth."

"Why go so far?" begged our poor mother.

Luke looked at Father and then at me. "The farther the better."

But later, in my small bedchamber under the eaves, Luke sat on the bed and told more. "I'm goin' to find Seth Harding if I can and join him. Failin' Seth, I enter the rebel service any way I can. I want to fight the king."

"Why?"

The baby was fretful in Mark's old room, and we heard Joanna stirring and dropped our voices.

"I'll show ye, Davy."

He stood up and tore off his tattered shirt—and I sat agape. His back, from neck to loins, was a mat of long, ragged scars laid crisscross fashion from each side, with irregular diamonds of skin between. Some of the scars were old and white, some new-healed and still red, but mostly old scars that had healed and been opened and healed again and opened again. The torn skin had dried in little dark knots along the edge of each livid track, like so many seed warts, shiny and hard. I thought of an old toad's back, but it was uglier than that. It was the ugliest thing in the world. The deepest scars were at the ends of the pattern, over the side ribs and under the armpits. Pieces of flesh there had been gouged clean out and healed in shiny white pits and troughs, fringed with the horrible dark skin warts. To show me this horror Luke raised his hands above his head until his body and arms made a rigid Y and held the pose stiffly, as if his flesh had come to expect pain in that attitude. I knew how he came by it but at first I could think of nothing but the stoical bronze figure on the crucifix that old Molly kept in her hut.

"You've been flogged," I muttered. The sight made me tremble all over.

"And flogged!" He abandoned that terrible attitude and flung himself on the bed, hands under head, looking up at me.

"It began as soon as I was taken aboard the tender. I'd made things lively for 'em in Market Square and in the boat, and they promised me, all the way, they'd teach me better manners. The tender was a schooner of five or ten guns. On deck an officer took a look at me— and at them—by the light of the gangway lantern and shrugged his shoulders and walked aft to his cabin. They took me below somewhere —there was a stink o' bilge water, I remember—and ranged half a dozen lanterns to give 'em light. My wrists were lashed together in front, and they rigged a line about my neck and fastened it to a beam overhead, so I could move about four feet along the deck, all ways, afore the line jerked me up. Then they tore off my shirt and began to play Hurry."

"Eh?"

"A game they play aboard English ships. I've played it myself. The lads stand in a ring, and one's in the middle, and there's a shoe, a big shoe for choice, passed from hand to hand around the ring behind your backs. The game is to keep the center man guessin' where the shoe is; ye keep yellin' 'Hurry! Hurry! Hurry!' and passin' the shoe, and when ye catch the feller back-to ye give him a lick over the rump and pass the shoe again quick as lightnin'. If he catches ye with the shoe ye take his place in the middle. They play the game a bit different with stubborn recruits aboard His Majesty's fleet tenders. Six men stood around me, each with a cat made o' trawl line, well knotted, with lashes about three foot long. They began to yell 'Hurry!' and o' course the fella behind gave my back a sharp lash. I turned quick and took a runnin' kick as he dodged back—and o' course the hang rope brought me up all standin'. By that time they were at my back on t'other side. So it went. I was mad clear through and made a fine fool o' myself, jumpin' and chokin' and cursin' 'em, and them roarin' with laughter and vowin' I was a reg'lar Yankee jumpin' jack and layin' it on.

"At last, what wi' the halter and all, I was half unconscious. I stood still then, and the fun went out o' the game, though they laid on pretty vicious for a time, tryin' to get me started again. They all went off somewhere to drink flip. In less than an hour they were back, pretty merry, and took up the cats again. But I set my teeth and wouldn't move, and o' course with those light cats they couldn't do much more'n bring blood. So one went off and came back with the ship's cat-o'-nine-tails, the real thing, that'll take the flesh right off a man's bones, well laid on.

"They pretty nigh fell into a fight over who'd have the first turn, but there was a thickset man with a black eye he'd got from me in Market Square, and they gave in to him. He peeled off his shirt, and they moved the lanterns back to give him a good swing, and he flogged till the sweat was runnin' off him the way the blood was runnin' off me. I couldn't keep my jaw shut after the first dozen o' that. I yelled, top o' my voice, hopin' the officer would hear, and kept on yellin' like a slut in childbed, every stroke. And Black-eye answered with all the fancy oaths he'd picked up between Portsmouth Hard and Halifax, round by the east. When he got tired another peeled shirt and began. Between turns they sat against the bulkhead, sweatin' and pantin' and swiggin' cold flip and goin' for'ard to the heads to ease 'emselves from time to time. I don't know how long it went on. They sent off a man once for fresh dips for the lanterns. I got so I couldn't stand and sagged more and more on the halter. I wanted to puke, but the rope was too tight around my neck. At last the place went dark, with fireflies skitterin' before my eyes, the way they do home, summer evenin's, sittin' on the back stoop.

"When I came to, they had me laid out on deck, slushin' water over me from the harbor, and one man sayin', over and over, 'The bloody fool's dead. We'll have the hide off our own backs for this. Topmen are scarce.' They felt over my heart and put their ears down to my chest and rubbed gun grease on my back for a salve, havin' a mortal fit, I tell ye. 'Twould ha' been funny if I'd felt better. Well, to cut a long yarn to a reef point, that was my introduction into His Majesty's service. The lieutenant came to look at me next day and went off without sayin' a word. I was kept below till my back healed. Then I went off with a party o' pressed men to H.M.S. *Centurion*. That was a life! I never could keep tongue in cheek and bide my time, like Father and Mark. I was there against my will and showed it, every chance I got. Shipmates warned me, and the bosun warned me; but finally I was taken afore the captain for insolence and marked down for three dozen o' the best.

"At the gangway next mornin' they took off my shirt and triced me up, and the bosun's mate straightened his cat, and the lieutenant stood by to count the strokes, and the captain came saunterin' along to read out the Articles o' War in the fashion prescribed by the Lords of Admiralty—and he saw His Majesty's badge on my back.

"'Hello!' says he. 'Here's an old offender, or I never saw one. That makes it different. That makes it six dozen, Mr. Smallman, and mark it down, please. Harkins, six dozen o' the best and lay 'em on well, or you'll take his place!'

"And that was my second tattooin' at the hands o' His Majesty.

"I've had plenty since. Why"—with a wild laugh that set my teeth on edge—"I've been flogged round the fleet in Boston Harbor. I'm famous!"

My skin crept at the sound of his voice, as much as the thought of his sufferings. But I said stubbornly, "You talk as if flogging were a personal vice of the king's. As if our own town hadn't a whipping post; as if Mark, ay, and you, Luke, hadn't taken a rope end to a surly hand many a time in the *Nan*. I dare say the rebels do plenty of flogging in their own army. How else can they keep law and order?"

"There ye go!" Luke jeered. "Order! Law and order! Just like Father and Simeon Perkins and the rest o' these smug Bible-thumbin' Yankees of ours. We mustn't hope for liberty—nunno!—but only for our rights as Englishmen, 'cause we've got to have law and order. Well, I say that's all bilge and to hell with it! What I want is independence for us and all America. I want to see British law and order and everything else o' theirs rooted out and chucked in the Atlantic. Some call that revolution and roll their eyes to heaven in holy terror, as if it meant the world's end. Bah! The world had earth and sea and sky long afore the English invented their precious law and order, and it'll have 'em when the English are just a bad taste in the mouth."

CHAPTER 11

His Majesty's Displeasure

WE HAD our first snow soon after Luke slipped away to Massachusetts, and the countryside turned bleak as our hearts and minds. But in mid-November we had another family reunion, for John walked in the door, in the queerest uniform I ever saw. He still wore his old hat and blue coat; but the hat had been cocked tightly with three brass buttons, and the coat cut short to a mock military fashion; and he had a warm waistcoat of yellow swansdown stuff and a pair of thick canvas breeches and black country-wool stockings, and over them a pair of long blue cloth gaiters that buttoned right up to the crotch.

"Look at your shoes!" Mother cried. Faith, they were worth a look —the soles worn through, the upper broken, and the whole bound together with strips of canvas. For that matter the only things sound in his whole equipment were the crossbelts, the bayonet and cartridge box, and the musket slung at his shoulder. Colonel Gorham had been obliged to buy the crossbelts and cartridge boxes with his own funds, John said indifferently. King George provided his Royal Americans with nothing but their muskets and bayonets.

We learned that the regiment—or the fragment that had been recruited—had been sent from Boston to Halifax, to quiet Governor Legge's fears—seventy Boston tatterdemalions and Colonel Gorham, together with two companies of the 14th Foot. Colonel Joe was now commanding the Halifax garrison—390 men, of whom only 126, John confessed, were fit for duty. General Gage had spared even these sorry troops grudgingly; the rebel invasion of Canada had emphasized the defenselessness of Nova Scotia, but he still thought he could crush the rebellion at the heart, in New England. All his officers said so, and the army was repeating it in the streets of Boston.

"It's nice to have you nearer home," Mother said, pleased.

John made a face. "I'd rather be in Boston. We'll see no fighting here."

"When I knew 'em in '58," Father said, regarding John's rig with one open eye, "the Royal Americans were a pretty smart lot. Maybe . . ."

"Oh, we'll be smart enough when the time comes. The regiment's not half recruited yet, and our uniforms are to come from England—green jacket, black leather cap, white waistcoat and breeches, black gaiters . . ."

"And shoes?" Mother said anxiously.

"And shoes—we hope!"

It was queer to see John with a sunburned face. He had spent the whole summer drilling on Boston Common and was brown as a smoked alewife. It seemed unnatural. I had a queer fancy that when he took off his hat the brown mask ought to come off with it, and my eyes kept going to his fingers, seeking the familiar inkstains. His thin frame was not built for soldiering, for any great bodily exertions; if he was a sample of the Royal Americans 'twas no wonder General Gage had sent them out of his sight. Father took him down to the store and fitted him out with two pairs of stout shoes, one for his feet and one for his knapsack.

"These," said John whimsically, looking at the spare pair, "will be stolen the first night in barracks. We're a rare lot of thieves in the Royals."

As he was leaving he asked casually after Joanna. She had been taken with a megrim about the time he came and stayed in her chamber with the baby.

Halifax remained mysteriously silent about the oath of allegiance. During November some American armed vessels sacked Charlottetown and carried off Mr. Callbeck, the administrator, and others and brought them to the American camp at Cambridge. We heard that General Washington released them, with harsh words for the men who had pillaged their brother colonists. But Halifax was alarmed and proclaimed martial law. Governor Legge was riding his spy mare furiously; innkeepers were commanded to report all strangers, and strangers were commanded to appear before not less than two magistrates and give an account of themselves. Business was at a sad pass. All commerce with the other colonies was at an end, except for smuggling, which labored under difficulties at both ends, with His Majesty's fleet in the middle. Supplies of manufactured things were very dear and hard to get; but the thing that touched us most was a sudden and complete scarcity of powder and shot. Our merchants could get none. We were told that it was due to the army and navy contractors buying up all ammunition in sight. The strange thing was that the Indians could still get plenty if they went to Halifax for it. Any lousy brown scamp in a blanket could call himself a chief and be sure of much rum and gunpowder, a fine red coat, and a gold-laced hat, in return for a vow of loyalty to the Great White Father in London. It amused us to see old Moise and others of our river Micmacs—heads of families no more—returning from Halifax with kegs of powder for their "tribes," while we, the suspect whites, could not buy it at any price; but 'twas a sour amusement, and the Indians, finding themselves with the upper hand after all these years, made us pay handsomely for the powder when we came to buy from them.

A week before Christmas a bombshell fell in our midst. A coaster from Halifax brought a message to my father, warning him that Governor Legge considered our town a "most rebellious place" and was sending a frigate to winter in our harbor. All of us knew what that meant. We had heard of such visitations elsewhere and the terror and misery they left in their wake. Dragooning, naval style, was a weapon that Governor Legge loved. Hoping to stave it off at the last minute, Simeon Perkins called a Court of Sessions to administer the oaths, and a number of glum people came and swore fealty to the king. But the rest stayed away, as before, and poor, worried Simeon had to adjourn his court.

We waited with a feeling of doom. That Christmas Day of '75 was as gloomy a day as our town ever spent. It was cold, with snow blowing. The young women as usual decorated the meetinghouse with boughs of pine and hemlock, and Parson Cheever preached a long sermon in the cold, while we sat with hands tucked in sleeves and watched our breath rising like smoke. 'Twas hard to believe in the Prince of Peace just then, with King George so insistent.

Two days later the frigate came in, H.M.S. *Senegal*, very big in our small harbor, with a crew on the same scale. There were more men within her wooden walls than in all Liverpool. She could not get over the bar and anchored off Ballast Cove, where for several weeks she contented herself with stopping every vessel going in or out, searching them for contraband and pressing their best hands. It was a neat way to strangle what trade we had left, and Captain Dudington informed each captain that he had come to stay the winter in "this nest of sedition," and that, by God, we'd remember him when he left. God knows that was true.

Week after week through the cold weather, H.M.S. *Senegal* sat in our town's throat. None of her crew were permitted ashore but the officers, who took a walk up the main street on fine days for exercise and stopped for a meal at one of the taverns. They were civil but let us see that we were under His Majesty's displeasure. Captain Dudington, stalking always a few paces ahead of the others, glowered and cursed at all who came in his path. The dogs took a particular dislike to him, and his progress along the street could be marked by the yapping of curs darting out of each dooryard. It got to be a byword amongst us—"There's another Injun come to town, or else it's Dudington!"—and our people could not hide their grins as the captain appeared, boiling mad and slashing right and left at the dogs with his rattan. Some in our town said he was the Dudington who commanded the famous *Gaspee*, which the Rhode Island mob burned in '73, a sensation well remembered in our town. I believe he was. The man had a downright hatred of Americans and shouted it to the winter sky and dinned it into the ears of every poor devil he pressed out of our vessels. I verily believe he would have burned the town over our heads if he'd had his way. But his orders kept his authority outside the harbor bar, and we took what comfort we could out of that. We could picture the temper of his seamen and marines, thus cooped between the *Senegal's* narrow oak walls, week after winter week, and wondered what would happen if the captain found excuse to employ them ashore. In January we heard there was smallpox aboard, with the men jammed up further to prevent its spread, and the air between decks choking with the tar pots they kept burning and the tart reek of vinegar, old and rancid, sprinkled daily through the ship. So she sat, through January, through most of February, a dark, floating hell, and so opened our year 1776.

Late in February, Governor Legge applied the screw. He had observed the reluctance of the militia to serve His Majesty and resolved to raise a regiment of his own. It pleased his malicious mind to see in our town, the biggest of the Yankee settlements, a source of recruits as well as military supplies. So now came a redcoat lieutenant, recruiting men for Legge's Loyal Nova Scotia Regiment, and with him came a Mr. Pollard, seeking timber and palisades for the defenses of Halifax. Lieutenant Cunningham got no recruits. He smiled and waited. Mr. Pollard was told that all our lumber was engaged for the West Indies. He smiled and waited.

One morning we saw three boats from the *Senegal* coming over the bar. They pulled up the river to one of the wharves and landed a strong party of armed seamen and marines, in charge of the frigate's master and a marine lieutenant.

The master went to Chief Magistrate Perkins and demanded search warrants for Captain Will Freeman's store and Robert Stevenson's— and the store of Mr. Perkins himself. Poor Simeon scratched off the warrants, and the search was made. In each store they found molasses and sugar, ay, even coconuts, which they declared contraband.

"From the West Indies?" gasped Simeon.

"From New England," they said with winks and guffaws. They found hogsheads of rum, too, which the seamen and marines were permitted to broach. All day these men, wild drunk, roamed the town seeking their fancy, while the officers drank at ease at Dexter's Tavern. None of the merchants' homes were bothered, but the men made free with the poorer folk; and in the evening, smiling and polite, the officers summoned Simeon and Captain Will Freeman to dine with them at the tavern and drink the health of the king. They went dolefully, and over the wineglasses Captain Dudington said casually, "As loyal subjects of His Majesty, gentlemen, you'll appreciate a bit of news I have. The rebel army before Quebec has been totally defeated; General Arnold is wounded desperately, and the renegade Montgomery is dead. If—ha!—any seditious gentlemen in Nova Scotia were inclined to look hopefully in that direction . . ."

"About our town," Simeon said, thinking of closer affairs. "Your men . . ."

"Aha! A little noisy, Colonel Perkins? You really are a colonel, are you? Well . . . Jack ashore, you know! Cooped up in the ship a whole winter . . . I mean to say, even a dog needs a run now and again."

Simeon tried again. "Some of our young women . . ."

Captain Dudington put back his head and laughed hugely. "I know! I know! But what can I do, damme? There's something about a sailor no healthy wench can resist, begad! And"—with the twist of contempt that never left his lips for long—"a strain of loyal English blood in your next generation won't do the town any harm, sir. Damme, no!

You should feel flattered. My best men, I mean to say. The pick o' the stud, so to speak."

"A gang of them took a young negro freedwoman," Simeon said slowly, "and . . ."

"Women," said Captain Dudington profoundly, "are all alike in the dark."

In a great rage Captain Will related all this at our house, and all the while he talked, my father sat raising and lowering his big fist slowly to the table before him and uttering oaths softly and saying through his teeth, "Sit tight! Sit tight! Sit tight!"

"Bah!" said Captain Will at last, and Father snapped at him, "Can't ye see the game? The governor's trying to goad us into some act of open violence, so he can make us an example for the rest o' the province. And Dudington's just the man for the work!"

So the goading went on. Dudington's men found "contraband" right and left, and the stores were closed one after another, with the broad arrow chalked on the doors and marine sentries posted over them. Then they went to searching houses and barns, armed with warrants got from the trembling magistrates. Some of our townsmen barred their doors against the search—and had them broken in and gangs of rough seamen making free with the house and all in it. Any protest brought a hard fist into the householder's face; resistance ended in a beating, and if the man were young and able he was lucky to be left free to recover. More than one was hustled down to the boats and disappeared over the bar into His Majesty's service. To make matters worse—and quite beyond Captain Dudington's intentions— these visitations brought the ship's smallpox amongst us, and some folk, half mad with fear of the disease, performed a horrible operation upon themselves—called "inoculation"—with scabs from diseased people and fell deadly ill in consequence.

On the seventh day of His Majesty's occupation of our town sleek Mr. Pollard called on Colonel Perkins, swept the hat off his curled white wig and bowed, and wondered if by any chance Colonel Perkins and his fellow mill owners would reconsider the matter of timber for the army. Simeon sighed and took quill and agreed in writing to provide palisade pickets at twenty-five shillings the hundred pickets and ranging timber at twelve shillings the hundred feet, running measure. The prices were Mr. Pollard's. The triumph was Governor Legge's.

On a Sunday in early March, Parson Cheever held meeting half the day, and our meetinghouse was full, with many people standing outside in the snow. Many and long were the prayers and longer the sermon. The preacher's text was from the ninth chapter of Isaiah, "The Syrians before and the Philistines behind, and they shall devour Israel with open mouth." 'Twas shrewdly chosen, caught as we were with the rebels before and the king behind, and Mr. Cheever enlarged upon it for three hours. He was a little drunk, but when Mr. Cheever was only a little drunk he was very eloquent indeed and a credit to Harvard. We came forth feeling that our increasing troubles were no less than the wrath of God, a thing to be borne with meekness. But Abdiel Bastick thrust his bitter old face into Father's, crying aloud to the people, "It's a jedgment! A jedgment fer the way ye used the 'Cajuns in '55! Ye devoured 'em with open mouth, like the Book says. Now we're to be devoured on account of it. That's what we get fer listenin' to ye all this time—fer comin' here with ye in the first place! Here we are with the Syrians afore and the Philistines behind—and I devoutly wish to God I had never left Massachusetts!"

Father pressed his lips white and managed to say nothing. He stumbled off, leaning heavily on his stick, refusing my arm, and when we gained the house he threw himself into his big chair with his head down and wept. That was a terrible thing to see—as if you saw blood flow out of a rock.

And the very next day our turn came. *Senegal's* boatswain, Mr. Jump, and half a dozen seamen came tramping through the slush to our door with cutlasses at their belts and bits of tarpaulin slung over their shoulders against the cold March rain. Jump was a thickset swarthy man with one side of his face dotted blue with old powder burns. He stood in our kitchen in a little pool of snow water and fished a paper out of his jacket. It was a warrant, signed by Magistrate Perkins.

"I'll send my son down to open the store for ye," Father said stonily.

"Save your trouble," Mr. Jump said carelessly. "We bin there. Busted the door a bit, but that's soon mended. There's ten 'ogs'ead o' molasses, six o' rum, and four o' sugar in that there store as looks to me like New England origin, not to mention the cloths and iron-mongery."

"Some of it's from New England," Father admitted coldly. "That's where we did most of our trading till last spring. Ye can't seize stuff that was brought in afore the trade with New England was forbidden."

"Can't we though?" Mr. Jump grinned, with the air of a man who has heard all this before and knows what comes next.

"Look, man. The rebel colonies 'emselves have proclaimed non-intercourse with us. They wouldn't sell us a spoonful o' molasses if we were starving for 't."

"I'm on'y tellin' ye what the lieutenant said. Tell it to 'im, sir. I got me dooty to perform and I warn ye ag'in interferin' with it. Lads, search the house fust, while Simms and me goes and looks at the barn."

Seamen tramped all over the house from garret to cellar, opening closet doors and peering in chests and drawers, while we stood in the kitchen and stared at each other's white faces—Father, my mother and me, and Joanna clutching her baby close, poor thing, as if she feared the child might be found contraband too. When I heard them in my mother's chamber a surge of rage welled up in me so hot that I could scarcely see. My eyes went to the gun of Louisburg, on the moose horns over the mantel, and Father must have noticed, for his hand closed tight on my wrist. I shook it off impatiently. I knew, and he knew, the gun was not loaded. There was not enough powder in the house to prime a pistol.

When the search party got down as far as our cellar they found the household rum keg with its spigot and mug, and soon through the floor came a chorus, all out of tune, of "Joan's Placket Is Torn," and Father stumped up and down the floor with his stick, lest the lewd old sea song come to the women's ears.

Mr. Jump appeared with the man Simms. Bits of straw stuck all over them, and by the muck on their shoes they must have searched our barn from loft to dung heap.

"Nothin' out there," said Jump, with a hard look at Father. He heard the song in the cellar and ran out to the cellar hatch, bawling down to his party to "come aloft, ye swabs, and stow the music!" They came up in file, with a comical, merry sheepishness about them, and Jump caught up the door prop and whacked the dust out of their shoulders with it. He left them there, leaning stupidly against the house, and went down to our wharf with Simms for a look at the *Nan*. They were gone a long time, and presently Joanna gave her baby to Mother and went out to milk the cows.

When Mr. Jump came back he beamed like a man who has found gold.

"Cap'n Strang, there's a bar'l o' molasses in that there schooner's lazareet, bearin' the marks of a merchant in Salem, Massa-chusetts."

Father lost his temper then. "Take it, and be damned."

"We'll take it awright," Mr. Jump said promptly. "The vessel too."

"What!"

"Lawful prize—found wi' rebel property aboard."

"But she's not! As I told ye before . . ."

"Tell it to the prize court in Allyfax," grinned Mr. Jump.

At this point I saw Lieutenant Cunningham tramping through the gray slush from the street. What with the coming and going of Mr. Jump and his fellows, all our doors were open to the wet March wind, and the soldier paused a polite moment on the threshold before coming in. A young man, not handsome by any means, though the gold lace and the red coat, the white breeches and long black gaiters set off his slim figure quite well, his clubbed white wig had come from the hands of an expert *perruquier*, and the sword at his side looked expensive. He must have cut quite a dash in Halifax, now that the regulars were gone. He regarded our little tense group curiously.

Mr. Jump was looking at me with a peculiar intensity just then and suddenly put out a hand like a bear paw, hairy and immense, and pinched my shoulders and the muscle of my upper arm.

"Now, 'ere's a fine strong lad, a rale withy lad as ever I see. Would ye be knowin' a mite about the sea, young man?"

Without thinking, I said, "I've had lessons in navigation, and I've been to sea a little."

"Ah! In the schooner, say?"

"Yes."

"That's nice. That's 'andsome. That's luck all round. 'Cause why? 'Cause ol' Dud don't like partin' wi' men to take captur'd vessels up to Allyfax, much as 'e likes the prize money, and 'ere's you as knows the 'ooker, and there's a couple o' these idle townsmen we can pick up in the back lanes, and wi' one or two o' 'Is Majesty's jolly tars to see all fair and no Yankee tricks, why, we'll get 'er to Allyfax 'andsome."

Mother rushed over to me and stood before Mr. Jump with her head thrown back. "You shan't take my Davy, you wicked man. The only son I have left—and hardly more than a boy."

Mr. Jump's heavy eyebrows went up. "A rale withy lad, ma'am. Proper young man, 'e is. Six foot if 'e's an inch. But when 'e gets to Allyfax, ma'am, 'e can turn round and come 'ome, I don't doubt. I don't doubt that fer a moment, ma'am. 'Andsome, I call it."

Father addressed Lieutenant Cunningham brusquely. "You, sir, you're a soldier—can ye tell me where in God's name all this is going to end? I served His Majesty faithfully in my time and am a hopeless, worthless hulk now from a wound received in that service. I've done my best to keep our people quiet, when all their natural sympathies were with their kin over Fundy Bay. And for that, sir, two of my sons have been taken by the press; my store is closed and half my merchandise seized on some quibble o' contraband; my schooner's to go before the prize court on the same quibble, and now this limb o'—this limb o' His Majesty proposes to take the last o' my sons. Ye know what that means. How many men does the fleet let go once they're between decks?"

"Um," said Cunningham, scraping a shaven blue jaw. There was a gleam in his eye. "Naturally we of the army don't like the navy's fashion of grabbing men under our noses, especially when we haven't the right to press ourselves. That brings me to a point I've been anxious to make ever since I arrived in your town, Captain Strang. I am recruiting on Governor Legge's behalf for the Loyal Nova Scotia Regiment, of which he's to be colonel. The regiment's being raised for the defense of this province. There's no reason to suppose it'll ever be required to go elsewhere. Strangely enough, we've had some difficulty getting recruits. I'm betraying no secret when I say that in all Nova Scotia not more than sixty men have come forward so far. Now it seems to me that your town, the second town of importance in the province, could easily provide thrice that. All it wants is a beginning, some encouragement from the men of influence amongst you."

"Hem!" uttered Mr. Jump, seeing where this was leading.

"Now," said the officer smoothly, "there's one sure protection against impressment by the fleet, and that, sir, is enlistment in the corps in which I have the honor to hold a commission. The pay—sixpence a day for a private, uniform and rations provided free by His Majesty—God bless him and confound his enemies—and there's no reason why a smart lad like your son here couldn't become a corporal at eightpence a day, in a mere matter of months—and in a year or two a sergeant, at a shilling a day. Think of it! A shilling a day! And all for garrison duty, for the mere defense of his own province!"

I looked at Father over my mother's trembling head. His eyes said No, but his lips were silent. It was my mother who spoke. She threw her arms about my neck. "Take it, Davy! Please! For my sake—you're all I've got left!"

I stuck out my hand over her shoulder, and the lieutenant fished in his breeches and placed in my brown palm a shilling and threepence, Halifax currency, the equivalent of the king's shilling. All seemed as final as death itself. I might have become a bored private of the Halifax garrison—or even a sergeant, at a shilling a day. But now came a sharp scream from the barn, and another.

I ran out into the cattle-stained snow of the barnyard and saw through the open door Joanna struggling with one of Jump's seamen. He had a leg behind hers and was trying to throw her on the hay beside one of the cow stalls. Poor Joanna was screaming her head off. I caught up the first thing that came to my hand as I charged into the barn—a flail, laid there from the fall threshing—and swung it with all my strength. It struck the fellow's head with the sound of a coconut under a hammer, and down he went. Joanna picked up her skirts for free running and scuttled away to the house. I heard an oath then and turned to see another seaman coming out of the stable shadows and swinging a cutlass at my head. And a voice was hailing from the house—"Look out, Davy!"—my father's voice. I glanced that way and saw Jump and another coming at me, whipping out cutlasses. I dodged the fellow before me and heard the sharp swish of steel past my shoulder. West of the barn lay our pastures and the grist mill brook and Peter Dekatha's hut and beyond them the woods. The woods!

I ran westward with a great thankfulness in my heart for the trees I loved, which seemed to stand waiting to protect me like a friendly army. It was touch and go. Jump and the others were at my heels, Jump calling upon me to stop or, by God, he'd cut my bloody head off. He would, too, I don't doubt, but Peter Dekatha came out of his hut with a gun and knelt in the snow. I saw the flash of the pan, the belch of flame and black smoke, and heard the bullet strike Jump in the head as you hear a snowball splat on a stone wall. I kept on and passed over the brook in a leap that I couldn't have done again in a month of Sundays. At the edge of the woods I paused and saw Peter still on his knees and trying to ward off with the empty musket the blows of three cutlasses. The seamen struck and struck, and I leaned against a pine trunk and was sick.

I dragged myself off. The snow was deeper in the shade of the tall woods, and I was terribly aware of the tracks I left behind. I had no notion where to go but instinctively struck up the river towards the Falls. After a mile or so I paused to listen and heard feet plowing behind and caught up a limb of deadwood to defend myself against the cutlasses. But it was young François, with a wild strained look on his brown face.

"Pe-poog-wess sent me with these things," he gasped; the gun of Louisburg was in his hand, my hunting bag slung over his shoulder, and in the bag I knew was my powder horn and shot pouch and my small brass compass.

"What happened?" I panted.

"The Old One is dead. They cut his head to a meat. Then the red-coat sagamore stood with thy father in the house door and commanded the ship men to take their dead and go. Later Pe-poog-wess sent me to thee."

"Thy mother . . ."

"Where thee go, there go I."

Somebody in the Scripture said that once; but it runs in my mind 'twas a woman.

CHAPTER 12

A Journey and a Pair of Shoes

As a boy, hearing my father's tales of winter forays against the French and Indians and Peter Dekatha's sagas of long, hard hunts in the snow, haunted by thoughts of the starving squaws and children, I had looked forward to a day when I might try myself against the wilderness that began at our pasture wall.

Now that I was faced with it the prospect did not please. The wind was shifting colder with an occasional large snowflake slanting down. The snow on the ground was sodden and heavy with the day's rain. The river was open as far upstream as the dark pines of Kebek, and doubtless Captain Dudington would send a boat party to push the pursuit, once it was seen that I had fled that way. They would have to leave their boats at Kebek and walk over the ice to the Falls, and I had no great respect for seamen hunting aland; but we dared not stop long near the river. The saw mills were closed, with snow drifted against their doors, and the homes of the few settlers there had a winter-bound look. We found a Micmac family crouching in a wretched little bark hut, banked with brushwood and sawdust from the mills and one end nigh buried in snow in the hollow where the Alewife Brook came down to the river, and borrowed snowshoes from them, also a chunk of *moosok*, lean meat dried in last summer's sun, pounded to powder, mixed with ripe blueberries, and pressed into a cake. The stuff was hard as a rock, with a fusty smell, and the snowshoes were poor things worn thin with a winter's hunting. They gave us three ounces of powder and a piece of wildcat fur which I twisted into a cap for myself. We were grateful for all these things and for their silence; white folk would have showered us with questions.

Outside, the snow was now falling fast, and the wind blew cold from the north. Where to go? That was a problem. François was for striking upriver to seek shelter with the Micmacs who wintered at the foot of the lakes, fifteen or twenty miles away. But that was not far enough. For a moment I thought grandly of following the river to its source and climbing over the height of land to Fundy Bay, a thing none of our people had ever done. But that meant a hundred-mile journey in a frozen wilderness where we must hunt to live—not to be undertaken with three ounces of powder and seven balls. I rejected the Fundy journey with a childish regret; 'twould have been romantic, a thing to talk about when I was old. Westward along the coast lay Barrington and Yarmouth, full of rebel sympathizers who would readily slip me over Fundy Bay in one of their smuggling vessels. But the nearest hamlet in that direction was seventy miles away through the pathless coastal woods. The third and last choice lay eastward, toward Halifax.

That seemed mad at first, but the more I thought of it, the more sensible it became. No one would think of looking for me there. Not more than thirty miles through the woods would take us to the Lahave, where the people were of a mind with ourselves and would give us any help we needed; and from the Lahave to Halifax ran a horse path with small settlements every fifteen or twenty miles.

In Halifax I would seek out William Smith, and he would shelter me for my father's sake. It was all quite simple and logical. But as we set our faces northeastward and the forest closed behind us I knew the real reason for my choice. 'Twas the yearning to see Fear Bingay. That alone.

Thirty miles is no great journey. I have footed fifty between sunrise and sunset in my time, and that through woods. But our march to the Lahave was nigh the death of us. The day was far gone when we started, and snowing hard, and night came early. For once we blessed our rocky countryside; there was a fine choice of big stones for shelter, some as big as a barn. Such a one we found, shelving deeply on its southern side, with a dry cave under the overhang. We scraped out the drifted snow and a litter of porcupine dung, and François took hatchet and hacked some chunks off a convenient red-pine snag. From the dry wood dust in the worm borings we got a handful of tinder, which we ignited with a little flash of powder in the pan of my musket. Carefully we fed it with small pitch-smelling shavings, got the chunks alight, and soon had a fire of birchwood, cut in four-foot lengths, throwing a fine heat against the rock. We gnawed our pemmican and, for our thirst, scooped snow into our mouths, a poor substitute for water.

The wind rose and backed to the northeast and blew a storm of snow that lasted the night and all the next day. When we left that place at last it was marked by the stumps of wire birch sticking out the snow for thirty yards around, all hacked off anyhow with the dull little hatchet, and the snow all beaten down like a moose yard by our fuel-gathering feet. Our hands were sore—each of those stumps was known to us by personal struggle and pain—and our mouths as dry as kilns. Never again in my life was I caught in the woods without a sharp hatchet and a kettle.

Within four hours of leaving our rock we came to the Medway River, by ill luck on a stretch of open rapids, and had to travel upstream some distance to find a frozen still water where we could cross. Such things upset all calculations, especially calculations made on a crude map in the mind. We were continually fetching a compass around bogs which the rains had turned to lakes of gray slush or seeking sound ice for the crossing of streams; and on some lakes the ice was sound; in others were long open stretches—from warm springs, François said—and on some the ice was black rotten, and we had to cut poles and go cautiously. The weather was medium cold and the sun bright—too bright. The upflung dazzle of sunshine set our eyes streaming—mine worse than François's. Micmacs call February *Abugunajit*, but March is the true "snow blinder."

The country between the Medway and the Lahave is a wilderness of lakes and bogs and streams. We welcomed the sight of a lake with good ice, for that was an open road with no trees, rocks, or windfalls to dodge, and we came to one that was pretty nigh the end of us. The ice looked good, and we slipped off our snowshoes with relief; but about two miles up the blinding white surface we came suddenly upon dark sun-rotted stuff where an old pressure crack had opened wide in a thaw and then frozen thinly. The rotten streak went right across the lake. 'Twas too far to go 'round, so we chanced it—and went through. The grasp of the icy water seemed to squeeze all the breath out of me. I went down to my armpits, with my musket stretched out before me instinctively to give a hold on the unbroken ice, and I gave a violent thrust with my feet as a swimmer does, hoping to vault out on the rebound. But when my full weight came on the musket the ice broke under it also, and this time I went under completely, gun and all. I would not let it go—the gun of Louisburg—and was like to have drowned if François had not found solid ice and came wriggling toward the hole where I floundered. He caught my jacket and dragged me to the surface. I opened my eyes, and the blast of sunlight along the level surface of the ice seemed to burn them out of my head. François bade me hold there and not move, while he went to cut poles. 'Twas a long teeth-rattling business, but he got me to shore at last more dead than alive. The gun was dripping water. We had lost our only means of making fire. Worse, our snowshoes were gone.

There was no stopping. It was move or perish, and we set off at once. The pine woods along the shores of the lake were piled deep with snow swept off the ice by the winds. We had to chance the ice inshore for the sake of easier footing. Water drained from our upper garments into our smallclothes, which froze and clashed like boards at every step. My eyes were fast swelling shut with snow blindness. François had to keep a hand under my elbow. Soon I could not make out the compass needle and had to rely entirely on François's eyes. I knew we could not be far from the Lahave. François thought the scene of our disaster was a lake called Minamkeag, not more than ten miles from the settlement at the head of navigation on that river. We left the ice and plunged into the woods. I could still make out daylight through the slits of my swollen eyes, but suddenly all was dark, and I thought I was gone stone-blind till the sharply increasing cold told me that night had come.

We stumbled along, François holding my wrist. There was a moon, he said. I told him to steer northeast by north, using the compass, but he did not understand, and I made a V with the first two fingers of my right hand and told him to ignore the little needle by so much on the side of sun rising. He grunted agreement, but I think he went by the polar star and his own notion of the way. He had never been in this region but he had a rude map of its lakes and streams in his head, acquired from hunting tales of the wandering Micmacs. Indians never forget that kind of thing, once heard, and you will see them getting the taleteller to illustrate his journey with a stick in the dust.

All through the night we crept along. In places the night's frost had put a crust on the snow which bore us fifteen or twenty paces before we plunged knee-deep, sometimes thigh-deep. But there were hellish places where one step held and the next went through—of all

traveling the worst: the legs set for one condition and finding another, like coming down an endless staircase in the dark, with some
steps steeper than others and landings in unexpected places. It was a
nightmare, but I said nothing lest François think me womanish.
Alone, I should have sat down and let the cold put an end to my
pains and weariness.

When I felt the morning sun on my cheek we were staggering
slowly from one tree trunk to the next. We had not spoken a word
in many hours. I was so far gone that I unslung the gun of Louisburg
and dropped it in the snow. François grunted. He was picking it up,
I knew, and I wanted to protest, but no words would come. The cold
was all through me, and movement was a pain without warmth. Men
said that freezing was a pleasant death once you gave yourself up to
it. I craved some sort of pleasure in this misery, if only the pleasure
of dying. I had lost faith in the compass, in François, in myself. The
very notion of endless sleep was comforting, though I blubbered once
or twice, from a weak self-pity, that no one would ever know what
had become of me.

Then I heard the sweetest sound in the world, a harsh clock-clock-
clock of Dutch ox bells somewhere to our left. François plunged off
in that direction, dragging at my wrist, and I followed blindly, col-
liding with the tree trunks that he turned and receiving the full lash
of bent twigs on my blind frostbitten face. We came upon a sled road
—I could feel the hard, polished snow of the runner tracks underfoot
—and heard somewhere to our left front, around a bend, I suppose, the
voice of a teamster crying, "*Huit! Huit!*" and cracking his whip. I had
a terrible fear that the team was moving away from us, but it came on,
a Lahave farmer going out to his wood lot for fuel: and that is all I
remember for three days.

The house was a small one looking down the slope of a snowy field
to the gray flood of the Lahave, just where it entered tidewater, a
dozen miles or so above its mouth. There were clearings and cottages,
some of logs, some frame and shingle, along the opposite bank and
behind them a steep, gloomy wall of pine-and-hemlock forest. Up that
bank and through that forest ran a narrow white trace, the horse path
to Halifax, seventy miles away.

Our farmer's name was Hessel, one of the Dutch settlers from
Lunenburg who had wandered up the Lahave. He spoke more Eng-
lish than most of his people, for the other settlers hereabouts were
Yankees and a few Englishmen run away from ships. Hessel was a

stocky slow-moving man with a yellow beard and long yellow hair and small twinkling eyes as blue as a summer sea. He was kind and asked no questions. I told him we had got lost while hunting out of the Medway settlement.

His wife was a strong blonde creature with no English. She was very good to us, but her eyes were suspicious, and she made François lie in the barn, as if he might rise and scalp them all in their beds if she let him sleep beside me on her spotless hearth. There were five children, solemn slow-smiling creatures, the girls with long, tow plaits. All wore wooden shoes. The youngsters slept in the garret, where they climbed in giggling file each evening by a ladder that stood in the kitchen corner. Hessel and his wife slept in a small chamber off the kitchen.

At the end of a week, by keeping my eyes bandaged most of the day and bathing them in warm water every night, I could see pretty well. I was anxious to push on, but my shoes were wrecks, and these folk were no hunters; there was not enough hide in the village to make a pair of moccasins. Frau Hessel was just as anxious to see the last of us, and small blame to her, for their store of corn meal was nigh gone and the salt pork low in the barrel, and for the long spring —always a hungry time in our Nova Scotia—there would be nothing but sauerkraut till the alewives came.

It was Frau Hessel who discovered, on a visit to a farmhouse half a mile down the west bank, the presence of a shoemaker in the settlement. I wondered what was up when she burst into the cottage with this intelligence but I could see Hessel looking at my feet, shaking his head doubtfully, and the woman pointing to my gun; and I knew before Hessel translated that she had sent word for the shoemaker to come—and for his pay I could sell my gun.

So the shoemaker came, a slender beady-eyed Yankee of the sort who wandered about the settlements, staying a day or a week as business warranted and welcomed as much for his gossip as anything else. He carried his outfit in an enormous pack on his back and bustled into the Hessel kitchen with a quick little smile and a "Haow-do?" that took in all of us.

Beside the fire he set up his bench, which was in two parts, one a low stool on which he crouched with his knees high and the other a sort of chest which he placed at his side. From the chest, one after another, he conjured a short hammer with a broad face, awls, a bag of wooden pegs, a polishing stone, a whetstone, several wooden lasts, nippers, a piece of brown beeswax, a bunch of hog bristles, a ball of homespun linen thread, a stirrup strap, apron and lapstone. He took one look at my shoes and pronounced, "Past prayin' for, friend. Ye want a new pair." And after some measurements, made, I think, to impress me, he pulled his stock of leather out of the inexhaustible chest, chose pieces for the uppers and soles, and began to beat the upper leather into a working texture against the smooth lapstone.

Hessel set out for his wood lot with the oxen and I sent François to give him a hand. They all went off together, the children riding on the sled.

As the shoemaker worked he talked, a stream of anecdote gathered all the way from Cumberland to Cape Sable, brought out in a droll way that was like to split my sides. Through it all, Frau Hessel bustled wooden-faced about her work.

"She speak English?" asked the shoemaker without lifting his head.

"Hardly a word," I said.

"Sure?"

"Sure."

He gave his nose an odd little twitch, closing one nostril and sniffing up the other. "Where ye from?"

"Medway settlement."

"Um. Know Silas Morang there? Nice man, nice place; treat ye clever there. What ye say your name was?"

"Smith."

He gave me a droll flick of his black eyes. "Never heard of it!"

I smiled. "It's well known down that way. There was a Smith represented the county in the assembly till the troubles began."

"Ah! Talked ag'in the king, didn't he? God bless him and confaound his enemies. What d'ye think o' things in Ameriky?"

I twisted my mouth and shrugged.

"Um!" He selected a hog bristle from his bundle, took a length of twine and raveled the end, twisted bristle and threads together until they were one point, and rubbed his lump of beeswax up and down the length of the twine.

"If ye hadn't said ye was a Smith from Medway"—he pierced the sole with his awl and a rap of the hammer, pulled out the awl, and thrust the bristle and thread through—"I'd 'a said, offhand, ye was a Strang from Liv'pool."

I felt my face go tight. "On what grounds?"

Another rap, another deft threading and pull through. "Knowed Cap'n Matthew Strang o' Liv'pool when he was plain Matt Strang o' Plymouth, Massachusetts. Never fergit a face, 'specially a face like his'n. Like a hawk's. That's what the Injuns called Matt, come to think on't. Yes sirree, young Smith, swan to man ef you ain't the spit'n image o' Cap'n Matt Strang, nose and all. Ever bin to Liv'pool?"

"Once or twice," I said uneasily. The kitchen had one small window, set high, and the shoemaker sat in the lower shadow, with only his hands and his work in the sunbeam. That and the weakness of my eyes kept me from searching his face as I wished. He had a foot in the stirrup strap now, drawing the half-made shoe down tight upon the last, and his nimble, hairy hands flitted back and forth, shifting swiftly from hammer and awl to bristle and thread and back again.

"Hear there's a frigate to Liv'pool."

"Heard that."

"Give Simeon Perkins suthin' to scratch his poll over."

"Reckon so."

"Tory, ain't he?"

"Don't know."

He paused and gave me a comical, sly look. "Don't know much fer a Medway man, do ye? On'y nine mile from Liv'pool!"

"I mind my own business," I said.

"Ha! Now if that don't sound like Matt Strang to the life ye can call me King George and kiss me!" He let out a long cackle of laughter and brought his hammer down on the sole with a whack that made me jump. "Mind me own business, he says. Oh, Matt, Matt, if ye could on'y see this feller. Spit'n image! Spit'n image! Ever see Matt?"

I hesitated. "Reckon so."

"What's he think o' things in Ameriky?"

"That's his business."

"Oho! Chock full o' business, ain't ye? Good thing too. Let every young feller stick to's business, the king to's throne and . . ."

"The shoemaker to his last!"

". . . the patriot to's principles. A close tongue's good as gold, these times. And speakin' o' money, I'm told ye've a musket to sell fer these shoes. Might I have a look at it?"

I passed him the gun—and wanted to kick myself. Against theft, long ago, my father had burned his name into the butt with a hot iron. The shoemaker, hunched at his bench, thrust the long barrel up into the bright motes of the sunbeam and squinted along it with an expert eye; he tapped along the metal with the handle of his awl and listened, as if for flaws; he tested the lock and the trigger pull with a careful thumb to ease the hammer. And finally he turned the butt to the light.

"How d'ye spell Smith down to Medway?"

"S-t-r-a-n-g," said I promptly.

He cackled and wagged his head, as if I were a very witty fellow, and laid the gun aside. The sewing was done on the first shoe; now he began to peg, first a tap on the awl, then a wooden peg in the hole, and a sharp tap driving it home.

"Fact is"—*tap!*—"ye're a son o' Matt Strang's"—*tap!*—"Liv'pool men don't hunt this side the Medway"—*tap!*—"And a face is a face" —*tap!*—"naow puttin' two and two together"—*tap!*—"I'd say you and thet Injun was on the run"—*tap!*—"'cause Dudin'ton's frigate is to Liv'pool"—*tap!*—"and that means hell to pay and no pitch hot."

He thrust his head sharply toward me, with one lank lock of hair in his eyes, and his neck seemed mighty long. He was like a snapping turtle thrusting out its hard, beady head, and I sat back instinctively.

"Right?" he snapped.

"That'll do to go on with," I said cautiously. Frau Hessel had gone out to the barn.

"I'm aheadin' fer Liv'pool, son. Got shoemakers there, but a good man can allus pick up a bit o' work, comin' spring. Might pick up some news too. Useful in my trade." He said this in such a fashion that the next remark sprang to my lips.

"Just what is your trade, shoemaker?"

He shut one eye and regarded me. "Friend of Ameriky?"

"Yes."

"How good a friend?"

"I'm going to New England, by the road around Cumberland, to fight for the rebels."

"Cape Sable's handier," he suggested shrewdly.

"So are the king's ships."

"Know anybody in Cumberland?"

I was about to say No. Then I remembered my tall Irish acquaintance of Market Square. "A young man named Uniacke—Richard Uniacke."

"Oho! So ye know Dicky, eh? Now that's rale convenient. That's luck—'cause I've a message fer Dicky."

I regarded him in silence, and he stared back at me. Gone was his clownish air. In his eyes was something bold, even desperate, but at the same time calculating.

"Who are you?" I demanded.

He put a hand to the side of his bench and slid a panel aside, a panel so neatly fitted and so like the rest of it that the sharpest eye could not detect it. Forth came a folded paper which he thrust at me, and all the time his cold eyes never left mine. The paper was worn and much thumbed and the writing finely penned. The superscription made my eyes pop:

> *By His Excellency George Washington Esq., Commander-in-Chief*
> *of the Army of the United States.*

To Aaron Trusdell, Esq.,

The honourable Continental Congress having lately passed a resolve that two persons be sent to Nova Scotia to inquire into the state of that colony, the disposition of the inhabitants towards the American Cause, and the condition of fortifications, dockyards, artillery and warlike stores, and the number of soldiers sailors and ships of war there, I do hereby appoint you, Aaron Trusdell, to be one of the persons to undertake this business; and as the season is late and the work of great importance, I entreat you will use the utmost dispatch.

Given under my hand this twenty-fourth day of November, 1775
                                    GEORGE WASHINGTON

I gaped at the thing like a bumpkin at a dancing ape. The words seemed to march across the paper like lines of men, with capital letters mounted here and there for officers, and they marched on parallel roads to some destination beyond the right-hand side of the sheet. That was what I saw—an army on the march. The spy's warrant had been written while Arnold and Montgomery lay before the walls of Quebec. Out of the whirl of my thoughts I blurted eagerly, "Is he planning to move on Nova Scotia? Eh?"

"General Washin'ton," Aaron Trusdell said, "sees the importance o' Nova Scotia as clear as you or me: the northern station o' the king's fleet and doorstep to all Canada. But he's insistin' on one thing— that us Americans mustn't put ourselves in the position of attackin' our brother colonists."

"He attacked Quebec," said I bluntly.

"I'm not so sure 'twas Washington's idee, that. But see what happened? A lot o' Canadians joined Arnold after Montreal fell, and many others gave the Americans help in one form or another. They're in a pretty pickle now. The American army on the St. Lawrence has received neither men nor supplies, must soon get out o' Canada, and leave its Canadian friends to face the music. That's what the general wants to avoid in Nova Scotia. One false move, and the Cause 'ud be ruined in this province."

"Why are you telling me all this?" I cried.

"Because I've a message for Halifax and I've got to trust somebody with it. You're a son o' Matt Strang's, and 'tain't in Strang nature to play false. Lookee here, son, ye won't find Richard Uniacke in Cumberland. He's stayin' at a tavern jist outside o' Halifax with certain friends o' the Cause. Here's what ye do. Make your way quietlike to Halifax, but don't go into the town. The south-shore road—it's no more'n a footpath really—forks at the head o' Nor'west Arm. To your left is a little valley that runs pretty well across the neck o' the Halifax peninsula. Foller that till ye strike the Windsor Road on the Basin shore. Take the Windsor Road towards town—there's mostly woods and a few Dutch farms—and on the shoulder o' the rise ye'll see a tavern with the sign o' the Blue Bell. Got that?"

"Yes, go on."

"Go in, and watch your chance to get Uniacke to one side. Says you, 'I saw the shoemaker.' He'll say, 'Is the shoe ready then?' And says you—mind this very careful now—says you, 'The shoe's laid aside for a time.' See? 'The shoe's laid aside . . .'"

"Yes, yes. But what's it mean, this gibberish?"

He cocked his lean turtle head and twisted the left side of his face till I thought the end of his long mouth would touch the tightly closed eye.

"That's none o' your business, friend."

I had to laugh, to find my own words stuffed so neatly down my throat, and the shoemaker gave vent to his peculiar cackle, and we were chuckling and slapping our knees as if this were the joke of the season when Frau Hessel came in. Like lightning the shoemaker was transformed. He fell into his professional jackknife posture and in a high nasal whine began to argue about the value of the musket.

"Old as Mother Carey's rooster . . . used in war . . . that's bad, sogers not bein' careful like you 'n me . . . stock scratched 'n marked with a name . . . hammer's stiff . . . trigger a mite weak in the spring and the cam worn . . . give ye the shoes 'n five dollars hard money . . . seein' ye've had a rough time."

"A hard bargain," said I, and it was—five dollars and a pair of cobbler's brogues for the gun of Louisburg!—but the good frau's shrewd eyes were on me. I nodded, and Aaron dived a hand into his gray homespun shirt and brought forth a leather purse, hung about his lean neck by the drawstring. From it he counted out five pieces of eight into my hand.

I greased the new shoes with mutton tallow and put on the old moth-bitten round hat that Hessel had given me and paid the good frau two of my silver dollars and sallied forth with François and Aaron into a sunny March afternoon.

The snow was going fast. We splattered our way down the slushy slope to the boat for the river crossing. There, in a clump of spruce trees under the high bank, we parted from the shoemaker. He was for the winding path downriver and the New Dublin shore, and I reckoned that what with his pack and his bench and the musket slung to his shoulder, Aaron Trusdell's nimble legs would be sore before his journey's end. But he was full of surprises, that man. With a swift glance over his shoulder, lest Frau Hessel be perched like a fat robin on one of the spruce branches, I suppose, he unslung the gun of Louisburg and pushed the barrel into my hand.

"Take it, friend, and when the time comes see that it speaks sharp for the Cause. Meantime, let the Injun carry it and call it his. An Injun's the king's own fancy. But nowadays 'tain't wise for a Yankee lad to tote a gun on the Halifax road."

With that we parted, and as François sculled the old boat across the Lahave I watched the wiry, purposeful figure trudging down the sled road to New Dublin with the great burden on its back.

CHAPTER 13

At the Sign of the Blue Bell

WE HAD ADVENTURES on the road to Halifax. We steered clear of the taverns, knowing that the keepers were now compelled by law to report all strangers. The shoemaker had given me the names of certain "friends o' the Cause" at Mahone, Chester, St. Margaret's Bay, and Nine Mile River, and to these we went for our food and shelter, warily, like thieves. At Mahone we lay at a smugglers' inn. At Chester, piously, we took shelter from the rain in the meeting-house on a Sabbath afternoon and heard the famous Parson Seccombe preaching a text from Proverbs: "And doth the crown endure to every generation?" His interpretation of that text was so revolutionary that I expected trouble and was glad that François and I had chosen to stand just inside the door; but his congregation seemed to be in accord with him, and I remembered that the men of Chester had refused to take the oath, and nothing happened. It was another winter before the Crown's long arm reached stouthearted Parson Seccombe and jerked him off to stand trial for "sedition."

On our way across the bleak hills between East River and St. Margaret's Bay we were caught in a snowstorm and providentially came upon a hut by the path. Three men were inside, and they were suspicious of us, and we of them, and none of us slept the night but sat choking over the fire, whose smoke had no outlet but a hole in the roof. By their looks and speech they were escaped American prisoners, making their way toward Liverpool and the western shore, but we asked no questions and heard no lies. In the morning we showed them how to twist the tough twigs of yellow birch into makeshift snowshoes and went our separate ways.

On the afternoon of the seventh day from Lahave we trudged wearily over the brow of a wooded hill and saw the Northwest Arm shining blue at our feet and beyond it the steep timbered slope of the Halifax peninsula. A brook rattled between icy banks to the end of the Arm. The track crossed it on a bridge of poles, and beside it sat fifteen or twenty bark wigwams whose brown cones smoked faintly, like dung hills on a frosty morning. A clamor of lean dogs announced us and were like to tear the breeches off us before we beat them off with sticks. Squaws peered from the filthy door blankets; a number of men and boys ran out, and we walked down to them crying the Micmac greeting, "Kway! Kway!"

These were not like our country Indians. A motley crew dressed in the castoff rags of Halifax town; squaws in tattered red or dirty white petticoats, and once-fine gowns that had passed from mistress to maid and from maid to squaw by way of the rag bag; men in old red army coats and gray blankets, all sorts of smallclothes, and one or two in greasy buckskins. One or two of the women looked wholesome under the winter's dirt, but without exception the men were bleary-eyed wretches, sodden with the cheap rum of the truck houses. The whole place was an offense to the eyes and the nose, for the slush about the wigwams was foul with the winter's easings of humans and dogs and stank the March wind. But François seemed quite pleased at meeting some of his brethren here, and I left him to stay with them, bidding him take good care of my gun. That was needless advice, for every one of those dissolute brown scarecrows had a good musket bearing the king's mark and powder to burn in it.

A path to the left took me up the shallow valley which forms the collar on the Halifax neck, through heavy pine woods where the dusk was already falling. A mile or so brought me to a road of sorts and clearings and small wooden houses in the German style, standing end to the road, with steep roofs and ornamental woodwork about the windows and heavy cornices and weathercocks swinging in the wind. The people called it Westenwald, but Halifax knew it as the Dutch Village, not to be confused with Dutchtown, the Halifax suburb.

The village street forked, and a road, ironed flat by sled runners and stained with the droppings of oxen, turned off toward Halifax through the woods. I ignored it, faithful to the shoemaker's instructions, and followed the main track northward to the Basin. The winter's ice had gone, and its broad water had a pink glaze in the last of the sunset. A few high feathers of cloud burned red in the western sky, and a band of yellow light lay along the southern horizon, saw-edged by the dark spruce tops. Overhead hung the apple-green stain which in our latitude heralds a frosty night, and in the east the first stars were shining.

At my feet lay the Great West Road, the only real highway in the province, by which Halifax tapped the rich farming country between Windsor and Fort Anne. Its snow had been packed hard by sleds hauling firewood to the town and by the cattle and sheep which summer and winter were herded to Halifax for transport to Gage's army in Boston, not to mention the smart sleigh turnouts of the Halifax gentry, driving out to Birch Cove for mulled wine and sillabub at the inn.

I paused a moment to admire the great anchorage, shut in by wooded hills. His Majesty's whole navy could ride there secure from all winds, but not a mast was to be seen. The lone sign of life was a prick of candlelight in the darkness far around the shore toward Sackville and another by Birch Cove. It seemed to me typical of our province and its people—a few candles glimmering between the woods and the sea.

I set my face townward with a high heart. There was danger along this road, but at the end of it lay my charming Fear. No young man could ask more. The track climbed abruptly from the Basin, and part way up the slope I came upon a small clearing and saw in the starlight the ruin of a blockhouse. I had heard my father speak of this place, built to guard the back gate of Halifax when the town was founded, and I remembered his grim story of the drunken redcoats he and his rangers had found scalped there one fine afternoon. 'Twas a ghostly thing in the early dark, and I was glad to put it behind.

On the edge of the plateau the woods opened into fields, and there was a hollow to the right of the road and a Dutch farmhouse and barn. This must be Philip Bayer's place, according to my directions, and the Blue Bell Inn lay not far beyond. Another quarter mile brought me to a row of winter-naked willows beside the road and then a gambrel-roofed house whose lower windows cast yellow beams along the snow. There was a shadowy bulk of stables and outbuildings, and a twist of the cold wind brought me a cheerful smell of wood smoke and the creak of a swinging sign. This must be the Blue Bell, as sure as God made little apples.

In the trampled snow before the door I hesitated. My clothes were rags, and my cheeks, which I had begun to shave last year, had known no razor since the good Hessel lent me his dull steel at the Lahave. Everything about me smacked of the vagabond—and the landlord would be full of the new law, so close to Halifax. Besides, young officers like an outlying tavern for an evening with the wine cups, especially with a petticoat along. But the night cold bit through my rags, and my empty belly shouted a pox on caution. I gave a bold rap on the door and entered, blinking, into the light and warmth of the taproom.

Clean sea sand gritted underfoot. Two brown-faced men in homespun and moccasins sat at a table discussing pots of ale and the shreds of a meal—drovers, by the look of them, homeward bound from the Halifax market. By the west window sat a round red-faced fellow of fifty, in a blue coat with brass buttons and a watered-silk waistcoat, both unbuttoned halfway down, and his stock loosened, and a great old-fashioned three-tailed wig hung on the chair post, addressing himself busily to a decanter of wine. There was no one else but a tall well-built man, back toward me, lighting a long churchwarden with a coal from the blazing fire in the hearth.

The landlord appeared from the kitchen, a sharp-eyed, lean fellow in a long, old-fashioned waistcoat and rolled sleeves, with blue breeches buckled above his knobby knees and the coarse stockings gartered over the breeches. He saw me with no great favor and bore down at once. I forestalled the question on his lips with the thickest Dutch accent I could muster.

"Blease, I must shpeak mit Mister Richart Uniag."

The man at the fireplace turned, blowing out tobacco smoke in a thin blue stream.

It was Uniacke himself.

"Who are you?" demanded the landlord, looking me up and down.

"Johann Tiel from de Deutsche Willage, blease," said I.

"I'm Uniacke," called the Irishman pleasantly, warming his back at the fire. "What is it?"

"A messitch vrom de zhoomekker, blease."

I saw his eyes go hard and wary. He dismissed the landlord with a wave of the pipe.

"Is the shoe ready then?" softly.

"De zhoo," I said carefully, "iss but aside vor a dime."

"Damn!" His eyes bored into mine like the awls of the shoemaker himself. He knew me—I saw the flicker of recognition and a glint of something else, suspicion, no doubt, or maybe anger at my news. A glint, anyhow.

"Come with me," he said abruptly, and loudly for the benefit of the taproom, "and I'll write ye a note for him."

He took a candle from the mantel and waved me ahead with it and on the upper landing of the stairs he gave my arm a squeeze and kept his hand there, guiding me to a chamber at the end of the narrow hall. There he flung open a door and nudged me into a comfortable scene. A Franklin stove blazed cheerfully before the chimney piece, and a four-poster bed sat in the midst of the floor with two men playing cribbage on it by the light of a pair of candles set on a chest of drawers. One was a tall fellow, about thirty, with dark brown hair tied loosely at his nape, and a pair of keen blue eyes very intent on the game. His waistcoat was too plain and too long to be fashionable, and his brown homespun breeches and gray wool stockings were those of a farmer. So were his hard brown hands.

The other man was back to and evidently did not intend to stay long, for he wore a three-caped cloak, unclasped, and I could see a pair of long, black riding boots with turned-down brown tops. That back, ay, and the cloak and boots were familiar, and the set of the unpowdered head. It was William Smith.

He turned his head and at sight of me sprang up, crying, "Strang? Matthew Strang's son, from Liverpool! What's this?" staring me up and down in a fierce and disconcerting fashion.

"He's seen the shoemaker," Uniacke said.

At that the other man jumped up. "And his message?" eagerly.

"The shoe is put aside for a time," said I like a parrot.

I never saw such consternation over a few simple words. The tall brown man glared at me. "Is he to be trusted?" he demanded of the others.

"A son of Matthew Strang's, at Liverpool," Smith explained. "Trusted? Yes, though his father's notion of the Cause isn't quite ours. It's David, isn't it?"

I nodded and at Uniacke's insistence told them what was going on at Liverpool and how I fled and met the shoemaker and how the shoemaker had shown me his warrant and given me the message.

"Why didn't he come himself?" snapped Smith. "A matter of such importance . . ."

"I think he planned to," I explained, "till he met me. He decided to go to Liverpool and judge what was afoot there. It seemed to be of some importance to him."

The brown-haired man was suspicious still. He talked with a faint Scots burr. "What! Is all our work to be put aside because the south-shore Yankees are watched too closely? We hadn't counted on 'em—under the fleet's thumb as they are."

"There's something else, depend on it," Uniacke said. And, "Davy, lad, let me introduce Mr. John Allan of Cumberland. John, shake the fist of as bonny a mauler as ever thumped a press gang."

Allan's face broke into a smile, and he put out a hand and shook mine.

"Dick told me that tale. Well, we've had no press gangs in Cumberland so far. It's about the only attention His Majesty's spared us."

"Let's to business," William Smith said curtly. "If we accept this message it changes all our plans."

"First," Uniacke said firmly, "when did ye eat, Davy?"

I made a mental calculation. "Forty hours ago."

He threw open the door and strode along the hall, a candle fluttering blue in his hand, and roared down the stair well for someone named Jupiter; and by and by a Negro came, all teeth and white eyeballs in the dark of the hall, bearing a tray with a knuckle of cold ham, a loaf, a chunk of cheese, a prune pie, and a bottle of Madeira. I fell upon these things like a wolf and for a time heard only the serious buzz of their voices somewhere beyond the champing of my jaws. They had a map spread on the counterpane and were squatting on the bed about it.

As my belly relaxed its demands and my wits crept back to my head I heard Allan say repeatedly, "Ay! Ay! But we must be sure."

That was what my father had said to the men of Liverpool, at that meeting in our kitchen in the fall of '74. 'Twas queer to hear the same words on Allan's lips.

Uniacke said testily, "Wait! Wait! Wait! That's all we do! I'm sick of waiting, Allan, man! Opportunity staring us in the face—not a corporal's guard between Halifax and the tip o' Fundy . . ."

"But in Halifax?" broke in Allan dourly.

"Gorham's Royal Rascals," Smith said crisply, "as worthless a crew as ever carried a musket for His Majesty, and two companies of English greenhorns. That's all. Not even a man-o'-war in the harbor. The defenses of Halifax on the land side were made against Indians in the first place—blockhouses and one or two small redoubts—all in ruins now. The naval dockyard's the only place capable of defense, and that only against musketry. Besides, Halifax is asleep. Governor Legge's cried 'Wolf' so much that it's become a lullaby. Look at the Windsor Road—not even a sentry to watch it! There should be a battery on Citadel Hill; there's nothing. Nothing! On a hill that looks down the very chimneys of the town! Not so much as a sentry box! Listen, Allan! A bold march from Cumberland will forereach any news of your rising, and three hundred determined men could seize Halifax in a night. The friends of the Cause in the town would swell your ranks to a thousand—for that matter the whole province will rise."

"Exactly!" cried Uniacke, eyes shining. "They're all waiting for a sign—and so, like fools, are we! A sign from the shoemaker, damme, when we can make a sign ourselves that'll set the province ablaze. Think of it, man! Nova Scotia, the last of the seaboard provinces, key to the St. Lawrence, to all Canada, throwing down the gage— begob, John, there's a pun for ye!—and leaving King George and his fleet without so much as a mooring post on the continent! A solid continent in arms, by Heaven, with one leader and one purpose!"

He snatched the map from the bed and flung it into a corner. "The devil with that! What we want is a map of North America!"

I jumped up, crying, "Here's with you!" caught by that marvelous compound of enthusiasm, humor, and purpose which was to make Dick Uniacke a great man in our Nova Scotia in the long time to come.

Soberly John Allan picked up the map and spread it on the bed again. It portrayed Nova Scotia, all the great sprawling mass of it— the peninsula, the islands of Cape Breton and St. Jean, the isthmus of Chignecto, the great forest wilderness which now is called New Brunswick, and a goodly section of what has since become the state of Maine. There was no particular reason why these earnest men should bother their heads about me, unless 'twas that I was Nova Scotian born, a symbol; for Smith was a New England Scot, Allan a true Scot—born in Edinburgh Castle, in fact—and Uniacke an Irishman barely three years away from the old sod.

"Davy," said John Allan, putting a brown finger on the map, "here's our province. Its westerly border is somewhere about the Penobscot, where the old French territory met the province of Massachusetts.

Years ago the Machias settlers petitioned Halifax for a township charter, but Halifax hemmed and hawed and nothing was done, and now Machias has declared itself part of Massachusetts. Mark that well, for the Machias men are in arms and ready to march to our assistance at a word. They've already raided as far as the St. John, which you see here, a great inland highway to Canada. There's a white family or two at the mouth of the river, but the only real settlement is Maugerville, upstream, where the people are openly for the American Cause. Now the bulk of Nova Scotia's population is in the peninsula. So run your finger up Fundy Bay—there—and you come to the isthmus, which is Cumberland County, where Uniacke and I live. It's guarded by Fort Cumberland, which the French knew as Beausejour. The fort's deserted now, like every other in the province outside Halifax. The people of Cumberland are mostly Yankees from New England, openly for the Cause. Three or four years ago that shrewd man Michael Francklin brought in some settlers from Yorkshire in England and planted them in our midst. They'll not oppose us in the Cause—many signed our petition against the Militia Act—but they'll not fight the king either. Now run your finger around Minas Basin. There's Cobequid and Truro—all Yankee folk and Scotch-Irish, all hearty in the Cause. Off to the left is the Annapolis Valley—Yankee folk again. They refused the militia oath, and several of their members in assembly have been unseated. Michael Francklin lives at Windsor and has great influence with them, but if our coup in Cumberland succeeds they'll join us. Very well. Run your finger around the western end of the peninsula. There's Yarmouth, Barrington, Ragged Island, and the rest, including your town of Liverpool—Yankee settlers all, but exposed to the king's fleet cruising between Halifax and Boston and closely watched by the governor—as ye know to your sorrow. Very well. Come east along the Atlantic coast, and there's Lunenburg, where the Dutch are. Most of 'em don't speak English and don't know what all the trouble's about and don't care. So go on—skip Halifax for a moment and look at the east end o' the province. A wilderness: a few Highland Scotch in the north of Cape Breton, a few scattered French, a handful of Yankee settlers about the ruins of Louisburg. Forget 'em. One place more—Pictou, on the Northumberland Strait. Some Pennsylvanians there, all strong for the Cause, and some Scotch, not so strong. Charlottetown in Isle St. Jean is nothing but an outpost in the Gulf, a handful of poverty-stricken French, English, and Scotch. Come back to Halifax, the capital of the province. Population—three thousand, say. A good half of 'em Yankee-born. Two classes: the rich and the poor—mostly poor. Halifax is bankrupt since the garrison went to Boston, and grass growing in the streets. But there lives the governor and his council and the circle of merchants who are now sharpening their claws for the fat army and navy contracts to come; in all Nova Scotia the only men strong for the king. That is the situation."

"And here's the plan," interposed Uniacke eagerly. "Nova Scotia's great weakness is the fact that most o' the population's scattered along the coast and under the heel o' the fleet. But men-o'-war don't like the fogs and tides in our Bay o' Fundy. None o' their first-rates'll venture beyond Annapolis. So our rising must have its root about the end of Fundy Bay, in Cumberland, and about Cobequid Basin. And in Cumberland we are ready. We've sent Jonathan Eddy to Washington's camp at Cambridge—he's there now, in fact—to beg arms and ammunition and, if possible, a few American troops for the look of the thing. All our people want is clear proof that the other colonies will support us in our struggle. It's little to ask, but we've got to have more than words. There! Any questions?"

"Yes," said I. "What is the end to be?"

They all shrugged, but Uniacke said after a moment, "Who can tell the end of a struggle like this? Such a thing's never happened before. But the end I expect—the end we all hope for, I think—is government by ourselves, for ourselves, within the empire. Anything else—anything else is unthinkable."

"Ay!" John Allan nodded firmly.

"Umph!" said Will Smith, and after a moment, "There's a fight to be won first. And it must begin soon. Time burns the fingers like a taper, held too long."

"Ay, and so does a coal," retorted Allan, "when ye try to pluck it out o' the fire barehanded. I'm not thinking o' my own safety, mind —I put that behind me long ago. It's our Cause in Nova Scotia. One false move, and the governor'll make Cumberland an example to cow the whole province. He'd like nothing better. For the past year he's been trying to goad some part o' Nova Scotia into a premature revolt. I say we must make no move till we've adequate means to carry it through. All else is folly."

"The shoemaker——" Smith began, with a curled lip.

". . . is Washington's own emissary. We've seen his warrant for that," John Allan snapped. "If he says wait, then wait we must."

"While Opportunity knocks!" said Uniacke dryly. "Lord, how blind they all are! The English take their garrison out of Nova Scotia for the fighting in Boston—and the Americans spend their reserve in a wild-goose chase to Quebec. And we must do nothing—we must let our fortune hang upon which of 'em wakes up first!"

They reminded me of something that Parson Cheever used to drone about in my lessons—an immovable object and an irresistible force—though Parson Cheever was talking of stresses on sails and hulls, and I now saw a stubborn Scot confronting a hot-tempered Irishman, with Will Smith playing devil's advocate. I was disturbed, for I was young enough to believe that all men who serve a Cause must be of one mind and purpose. I loved Uniacke's fire and fearlessness; yet Allan's canny policy sounded so like my father's grim "Sit tight! Sit tight!" that I gave him an instinctive respect. Here was trouble. But William Smith, the shrewd weigher of men and chances, now stepped in, with an almost audible swallowing of his own opinions.

"Uniacke, I'll not deny that Allan has some logic on his side. We can't risk a flash in the pan."

"You too!" cried Uniacke, all fists and fury. "Then I'll do it alone! Damme, I'll start for Cumberland tomorrow! Wait? Not if Washington himself got down and begged me on his knees!"

"You'll at least wait for Jonathan's opinion?" Allan begged.

"Jonathan? Aha, Jonathan Eddy's a firebrand like me, Allan. He'll say fight—guns or no guns, powder or no powder. A man after my heart is Jonathan!"

Uniacke's voice had reached such a pitch as to make the room ring, and cautious Will Smith flung open the door and peered into the dark hall. No one was there. Allan brought a candle to make sure. But Smith was uneasy.

"I must go," he said abruptly, and clattered downstairs in his riding boots, bawling for the hostler. The rest of us stared one at another.

"If ye go to Cumberland in the morning, here's with ye," Allan said to Uniacke somberly. "Hang one, hang all—but we're fools."

"It'd be a dull world without fools," Uniacke flashed.

A word from him got me a chamber next his, and a drowsy slattern came up with a warming pan full of coals from the dying taproom fire to rub the chill out of the bed sheets. I chased her out and jerked the sheets from the bed lest my dirty body soil them, and I tore off my rags and rolled into the quilts and slept like the dead.

Chapter 14

I Join a Cause

I wakened to find Uniacke dressed and shaking me, with day-dawn making a gray smudge on the frost-furred lattice panes. Allan came in with a candle, and I crawled out bashfully in my grime and nakedness. They took a look at my rags on the floor, and Uniacke fetched a pair of spare breeches, stockings, a shirt, a worn but warm swansdown waistcoat, and a round jacket of blue fear-nought stuff. They fitted me quite well, for we were much of a size, though there was more flesh on his bones. The Negro Jupiter carried breakfast to their chamber: fried bacon and eggs, a loaf, a round of pale country butter and—a luxury I'd never tasted in my life—a pot of steaming coffee; our three countrymen's appetites finished the lot. Outside, a shivering hostler was holding three horses saddled for the road. The sun was just up, sending a bleak yellow ray along the snowy road from town, which lay hidden below the distant white cone of Citadel Hill. Overhead was a roof of gray cloud moving slowly with the northeast wind, which whipped a few specks of small snow about our ears. Yesterday's slush had frozen in the night, and the snow crunched underfoot like caked sugar. The landlord brought forth a bottle of Jamaica rum for the road, which Uniacke slipped into his saddlebag ("Aha, friends, the champagne of Acadia, the wine of our fair province!") and we mounted.

Mine was a big hammerheaded nag with a gait like the town pump, and I speculated sadly on the long road to Cumberland.

As we ambled abreast down the hill where the Windsor Road meets the Basin shore, I thought of François waiting for me in those flea-bitten wigwams at Northwest Arm. I said to Uniacke, "I left an Indian at the Arm and must tell him I'm for Cumberland. Ride on—I'll overtake you along the road."

He looked a little surprised, but nodded. I reined my nag into the path across the isthmus, but just as I did so there was a sound of thunder from the southeast. Thunder was so uncommon on a cold March morning that we all pulled up together.

It came again, dully, a steady thud-thud-thud.

"Gunfire," Allan said. We looked at each other. The sound echoed along the empty hills about the Basin as if invisible armies were at strife.

"A ship saluting," I said.

"A fleet, more like it!" Allan exclaimed.

"Something's up, anyhow," said Uniacke, eyes alert.

"Maybe Washington's come to take Halifax—what he should have done long ago," suggested John Allan, with a pawky grin.

"If only it was, man!"

"There's one way to find out," I ventured hopefully. A ride into town might give me a glimpse of Fear. The notion of coming so near to her and leaving without seeing her had given me my one regret at joining the Cause.

"Come on!" Uniacke cried. We wheeled about and galloped up the hill past the inn, past farms and spruce clumps and fields whose straggling walls of loose field stones barely showed above the snow. Our hoofs rang on the icy road. We skirted Dutchtown well to the west and followed a narrow sled road to the common, whose bare alders and huckleberry bushes and marsh grass bristled in the snow. Ahead, Citadel Hill rose like a great wigwam white with snow, and we put our blowing horses up a path over its northerly shoulder. Like magic the town appeared under our noses, roofed with the smoke of morning fires. But we had no eyes for the town.

The wind here had an easterly slant, and it wafted up the harbor a procession of sails that seemed endless. A fleet—and what a fleet! Apart from men-o'-war, there were ships, brigs, snows, brigantines, sloops, ketches, schooners of every size and rig from our own bank fishers to the Baltimore pilot kind; and a host of smaller craft—Chebacco-boats, luggers, jiggers, shallops, and whaleboats—anything that could swim and carry sail. Those with guns saluted the rotten-log ramparts of Fort George as they came abeam, with a ripple of smoke puffs running along the sides and a delayed thud-thud-thud coming up to us across the wind. Below, the town was all astir, and we could see heads pouring like handfuls of shot down the steep streets to the water front. The wharves were black with people. In the waist of one transport we could see a mass of redcoats and the glitter of weapons —or perhaps musical instruments, for we could hear faintly, now and again as the wind lulled, the brassy notes of a regimental band.

My first wild thought was that England had sent a new army and fleet to finish the war in America, but when I looked again at the motley craft I knew that very few of them could have made the western ocean passage in windy February and March. We looked at each other and back to the spectacle below.

"By God!" Uniacke exploded. "It must be Gage, back from Boston! But why?"

Why indeed? All the news had been of Gage's success. He had beaten the rebels off Bunker Hill last summer and kept them freezing outside Boston all winter. I remembered what Captain Dudington had told our Liverpool townsmen—the rebel army melting away, rebel leaders at loggerheads, the Congress bankrupt, snowed under with its own worthless currency, and Tories everywhere rising to arms for the king.

"Whatever it is," Allan said dourly, "this changes all plans for our rising, Dick my boy. Yon's force enough to crush us like a toad under a stone drag. Will ye listen to me now? This is what the shoemaker knew. This is his reason why we must 'put the shoe aside for a time.'"

Uniacke said nothing for a time, staring and frowning at the ships. At last, "Right you are, John—damn your hard Scotch head. We must ride to Cumberland and head off Eddy, or he'll be raising the wind, specially if Washington gave him any encouragement."

"We must leave word with Smith too," Allan said, looking at me meaningly.

"Go on to Cumberland," said I promptly. "I'll find Smith and tell him."

They hesitated. Allan said slowly, "Understand, David, Smith's a fanatic in the Cause. And he's watched. If he thought ye endangered him or the Cause he'd not think twice about throwing ye to the dogs."

"I'll chance that!" I said gaily. I was feeling very heroic that morning.

I put my nag down the steep hillside to Barrack Street, which was deserted. The dram sellers, the trollops, ay, the very dogs had joined that human flood to the wharves. Buckingham Street was the same: silent houses, doors left open in the rush, an empty thoroughfare, a town gone dead in a moment. Albemarle Street, Argyle Street, all the same. I wondered if Smith himself had joined the curious people at the waterside. I rode past his house cautiously, with no more than a side glance. I rode back again, with a sharper glance in the passing, and two or three houses up the street a black boy ran out of an alley and caught my bridle, whispering swiftly, "This way, sah, this way!"

Up the alley we went, treading a pudding of discolored snow and garbage from the houses on both sides. About a hundred feet from the street it turned at right angles, and we came to a stable, and I had to duck my head quickly, for the boy led my horse straight in. In the warm horse-reeking gloom within stood William Smith, face like a thundercloud. Evidently he had seen the fleet.

He rapped out, "What are ye doing here, ye young fool? What are the others doing?"

I got off the horse. "We saw the transports from Citadel Hill. Allan and Uniacke are off to warn Eddy and the others in Cumberland. That's what I came to tell you."

He considered that a moment. "Well"—disapprovingly—"you'll have to stay here now, out of sight. Pompey, you take this horse back to the Blue Bell, on the Windsor Road. Say the young gentleman didn't like it and changed his mount at Birch Cove. That's all ye know—mind!"

The stable was surrounded by a high, paling fence, but a small gate gave upon a garden deep in snow, and I followed William Smith into the house.

I came to know that house well—too well for my peace of mind. Mrs. Smith was a quiet woman with kindly eyes, very much under the domination of her resolute husband, and the servants appeared to be an old mulatto man and woman and the Negro boy Pompey. The house was a large and gloomy thing of wood, with windows too few and too small for the size of the rooms. I was given a chamber in the attic and told to stay there until Smith judged it safe for me to remove. The old woman brought my meals and made the bed and tidied the chamber each morning, and at my shouted request—she was hard of hearing or pretended to be—furnished me with a couple of clays, tobacco, and a tinder box and candles. Smith sent other things for my use; for the first time in many days I had a clean face, well shaven, and my hair brushed and decently tied, and I wore clean linen on a clean skin. I asked for something to read, to while the time, and Mrs. Smith herself brought me a well-thumbed copy of *Joseph Andrews* which, she said regretfully, her husband used to read and enjoy "before he became absorbed in these troubles in America."

Joseph Andrews seemed to me a fool, and I had small patience with his adventures; but on the third day Smith sent up by the old mulatto something new, a pamphlet by one Thomas Paine entitled *Common Sense* and published lately in America. I read it diffidently at first. A flood of pamphlets printed in Boston had gone the rounds of our Nova Scotia settlements the past ten years, bombastic things, ill conceived and worse written. But *Common Sense* was written in

simple words that rang in the mind like bells. I read it again and again,
until I could quote many a passage by heart. Till then, the Cause
had been something mysterious that had to do vaguely with Tories
and Whigs in America and the king in England. In the light of *Common
Sense* it became something real and plain to be seen, a thing to
believe in and swear by and fight for. I came to know later how it had
aroused men everywhere in the colonies like a bugle call; I was to hear
it quoted constantly in argument, to hear particular passages preached
upon by godly men as if it were Scripture, to hear men questioned
on Tom Paine as a test for faith in the Cause. For me and for many
another in our America, *Common Sense was* the Cause.

My garret had a small gable window looking down upon the snow
of the small garden where each night, like any dog, I was allowed a
run. In the daytime there were street sounds from the front of the
house, sleigh bells ajingle, the clack of passing voices ringing high
in the frosty mornings, and the tramp of soldiers' feet—for the town's
main guardhouse was not two hundred yards away.

The house itself was full of rustlings and creepings, as if 'twere
haunted. I verily believe those people talked with signs, like mutes,
for I rarely heard a voice downstairs. It occurred to me after a time
that I was a prisoner, kept hidden in this house in the heart of Halifax
less for my own safety than for William Smith's. It chafed me, this
enforced idleness, when *Common Sense* was speaking to me like a
voice. And one evening, with dark rafts of cloud floating on the sea
of stars overhead and a softness in the air that set all the icicles on
the eaves and cornices adrip, I refused to leave the garden when the
mulatto man pulled my sleeve.

"You got to come," said he doggedly. I struck him out of sheer
vexation, and harder than I meant, for he fell in the snow and cried
out.

Mr. Smith came rushing out of the back door in the nightcap he
wore every evening after doffing his wig and thrust me toward the
door with an urgent hand on my shoulder, berating me all the while
in a harsh whisper.

"Take your hand away," said I, "or I'll cry Murder or, better, I'll
strike you down and you can cry. One good shout'll bring up the
guard."

"But why?" asked a quiet voice behind. A man had come through
the gate in the fence by the stable.

"Because I'm sick of being penned up here like a goose for slaughter," I sputtered.

Other men were coming silently through the gate, in file, and "Come inside, lad," said a voice, "and let's have a look at ye."

In the back parlor, whose windows were closed against the cold of an April night and screened with heavy velvet curtains against the prying eyes of Halifax, I discovered the owner of the first voice to be an old friend of my father's, a merchant of Halifax named Malachi Salter. The others appeared by their dress to be merchants also, with one or two obvious sea captains. A baker's dozen in all. Salter knew me "by the cut of my jib," as he said, and turned a look of half-humorous inquiry upon Mr. Smith.

Said Smith, "David's wanted for the killing of a seaman of H.M.S. *Senegal* some weeks ago. The governor has handbills out, and there's a reward. For his father's sake I took him in and kept him hid—and for all our sakes, come to the fine point. He knows the shoemaker and Uniacke and Allan, who were unwise enough to tell him all our plans. He could ruin us, if caught."

The insult implied in that made me boil, and I made toward him in a rage, but Salter caught my arm.

"Tongues can be loosened," said Mr. Smith darkly. "In the Cause we can't afford to take risks, lad."

"You seem to have news from Liverpool," I said sulkily. "What about my family?"

"They are well—your father and mother, anyhow," he said. "There's no news of your brothers except the one in the Fencibles. I understand there was a scene between Captain Dudington and your father over the seaman's death, but a Captain Cunningham of the governor's new regiment intervened. Of course, Liverpool is still in the possession of Dudington's seamen and marines, and your father's schooner has been seized, together with most of his merchandise. She's in Halifax now, with a vice-admiralty court monition nailed to her mast. And now, David, you'll please remove to your chamber. I have important affairs to discuss with these gentlemen."

I caught a gleam in Salter's eye and blurted, "Let me stay. I know what your business is—the Cause, which is mine as much as yours."

Led by Salter, there was a chorus of agreement amongst the men. I liked that man Salter, and all I heard of him made me like him better. Lately he had been hauled before the Council for sedition and managed to win clear, like Smith and Fillis before him. I believe he made the Council feel like interlopers; for Malachi Salter was using the great harbor for his fishing business when Halifax was still a forest, with no sign of other white men but the moldering skeletons of D'Anville's dead on the Basin shore.

Having accepted me, they plunged at once into a survey of recent events, and I sat there drinking it in.

General Gage, who had energy and no brains, was recalled to England, his place taken by General Howe, who had brains but no energy. Howe had sat in Boston till the Americans mounted cannon on Dorchester Heights and shelled him out of the town. Now he had withdrawn his whole army to Halifax. The ships I had seen from Citadel Hill were only the vanguard, bringing mostly Tory refugees. The other fifty or sixty ships had arrived a few days later. All this had wrought a mighty change in Halifax. The ramshackle, half-deserted capital of our province was suddenly a teeming city, with rents and the price of provisions soaring to the skies. Tory men, women, and children from fine homes in Massachusetts were huddling in every second-rate chamber and garret like sheep in winter pens. The best houses available had been taken over for Howe's officers. The army was encamped on a low hill at the south end of the common, called Camp Hill, making free with farmers' fences for fuel and removing stone walls from the boundaries of the farmers' fields to fill hollows and make roads. An inoffensive Dutch farmer named Chris Schlegal had objected to such liberties and was killed, and three soldiers had been "tried" for the murder and acquitted.

The soldiers appeared to be smarting still from the insults of the Boston mobs before the fighting started and from defeat afterward and, finding themselves now in a town whose accents were those of New England, sought their revenge upon it. Street robbery by men in red coats was a commonplace. Ay, and worse. The drabs of Barrack Street were not enough for this lusty swarm. No woman was safe on the streets after dark. And no man in common dress was safe at any time, what with His Majesty's hard bargains picking quarrels at every street corner and the press gangs busy after dark. And in and through it all moved the Tory refugees in their hundreds, mournfully, disgustedly, wondering what was to become of them in this roaring, bawdy, stinking, rickety, wooden hell on the side of Citadel Hill.

I marveled at their hardihood in leaving good homes for this. Afterward I came to know that they had fled of necessity, their homes wrecked and pillaged by mobs, themselves frequently beaten, stoned, tarred-and-feathered. And the homes and properties they left in Massachusetts were even now being confiscated by Committees of Safety and sold to selfish camp followers for a song.

There was nothing about this in *Common Sense*. But, argued the men in Smith's parlor, with shrugs and pursed lips, that was what came of making a civil war out of a simple struggle between Americans and the king—the Tories had nobody but themselves to blame. Perhaps they did. They looked sad enough.

The talk turned to Cumberland. Jonathan Eddy had returned there from Boston empty-handed. The General Court of Massachusetts was glib with promises of support—but the rebels of Nova Scotia could not load their empty muskets with promises. The men of Machias, led by their fire-eating preacher James Lyon, were eager to join the expedition to Nova Scotia and had even submitted a plan of campaign to General Washington. Eddy had brought back a copy of it and a copy of the general's reply, which he had sent on to Salter in Halifax. Salter opened it on the table now, and we all craned to read:

Camp at Cambridge, Aug. 11, 1775

Gentlemen:
  I have considered the papers you left with me yesterday. As to the expedition proposed against Nova Scotia by the inhabitants of Machias, I cannot but applaud their spirit and zeal, but I apprehend such an enterprise to be inconsistent with the principle on which the Colonies have proceeded. That province has not acceded, it is true, to the measures of Congress, but it has not commenced hostilities against them, nor are any to be apprehended. To attack it therefore is a measure of conquest rather than defence, and may be apprehended with very dangerous consequences. It might be easy with the force proposed to make an incursion into the province, and over-awe those of the inhabitants who are inimical to our cause, but to produce any lasting effect the same force must continue. And our situation as to ammunition absolutely forbids our sending a single ounce of it out of the camp at present.

I am, Gentlemen, &c.,
GEORGE WASHINGTON

Out of a stunned silence I said hopefully, "That was last year. Washington has sent the shoemaker and others to spy out the province since then."

"Ay," put in one of the sea captains, "and he's chased Howe out of Boston and into Halifax."

Several voices took up the implications of that. It looked as if Howe had abandoned all America south of Fundy Bay to the rebel armies. That was such an enormous success for the Cause in general that we could not grudge the ruin of our own little cause in particular. But was it ruined? While the English foothold remained in Nova Scotia, Howe remained a menace on the north. Washington, the shrewd weigher of chances, could not ignore that. He had been sending gifts to the Indians of Nova Scotia. Was he planning another swift move like the daring attack of Arnold and Montgomery on Quebec and with a bigger and better equipped army? That was what we all hoped.

Michael Francklin's name was mentioned. That able Englishman had a finger on the pulse of the province and seemed to sense the forthcoming trouble in Cumberland. Why else had the 17th Light Dragoons, Howe's best cavalry, been sent to the convenient port of Windsor on the Bay shore? To ease the forage situation in Halifax, someone said. But Lieutenant Governor Francklin lived at Windsor and had a manor in Cumberland. 'Twas an odd coincidence.

Another point: Michael Francklin was still at loggerheads with Governor Legge and was known to be urging London to recall Legge before that choleric man goaded the Nova Scotians into open revolt.

Salter mentioned this, waggling a finger. "Gentlemen, Governor Legge is the greatest possible asset to our Cause. He creates more hatred of the king in a week than we could do in a twelvemonth. But, by the same token, Michael Francklin's most dangerous to us. That man's clever, and he's popular, even with our Whigs. Why, I think a lot of Michael myself! That's bad, seeing he's a king's man."

And what was General Howe doing in our midst? His soldiers had built a blockhouse at Fort Needham above the dockyard and another at Three Mile House on the Windsor Road. Another was to be erected on Citadel Hill—Howe with his painful memories of Dorchester Heights!—but all these were insignificant works. The troops remained in their tents under our April rains and snows. Was Howe going to sit here all spring and summer with his women and wine, as Gage had sat all fall and winter in Boston?

As for the American army in Canada, it was still holding Montreal; but with the ice going out of the St. Lawrence the British could soon reinforce Quebec by sea and might thrust up the great river and cut the slender American communications along the Richelieu. Washington, with his instinct for a situation, would scarcely leave the American force in such a danger. Yet if they withdrew they must leave to the king's mercy the Canadians of Montreal, Three Rivers, and elsewhere who had joined their ranks or supplied them, even to ammunition for their cannon.

'Twas a nice problem, and Washington must be scratching that steady poll of his, even now. Also it was well known that Congress had sent Benjamin Franklin and Silas Deane to persuade France into war with Britain—and doubtless France would want her old possessions in Canada as the price.

When the sober discussion in the shrouded chamber reached this point I noticed a change in some of the voices, a note of doubt for the first time. We Nova Scotians had no love for the French. The old bloody memories were too close. If Canada went back to France . . . but William Smith adroitly shifted the subject, and soon after the meeting closed.

CHAPTER 15

In Which I Meet My Love

MALACHI SALTER rescued me from my garret. The Salter home was a sturdy wooden house at the corner of Barrington Street and a lane which the townsfolk had begun to call "Salter's Street." There I had a comfortable bedchamber and became one of the Salter family. I begged to have something to do and liberty to walk abroad, for the longing to see Fear filled all my thoughts when alone. So 'twas arranged that I should work as a clerk in Salter's store under the name of "Japhet Moreton." The store was a busy place in these rushing times, for the town was suddenly glutted with money, and I penned invoices and letters and bills of lading and kept the ledger and often took a hand behind the counters selling everything from cod lines to petticoats; and sometimes I went aboard ships in the harbor with Mr. Salter, carrying papers, inkpot, pens, and sand caster in a satchel slung from my shoulder.

With the swarm of Boston refugees roaming the muddy streets, a stranger could move at ease, and on Sundays at ease I moved. One of my first excursions was to the Indian camp at Northwest Arm, where François greeted me joyfully. He was not so joyful when I told him he must stay there and learn what he could of their attitude toward the war. But he consented glumly.

Mrs. Mawdsley's select school for young ladies was in a big yellow clapboard house in Bedford Row, not far from the Commissary Offices, and on Sunday mornings the young ladies walked two-and-two, laughing and chattering in their Sabbath finery, to service at St. Paul's. On two successive Sundays I stood amongst the town idlers and watched them pass and looked in vain for Fear. Was she ill? I was in misery at once. Perhaps she didn't care to walk in that giggling procession and rode to church in the carriage of one or other of her family's friends in Halifax. To satisfy this hope, upon a Sunday I followed them into the church, where the pews were filled with scarlet uniforms and gold lace and silks and ribboned caps and flounces and capes and wigs, wigs, wigs. There was enough flour in those beautiful male wigs and in the high-piled hair of the ladies to feed the town's poor for a day, or so it seemed to me. 'Twas my first sight of wealth in our Nova Scotia, and I stood at the back with the poor folk and gaped as much as they. And I heard their whispered comments: the scandal about Major This and Mrs. That and the money that Lieutenant So-and-so lost at cards and what a naughty little puss old Fatback's daughter was and the duel that Captain Blank and Major Deuce had fought over her by the pond in the common and the money that Merchant Chillgaze was scooping out of army contracts. And I learned how the magnificent white coiffures of the great ladies were built over frames of thin basket-work and could not be taken down any more than a house, and when lice got into them those prolific insects could live at ease, except for an occasional delicate prod from a bone skewer that the lady kept in her muff.

Common soldiers sat in the gallery, infantry on one side, artillery and cavalry on the other, and they seemed to cough in unison, by companies; and the bell clanged and the organ boomed and the ladies and old gentlemen snuggled their feet down upon the hot bricks in the straw of their foot warmers and hitched their fur-trimmed cloaks about their shoulders and hands into muffs—some of the gentlemen had muffs—and all the breaths rose in one mist in the dank April cold.

At the close of the service, servants made way outside the great doors for their masters and mistresses while the carriages came down from Argyle Street; and the troops formed up and marched off to their barracks behind the bands, followed by a scamper of dogs and small boys and servant girls. A grand spectacle from first to last, and small wonder that Halifax lived for it from week's end to the next.

As Mrs. Mawdsley's girls emerged into the pale sunshine, like a little convoy of schooners under the watch of a square-rigged broad-beamed seventy-four, I searched each passing face again at close range in the throng. At the end of the procession, straggling some distance behind the rest, was a plump merry-faced girl whose large blue eyes had met mine the Sunday before down in Bedford Row. Now they met mine again. She glanced ahead warily and halted with an impish grin and chanted mockingly,

> "*Stare, stare, like a bear*
> *Then ye'll know me next year.*"

My face went hot, but I looked at her earnestly and pondered how to say what was in my mind without telling all Halifax. But now the crowd was breaking up, and people jostled past us, chattering about the service and the cold and paying us no more attention than if we had been a pair of hitching posts.

Said the girl pertly, like a 'prentice boy outside a shop, "What d'ye lack, sir? What d'ye lack?"

"A young lady named Fear Bingay," blurted I.

She made her mouth very small and round and looked a little disappointed.

"Pooh! She left Mawdsley's long ago. Her aunt's here from Boston, and Fear's living with her in Granville Street. Sweetheart?"

"Something like that," I confessed, blushing.

"Then I'm sorry for you, Bear."

Down the hill the big seventy-four had hauled her wind to count convoy, and evidently the plump girl was missed, for Mrs. Mawdsley showed every sign of bearing down upon us. The girl caught up her gown and scuttled off without another word.

Aimlessly, instinctively, I suppose, I made my way toward Granville Street and ran into Fear herself at the corner of George. She wore a fine red cloak over a gown of printed stuff and carried a muff and wore a small feathered hat tipped forward coquettishly on her powdered hair, and her silken shoes were strapped to a pair of muddy pattens that made her look very tall—as tall as the officer at her side. He looked hard at me, and I at him, as I suppose men anywhere regard each other over a pretty woman's shoulder. He was a man of thirty-odd, well built —a little thick in the neck, it seemed to me—with a strong-boned face and a pair of lively blue eyes. His uniform was unusual in these streets which swarmed with redcoats, for his jacket was short and round and grass-green, with black facings and silver buttons, and he wore an elaborate white stock, a white silk waistcoat, white buckskin breeches so tight that I wondered if he could mount a horse, and polished black riding boots. Upon his head gleamed a black leather helmet or cap, shaped like a chamber pot with a glazed visor in front to shade the eyes, a glossy black plume, and a black leather chin strap that came no farther than his lower lip. No English regiment wore such a dress to my knowledge. A provincial corps? It must be, though few provincial officers could afford the gold-hilted sword he wore at his side. An Englishman then; doubtless one of the titled adventurers and younger sons who were swarming out to take commissions in American-Tory regiments, since the War Office believed that no colonial was capable of leading men—even colonial men.

I disliked this man—ah, let me be honest, I hated the man at first sight—and looked my thoughts. The familiar mockery was in Fear's clear-cider eyes, reading his face and mine. But nothing else about her was the same. She had grown up. Worse, she had leaped from seventeen to something like five-and-twenty in less than two years, while I at nineteen felt more like a gawky boy than ever. I was mighty conscious of my pinchbeck shoe buckles, my white cotton stockings (all spattered with the black slush outside St. Paul's) and the plain black smallclothes, the snuff-colored waistcoat and horn-buttoned blue surtout, the loosely cocked hat—all from Mr. Salter's shelves and made up by the little Swiss tailor around the corner who catered to the ship trade.

"Why, it's Davy!" she cried, and took her hand in its yellow wool wristlet from the crook of the officer's arm and held it out to me. I took it and didn't know what to do with it, any more than I'd known that day of the strawberry frolic. Shake it, like a man's? That seemed crude and all wrong. Stoop and kiss it, as one of the hand-bussing silk-and-powder fops of wartime Halifax would have done? That was impossible. She came to my rescue and put it into her muff.

"Jack, let me present David Strang, a very dear friend from Liverpool. Davy, this is Captain Helyer, of the Royals."

The soldier gave me a stiff little bow—I think he dared not bend far in those breeches—and I gave him a nod as stiff. We eyed each other like a pair of strange dogs.

"Run along, Jack, there's a dear," she commanded. "Davy shall see me to Aunt's—we've so much to talk about."

"I bow to old acquaintance," said Helyer pleasantly enough, and bowed—not so stiffly—and marched off toward Barrington Street and the Parade.

Fear slipped her hand in my arm and gave it a little squeeze. "Aunt wanted me to drive home in the carriage, but it's not far, and I love to walk."

"With a handsome soldier!"

She tossed her fashionable head. "Why not? Oh, Davy, let's talk about each other; it's been such a long time—and how you've changed.

You look—I don't know—a little hard somehow, like your father and Luke. You used to be more like Mark."

"It's been a long time," I said.

"Has it really seemed so, Davy? Have you thought of me much? What a little prig I was, that day of the strawberry frolic! And poor Mr. Cheever!" She tilted her head and laughed merrily.

"I've thought of you ever since that day."

"You're just saying that to be nice. I'm a hussy, really."

"You're beautiful," I said.

We had turned along Granville Street, stepping warily over the uncertain wooden cellar traps and the rotten footboards that ran from the doors to the churned black slush of the roadway. Once we were safely around the corner from George Street she gave me a quick side glance. "David! What are you doing in Halifax—of all places? Mama wrote and said there'd been trouble over smuggled goods at your house, and you and your father's Indian had killed two seamen from the *Senegal*. I didn't believe the part about you—Mama takes her politics from Papa, and he's *so* prejudiced against Whigs—but Sue Tinkham wrote and told me the same and said you'd run away into the woods. Davy, is it true?"

"I struck a man," said I dourly. "I didn't wait to see if he died or not, for his friends were after me with cutlasses. Peter Dekatha shot one of 'em—and they chopped Peter to death there in the snow, under poor old Molly's eyes. I'm here . . . well, because it's safer amongst all these strangers—these refugees."

"And you're really a rebel, David? That's true?"

"Yes."

We splashed along without words for a few paces, Fear's iron pattens clinking on the stones under the slush.

"Do you mean, Davy, you're going to fight against us—I mean, the king?"

"As soon as I can get where there's fighting."

"Your poor mother!"

"We're going to win this war," said I angrily. "When that time comes . . ." She gave my arm an angry little shake. "That time will never come, Davy, and so long as there are willful, misled boys like you to join the rebel armies, the war'll go on and on. You can't beat the king and all that's behind him."

"The rebels have done very well so far."

"Pooh! Boston! But there are more troops on the sea. The affair at Boston has opened English eyes. General Howe says . . ."

"Yes?"

Her sudden coldness chilled me. "I'm forgetting . . . you're a rebel, David."

"Let's not talk about that," said I desperately. "Let's talk about ourselves. What are you doing here? Staying with an aunt, someone said."

"Aunt Anne—she's a refugee, the widow of a rich Boston merchant, Gideon Shaddock. Uncle Gideon never had much to do with the Tory group there, and I can't think the rebels would have molested his widow; but poor Aunt Anne says they're all levelers and sooner or later they'll take everybody's money and divide it up, and she wasn't going to stay and see poor Gideon's hard-earned fortune scattered to the rabble. She had to leave the house, of course, but she managed to ship her furniture and things and she's got most of Uncle's money in good credits on London. When Papa heard she'd arrived in Halifax he insisted I must stay with her for company in her loneliness—she's his sister and has no children."

I seemed to see James Bingay sitting in his countinghouse in Liverpool, considering Aunt Anne's fortune, and his own ambitions for Fear and adding one and one and making a satisfying two.

"Does your aunt propose to stay in Halifax? Most refugees despise the place."

"Of course they despise it, after Boston. Most of the poor things don't know what to do. They don't like this province—they call it Nova Scarcity, Davy; doesn't that make you bristle?—but the West Indies are too hot, and England's too far, and of course there's no safety for a Tory in any American colony but this. I think Aunt Anne plans to stay here till it's safe to go back to Boston, whenever that may be."

"About this soldier . . ." I began bluntly.

She looked at me steadily. "I like him, Davy. Of course, Aunt Anne's full of his family in England, and so on, but that means nothing to me. Governor Legge's got fine family connections too—but what a horrid, puffy, jowly, popeyed creature *he* is! No, I like Jack Helyer because he's charming and because he's a brave soldier—he was wounded at Bunker Hill, and some say he was the first man into the rebel trenches, wound and all, and shot down the rebel Doctor Warren with a pistol. . . ."

". . . Not to mention he's dashing with the ladies and sings a good song and cuts a fine figure ahorseback, and chucks a guinea over the gaming table as if 'twere sixpence and knows a south-side Madeira from a north-side by a sniff at the bottle and has every Tory miss in Halifax setting her cap for him!"

"What an explosion! How do you know all these things, Davy?"

"By the look of him."

"Then his looks deceive. He can't sing for sour apples, though he gets the words out in a jolly sort of way and makes you laugh. He rides well, I grant you, and I wouldn't know about the gaming, though I doubt if he's any guineas to throw away. Wines? . . . He knows one wine from another as your father and mine know genuine Jamaica rum from Demerara . . . is that a crime? As for setting caps, it's well known amongst the Tory girls in Halifax that Captain Helyer hasn't a penny but his pay."

"Then maybe the cap's on the other head," I grunted.

"I don't know quite what you mean by that," she said, displeased, "but I don't like that way you say it. And here we are at Aunt Anne's."

We were outside a tall, narrow wooden house whose clustered chimneys smoked furiously and proclaimed a fire in every room, a sure sign of wealth in Halifax in the spring of '76. Two burly fellows trudged past with a sedan chair, sweating in the cold wind along Granville Street, and a very grand dame with a mountain of powdered, ribboned, and lace-frilled hair leaned out and gave Fear a nod and regarded me with a bright round hen's-eye.

"I can't stand out here talking to you, Davy. Do come in—there's so much to say, and I want you to meet Aunt Anne."

I went in for the sake of the extra minutes, feeling like a fish out of water. The parlor was small, like most Halifax parlors of that time, with a cheerful fire and a great deal of mahogany furniture and a flowered wallpaper almost wholly obscured by portraits in large gilt frames—men with shrewd Yankee faces and women looking very prim, the bygone Shaddocks whose faces and fortunes Aunt Anne had saved from the levelers.

Fear went off, pattens and all, to warn Aunt Anne of a guest in the house while I stood in mid-floor under the grim gaze of the exiles. She came back without the cloak, the pattens, the hat, and the wristlets, a bit more like the Fear I had known. I had a temptation to seize her in my arms before the aunt came, to go on where Parson Cheever had interrupted us that day of the strawberry frolic. I don't know what stopped me—the painted Shaddocks perhaps. Fear came toward me slowly with hands behind the panniers of her gown, her powdered head tilted to one side, regarding me with a look I could not fathom. The laced velvet bodice made her waist a sweet temptation to a hungry arm and gave a charming mold to her bosom that I'd never noticed before. The low cut of that gown would have been damned as indecent in our country town. It delighted me; I was fascinated with the treasures it revealed; yet I felt a furious resentment that any eyes but mine should behold them and thought of Captain Helyer and hated him worse than ever.

"Well, Davy?" she said, standing before me.

"I love you," I said. I did not move. Looking back on it, after all these years, I can laugh at myself—standing there with fists doubled, face angry and red, more like the prints of Jack Broughton in the prize ring than a lover greeting his love. She looked away, and her long, slender hands appeared from nowhere, fiddling at a ribbon, after the manner of all women when a bosom has been seen and appreciated and must now be defended against too-ardent eyes. But there was a sadness in her averted face, it seemed to me, and I could not understand. She had all a little country miss could dream about—a pretty face, a charming figure, health, clothes, and beaux—and a widowed aunt worth a fortune.

I had nothing but the clothes I stood in and a price on my life. I felt like a beggar who has called attention to his poverty and now boggles at asking alms. In a long silence the clock on the mantel rang like the hammer strokes of a forge. I uttered no word. She made no move.

"Davy," she said at last, evading my eyes. "There are two Me's. One loves excitement and nice things to wear and Sunday service at St. Paul's and routs at the Pontac Inn or the Golden Ball and handsome young men saying things they don't mean and looking things they do and envious pussy cats making remarks—in short, one half of me adores Halifax and wouldn't be anywhere else in these times. The other half—I don't know so much about that other Me; it seems to belong in Liverpool. Because that's my home, I suppose, where my parents are. And you—I don't know what to think or say, Davy. When I met you this morning, 'twas like stepping out of a hot room full of people—very nice-smelling people, mind you—into a strong west wind down the river at home."

There was a brisk step in the hall, and we sprang away from each other self-consciously. Aunt Anne surprised me. I'd expected a pomposity like her brother James Bingay. Instead a small, lean woman came into the room—sideways, to clear her panniers—in a swirl of silk gown and quilted petticoats. There was rouge on her small wrinkled cheeks, and her hair would have been mouse-gray, I fancy, had it not been piled high over a framework and stiffened with pomatum and flour and figged out with ribbons and a bandeau of pearls. Her bodice had the same fashionable cut as Fear's, but what it exhibited was a pair of flabby white purses propped and made prominent by wooden brackets and pads that the tight bodice clearly revealed. Her bony fingers were laden with rings. She was grotesque, and I wanted to laugh at her—this little old partridge hen dressed in peacock feathers, strutting painfully across the floor to us on a pair of tiny pointed shoes.

"So this is David!" She gave me a hand and a look, and I took the hand and bent over it clumsily and pondered the meaning of the look.

"Do go, Fear darling, and find that wretched girl Meggie. Just when Cook's all but ready with dinner, she disappears; and Toby's down cellar for the wine, and I've no one to send. And the rector coming any minute!"

Fear fled on her errand, and I turned to go. That last sentence had been aimed at me like a musket.

"Don't go yet, young man—David, I mean. You're from Liverpool? An old swain of Fear's, I suspect."

"Something like that," I mumbled.

"Ha! Well, things change a good deal between an outport and the capital, young man. The girl's not the same creature you knew, though giddy, still giddy!" She fixed me with the mildest pair of pale blue eyes that ever looked out of a shrewd face. "My brother—James Bingay, you know—my brother thinks I've got half the money in America and one foot in the grave, so he's put Fear on my hands. A dear girl, I'm really very fond of her and intend to do my best for her. But I'm not rich, far from dead, and may even marry again—lor, who knows in these times and amongst all these fascinating men?—and Fear's a responsibility in this naughty, naughty town. Now, young man, what's the answer to that?"

"Send the girl home," I suggested.

Up shot the little woman's eyebrows in horror. "To Liverpool? That jumble of fish-reeking hovels in the edge of the wild woods? La, boy, I thought you were serious! Marriage—marriage is the answer! There's many a good match going begging in the streets of Halifax just now—some of the handsomest men in England or America—not to mention money. There's young Carter Whitfield, who'd give his fortune for a kiss of her finger tips, and James Mayes the Halifax merchant, who's a big stone house empty in Prince Street and keeps his carriage and four, and Major Bewlby of the Seventeenth, that's heir to a title and a cool four thousand a year. But Fear—contrary creature—won't give 'em a morsel of encouragement, young Swang, or is it Shring? The only one in the swarm that seems to strike her fancy at all is Jack Helyer of the Royals. Hasn't a penny, of course, but the family's a good 'un, and you can't beat the English breed, horses or men, I always say; and everyone says Jack Helyer will make his mark in this war if it lasts long enough."

"Every officer in the English army thinks that," I suggested harshly.

The little woman shrugged. "The fact is, young Slang, he's the very man for her: a bit older, a man of the world with good connections, a dashing soldier, just the right husband for the sort of girl she is. I think Jack's pretty well made up her mind. . . ." She cocked a bright challenging eye at me. "Now a vivacious creature like Fear, that's young and don't know her own mind, is easily upset at a moment like this. You know how young girls are when they've more spirit than sense—touchy's the word, all ready to fly into the laughing convulsions and cry for the moon."

"Moon?"

"Yes. A moon like you, for instance, or some other lad with no prospects. You look like a young feller with common sense. I'm sure you see what I mean?"

"I do," said I coldly, and picked up my hat. Aunt Anne let me out of the street door herself, with a satisfied smile that set all her rouged wrinkles in motion like a stone cast into a pool.

"You needn't worry about me," I told her, looking up, hat in hand, from the lower step in Granville Street. "She thinks I'm just an off-shore wind. She told me so."

And off I went, just as the rector's carriage came splattering down the hill, with slush flying from all its spinning spokes.

CHAPTER 16

The Festival of St. Aspinquid

REBELLION needs a hearty hatred for success. For such a business commend me to a young man crossed in love. I looked upon our America and King George in the light of Fear and Captain Helyer, with a scheming Tory aunt playing the same part in both pieces, and threw myself heart and soul into the Cause.

One of the things our rebel friends in New England stressed in every smuggled letter was the need of competent officers when the time for fighting came, and I joined a group of young men in Halifax who were studying earnestly the art of war.

Malachi Salter got for us some of the textbooks that British officers used: a manual of arms, the important *Treatise of Military Discipline* by Humphrey Bland, and several works on field maneuvers, mostly translated from the German. The English officers appeared to think mightily of the Prussian military system. Indeed, we heard that whole regiments and brigades of Germans were being hired by our king for the war against us. I burned many a candle over my military studies and soon could quote the textbooks very wisely when we discussed the forthcoming campaign in Nova Scotia. None of us doubted that our province was to be the next, ay, and the greatest and final battlefield of the war. The British army was here, and General Washington must follow them and repeat at Halifax the triumph of Boston.

General Howe seemed to think so, too, for with the melting of the snow he began to exercise his troops on the common and the slopes of Camp Hill. I used to squat with other curious townsmen in the sunshine on the west slope of Citadel Hill and watch the masses of redcoats and bluecoats and greencoats marching, wheeling, extending —but never retreating—all in an impressive glitter of musket barrels and bayonets. Howe's favorite exercise was the storming of Camp Hill from all sides, a fine spectacle: each regiment in line, with its light company skirmishing ahead, its tall-capped grenadier company in reserve at the right-flank rear, officers galloping back and forth on fine horses, horse artillery rattling over the hummocks and bushes—and getting sadly bogged in the muddy stream that flowed between the Citadel and Camp Hill. The quiet common, where in summer the town's butcher boys kept cattle and sheep and in autumn the officers of the garrison hunted woodcock in the alder covers, had never received such a trampling.

At sundown the troops marched back to their tents and barracks, cursing the rents in their breeches and the mud plastered on boots and gaiters which would have to be scraped away for next morning's inspection and panting for their rum and beer.

They looked their dislike as they marched past our idle groups— and we gave them look for look. No love was lost between Howe's soldiers and the population, Whig or Tory. To the army we were all rebels at heart, held passive by their presence. And their scarlet backs still stung with the smart of Boston, and all these maneuvers were a constant reminder; the repeated full-dress attacks on Camp Hill were simply Bunker Hill over and over again. Any fool could see that. General Howe acted as if the war in America were to be nothing but Bunker Hills, with the rebels repeating their mistake of standing on easily flanked positions and the British avoiding theirs of marching in column of companies against rifles.

The more I saw of it, the madder it seemed; and at last I threw the books away. The less we knew of these stiff European tactics the better. Our ignorance was our strength, and if the British persisted in fighting an American war along the lines of a Prussian drill book our ultimate success was sure.

Once or twice I caught sight of Captain Helyer at these affairs, but the rank and file of the Royal Americans were still in their assorted rags, and General Howe always kept them far off on the flank, out of sight. By cautious inquiry I found that my brother John was away on a recruiting party. 'Twas open gossip in Halifax that Colonel Joe Gorham, unable to raise more than a handful of recruits in Nova Scotia for his ragamuffin regiment, had sent to Newfoundland in better hopes. So, too, had Governor Legge, who had met with no better success in raising his Loyal Nova Scotian Regiment. The army hated Halifax and wished itself out of Nova Scotia. Some officers declared that in a few weeks Howe would take ship up the St. Lawrence, drive the Americans out of Montreal, and follow hard on their heels down the Hudson Valley. Others pooh-poohed and said that Canada was Guy Carleton's nut, and he must crack it with his handful of Highlanders and sailors; these declared that Howe was only waiting reinforcements before sailing to retake Boston. Some even said New York or Philadelphia.

The northwest wind brought a steady whiff of sedition from Cumberland, but no one outside of the rebel circle in Halifax gave it the least attention—except Michael Francklin. The presence of Howe's army made the notion of revolt in Nova Scotia a sorry jest, though 'twas no joke to us. Yet from Cumberland came a merry epistle of Uniacke's, telling how he and Allan had toured the muddy roads in a coach and six, waving the pine-tree flag of Massachusetts and bawling to every farmhouse that Washington had driven the lobster backs from Boston to Halifax and would soon follow them here. Jonathan Eddy was back from another visit to Congress, declaring that, just as the colonies had rallied to Massachusetts in her hour of need, so they would rally to Nova Scotia in our effort to throw the king's troops off the continent. Uniacke did not say how much of this he believed, but he wrote significantly that gunpowder remained our urgent problem "especially now with so many more redcoats to shoot at!"

Because I knew the Micmac tongue and had an ear (in the person of François) in the Indian camp at Northwest Arm, our Halifax committee put me in charge of Indian matters in the district. I was not pleased. I had my father's low opinion of Micmacs as a tribe and since meeting Richard Uniacke I had come to see the Cause as something shining and glorious—much too good for an Indian. But there was a more practical side to my objections. The Micmacs and Malicetes had never lost their love for the French king, their hatred for the "Yengees," and they clung to the faith of bloody-minded Father Le Loutre, who had taught that a Protestant scalp was a sort of passport to heaven, not to mention its value in hatchets and blankets here below. Le Loutre had fled the country long ago, disowned by his bishop at Quebec, but the Micmacs and Malicetes still saw all English-speaking folk as deadly enemies of their race and their adopted religion. It seemed to me that if they took the warpath it might be a bloody day for all of us, Whig or Tory.

And about this time we heard that General Washington had again sent wampum and letters to the Nova Scotia tribes, without consulting us, who were so intimately concerned. My first task was to find out what those letters contained, and fortunately the chance came soon.

In the time of the new May moon each year it was the custom of the Micmacs to gather and celebrate the feast of St. Aspinquid, the patron awarded them by the old French priests. The English governors had looked upon the affair with suspicion, chiefly because 'twas "Popish"; but wise Michael Francklin had encouraged the Indians to go on with it and, more than that, to celebrate it on the shores of Northwest Arm, under the careful eye of Halifax. Already the Micmacs were journeying to the festival, and I found the squalid camp at the Arm head multiplied by four or five times, with other smokes rising from the trees along both sides of the blue water for a mile or more. The shore was dotted with bark canoes drawn up, and others were slipping into the harbor from the coast in both directions or coming over from the Fundy side by way of the Shubenacadie River and the Dartmouth lakes.

Malachi Salter gave me leave of absence from the store, and I joined François in the worst rags I could find, with my face and hands almighty dirty and my hair parted and twisted into a pair of thin black pigtails. My blue eyes passed without comment, for I spoke the bastard idiom of the Cape Sable tribe who intermarried with the French a good deal in the old days, and François was my sponsor. We shared a filthy wigwam with an Indian named Penaul and his squaw and two children. We had other guests from time to time, each with news from far places like Cape Breton or Isle St. Jean or the Gaspé, each with a contribution of insects toward the itch of our days and nights. I remember an Indian from Miramichi, a stout pock-marked jester named Bigtook, scratching himself one evening and giving us a comical discourse on the virtues of the louse as compared with the flea. (The louse—*waagookwe*—was an Indian insect, he said, a companionable beast which shared one's sorrows and fortunes till death, and was not too demanding in its appetite. Whereas the flea had come with the French, a leaping, restless, ravenous creature, forever wandering from one body to another in search of a new taste and never satisfied. He offered in proof of this the fact that the Micmacs had no name for the flea, calling it *pis*, the nearest their tongues could come to the French *puce*.)

Bigtook informed me carelessly that John Allan had been to Miramichi, sounding the large tribe there on their attitude to the war. This was news. I drew him out, François helping, while Penaul and his squaw shared a blackened clay pipe and watched us with unemotional eyes. Bigtook declared that the Micmacs had a great respect for John Allan; so had the Malicetes; also Allan knew the Passamaquoddies. In fact he had influence with all the savages between Cumberland and Machias. If I had been less stupid I might have foreseen, even then, what part John Allan was to play in the struggle for Nova Scotia.

The day before St. Aspinquid's, the Indian women were sent to gather lobsters and dig clams at low tide; you could see them all along the shores, old and young, with their ragged petticoats or greasy buckskin smocks tucked up, like so many stocky-legged herons wading about the narrow shore flats, stooping over their clam sticks or lugging maple-splint baskets to the nearest spring, to wash away the black mud and grit from a clicking, bubbling, squirting mass of clams. About halfway down the Arm on the east shore lay a large clearing with a couple of houses, a big shed, and a wharf, the station of two whites in the fishing business, a Captain Jordan and his Hebrew partner Nathan Ben Sadi Nathan. They were friendly to the Indians and encouraged them to hold their feast at this spot, where the fish and lobsters and clams could be stewed in the huge, iron, net-dyeing pots. I suspect that Jordan and Nathan did this at Michael Francklin's urging. Francklin's hand was there without doubt, for as the canoes gathered about the wharf and Indian men, women, and children swarmed about the field and in and out of the shed and the houses, I noticed several barrels of rum in a lean-to, guarded by a group of stout warehousemen from the

town; and there was a pair of cannon, with gunners in common seamen's clothes, to fire a salute for every chief, great or small, as he came
up from his canoe with his squaw and youngsters in file behind. The
Indians loved that.

The weather was fine, a perfect May day, with the sun falling hot
in the clearing and the tall trees warding off a cool westerly wind. The
hardwoods had no leaves yet, but their breaking buds spread a pale
green blush over the hillside below the pines, and the feel of spring
was in the air and the earth, with the brooks running bankfull and
robins whistling about the clearing and swallows darting in the sunlight. Now the alewives were coming into the streams from the sea,
with the shad behind, and there would be mackerel schooling just
offshore and cod and pollock in every bay and inlet. This was the fat
time for the Indians, the easy shore time, after the winter's storm and
cold and semistarvation inland. I suspect that they had always cele-
brated a day like this, and the wily French missionaries had given them
a saint to call it by.

All the long morning they danced and chanted and sweated in the
sun. The men did most of the dancing; but now and again the squaws,
old and young, lined up and went through a queer, shuffling rite, looking very solemn and hot.

The white guardians of the rum supply ladled out drinks for the
panting male dancers, but sparingly—I saw none drunk until after
nightfall, and then not many. In midafternoon they fell to feasting
on the steaming chowder in the great pots, and I noticed many town
folk arriving by the wagon road through the woods to watch the fun,
plain citizens afoot, gentlemen and a number of young ladies ahorseback, and several carriages were drawn up in the shade of the trees.
Then I noticed Michael Francklin, my first sight of the man at close
range. I studied him carefully. He was walking carelessly amongst the
throng, now chatting in fluent French with one of the half-breeds from
the Bay shore, now setting one of the chiefs in a cackle with some quip
in Micmac. A handsome man with bold black brows, a slim straight
nose, and a full mouth that smiled warmly and talked wittily, and a
pair of eyes now gay, now grave, and missing nothing.

Malachi Salter had called him the most dangerous enemy to our
Cause. Governor Legge was denouncing him to London as a rebel
sympathizer. The truth was that Michael Francklin was working desperately for a middle course between the king and rebellion—which
made him the king's enemy no less than ours. I gave him a grudging
admiration, for it seemed to me that he risked his wealth and position

whichever way the war went, and how many rich men in America had been willing to do that?

But now a new troop of ladies and gentlemen rode into the clearing from the town road. One of them was my Fear. The full skirts of her riding habit fell like a green waterfall over the gray flank of her horse but did not conceal the neat and expensive riding boots. Her jacket was cut in the tight-waisted military fashion, with large, gold-braided frogs and silver buttons, and upon her hair (all stiff with powder) sat a jaunty wide-brimmed hat with an enormous feather drooping back over her shoulder. Her party sat in the saddle, unwilling, I suppose, to dismount and rub shoulders with the smelly multitude. She was lovely in that costume, well cut to the slim lines of her long waist and the sweet swell of hip and bosom, and all eyes went to her. She seemed quite unconscious of the stares. She herself had no eyes for anyone but Captain Jack, whose glossy black mare was dancing beside hers and whose green jacket was a perfect match for hers.

They made a handsome and spirited pair, and in a chaise near me a middle-aged male voice said so. Another voice agreed, rather coolly —I could see the owner, a large, fair woman in shalloon, with a port-wine complexion and a cold blue eye, as she declared, "The match of the month, Captain Molyneux—is it possible you haven't heard? Jack Helyer of the Royals, and a little country baggage named Bingay from one of the outports. She's a nobody really—but with a rich aunt, a refugee from Boston. Jack's a good fifteen years older than she, but a handsome figure of a man, and they're quite fascinated with each other as you see. How long it'll last one can't say. Jack's a charming fellow with expensive tastes and only his pay to indulge 'em. Loves the girl, of course—Jack always loves his girls very passionately, I'm told, and quite sincerely—but thinks he's marrying the aunt's fortune as well. Whereas the aunt's practically pushed the little Bingay at him— anxious to get the girl off her hands."

"Pooh!" declared a second female voice in the chaise. "Fear didn't need pushing, my dear. Look at the girl—she can't take her eyes off that handsome devil, and no wonder. Half the girls in Halifax 'ud die for the sake of twenty-four hours in her stockings."

"All very charmin'," said the male voice lazily. "Bit sad, though, to think of such lively creatures doomed to be tamed by marriage and a lack of dibs. The war'll be over in a year, and commissions in these mushroom provincial regiments won't be worth a penny. What then, I wonder?"

"What's to become of half these Halifax marriages?" demanded the plump shalloon.

"What with the army and fleet, and the town full of refugee girls and matchmaking mamas, life's one peal of wedding bells. After the war . . ."

"Gettin' back to Helyer and his charmer," said the lazy voice again, "there's a rumor blowin' down the Spring Garden Road that the Royals go upcountry very soon. The general's tired of seeing Gorham's tatterdemalions about the streets, and our dashing captain will have to follow the regiment into the wilds. In that case, the lovebirds yonder will have a chance to reconsider. Absence don't always make the heart grow fonder."

"Too late!" giggled the younger female. "Captain Molyneux, haven't you heard? They've been married a week or more, and look at 'em! Young love grown nine days old!"

CHAPTER 17

In Which There Is Another Kind of Wooing

I TURNED AWAY, sick. Ay, that light voice smote me as a spring cold often does, with a chill and then a fever and an upheaval of the stomach. I slipped through the trees to a quiet part of the shore. I felt as I suppose any man feels at the sight of his love, blithe and smiling, beside the rival who has claimed her in marriage bed. But I did not tear my hair nor cast myself down and wish I was dead nor any of the things that hopeless lovers are said to do. I sat on a rock by the water and waited patiently for that sick feeling to pass, like a boy suffering out a green-apple bellyache. And before very long the logical side of my head, the side that belonged to the Cause, was turning over that lazy remark of Captain Molyneux.

General Howe's headquarters were in Spring Garden Road, just above the governor's garden for which that rustic lane was named. A rumor "blowing down Spring Garden Road" was like a whisper from the throne itself. So the Royal Fencible Americans were going upcountry! Where was that? Did Howe propose to regarrison the empty fort at Annapolis with Gorham's men? Or deserted Fort Cumberland? Or were they to relieve the 17th Dragoons at Windsor? They would make a poor substitute for the cavalry there. The Dragoons had been sent to Windsor "to ease the forage problem in Halifax"; but their real purpose was to overawe the Yankee farmers of Minas Basin and the rich Annapolis Valley, the chief source of Howe's supplies this side of England and the only part of our Nova Scotia suited to cavalry operations. If the R.F.A. went to Windsor, where were the Dragoons going? It seemed to me that in the movement of Colonel Joe Gorham's regiment we might find a key to the riddle of Howe's future plans.

At sundown, guessing that the townsfolk had by that time wearied of the spectacle and gone, I returned to the feast. A few silks and fine feathers lingered in carriages, watching the savages still busy about the big pots, scooping boiled fish and lobsters and clams with dippers of birch bark, and gobbling the scalding stuff. But Fear and her captain were gone, and soon the last chaise vanished into the dusk, with a parting sally anent the table manners of "Michael's protégés." Of the whites, only the guardians of the rum remained, and Nathan and Captain Jordan—and Michael Francklin. Nathan and Jordan were busy lighting candles and lanterns in the big shed, where Indian men of all ages were now gathering and squatting with their faces toward the middle of the rough plank floor, where a circle of squatting chiefs made a space for the orators to come. I entered with François and Bigtook and found a good vantage near the south wall. There was little or no talking, but a great chorus of belchings and tooth suckings bore witness to the abundance of the feast. The wide shed reeked of ancient fish smells and the sour Indian sweat. It seemed an odd place for a fine gentleman like Michael Francklin, squatting at ease on his silken calves within the circle of chiefs.

There was a stir at the door, and an officer came in, wearing the green coat and white breeches of the Royal Americans, with a dress sword at his side. "Gollam," grunted Bigtook. Gorham it was—Colonel Joe himself, with his gaunt blue-shaven cheekbones and amiable but indecisive mouth. He made his way through the throng to the inner circle, bowed to Francklin and the chiefs, and took his place, squatting with the sword in his lap and his laced hat tucked under his arm. A long, expectant silence followed, Francklin and Gorham obviously waiting for the Indians to speak and the Indians waiting, tribal chief for tribal chief. At last a Micmac of the Bras D'Or people arose, a muscular brown man naked to the waist, with a red blanket draped about his hips over the buckskin leggings. He addressed the gathering pompously as "My brothers," talked at some length of his pleasure in the feast in the company of his brothers, and sat down.

Another stood up, said much the same, and sat down. Another. Another. It became monotonous. All were Micmacs, representing various tribes from Gaspé to Cape Sable. Three things I noticed. Not one of them by word or glance recognized the presence of Francklin and Gorham under their brown noses; not one of them mentioned the war; but the word for priest—*paduleas*—the nearest their tongues could come to the French padre, was sprinkled all through their talk, and at every mention a murmur went round the shed. They wanted priests, denied them ever since the days of '55, except for saintly Father Maillard. It was a striking proof of their devotion to the Catholic faith which had been theirs for more than a hundred and fifty years. Once or twice I saw Gorham glance at Francklin, but Francklin kept his eyes on the orators. Governor Legge had set his violent will against priests for the Indians, and nothing could be done about it—now.

Colonel Joe stood up and talked to them in fluent Micmac for half an hour, but he was no orator, and the talk was dull. The burden of it ran that the Great White Father over the Big Water was in trouble with some of his Yengee children, especially the one called Wachita (Washington), and he, Gorham, hoped with all his heart that his brothers the Micmacs would take the part of the king. He reminded them of His Majesty's gifts of guns, powder, blankets, and food, made yearly ever since the province was won from the French and lately much increased. He made a long harangue about loyalty— a word which has no natural counterpart in the Micmac tongue and must be described in a made-up word as long as a rainy Sunday— *ked-la-wa-e-tu-la-de-gem-ka-wa*. Colonel Joe, trying to put English oratory in Micmac, always a mistake, succeeded only in making those grave brown faces smile every time he rolled that immense word off his lips.

When he sat down I felt assured about one thing. We need not fear Joe Gorham's ancient friendship with the Micmacs. They accepted his words as a duck accepts the rain from heaven and they went no deeper.

I was anxious to hear Francklin. I wanted to weigh him in the same scales. The Indians had a great weakness for oratory; a man with the right kind of tongue could set them on the warpath against the king or against the Americans as he chose. But the Indians were not yet looking at Francklin. I followed their quiet side glances to another part of the crowd, just behind the inner circle, and saw there a pair of Malicete chiefs. Malicetes at a Micmac feast! François whispered their names in my ear. One was familiar. Pierre Tommo had been an early seeker after the king's bounty at Halifax, and I remembered my father telling how Pierre Tommo and some other Malicetes appeared in canoes just when our Liverpool settlers were cutting their first clearings by the shore. The Indians were on their way back to the St. John River by way of our river and Fundy Bay, the ancient Indian route to the Big Water, and one of the Malicetes was sickly and died that night, the first death in our town of Liverpool. Our people buried him next day with a Christian ceremony which impressed the savages very much, but first Pierre Tommo cut off one of the dead man's hands, to take home with him in proof of his death.

That was seventeen years ago. Now Pierre Tommo was one of the foremost chiefs of the Malicetes. Only one had more power, and that one sat beside him, a noble old man with the French name of Ambroise. What was the meaning of their presence here? The Malicetes, less spoiled by white vices than the Micmacs, were the better fighting men. Their hunting ground was all the great St. John Valley, extending into Quebec province itself, and they had a blood alliance with the Passamaquoddies and Penobscots, whose hunting grounds joined theirs on the west and reached into Massachusetts. All the country east of the St. John was Micmac ground. The four tribes were natural allies—they had fought for the French against the English for a century—and they held between them the land route from Nova Scotia to New England. I had hoped to see them at peace with us and with each other, so that we could count on this one safe road, the sea route being barred by the king's ships. But now I saw that the stake was higher. If the British could set these tribes on the warpath westward, then the whole frontier of Massachusetts—that part which the French called Maine—would become a horror of blood and flame. On the other hand, if the Americans turned the faces of the tribes eastward, the horror might be ours. Was this what they were playing for—George Washington and Michael Francklin?

Old Ambroise arose, clutching his blanket about his skinny body against the drafts. There was a brass crucifix slung about his scraggy neck by a thong. He spoke slowly in a high, thin voice that carried well in the respectful silence. The Malicete tongue is much like Micmac, and many words are the same. The Micmacs in the shed seemed to understand him well enough; indeed, he spoke to them in their own idiom for a time. Colonel Gorham's face was a blank. But Francklin followed the old chief's lips with eager, understanding eyes. He had a gift for languages, that man.

Ambroise addressed himself bluntly to Colonel Joe.

"Gollam, I hear your words. You speak for the king, yet you do not wear the red coat of the king. You wear *wisawek*, the green cloth of those who in the olden time scalped our women and children for gold. Gollam, you were one of those who took the scalps of our people in those days. I remember that time, but there is no hate in my heart. You were young then, and a young man's heart is fierce. When a man grows old the frost creeps into his blood; he seeks the peace of the fire and the wigwam. Now you are our friend. That is good. But you say we should paint our faces and take the warpath against the Yengees for the sake of the Great White Father across the Big Water. You say the Yengees have evil in their hearts. Behold, certain Yengee men have come to us and told that the redcoats are the evil ones, and we must fight against their king. Gollam, this is strange. In the old time when our country was ruled by the Wenjoo [French] we took the warpath many times against the Yengees and the redcoats. They were our enemies together, and together they conquered us and the Wenjoo and burned our camps and killed our women and drove the Wenjoo back across the Big Water. Ayah! The crows picked the bones of our people. With the downfall of the Wenjoo passed the greatness of our tribes. The Great White Father sent our priests away because they were Wenjoo men. Now there is none to make us Jesus-talk, and we are poor and must come and beg for gifts at Chebuctook [Halifax]. It was not so in the old time. All these evil things have come to pass because we fought for one white man against another. Now the Yengees and the redcoats fight each other. We are a simple people and cannot understand these things. How comes it that Old England and New England quarrel and come to blows? For the father and son to fight is terrible. Old France and Canada did not do so. How then can we join this war where we know not who is right and who is wrong?"

Colonel Gorham stood up and gazed across at solemn old Ambroise. "When the son makes a mischief in the lodge, then the father must chastise him with the nearest stick," he said sharply. "You, my brothers, are the stick. Be assured that you are not alone. You have seen the throng of redcoats in Chebuctook. They are as the red maples of the forest in autumn. Yet a greater army of redcoats is on the Big Water. You shall see how strong is the Great White Father's wrath."

Pierre Tommo jumped up and sneered, "Why have the redcoats run away from *Bostoon*? Does the son chastise the father?"

Ambroise turned slowly and silenced Pierre with a look. He addressed himself, not to Gorham, but to the whole gathering.

"See!" He flung open his blanket and held up a magnificent belt of wampum, whose hundreds of small beads, all of the valuable purple kind made from quahog shell, glistened in the light of the fluttering candles. Holding it aloft by one end, he drew a folded paper from his waistband with the other hand and flourished that also. He turned slowly around, so that everyone might see. I could hear the savages murmuring in awe. Three times he turned completely around, and the polished wampum beads gleamed richly, and the letter crackled faintly in his fingers.

"These," he announced in his reedy voice, "are from Wachita!"

The shed buzzed. Such a mass of the prized purple beads had never been seen in Nova Scotia. I knew that wampum had been the ancient Indian currency and that fine belts of it were always presented with important treaties and suchlike and the story of the treaty told in certain intricate arrangements of the beads. Customarily the messenger who brought the wampum recited its message, that there be no mistake, and doubtless Washington's messenger had done so; but the American general had put the matter in writing also, and in English, as if he guessed that Ambroise would bring the matter before the gathering of St. Aspinquid, where the English governor was sure to be represented.

"Gollam," declared Ambroise without looking at Colonel Joe, "has told us that we must fight against the Yengees. Now hear the words of Wachita, who is wise and is the great sagamore of the Yengees:

"'Unto my Penobscot brothers, greeting. Unto my Passamaquoddy brothers, greeting. Unto my Malicete brothers, greeting. Unto my Micmac brothers, greeting. Behold there is war between the Yengees and the redcoats because the Great White Father demands tribute beyond his right. It is a war between white men. So be it. I, Wachita, want only peace with your peoples, and should my brothers be molested by the redcoats I will surely come to their defense. I send this wampum in token that my heart is good. There shall follow gifts to bear witness for the Yengee people. Peace!'"

Ambroise paused significantly, then strode across and thrust the paper under Gorham's long nose. "See! Here is Wachita's message made with the white men's marks! Does he speak with a split tongue?"

Colonel Joe took the paper, read it with an impassive face, and passed it back. He made no answer. Evidently Wachita spoke with a single tongue.

"Now," said Ambroise scornfully, "who has evil in his heart? You who say we must take up the hatchet, or Wachita who says we must remain at peace?" He paused, and there was a tremendous silence.

Then in a lower voice, "Behold we have dismissed one of our chiefs who spoke ill of Wachita. We have sent Jean Baptiste and Mattua to Boston with our answer to this wampum to say that our heart is good towards Wachita and the Yengees." He flung up his noble old head and cried to the crowded shed, "Have we done well?"

"Ayah!" they chanted.

Colonel Joe looked unhappy, and small wonder. I suppose it was the most crushing rebuke ever given by a so-called savage to a white man. And the irony of it was that Gorham was only doing what he conceived to be his duty, against his own instincts, for he was too lazy a man, too amiable, too old, and too anxious to enjoy his long-sought offices in peace and quietness, to stir up such a hornet's nest as an Indian war. And on the other hand there were the *Bostoon* eagerly stirring up such a war against the king, without consulting Washington or anybody else. 'Twas a queer tangle, and when Michael Francklin arose I wondered what he would say. He did not talk very long, but what he said surprised me.

After the opening compliments, bowing in his courteous way to each of the circled chiefs and calling them by name, he said quietly, "This is a good wampum from Wachita. Wachita is my enemy, as he is the Great White Father's enemy, but his words to thee are wise and good. I send no wampum. I come to speak my message face to face. It is this. Let my brothers remain outside this quarrel between white men. Terrible it is for the son to fight against the father. How much worse then, if the son call in a stranger to help in his struggle? Behold, it has come to my ears that certain of the Yengees have sent gifts to my brothers. That is good. But why do the Yengees send gifts only in time of war? Was there no hunger and nakedness amongst thee in the time of peace? I have known thee many winters—twice ten, and three. Men have been born and grown to manhood in that time. In all that time, when ye were naked and hungry it was to Chebuctook that ye came. Were ye ever refused bread for your mouths? Blankets? Guns and powder and shot for your hunting? Ye know these things were granted without fail by the Great White Father—through me, his servant."

"Ayah!" they cried together.

"Who then are your true brothers—the redcoats or the Yengees?"

A shrewd thrust, that. The Nova Scotia tribes knew nothing of the more southerly American colonies; for them all Americans were Yengees, the deft and pitiless frontier fighters who had lifted their scalps in the long struggle for Nova Scotia. They had sucked in hatred

and fear of the Yengees with their mothers' milk. For the English on
the other hand, the redcoats, so easily vanquished once they entered
the woods, the Indians had a faintly contemptuous affection.

Nevertheless, this brown-skinned crowd refused to make the choice
that Francklin put to them. They chanted, "*Wel-sut-ak* [I hear this
man with pleasure]," or "*Weltaak* [it sounds well]." I watched Francklin's face for sign of disappointment. He was calm, easy, smiling a little.
He knew (what we all knew) that the Indians still counted the French
their true white brothers, and nothing would change them; but he was
content. He and Washington were working to the same end, to keep
the eastern Indians quiet. That was plain. And that was what we
wanted, too, we Yankees of Nova Scotia. But how far would Francklin
and Washington succeed when lesser men, English and American,
were working furiously to get the Indians on the warpath?

Time held the only answer to that. Michael Francklin sat down, and
the conference closed in polite compliments and a distribution of gifts
from the Great White Father George—gold-laced hats and rich red
cloaks for the chiefs, blankets and hatchets for their sons, and clay
pipes, beads, and other gewgaws for the rest. The Indians took the
things thanklessly, as always, as if the gifts were theirs by right, and
the young ones clamored for more firewater. But old Ambroise jumped
up crying to Francklin against it, and Francklin held up a closed fist
to his warehousemen beyond the open door. The young bucks
grumbled and spat at the feet of the warehousemen. But no more
rum was given, and they went down at last to their canoes, family by
family, and returned to their wigwams about the Arm shore. By the
next evening all but the group at the Arm head had vanished, and
only the trampled grass, the ashes of their fires, and the white heaps of
clamshells remained to mark where they had been.

CHAPTER 18

All in the Merry Month of May

SOON AFTER St. Aspinquid's Day there happened a thing that I had
never expected to see. Governor Legge left for England. There had
been rumors, but they never came to anything. Michael Francklin had
worked long and earnestly for that end, had even sent a delegation of

Halifax merchants to London in January to press for Legge's recall. No one expected fruit of these endeavors. That flabby, violent man was known to have powerful friends in England, and 'twas an axiom well tested in the colonies that an officer with influence in London could stay in office though the heavens fell. It amused our cynical minds that when the American sky fell, Governor Legge, who had done more than any man to goad our province into rebellion, actually boasted to London that he and he alone had kept the fourteenth colony loyal to the king, and it amused because we thought that London would believe it. The news of Legge's recall fell upon our rebel group in Halifax like a bombshell.

As wise Malachi Salter had long since pointed out, Francis Legge was worth his fat weight in gold to our Cause. The mere look of him was an incitement to revolt. Now he was to go, and able Michael Francklin would step into his shoes. Even the stupid heads in London must recognize Francklin's right to the post, if only on the score of long service. He had been lieutenant governor ever since '66, working like a beaver for the loyalty of the province. For the king's Cause he was so obviously the right man, and Francis Legge so obviously wrong, that London's sudden gleam of intelligence astounded us.

But we were relieved almost at once. John Fillis burst into the room where we sat, sailed his hat jubilantly over our heads through the tobacco smoke, and cried, "Francklin's out!"

We jumped up, shouting unbelieving questions.

Fillis' eyes were sparkling. "It's true, I tell you. Oh, it's rich, rich! Legge's recalled; they couldn't keep him here any more—even General Howe saw through the man. But have no fear, boys! Our Lords of Misrule in London remain in office—and Legge is still a cousin of the Earl of Dartmouth and must be taken care of. He's to sit in England —retaining the governorship, mind you—and draw the dibs, while the lieutenant governor does the work."

"But that's Francklin!" we cried.

"Nunno! Francklin's out—given the Order of the Boot, to satisfy Legge's friends. The lieutenant governorship goes to a naval officer on the station—Arbuthnot probably, but anyhow some steady-going Bill Bowline who'll thank God for the extra pay and never worry his head about what's ado outside the dockyard gate."

For a moment there was silence. Then someone laughed, and another, and in a moment we were all sprawling in our chairs, leaning against Salter's walls, rolling on the carpet, punching each other, pulling wigs and queues, roaring, hooting, howling with laughter. Mrs.

Salter and some of the family came running to know the matter, and we told them, with tears in our eyes. Off went good Ma'am Salter for wine and glasses, and Fillis gave us a toast: "Long live the king and parliament!" We clinked our glasses and drank heartily. So long as they lived, our Cause would prosper.

I shall never forget Governor Legge's departure from our shores. It was the morning of May 12th, 1776, and out of curiosity I went to see the last of him, in Market Square, where Mark and Luke and Uniacke and I had battled with the press gang just a year before. The word had gone all through the town, and every street and alley poured its people toward the water front—common folk for the most part; the gentry apparently had decided to give Francis Legge a cold shoulder to the last. The ship lay at anchor abreast of Market Wharf, where a barge with a smart crew waited for the distinguished passenger. He came down the muddy street in a carriage, gloomy and alone, though his plethoric features seemed to brighten a little at the sight of the populace gathered to see him off. The guard at Market Slip turned out and made a little lane of redcoats and glittering steel from the carriage to the wet harbor stairs. Legge ran his eye over the soldiers as he descended heavily from the carriage. Only the officer of the guard was there. I fancy General Howe and his officers despised the man as much as we did. Francis Legge drew his heavy blue boat cloak about him and stumped down to the barge, his big jowls quivering at every step. The multitude was stiff and silent. You could have heard a pin drop anywhere in Market Square. He went down the slippery stone steps cautiously and took his seat beside the coxswain, looking over the man's blue shoulder at the people. In the great silence the sailors shoved off, and we heard the coxswain's low, "Give way, lads."

Then the silence was broken, was shattered, was torn and flung to the cool May wind down the harbor by a chorus of boos and hisses from hundreds of throats, breaking into individual shouts and execrations. "Yah, good riddance!" "There goes old Fat-and-Fury!" "Here, old Take-the-Oath—take this!" (And "this" was not the oath of allegiance!) "A fair wind for a foul cargo!" and a chanted chorus of "Legge—Legge—Legge!" which, by the mere repetition of the hated name, seemed to sum up all they thought of him. The officer of the guard looked flustered—and did nothing. Some of the soldiers grinned; others stirred and muttered; they were still holding their muskets rigidly at the present. I dare say the sound of the mob held painful memories for those who had served in Boston. Someone threw a handful of mud. It fell short and made a little bright splash in the water. The crowd caught up the idea gleefully. Balls of mud began to fly, and some stones. I could see the coxswain urging his crew to greater effort. The captain of the guard, a young, bewildered man, began shouting in a high voice to the people. Some of them caught sight of a country-man's cart full of potatoes for the market. They swooped upon it, and in a moment the cart was bare, and the air thick with flying potatoes, and like a thin hem on the uproar I could hear the farmer's cursing protest. Now the young officer gave an order. Not to fire—the army had learned something from its Boston experiences—but to disperse the mob with their gun butts. Instinctively I looked up the square. Others were doing the same. The guard at Government House, around the corner of Hollis Street, would be turning out any minute. There would be arrests and questions. 'Twas no place for a man with a price on his head. I took a last look and saw Governor Legge standing up in the boat, his puffy face purple with wrath, shaking a fat fist at all Hali-fax. Then I ran, chuckling—and still amazed. I had not realized how deep a hatred our people held for furious Francis Legge. I only wished that Uniacke could have been there; it would have been good to hear his Irish laughter.

I was sick of Halifax. The presence of the army and the horde of Tory refugees from Boston had given it a prosperity and a polish that seemed to me equally false. I suppose there was not a gayer town in all America. There was a constant round of routs and assemblies at the Pontac, the Golden Ball, and other hostelries, and the townsfolk thronged to gape at the carriages and chairs arriving with their scented and glittering freight of officers and ladies, to hear the strains of cham-ber music within, and the efforts of the regimental bands outside, to sniff hungrily the smells of rich cooking borne high on trays by serv-ants, not only from the tavern kitchen at the rear, but from confec-tioners and bake houses all over the town, and to watch the company of bored redcoats formed up in the courtyard, firing a methodical *feu-de-joie* at a signal from a window, to mark each toast at the table. And when the admiral gave a dinner at the Pontac he did not trust the cooking ashore at all but had the food prepared on board the flag-ship, whence it was rushed in covered dishes, by boat to the Market Slip, and then up to the big inn by a hurrying file of seamen and stew-ards, with an armed party ahead crying way for them.

There was a constant coming and going of packet ships and cartels and naval dispatch boats and a constant thunder of salutes in consequence. There was enough good powder wasted in salutes and *feu-de-joie* nonsense every month to fight a battle—or so it seemed to me, seeing our Cause held up for lack of it. The merchants of Hollis and Granville streets were doing a roaring trade, with hard money rattling on the counters, the first real sight of yellow guineas in Halifax since Wolfe came there in '58. Army and navy contractors waxed fat, and the vintners could not import stocks fast enough. And the stews of Barrack Street, recruited with new flesh amongst the poorer refugees from Boston, strove lustily to cope with the needs of Howe's nine thousand men.

The grass was gone from the streets of the lower town, and many houses were being actually painted, some red, some white, but most of them brown or a light, flaring yellow, so that from the harbor Halifax on its steep slope resembled a loamy bed of daffodils.

It did not smell like daffodils. The streets were deep in the flung slops of the swollen population, and privies in yards and alleyways stank the air. The constant traffic of country carts, and the chairs and chaises and carriages and coaches of the gentry and the riding horses of the officers and young bloods and the ceaseless wandering of soldiers, seamen, refugees, and citizens had deepened the holes in the streets and churned the roadways to rivers of reeking muck. The tents of Howe's soldiers on the common and Camp Hill stood in a man-made quagmire after every rain, bordered by brushwood latrines which the men used or ignored as they chose, and the whole camp gave off a miasma which the warm southwesterly airs carried over the town.

The scents and pomatums of the fine folk of Halifax gave these things a false crust, like a gilded lid on a chamber pot.

I wanted a smell of clean air, a breath of the woods, and kindly Malachi Salter gave me leave for a few days' fishing and provided me with a horse.

I picked up François at Northwest Arm—riding behind with lean arms clutched about my waist, his first experience ahorseback—and turned along the Dutch Village path to the Basin. There was food for four days in the saddlebags and a pair of blankets and lines, hooks, angleworms, and a few painfully made flies.

I followed the Windsor Road ten miles along the wooded shore of the Basin to the mouth of the little Sackville River, where I left my horse at the inn. We cut rods in a birch clump, rigged our lines, and fell to fishing. Black flies were at their thickest, but we smeared our faces and hands with pork rinds to keep them off and were tolerably comfortable. At the first day's end we were well upstream and had three salmon and thirty or forty trout. We lit a fire and lay the night in the edge of the woods. The black flies subsided at dark, and the night was too cool for mosquitoes.

"This is good," said François in Micmac, sucking his little black clay.

It was good. I felt as if I had lived many months in a madhouse and suddenly wakened in the woods by home. There was the same wild pear in snowy bloom, the slender white birches just breaking into leaf, and the sheep laurel all a purple flame above the river. After dark the frogs sang a chorus that filled the night, and somewhere a bittern boomed—*boom-snick-boom-snick-boom-snick*—like a man driving a stake into the earth with the sound of his maul strokes echoing against the woods. An owl hooted, and for fun we called him up—*hoo-hoo, hoo-hoo, hoo-hoo-awrrr!*—and he came and sat in a tall pine over our heads, and our clamor brought up others to join the conversation, until the whole dark wood was alive with owl voices, some with a deep note, some with high, some loud, some soft, hooting and muttering and screeching down at our fire. Ay, it was good. Familiar sounds and familiar stars, shining between the dark pine branches, and the river running and the rustle of small creatures in the grass by the waterside and the breath of the forest, the clean medicinal smell of spruce and pine and fir. There was a bush of sweet fern beside me, and I reached up and pulled off a handful of the fragile twigs and buds and crushed them in my fingers and thrust my face down into them, sucking in the perfume that to me is more fragrant than anything in the world except the hair of my love. I could persuade myself that I was happy.

I had not seen Fear since St. Aspinquid's Day; indeed I had avoided the merchants' walk in George Street and the Parade and St. Paul's of a Sunday and other places where officers and their ladies strolled or passed their time. That was not difficult, for the scurry of business kept me busy in Salter's store till any hour short of midnight, except on Committee nights, when the Cause absorbed my time and thoughts. On Sundays I went with the Salters to Mather's Meetinghouse. Almost the whole congregation—and the preacher—lay under suspicion of the Council for sedition, because so many were natives of New England. Salter was the great man amongst them, foremost in contributions to the meetinghouse expenses, but more than that a true and fearless Christian. He proved that almost daily in his visits to captured Americans in the damp and gloomy jail on Hollis Street, carrying parcels of food and wine for the sick and quilts and suchlike. A lesser man, playing the dangerous game we all were playing there in the provincial capital, would have shrunk from calling attention to his sympathies.

Occasionally he got word in some roundabout way of Liverpool affairs and told me that my father's health was failing, that Joanna's child was growing lustily, that Captain Dudington and the *Senegal* had been withdrawn from our town late in April after a reign of terror lasting one hundred and twenty-four days, that Luke had got to Boston, and Mark had been heard from, serving in one of His Majesty's ships.

On the following afternoon François and I were busily fishing our way downstream when we heard the rub-a-dub-dub of a drum in the woods to the east. The Windsor Road, which Halifax grandly called the Great West Road, lay up there, not far, winding along the slope of the narrow Sackville Valley.

At once we threw down our rods and crept through the trees toward the road. We came upon it even sooner than I expected, a narrow track in the forest that was little more than a chain of mud holes linked by deep ruts whose ridges were just beginning to dry. The drum came steadily toward us from the direction of Halifax and behind it the tramp and splash of many boots and the clip-clop of horses and rattle of wheels. We peered from the bushes. Two mounted officers came at the head of the column. They were Colonel Gorham and Captain Jack Helyer. So the "Royal Rascals" were indeed moving upcountry, as the gossip had prophesied!

All the officers were mounted on fair enough nags, and they rode and talked together in twos and threes, looking very fine in their green jackets and white breeches and glossy, black, leather helmets. A few of the men at the column's head wore uniforms of the same kind, enough for a sergeant's guard perhaps; I suspect Colonel Gorham had provided them out of his own pocket for the sake of appearances. But after seven months or more in His Majesty's service the rest of his Royal Fencible Americans were in their original rags: coats and breeches of all sorts, colors, and sizes; some in waistcoats and no jackets and vice versa, and all were ragged and patched and ragged again; there was scarce a pair of gaiters in the whole column beyond the uniformed few, and their coarse wool stockings, some black, some gray, were already well spattered with the Great West Road. There was nothing respectable about them but the muskets on their shoulders and their belts, bayonets, and cartridge boxes. But it was their shoes I noticed most. They marched in the things they had been issued the previous fall, wrecks after the winter in Halifax and the spring maneuvers with Howe's troops in the mud of Camp Hill.

The road wound forty-six miles from Halifax to Windsor, and they had covered twelve or so, marching at ease and sweating freely in the hot sun. Their feet pattered all out of step—'twas impossible to keep step on such a road—and some were limping already. I wondered how many would reach Windsor on those feet and in those shoes.

Fortunately for them, 'twas customary to break the Windsor march at the sorry wayside inns which marked the fifteen- and thirty-mile stages of the journey. They were nearing the first night halt and thanking God aloud in all accents from Swiss to backwoods Massachusetts. I looked for John's face, but he was not amongst them. There were not more than two hundred of them, and in the hot sunshine the black flies hung over the column like smoke. Behind came the transport, country carts for the most part requisitioned in the Halifax market place, a queer collection, splashing in the holes and jolting over the stones, some drawn by horses, some by oxen yoked in pairs with heavy birchwood horn yokes of the German kind. Some had canvas tilts, and in these were the regiment's women and children, a mixed lot like the men. Captain Helyer came trotting back along the column, the men drawing aside to make way and taking the splash of his fine black's hoofs. He pulled up before the very bank where François and I lay, and I thought for a moment we were discovered. But he was looking down the road past the lumbering carts, and we perceived at the column's tail a coach and four, of all things, driven by a Negro in a white wig and a green-cockaded hat. The coach top was a clutter of trunks and boxes and travel bags lashed on with stout rope.

The Negro pulled up and doffed his hat, and Captain Helyer leaned over to speak to his passengers. They were women, three or four of them, but I saw only the one whose face appeared at the coach door, the charming face of Fear laughing up at the athletic man on the horse. I thought with a pang that she must love him very much to give up the merry round of Halifax for life with him in some dull provincial outpost.

"Tired, my dear?" asked Captain Jack.

"Not at all. But . . . 'the Great West Road' . . . good lack!"

"Oh, come, Fear, darling," protested a female voice within. It was pleasant. It tinkled. But there was a touch of malice in it. "They tell me the south shore has no roads at all."

"On the south shore," Fear answered, smiling up at her husband, "we call a horse path a horse path and have done with it."

"The first stage is three or four miles ahead, my dear. There's a bit of an inn, and we'll make a snug party of it. The men and their families'll have to pig it in the barn, poor devils, but they're used to hard lying. You'll have room to pass the column there, and in the morning Sip can put the coach ahead."

"Does the road improve with distance?" asked the tinkling voice.

Captain Jack made a comical grimace. "The middle stage is the worst, I'm told."

"Thank heaven we go from Windsor to Cumberland by boat!" said the tinkle piously.

Cumberland! As soon as they were out of sight around the bend I snapped, "Come on!" to François and scrambled down to the river for my knapsack. All the way to the Sackville Inn I racked my wits for a means of getting a warning to Uniacke and Allan. I could overtake the column on Mr. Salter's horse and probably pass it at the post inn but I should be recognized, and Helyer would question my hurry and doubtless guess my errand. François? The Indian couldn't stay on a horse to save his neck. Afoot through the woods he could outpace Gorham's sore-footed soldiers as far as Windsor but there he must take the long way around Minas Basin while they were sailing direct to Cumberland.

But in the yard of the Sackville Inn, just where I was making up my mind to chance it on Salter's horse, I saw the one man who could do it—and the last I had expected to see. Aaron Trusdell, sitting a fine bay mare by the inn pump, where a lame Negro boy was filling the trough to water his horse. Gone was the shoemaking pack, the shabby homespun jacket and smallclothes, the wheedling, Yankee-peddler manner. He was dressed like a country squire, with the satisfied, self-respecting, guinea-in-pocket air of a man coming from successful business in the town.

He got rid of the Negro swiftly—"Boy, fetch me a bottle of brandy for the road." And as the cripple hobbled indoors, "Well, David, why so hot?"

I stood close to his knee and muttered up to him, "Gorham and his Fencibles are on the march for Cumberland. We must warn Allan and Uniacke."

"And where d'ye think I'm bound, David?"

I looked away from his quizzical eye. "You know everything," I said uncomfortably.

"No," he said seriously. "If I knew everything, lad, there'd be an end to General Washington's uncertainty. Howe's here waiting orders

for his next move, and on that move may hang the war. Now I must
drop everything and gallop to Cumberland and warn that hothead
Jonathan Eddy lest he do something rash and hazard the whole Cause
in Nova Scotia. For that's at stake in Cumberland, David. One mis-
fire and all's lost in this province."

The black boy appeared with the bottle and stowed it in Aaron's
saddlebag and caught the tossed coins deftly. The spy leaned over and
put a hand down to me, and I shook it hard.

"Take care of yourself," I said.

"Take care of the Cause," said Aaron Trusdell, and spurred off.

CHAPTER 19

A Rift in the Lute

WE WAITED on tenterhooks for news from Cumberland. It came on
one of the early days of June, as cold a June as I can remember, with
raw, easterly winds and rains and fogs and sometimes a sharp frost at
night. And the frost entered our souls, for the news was bad. Gorham's
troops were in Fort Cumberland, putting it into a state of defense.
Several of the king's ships had appeared at the head of Fundy Bay.
Michael Francklin was there, urging the people to put aside their rebel
sympathies and enlist in the militia "for the defense of Nova Scotia."
The small Tory group in Cumberland was jubilant. Jonathan Eddy
had gathered up his family and fled the country, together with two
other leaders of the movement in Cumberland, Sam Rogers and
Zebulon Rowe. John Allan and Richard Uniacke were sitting tight,
under suspicion. Our little Cause had been nipped in the bud.

But the big Cause was itself in danger, for now arrived in Halifax
a fleet of transports from England, crammed with reinforcements for
General Howe. They seemed to fill the great harbor, their decks a mass
of redcoats, and boats fled from ship to shore bearing officers on mysterious and important errands. Howe's headquarters on Spring Garden
Road buzzed like a hive.

Rumor flourished. The army was for Canada, to drive the Americans off the St. Lawrence. It was for Boston and a final decision with
Washington's army there. It was for a descent on Philadelphia, the

home of the American Congress. We watched its movements as a treed cat watches a dog.

Howe did not keep us long in suspense. His orders had come in the fleet, and he moved with surprising energy. One day the tents on Camp Hill were struck as if by a hurricane, and the next day—June 7th—their late tenants, the veterans of Lexington and Bunker Hill, marched down the steep Halifax streets to the squeal of fife and drum and embarked. They were glad to be on the move and said so in their ribald farewells to the sluts of Barrack Street as they passed and to the silent citizens. The fleet lay three days waiting for a wind, and when it sailed I rode with young Micah Smith around the Arm and through the woods to Sambro, eager to see which direction the ships would take. But the sails stood straight out to sea and vanished, and we returned no wiser.

The town was strangely empty. Most of the Boston refugees had gone with the army, in hopes of a triumphant return to their homes. There was a hush in the streets like the hush before thunder.

Now came a cheerful dispatch from the irrepressible Uniacke, saying that Michael Francklin had been unable to get a single recruit for his militia in Cumberland and was gone to Windsor and lay ill there. Gorham's soldiers were "an ill-assorted lot of bog trotters engaged in quarrels among themselves," and Fort Cumberland could yet be taken by "three men and a boy with pistols." He added, "If Howe goes to Boston, as some think he will we can do nothing, for our revolt depends on help from Massachusetts. But if he goes to Canada or south as far as New York or Philadelphia we shall have such an opportunity as we had in the summer of '75. The one good regiment left in Nova Scotia is the 17th, at Windsor. Watch 'em!"

Transports laden with troops from England continued to put in and sail again. Some of the regiments came ashore to stretch their legs after the long voyage. We saw the 72nd Highlanders parading the Halifax streets, and one Sunday a regiment of Hessians in blue coats and with their pigtails done up in eel skins marched to St. Paul's, where Dr. Breynton addressed them in their native German. They had a much more rigid discipline than the rigid English troops and marched like so many wooden puppets on a single string; I wondered what would happen to them when they met the American rifles. But every one of these transports was a new burden on the American Cause, and we watched them gloomily.

The news continued bad. Late in June we learned that the American army in Canada had abandoned Montreal and was in full retreat for home, and the Canadians who had fought beside them and assisted them in so many ways were left to their fate.

In all America the Cause seemed doomed. Yet our stubborn Nova Scotia Yankees clung to their belief in it, and in reprisal the assembly, sitting in the old building at the corner of Hollis and Sackville streets, a former guardhouse, solemnly declared vacant for "non-attendance" the seats of Annapolis, Cornwallis, Horton, Cumberland, Sackville, and Yarmouth. What remained? The Dutchmen of Lunenburg and our Yankees of sprawling Queens County were "represented" by Halifax merchants forced upon them by pressure from the Council. The assembly was a hollow, Halifax sham that deceived nobody but the smug statesmen in London. The rule of Mariott Arbuthnot the sailor, our new lieutenant governor, was quiet after Legge's bombastic days, and 'twas said that Michael Francklin had his ear. And General Massey had arrived to command the handful of troops that remained in Nova Scotia. An able man, as we learned later to our cost.

On a hot July afternoon young Micah ran into Salter's store and dragged me into the countinghouse. "The Light Dragoons, David— they're coming through the town! And there's a transport waiting at the governor's wharf!"

I snatched up my hat and went out into the streets with him and presently saw the 17th coming down George Street, a fine sight, even to my rebel eyes. They were well mounted, the horses fat and sleek with the fresh green pasturage of Windsor. The men looked immense in tall brass helmets that glittered in the sun and redcoats and cloaks and white breeches and polished black jack boots. From the top of each helmet a scarlet-dyed horse tail hung to the trooper's shoulder, and in front grinned their ghastly badge, a white skull on a black plate with the words "Or Glory" underneath. All Halifax knew their history—a regiment raised by one of Wolfe's veterans and the badge designed in Wolfe's memory. They poured like a red fire down the narrow street past the governor's mansion and turned along Hollis to the entrance to the governor's wharf. The hoofs clip-clopped and struck sparks from the stony street, and girths creaked and sabers clanked, and the crowding people buzzed. Beyond doubt the finest corps in Howe's whole army, even including his regiment of Guards. By Michael Francklin's wit they had been stationed at Windsor, where they could strike swiftly at rebellion wherever it showed on the Fundy side, until the last possible moment. Now they were off to Staten Island, where we now knew Howe had landed, intent upon the capture of New York.

"They'll make good targets," young Micah said contemptuously.

"Don't be too sure of that," muttered I. "A horseman's hard to hit, and he can move fast and far. If Howe had more of 'em and less of those wooden infantry I'd not give much for Washington's chances."

I felt a tap on my shoulder, and there was Charles Trider, one of our Halifax committee, growling, "Well, what are you waiting for?"

We made for Salter's house at a run and, as we approached the house, saw half a dozen other committeemen on the same errand, throwing all caution to the winds. Inside, the big parlor was full of excited voices, Smith's loudest.

"Gentlemen, the time has come! No garrison in all the province now but Gorham's rabble at Fort Cumberland and a handful of Highland Emigrants at Windsor. And the fleet's at New York with Howe. It's now or never!"

"What about Legge's Loyal Nova Scotia Regiment?" a voice demanded.

That raised a laugh. The "regiment" numbered a scant hundred, mostly rogues from the streets of Halifax anxious to avoid the press, but it served Legge's purpose. Far away in England he was drawing full pay as its colonel.

The lift in our spirits was miraculous—all the hopeless waiting past and the prospect of action firing every face in the room.

"What's the plan?" I asked eagerly.

"The old one. Jonathan Eddy's been made a colonel in the Continental Line and is raising a force in Maine. They're to march around Fundy Bay by way of Maugerville—the Maugerville men are cutting roads already—and when they appear at the head of the Bay, all Westmoreland and Cumberland are to rise. The men of Truro, Onslow, and Londonderry will march to Cumberland to join 'em, and together they'll storm Fort Cumberland. Then on to Windsor, where there's nought but an earthwork and a barrack, held by a handful of Scotchmen that call themselves the Royal Highland Emigrants. They'll fight well enough but they're not enough to stop us. With Windsor in our hands, the whole Annapolis Valley's to rise; then a swift march on Halifax, where there's nothing but Howe's new blockhouses and a handful of Legge's regiment and the governor's guard—say one hundred and fifty men. Against them Colonel Eddy will have a thousand at the very least—and inside the town we'll be waiting, ready for the word. In thirty days at the outside the province will be ours, and we'll be sending a representative to the Congress."

"What do we use for powder?" I asked bluntly.

"Powder?"

"Gunpowder—the stuff that wars are won with. There's none in the province, outside the king's magazines. Massey's ordnance officers are even attending the prize sales now, buying everything that smells like powder, just to make sure it doesn't get into the wrong hands."

William Smith said coldly, "The General Court of Massachusetts has promised Colonel Eddy a supply—enough to take Fort Cumberland. And in Fort Cumberland we'll find enough to blow Halifax sky-high. Eh, Malachi?"

We all looked at Mr. Salter then. 'Twas strange that we had overlooked him in our babbling, the great man amongst us. And now his appearance stopped all our tongues at once. He sat staring at the litter of papers and maps with a face as dark as thunder. His long gray hair had escaped its ribbon and was all awry and wild, his shrewd and kindly features distorted with a mixture of anger and distress that set me wondering what disaster had befallen. 'Twas a long time before he spoke, and then his voice shook.

"Gentlemen," he said slowly, "no man has worked harder or risked more for the Cause than I. I've believed in it—I've *lived* it, these eleven years, ever since the Stamp Act was proclaimed." His lips twisted in a small wry smile. "I was here in this harbor before many of you were born. I had a fishing station here when D'Anville came to conquer America and saw his Frenchmen die by thousands on the shore of the Basin, swept off by a ship fever sent by God in answer to New England's prayers. That was in '46. I remember how the remnant of 'em buried D'Anville out there on George's Island and burned the ships they couldn't man and sailed back home to France. The greatest danger the American colonies ever knew—all swept away by God; and I, the lone Yankee fisherman, left in possession of this great harbor as before. I was a religious man after that. In '49 Cornwallis came with his ragtag and bobtail English settlers and soldiers and built this town, this Halifax. I liked Cornwallis. He was hot-tempered but able, and not afraid of anyone, not even the king. One of his first deeds was to call together representatives of the other settlements in Nova Scotia—the first government of this province. What's more, he listened to what they said and wasn't afraid to back their opinions against those high and mighty Lords of Trade and Plantations, in London. A great man. We've never had a governor like him since. The rest were just dullards or stiff soldiers who stood with their backs to America and their eyes fixed across the sea. The Council drifted into the hands of a group of greedy men, fawning on each successive governor for their own ends, bleeding the province dry, and singing 'God Save the King.' That couldn't go on forever—not in a province that was settled by New England Yankees. The Stamp Act set us thinking—set all America thinking, come to that. Up here we didn't lose our heads, Boston-fashion; no mobs, no stoning redcoats till they fired in return, no burnings, no beatings—none o' that. British law was good-enough law. We wanted to administer it ourselves, for ourselves; we wanted the king and his governors and bloodsuckers to keep their hands and teeth off. That was reasonable, I think. 'Twasn't anything to do with loyalty. We were far more loyal to the king, I reckon, than the governors and their friends who worshiped only his image on the guinea."

"Speak for yourself, Malachi!" warned William Smith's harsh voice.

"Very well. I like the British flag. I've seen a lot o' good men die for it, and because of them we've been able to make an English-speaking world here on the shores of America. I'm an old man, and old men can't forget those things. It's always seemed to me that if we fought the king for our rights we'd be fighting for British law. 'Twasn't my idea alone. Over in Boston, Sam Adams and the rest insisted right along that Americans were fighting for just that—their rights as Englishmen. Very well. On that ground I've risked everything in the Cause. On that ground I'm willing to fight still."

"Then let's get on with it!" cried young Francis Moseley fiercely.

"One moment, young man. Here is a Pennsylvania *Evening Post*. It says that on July the fourth the Congress solemnly declared the American colonies forever separate and independent of Great Britain!"

He stopped there and gazed from face to face, in a room so still that the tall clock in the hall corner ticked loudly through the closed door, and we could hear the clatter of dishes in the distant scullery, where the maids were readying supper.

"I don't believe it!" Wynn Carten yelled.

"It's the truth, sir! But it makes a lie of all we agreed upon when Massachusetts raised the flag of rebellion. Sam Adams' promises! We had 'em by word of mouth; we have 'em on paper now—on a sea of papers and pamphlets poured upon us from Boston the past five years. Now"—he shook the newspaper in our faces—"you see how much they mean!"

At once a clamor broke out all over the chamber, voices crying Salter down, voices giving him the right of it, and others—a majority, it seemed to me—commanding Salter to go on and finish what he had to say. 'Twas some time before he got a hearing. Then he said grimly,

"Of all the fourteen colonies we have the most thinly scattered population and we face the greatest danger. That's something to consider. We considered it and were willing to take the risk—if the other colonies would send help. For help, the Congress referred us to Massachusetts, and Massachusetts gave us promises—Sam Adams' kind. Ay, Sam and his General Court declare even now that we shall have everything —troops, arms, and ammunition. General Washington tells us to expect nothing. Who do ye believe, the men who stand convicted liars at Philadelphia or the soldier who tells the uncomfortable truth?"

Again uproar, Moseley, Smith, and others shouting that the time had come to fight and have done with all this jawing; some (these mostly older men) crying that Salter was right and to hell with Sam Adams, the General Court of Massachusetts, the Congress and the rest, and there were some—and I was one—who saw only the tragedy of a split in our devoted band and cried all sorts of hasty compromise to patch it up. Amongst us we made a hubbub fit to wake the dead in St. Paul's burying ground up the street, and Mrs. Salter put her head in the door, regarding us like a lot of schoolboys, and asked severely, "Have you forgotten the town guard?" That sobered us a little, and the voices dropped to grumbling.

William Smith stepped up to the table. "Let's have a show of hands, all who favor fighting—fighting now!" He thrust up his own for a start.

Five other hands went up at once, all young men hot in the Cause.

"Now those who follow Malachi!"

Mr. Salter's hand went up firmly, and I saw John Fillis' and two or three more.

"What foolery is this?" snapped Will Smith. "There are fifteen men on this committee. Where d'ye stand—you others?" He looked straight at me.

I said earnestly, "I stand for unity in the Cause. Unity somehow or anyhow. Otherwise all will come to nothing. 'Tisn't fair to put it to a vote now, when we're all hot or bewildered by the turn of events. Give us a chance to cool, sir, to sup and sleep on it."

"A chance to cool! That's just the trouble! Nunno! We must make our decision here and now. Time won't wait. And—there's no middle road, gentlemen. Not in the Cause! You know that. Tell them—tell them, Malachi!"

Mr. Salter's tired old voice said bitterly, "He's right, lads. No middle road. Ah, good God, the tragedy, the tragedy! So many people here and in the rest of our America want a middle road, and nothing for them but a hard choice in the end. God knows I don't love the king nor his rotten parliament. But to cut ourselves off forever from the British people, the men and women who speak our tongue in every part of the world—no! Not that! Anything but that!" Tears rolled down his cheeks, and to see an old man cry is terrible.

Will Smith called out resolutely, "Show hands, all true Friends of America!"

Up went the original five, then mine, and slowly, three more.

Nine—nine of fifteen. There was the measure of the breach, not merely in our small committee, but in the ranks of all who favored the Cause in Nova Scotia.

Smith turned to Mr. Salter. "Sorry, Malachi," he said, not unkindly.

We followed him out of the room, but in the doorway I paused and looked back and met the old man's eyes.

"Is it good-by, David?"

"Yes."

He rose and came toward me, putting out his hand. I took it.

"God bless and keep you, David. God make His light to shine upon you always and give you peace."

"Amen," I said huskily, and fled.

CHAPTER 20

The King's Messenger

I TOOK THE ROAD for Cumberland in the morning, on a horse hired at the Crown Coffee House near the water front. My eyes were heavy, for we had sat up all night talking at Will Smith's, but my heart was light enough. No man can be a pessimist at nineteen, on a bright July morning, with a good breakfast under his belt and somewhere ahead a Cause to fight for.

I was glad to put Halifax behind me and with it my love pains and all the dull waiting and argument. I rode across the common and down the track to the head of the Arm, where I found François preparing to go codfishing in a newly made canoe. He read my errand in my face, and his black eyes glowed.

"We go to fight?"

"To fight."

He dived into a wigwam and brought forth the gun of Louisburg

and my powder horn and bullet purse. The gun shone with bear grease.
He had kept it well.

A young squaw came out of the wigwam in an old red petticoat
that bulged eloquently below the waistband. She called out something
in Micmac, and François hesitated and went back to her. I could not
catch the words but I knew she was begging him to stay. He stood a
minute, scuffing the ground with his moccasin toe, and at last shook
his head stubbornly and came to me.

"Get up behind," I said.

He looked at the horse dubiously. "I do not like these things. They
make me sore behind. Do we go far?"

"Four days," I said. "Or five—or six. I do not know myself."

"That is not far to walk," said François proudly. So we set off along
the path to Dutch Village and the Basin, with the horse at a walk and
François moving with his light step at my stirrup. He did not look back,
but I did and saw the young squaw standing with her face screwed up
like a child's, weeping. I had a twinge of remorse then, but only a
twinge. In thirty days we should be marching into Halifax in triumph,
with the troops from Massachusetts and an army of our own.

The Great West Road had dried since Gorham marched that way,
and the traffic of supplies from Windsor to the capital had leveled the
ruts with dust. Some ragged children and a noisy dog ran out to greet
us at the wayside inn of Lower Sackville, but we traveled on. 'Twas
past nightfall when we reached the thirty-mile inn, and I was glad
enough to 'light and bait, though François seemed unwearied. The
place was no more than a small frame house in a clearing at the roadside, with a log stable and barn behind. A frowsy woman came to my
knock with a tallow dip flickering in her hand.

"The Injun'll have to sleep in the barn," she said at once.

"He's my servant," said I pleasantly, "and used to civil treatment."

She sniffed. "If our barn's good enough fer His Majesty's sogers
it's good enough fer an Injun." And I thought of the march of the
Royal Americans.

"Barn good," François said to me. I went out with him to put up
the horse and found a big roan in the stable with the king's broad
arrow branded on his flank. Evidently there was company at the inn.
I pointed out the brand to François and put a finger to my lips. At
the kitchen door the woman handed François a plate of cold roast
pork and a hunk of bread, and with it he vanished into the shadows.

The inn parlor was a small room, furnished with a round table and

a few chairs handmade out of birchwood. There was a scatter of sawdust over the floor, from the sawpit in the edge of the clearing, and a
lamp hung from the ceiling, giving off a fine stink of whale oil and
precious little light. In the little disk of shadow directly underneath
the lamp sat a lone fellow traveler, a lean, pasty-faced fellow of five-
and-thirty in a red coat and white breeches—the coat unbuttoned for
comfort in the hot July night and the breeches soiled with the dust of
the road. His big boots lay in a corner, and his stockinged feet stuck
out beneath the table, toes wriggling comfortably. There was an earth-
enware jug on the table and a glass of dark liquid at his hand. He regarded me with a pair of bloodshot eyes.

"Who the devil are you?" said he.

"Name of Japhet Moreton," said I easily, taking a seat at the table.
"Bound for my farm in the Valley, from Halifax, and glad of it. And
you?"

He gave me a comic leer. "Nemmind!" He took a long pull at the
glass.

The woman brought my supper—cold roast pork and bread and
cheese, doubtless the only fare in the house. I asked what she had to
drink.

"There's grog," she said. "Or I can make ye a dish o' tea."

"Grog and cold pork don't sit well with me, ma'am. And I'm not
rightly partial to tea."

I watched her as I said that, and her eyes narrowed. She said,
"There's milk in the big crock in the kitchen if ye'll help to pour it."

I went out with her, and she swept the door shut and faced me.

"Why don't ye like tea?" in a fierce whisper.

"For the tax on it."

"Give me the word!"

"Liberty."

She clutched my shoulder with her hard brown fingers. "Listen,
then. That boozy fool's a king's messenger, with a dispatch for the
Royal Americans at Cumberland."

I opened my eyes and clamped my jaw.

"Don't ye dast touch him in my house, mind!"

"All I want's a look at his message," I said, and returned to my
supper with a pitcher of milk. Redcoat regarded it with immense disgust.

"Milk!"

"Yes, with food always. I'll join you later in a glass of grog if I
may."

He made a large-handed gesture and poured himself another drink.

When I finished eating he summoned the woman with a whack on the table and demanded pipes and a coal. He passed one of the clays to me and produced some tobacco wrapped in a handkerchief.

"Can't get nothin' but that damned navy twist at these country inns —strong enough to kill an 'orse. Fill your pipe, Mister What's-your-name, while the coal glows. It's proper 'baccy, real Virginia—the only thing good that ever come out o' Ameriky. Fill your glass wi' this punch too. I allus carry me own lemons in the 'ot weather, but the rum's some o' that rot gut from old Mauger's distillery in Allyfax, the on'y stuff in the 'ouse. What a country! Flies in the air"—he looked up disgustedly at the insects fluttering about the lamp—"fleas in the beds, and flux in the drinkin' water—if ye're fool enough to drink it. Wintertime ye freeze to death. Well, 'ere's long life to 'Is Majesty, and Gawd defend the right!"

I drank that pledge in all sincerity; some of the others—the many others—I drank tongue-in-cheek. We toasted the whole royal family one by one and Old England, God Bless Her, the Empire, the Army, the Navy, the Governor, the Council, Damnation to All Rebels, Departed Friends, Days of Ease and Nights of Pleasure, Honest Men and Pretty Women, the British Constitution, Your Love and Mine, and some others I cannot remember now. Redcoat drank a great swig for each, but I sipped gingerly, protesting I was only a simple country-man with a poor head for liquors. "The more fer me," he grunted, and, seeing in my remark a compliment to his own head, he went on to demonstrate how good it was. And I was impressed. The fellow drank enough to stupefy a boat's crew before he fell to the floor in an attempt to get a foot on the table for another bumper to " 'Is Majesty," and there he lay, with a great sigh, and fell to snoring almost at once.

I sent the woman upstairs to rummage his saddlebags and set about the sodden carcass on the floor myself. There was nought in his pockets but a purse containing eighteen shillings, a battered silver watch, a soiled handkerchief, and a horn snuffbox. In his coattails the piece of Virginia tobacco, a red garter—from the plump leg of some Halifax serving wench by the look of it—and a much-thumbed paper which I fell upon greedily. 'Twas not what I sought, merely a passport made out by Governor Legge last year, setting forth his own titles and dignities and requiring in the name of His Majesty "all those whom it may concern to allow our good and trusty messenger Bartholemew Prout to pass freely without let or hindrance and to afford him every assistance and protection of which he may stand in need."

I had half a mind to steal it, for it might prove useful at Windsor if the Highlanders were watching the road, but I thought of the woman's danger and put it back. She came downstairs, reporting nothing in his bags or about the chamber.

"Feel his riding cloak for a crackle of paper," I suggested. "And the lining of his hat." These hung just outside the parlor door and were soon examined. Nothing there. I straightened up and stood over the man, baffled. In a corner lay his dusty riding boots. Boots were so obvious and old-fashioned a postbag that I dismissed them, but after another careful search of the good and trusty Prout, without result like the first, I went over and capsized his boots. Out dropped the thing I sought, a folded sheet superscribed to Colonel Gorham at Fort Cumberland and caught together with a great lump of red wax, impressed with the governor's seal. I turned it over in my fingers. To break the seal would betray the woman. She read my thoughts and snatched the thing from me. I followed her swift skirts to the kitchen, where she heated a thin knife in the embers of the supper fire, wiped it carefully, and then slid the hot blade expertly between paper and seal.

"Where did you learn that?" I asked curiously.

"From a shoemaker."

"Ah!"

"They're handy with knives and wax in the way of their trade."

"Of course."

"I can set the seal back the same way."

There were two letters, one folded within the other. The first ran:

My Dear Gorham:

I trust that by this time you are well established in Fort Cumberland and making some repairs to the buildings. I scarcely need remind you that winter is long and severe in those parts, and effort made now will repay itself a thousand-fold after October. You may take some local carpenters upon your strength until winter sets in. I note what you say about the condition of the ramparts, curtains, &c., but I am held to narrow funds and you will have to make what repairs you can to the earthworks and palisades with the labour of the troops themselves. I may say I have taken a great risk in sending your entire regiment to Cumberland. For the rest there is little but the grenadier company of the Royal Highland Emigrants at Windsor. They can support you at need, while still within quick recall of Halifax, which is nigh naked. I have here none but Legge's handful of hard-bargains, the town guard, and a few Highland recruits. Francklin's militia looks well on paper, but is worthless against an uprising within the province, indeed I would not trust most of 'em with arms in their hands. The whole province is a nest of sedition. Our recruiting officers returning from various parts have got few or no men, and report disaffected persons everywhere ready to join the rebels at the first opportunity.

As for Cumberland, you are the best judge what is afoot there. The presence of yourself and troops should overawe 'em sufficiently, but do not mistake your function at Fort Cumberland. It is to guard the isthmus against rebel invasion. If sedition alone were warrant for sending troops I should have our forces scattered from Cape Sable to Canso.

But all this is by the way. My real message is a despatch received from England yesterday, marked urgent. His Majesty has been pleased to issue a command that henceforth the hair of all Infantry shall be dressed in the mode called Clubbed. You will please see that this instruction is carried out.

With Compliments, &c., &c.,

> *I am Yours, &c., &c.,*
> EYRE MASSEY, *Major General.*

P.S.

No uniforms for your corps yet. I am in hopes of a supply of shoes for 'em before the autumn rains.

I lowered the sheet and gazed at the woman solemnly.

"What's it say?" she cried, vexed at my silence. I sank into the nearest chair. Expectancy had wound me up like a clock spring, and now the spring ran down—in laughter. I let my hands droop to the floor and laughed myself to tears; and whenever my sober senses began to take hold, a glance at the woman's angry face, a snore from the sot on the floor, or the thought of His Majesty's pigtails sent me off again.

The woman snatched up the inner sheet, gave it a quick glance, and thrust it at me like a dagger. 'Twas a post-postscript, not nearly so amusing. It wiped the grin off my face like the sum from a slate. It was an order to post rewards for the arrest of certain "leaders of sedition" in Cumberland. Uniacke was not mentioned, but there were £100 each for John Allan, Rogers, and Howe, and £200 for the person of Jonathan Eddy. I sat there staring at it for a time, then held it to her candle's flame until it was a black wisp floating slowly to the floor.

The outer sheet she resealed, and I returned it carefully to the messenger's boot; and then in the true spirit of conviviality I helped Bartholemew Prout to bed.

CHAPTER 21

Cumberland

WINDSOR'S OPEN FIELDS, rich and green in the sunshine, were a pleasant sight after the long journey through the woods. The Fundy tide had gone out, leaving the river a mere trickle in a chasm of wet red clay that shone like new paint. The soil on this side of the peninsula was rich—rich as our stony south-shore fields were poor—and small wonder that Michael Francklin and other well-to-do Halifax merchants had established here their country residences. Thirty or forty houses made the village, but they were good houses, and the people had a prosperous look. I could see the British flag drooping over the blockhouse and simple earthwork which would be the only barrier on our victorious march from Cumberland, and some of the small garrison wandering aimlessly in the red dust of the one straggling street. They did not look a bit like the Scotch I had seen ashore from Howe's transports in Halifax Harbor. These fellows wore breeches of some coarse white stuff and country-knit stockings and waistcoats (all unbuttoned in the heat) of spotted swanskin cloth and any sort of headgear from a battered old hat thrice cocked with horn buttons to a home-tanned leather cap.

I rode past them at a good pace, with François trotting in the dust at my stirrup, and every moment expected a hail and a command to stop. None came. Even the villagers saw us with indifference.

There were good friends of the Cause in Windsor, and I had a list of their names in my head, but for their sake and my own I decided to make my own way to Cumberland if I could. I left the horse at the post inn and went afoot to the riverbank to look for a boat passage up the Bay. A few shallops and a small sloop lay on their beam ends upon the red-clay flat below, but a fellow with a load of pea brush on his shoulder told me there would be nothing for Cumberland till next week. I turned away, half minded to steal one of the shallops when the tide came in, but as I was passing a farmhouse I heard a sound that wakened instant memories—the tap-tap of a cobbler at work and a nasal Yankee voice telling some whimsical yarn that set his hearers cackling. I walked up the lane to the barnyard and came upon Aaron Trusdell sitting on the worn doorsill of the barn with his little bench before him, foot in stirrup strap and tongue and hammer going busily together. The farmer and his sons stood by, hands in homespun pockets, grinning at his tale. Aaron looked up as I approached, with not the least flicker of recognition on his lean face, and his audience regarded me with lazy, good-humored eyes.

"Naow," he said, indicating me with the hammer, "here's a gen'le-man bin aridin' and got a heel loose o' his right boot and wants me to give it a lick or two. Right?"

"How did ye know?" I smiled, nodding and winking at the others.

"Easy. Ye walk like a man that's jist got down off'n a horse, and there's the inside o' your knees still dark wi' the horse's sweat. Stirrups is a tarnation thing to pry off heels, and ye're favorin' the right foot. But—hey!—look there, Mister Carson!—swear if there ain't a brindle cow in your sarce patch!"

All our eyes followed the thrust of his hammer toward the farmer's flourishing vegetables. The fence was unbroken, and there was no sign of a cow. Farmer Carson said so, though he looked fierce enough to have seen a troop of Indians.

"'Course ye can't!" snapped the shoemaker. "She's over the rise now. Take arter that there caow, boys, or ye'll want for cabbages next winter sure as death!"

Off they went, running and shouting angrily, and Aaron turned to me with a sly wink. "They'll be back in five minutes, hot under the collar, and I'll have to own up, shameful-like, that porridge fer break-fast gives me spots afore the eyes." His manner changed abruptly. "Come, David boy! Ye waste time! What's afoot? It's to do with the dragoons that left here, I know that."

"They're gone to join Howe, New York way, and I'm for Cumber-land to give the signal for revolt."

"On whose authority?"

"The Halifax committee's."

"Umph! The Cumberland committee'll have to pass on that."

"What about these soldiers at Windsor?" I asked.

He scraped his sharp chin. "One company of the Royal Highland Emigrants, far's I can find out. New regiment raised amongst the Scotch in this country. Colonel's a feller named Small, but he's off tryin' to get clothes for the regiment, and the man in command here is a Captain Alec MacDonald. A hustler, I tell ye, and a fighting man that hates the sight of a Yankee. Most o' his men are from Isle St. Jean—Clanranald's settlers—speak Gaelic—hardly a word o' English in the lot. Some riffraff amongst 'em—American deserters and such—but don't judge 'em by Gorham's lot. Scotch make good fighters, and this lot's hard as nails."

"A handful of nails won't save the king in Nova Scotia," I said stoutly. "When we've taken Fort Cumberland we'll not be long over that mud work on the hill. Then for the open road to Halifax."

"Confident, aren't ye, David?"

"Why not? Tell me, how am I to get quick passage to Cumberland?"

"Easy. Some fellers here are just startin' a boat ferry across Minas Basin to Partridge Island—that's right opposite Cape Blomidon. Go to Partridge Island, and ye'll find a path through the woods to River Hebert. Any farmer at Hebert'll lend ye a dugout to paddle downriver to Cumberland. I see my friends returning—and no brindle cow. Off with ye, boy, and good luck. Ye'll need it!"

So we took passage, François and I, in the ferry shallop across Minas Basin, with the great hump of Blomidon steep and blue under thunderclouds to our left. The water had a hard glitter in the sunshine, and when we were well out from shore the land shuddered in the heat haze as if rocked by earthquakes, but the hot breeze bowled the shallop along famously. We made the thirty miles to Partridge Island just before dark. The settlement was not on the island itself but a couple of miles up the river and consisted of half a dozen poor huts by the shore, with a range of wooded hills behind. We lay the night there and at daylight took the path through the hills. After passing the first range it followed a narrow gravel ridge called the Boar's Back, a strange thing, a roadbed laid by nature as if for the purpose of human travel and a favorite hunting trail of the Indians. Then we saw the Hebert River, a small stream now in the summer drought, running thinly over wide gravel bars until it reached tidewater, where it became the usual Fundy creek, wide and deep, with red-clay walls. We had walked twenty-five or thirty miles when the banks began to recede, leaving considerable marshy flats, and here the shore had a scatter of farms.

The owner of the first was one Thornton, a Friend of America, and we stopped there the night and had a fine supper of alewives, salted lightly and smoked just enough over a green-maple fire to give them a sweet, nutty flavor. Our host was a Connecticut man, ten years in the country, and called the fish "*gaspereaux*" after the French fashion. I kept my errand to myself but let him know I was on business of the Cause and must have his canoe.

'Twas a poor thing in the light of morning, hollowed out of a pine

log in the old Indian fashion, by charring the wood with repeated
fires and hacking out the soft, burned wood with an adze—a very dull
adze by the look of it. A tipsy thing it looked, and I stared down the
broad tidal reach of the river and was doubtful, but François stepped
into the bow, ready enough, and Eben Thornton took the stern paddle, and away we went, myself sitting on the bottom for ballast.

Thornton pointed out two estates of some size on the left hand,
just past the point where the river became swollen by its juncture with
the Maccan stream. "Tories!" he said, and spat. "Nigh one is Barron's
place. Young Barron got a commission in an English regiment—an'
got a ball in the leg at Bunker Hill. Bin home ever since, gittin' well,
an' now Gorham's made him engineer off'cer over to Fort Cumberland. Place beyond is Francklin Manor—Michael Francklin's. Big
place, twenty thousand acres, mostly good ma'shland. Raises hay there
for his stud farm over to Windsor. Them smaller houses belongs to
his tenants. Downright sinful, ain't it?—one man ownin' sich a sight
o' land!"

"You're a leveler," I suggested.

"Ain't we all?" he asked, surprised.

The tide was in, covering the wide flats of Minudie, whose red mud
seemed to dye the sea itself, and as we swept down the estuary and
put Amherst Point behind us I gazed eagerly over the starboard gunwale for my first sight of Fort Cumberland. It had occupied my
thoughts for months, ay, for years; my father's tales of the fort's capture
from the French in '55 had fired my mind since childhood.

Cumberland Basin, upon whose flood we now paddled, lies curled
like a great pink shrimp about the headland of Minudie. The shrimp's
tail is formed by the confluence of the Hebert and Maccan rivers, and
there must be all of sixteen miles around the ship channel to its head
at Cape Maringouin. This is the end of the great Bay of Fundy, the
lash on the whip of the famous Fundy tide, which here rises and falls
on the average forty feet. Forty feet! On our south shore an eight-foot
tide is a big one. The "basin" of Cumberland is more like an enormous
platter, for the land rises so gently from the sea that a vast expanse
is salt marsh covered at high water by the red Fundy flood, which also
penetrates far up the little rivers into the isthmus.

"I'd expected higher land," I said, and our guide grunted, "Everyone does, that's on'y seen it on a map. Ye ain't seen nothin' yet. Them
Tantramar ma'shes goes back miles 'n miles, flat as a pancake, all
thridded with little red streams like the blood in your veins. Ye've got

to travel halfway 'crost the isthmus to git dry footin' around 'em." He pointed suddenly to the right with his crudely whittled paddle.

"Fort Cumberland!"

A narrow ridge of upland lay in the marshes like a finger pointed at Minudie across the basin. It was cleared for the most part and dotted with houses and barns along the slopes above the marsh, and near the end, like the last knuckle on the finger, was a small green knoll from whose midst protruded a cluster of wooden roofs and red-brick chimneys, like a little green volcano which in some fantastic manner has begun to erupt a village. From this knoll to the point where the ridge dropped seaward to the marsh extended a shelf of earth, bordered by barracks and enclosed by a new and gleaming wooden palisade. I have likened the ridge to a finger; Fort Cumberland was the last knuckle, and its parade ground was the nail, and the whole thing was so small and insignificant that I could scarce believe my eyes.

"Why, it's a paltry thing!" I exclaimed.

"In a way, yes. The fort itself don't measure a hundred yards from rampart to rampart, an' the Frinch kep' three hundred men jammed up in there like rats in a box. When Monckton's mortars got to heavin' bumshells in, the Frinch surrendered pretty prompt. Wa'n't anythin' else to do, I guess. Arter the English got it they made that there parade ground on the back an' built extry barracks there, to give 'emselves more room."

"It's pretty exposed," I suggested.

He chuckled. "If ye mean to the weather, yes. Gits every wind that blows, stuck out in the ma'shes that way. Yes sir, I reckon from October to May, Fort Cumberland is the coldest, bleakest, Godforsakenest post in all Ameriky. Them sogers o' Gorham's'll find *that* out afore spring comes round ag'in." He ceased paddling and nudged my shoulder with his knee. "*If* they're still inside, come spring."

I had not told him my mission and I made no comment. He went on. "But if ye're talkin' military-fashion, why, that's diff'rent. Take the waterside, naow. Fust place, a ship of any size has got to come in with the tide an' git out on the ebb, and ye can't besiege a fort with any sich off-an'-on business. I'm talkin' o' men-o'-war naow. Second place, a ship couldn't raise her guns that high an' do any damage."

"But a bomb ketch could," I suggested.

"Third place—seein' ye mention it—the fort's out o' proper gun range from the water. Fourth place, there's the ma'shes. The Frinch had them ma'shes diked an' dreened pretty well, I guess, includin' the ma'sh between the fort an' the shore. Arter '55 the dikes went down, an' the *'boiteau* gates rotted aout, an' it's on'y lately we've got onto the hang o' fixin' 'em. Takes time, that does—an' money. So we ain't done much. Consequent, the ma'shes is pretty well flooded at high tide an' mighty treacherous walkin' at low, on three sides o' the fort. Fact is, the on'y way ye can come at the fort is from the nor'ard, along the ridge, same as Monckton did in '55. Smart man, that Monckton. Ef I was agoin' to 'tack that there fort naow I reckon I'd foller his plan right through."

I heard that treasonable suggestion repeated, almost word for word, at Robert Foster's house in Sackville that night. There I met the Cumberland committee and gave them my news. I was anxious to see what sort of men favored the Cause in Cumberland, because so much depended on them. The faces in the light of Foster's kitchen candles were reassuring. These were no sulky ne'er-do-wells at odds with law and order and out for excitement, but steady-going farmers, smelling of the rich Cumberland earth as our Queens County men smell of fish and balsam, lean brown men with cool eyes and hard hands. They had a lot to lose by their devotion to the Cause, and I did not blame them for plying me with sharp questions. I answered them as best I could and studied them at the same time, for here were the men I was to fight beside—Elijah Ayer, Obed Ayer, Nathan Reynolds, Eben Gardner, Will Maxwell, Simeon Chester, Robert Foster—and they represented something like three hundred patriots, all the men and boys in the isthmus capable of bearing arms, barring the Yorkshire immigrants.

I asked about the Yorkshiremen.

Elijah Ayer struck the table with his bony fist. "Michael Francklin planted 'em amongst us apurpose, damn his schemin' eyes. Them and this missionary John Eagleson who's their preacher. The Society for Propagatin' the Gospel sent him out to 'em, and he spends half his time with 'em and t'other half in the officers' mess at Fort Cumberland. Most o' his propagatin' is on behalf o' King George. Ah, the Yorkshiremen are good men, o' course. Good farmers, good workers, good husbands and fathers—all that, I grant ye. But they're on'y three or four years in this country and they dream of England when they go to bed o' nights."

"But they'll not fight against us?" I asked quickly.

"Reckon not," Will Maxwell put in. "They just want to be let alone. Some of 'em signed our petition against the Militia Act."

The door opened, and more men arrived. Their names were not on the committee, but I knew them for the real leaders of the movement in Cumberland. John Allan, who greeted me kindly, and Will Howe, Sam Wethered, Benoni Danks the old ranger captain, Josiah Throop, who had been engineer officer at Fort Cumberland in my father's time, Will Scurr, the unseated assemblyman for Cumberland, and swarthy Isaiah Boudreau, the Acadian who accompanied Colonel Eddy on his first visit to the American Congress.

For them I repeated my message and submitted to the same sharp questioning.

Finally sly old Benoni Danks said through his nose, "What have we got for proof that ye ain't a royal agent, sent here by the governor to stir us into the open so he can hang us all?"

"The proof of my own neck and hide," said I hotly. "I've come to fight beside ye. Put me to the test tonight if ye like. Why wait?"

There was a gleam in his sharp eyes and in the eyes of many another in Foster's kitchen. They were weary of the long waiting and empty discussions.

But Uniacke, who had not spoken before, now surprised me with a sober, "At least we'll wait till Eddy gets here with the Massachusetts troops and supplies."

John Allan spoke, his faint Scotch burr very noticeable in this room full of Yankee accents. "Well said, Dick, lad. Yon fort's in bad repair, true; but there's a couple o' hundred men inside, well armed and ammunitioned."

"Two hundred riffraff from the streets of Boston and Halifax," I scoffed. "And a good half of 'em deserters from the American army."

"That's good reason why they'll fight like devils when the time comes. D'ye think they'll let themselves be taken cold by a rebel force, David? No, I say. And I say No to this notion of attacking the fort by ourselves and now. We may not need the Massachusetts troops but we must have their powder anyhow. More than that, we should have cannon. All else is folly, and I'll have no part in it."

There was no selfishness in John Allan, yet I could not help thinking that his fine farm, Inverma, lay on the Baie Verte Road within two hours' quick march of the fort. And that reminded me. I blurted out, "I must tell you, Mr. Allan, that the Council's offered £100 for your arrest."

The whole gathering gasped, and I watched Allan's blue eyes going bleak and hard and the stiffening of his jaw.

"How much time have I got?" he asked.

"I overhauled a king's messenger on the road and stole and burned the order. But there's sure to be a duplicate in the next postbag for the garrison."

"That might come any time." He turned to the grim men in the kitchen. "So I must go. This is what Eddy foresaw." He threw up his head proudly. "But I'll not go bag and baggage, as Eddy did. I leave my wife and family in your care—as a pledge of my faith in the Cause. I'll come back when I can come with force enough to make our venture good. Until then"—his eyes went to me—"let no one persuade you into a rash move which will ruin all, and for God's sake guard well my wife and youngsters!"

We poured out into the starlit farmyard and crowded about him as he mounted his horse, and "There goes a damned brave man!" said Richard Uniacke.

I sat up late with Uniacke in a bedchamber of the hospitable Foster house. I gave him various news from Halifax, and he said, "You're holding something back, David. Out with it, man!"

I considered a moment. "Well, there's news from Philadelphia. The Congress has declared the American colonies free and independent."

"Phew! Now why didn't ye tell that to the committee?"

"Because," I snapped, "my instructions were to give Cumberland the word to rise, and I'm for fighting and no more quibbling."

"There's more," he said. "Out with it!"

"Well, the Philadelphia news has split the Halifax party. Malachi Salter's withdrawn, and nearly half the others. They're willing to fight the king for self-government but not for utter separation from the empire."

He was silent a minute. Then, "They're right, David."

I gaped at him. "What's happened to you, Uniacke? Only a few weeks ago you were for fighting, come what may."

"But not for separation. Does that sound queer, coming from an Irishman? I'm thinking of this province, David. The other colonies are looking out for themselves. So must we in Nova Scotia. We can't live after the war on the resolutions of a Congress in Philadelphia. Our business is fish and timber and farm produce, and our market's in the British West Indies for the most part and in Europe. And why? Because the other colonies have their own timber and farmstuffs, and Massachusetts supplies the fish. Suppose they win this war and their independence. Think you they'll buy our wares out of sheer love for us? You know they won't! What have they given us in this matter of rebellion? Pious resolutions from the Congress and empty promises from Massachusetts! The back o' my hand to both! They care no more about us than the king does."

'Twas on the tip of my tongue to cry out something of Judas and the silver pieces, hearing this cold talk of trade versus liberty. But I said blankly, "What do you think we should do, then?"

Uniacke leaned forward eagerly. "First let me say this, David. If the Cumberland men rise, with or without help from Massachusetts, I'll fight beside 'em—and the devil with my principles! But suppose no help arrives and our people wisely decide to leave the old gun over the mantelpiece? Then, David, Nova Scotia must bide her time. The other colonies will win their war—their independence. And that'll shock the British nation to the roots. Remember the old Jew in Halifax—what he said? The English people themselves are crying for freedom, for a better kind of government. And they'll get it, just as surely as the Americans get theirs. Only they'll get it by the only road they know, the long road, the road of vote and parliament, without bloodshed. It'll be a struggle. But it'll come. And how will that affect us across the sea? The American affair will force the parliament to take stock of its colonial policy. That means they'll listen less to governors and more to the people. It'll be up to the colonial people then to make 'emselves heard. The good God gave us tongues to speak and hands to hold a pen, and we'll use 'em for all they're worth."

"A game for lawyers," said I contemptuously.

"True! Did I ever tell ye how I started out to be a lawyer, Davy? I spent four years reading law in Dublin. Listen! I'm going to work like an ox on this farm of mine and when I've saved enough money I'm going home, to finish my education and get a law degree. Then for Nova Scotia, to fight the thing out in a wig and gown, if it takes my lifetime. And I won't be alone. There'll likely be sharper tongues than mine. The breath of revolution's in the air. It'll be a strange thing if we can't get some kind of home rule out of it."

"What you mean," I said bitterly, "is that we'll let the other Americans shed their blood for liberty and get our own on the strength of it."

"Begob," grinned Uniacke. "Ye talk like a Boston pamphlet!"

CHAPTER 22

Schemes and Stratagems

I WAS UP at cockcrow and after a stout breakfast of fresh eggs and thick slices of country bacon took horse for the Cumberland Ridge. The road from Sackville followed the upland northward along the edge of the marshes for six miles, then crossed the Tantramar River by a log bridge and turned northeast through the hamlet of Mijik, winding like a thin red snake through a maze of streams and reedy ponds. Along those first six miles were fine farms and orchards looking out upon the broad green table of the marshes. This was the old *Acadien* country, taken over by New England settlers after the great expulsion. The marshes afforded hay and pasturage for big herds of horned cattle, horses, and sheep; hogs squealed and rooted in every farmyard and in newly broken upland, and there were flocks of hens, geese, and turkeys, though why they bothered with poultry I don't know. The marsh pools were alive with wild fowl, rising in dense clouds every few minutes at some petty alarm and settling again with such a quacking and honking as I never heard in my life, not even at our Port Joli, where the wild geese winter from the North.

Past Mijik the road twisted through a district half marsh, half woodland, with long stretches of hoof-splintered corduroy laid down in the boggy parts. Then a log bridge crossed the upper Aulac stream, and the road followed an old French dike to reach the Cumberland Ridge. I noted all this with care, for here was our line of retreat if the attack on Fort Cumberland failed.

The ridge itself was low and quite flat on top and traversed by the Fort Cumberland—Baie Verte Road, with prosperous farms on either hand. There was a settlement called Point de Bute, mostly inhabited by New England folk, and farther toward Baie Verte was the village of Jolicoeur, where a number of *Acadien* farmers lived. All of them, French included, were heart and soul for the Cause.

John Allan's farm, Inverma, lay upon an old French lane at a place called Bloody Bridge, where the French and Indians had ambushed a party of soldiers from Fort Cumberland in the old war. Allan disliked the grim name and had dubbed the place Invermary in honor of petite Mary Patton, the Yankee girl he married, but everyone in Cumberland called it Inverma. It was one of the finest farms in Cumberland, and Allan lived as a sort of backwoods baron, with a number of *Acadien* families as tenants. The big farmhouse, the seven houses of the tenants, the two large and two smaller barns, and various wagon sheds and outhouses made Inverma a little village of itself.

The whole family came out to greet me in the lane, and I was surprised to see Allan himself with his strong arm about Mary Allan's slim shoulders. He had risked another day with her and the children. Mary held in her arms their lastborn, proudly named George Washington Allan, and there were William, John, Isabel, and Mark, whose ages ran from eight to two.

"My hostages to fortune," Allan said, and squeezed his wife's shoulder, and she turned her dark head to him and smiled, with a haunting mixture of courage and sadness. I told him my errand, and he insisted on coming with me, scouting the notion of danger till the post arrived. An *Acadien* farm laborer brought him a saddled horse, and we two rode off toward Fort Cumberland.

The road followed the ridge faithfully past farms and patches of woods, and after an hour we emerged upon a shoulder of cleared land which dropped sharply southward to the spur on which Fort Cumberland stood. The fort itself was hidden from our view by scrub spruce and fir trees in the pastures along the spur. To our right lay the little Aulac stream, a red-clay gash in the green of the Tantramar marsh, and to our left the Missaguash flowed through another green sea.

"This is Camp Hill," Allan said, and I thought of Howe's Camp Hill at Halifax.

"Why 'Camp'?" I asked idly.

"Monckton's force camped here in '55. His headquarters were about where we stand. The redcoats pitched their tents in regular lines along the crest, but the rangers like your father weren't so military and pitched all over the lower slope, wherever they found good lying."

We dismounted and wandered in the pastures, leading the horses. Twenty-one years had gone by since my father camped here with the besieging army, and there was little trace of that bygone swarm; a few faint gutters, grass-grown now, where the methodical regulars had made drainage for their tents, and some shallow pits in the edge of a field which might have been the regimental privies. Mounting again, we rode down the west lane to the fort. This spur of Cumberland Ridge was narrow, but we were screened from the main road on the other flank by the crown of the ridge itself and by the scrub woods which had sprung up in the abandoned French fields. The New England settlers had mostly preferred to farm inland, where the soil was better. At last we stopped and tethered the horses in a thicket and crept afoot to a small clearing in the midst of the woods, where an old log building of some kind had long since moldered down to earth and made rich food for the greedy laurels.

"Monckton's blockhouse," Allan said. "He built it to protect his sappers while they dug approaches for the mortars. Mark it well."

'Twas still possible to follow the old line of the sap, though Monckton's men had filled it in after the siege, and presently we stood on a bushy mound in the woods, the site of Monckton's siege battery, which had compelled the French to surrender the fort. I was thrilled. In this place, exactly located for us by Monckton's careful engineers, we, too, when the time came, would set up our cannon.

We crept forward like a pair of Indians through the thinning trees and came upon the elaborate outworks of the fort, which Monckton had built after he took it. This was what I had chiefly wanted to see. A glance was enough. Nothing had been done here since Monckton's time. The frosts and rains of twenty years had crumbled the sides of the deep fosse, and the earth-filled gabions of the battery positions had rotted and spilled their contents into the trench below. A rank growth of bushes covered the half-filled musket pits, and grass grew in the choked trenches. We were amused to see a pair of soldiers' wives picking blueberries on the site of the central redan. And the scrub trees continued to within easy musket shot of the very ramparts of the fort itself, where the roofs of the barracks showed over the sunken parapet and new shingles gleamed in the sun. Borne on the sea breeze we could hear the tap-tap of Gorham's carpenters at work within. But the green turf of the glacis was seamed with deep, red gullies where the rains of twenty years had been at work; the log revetments had rotted away, and the naked earth had burst out of them like a fat woman out of a split bodice, and the ramparts in consequence had sunk so low that we could see the upper range of windows in one of the barrack blocks. A good rifleman hidden in these trees could put a bullet into the very barrack room.

"Why," I said contemptuously, "the place is nothing but a trap."

John Allan was gazing absently at the union jack, a new one that made a fine spot of color at the fort's masthead, snapping in the sea wind across the marshes. "As it stands now, yes. Of course, Gorham's got two or three hundred men in there, and if he put 'em all to work with mattocks and shovels and axes you'd see an almighty difference in a month's time. If I were in his shoes I'd have 'em at it now, and the

devil with shingling the roofs. I'd have 'em cutting logs for new revetments and making gabions of maple withes and filling 'em with
earth to stiffen and raise the ramparts; I'd have axmen clearing away
these trees right back to Monckton's old outworks, ay, and beyond,
to give a field of fire from those same outworks. Monckton knew the
fort's weakness—the approach along the ridge from its rear; that's how
he took it and that's why he made those outlying trenches and batteries
afterwards. If I were Gorham I'd hire every man and boy in the countryside to work on those outer trenches."

"Who'd he get?"

"The Yorkshiremen."

We returned to the horses, but as we led them toward the lane there
was a faint clop-clop of hoofs in the red dust, and we halted in a
clump of young maples. The hoofs approached slowly along the lane,
as if the riders were admiring the great sweep of marshland to the
west. Then they came in sight, and a hammer began to beat in my
head. The rider on the near side was an officer wearing the green
jacket of the Royal Americans, and the woman beside him wore a
green riding habit that cast my mind back to St. Aspinquid's feast.
Their faces were turned away from us. The woman sat her horse facing
the open sunlight of the wide green marsh below—but she was seeing
very little of the marsh. She was leaning backward on her saddle,
held and supported by the man's arm. His knee was being squeezed
between the horses, but he did not seem to mind, for her head was on
his green breast, and her wide hat dangled from her hand. They halted
—and small wonder, for 'twas an awkward way to ride or to make
love.

"Naughty man!" she said, and laughed, a familiar tinkling that cast
my mind back to the gossipy chaise at St. Aspinquid's feast and again
to the coach at the tail of Gorham's marching column on the Great
West Road. It was the cool voice of the coach. She lifted her head
with its golden waterfall of curls and turned her face up to him, laughing softly. Her eyes were large and blue, and her face was handsome
in a sharp-chinned high-nosed English fashion. In town, with that
yellow hair turned white with pomatum and flour and stiffened and
piled high, she would be like a dashing captain of Grenadiers mas-
querading in feminine clothes, and at sixty she would be a witch out
of a book. But here in the speckled shade and sunshine of a Cumberland lane she was fetching enough, and the breasts that promised to
burst out of her bodice in this posture were feminine enough, and her

low, challenging laugh was invitation enough, that I scarcely blamed the man for his swiftly bent head and his long, thirsty kisses.

His jacket and his white buckskins marked him as an officer of Gorham's, though he wore any gentleman's thrice-cocked hat. I was amused and even a little envious. No young man in hard health, foot-loose and fancy-free, could have witnessed that encounter without fancying himself in the actor's shoes.

But these idle fancies gave way to alarm, for it occurred to me that no man can make love very long on horseback, and there was an inviting patch of greensward in the shade of our maple clump. I could hear the fellow's low, urgent voice, and again that Eve's laughter of hers, and then her clear voice, "La, Jack, what a hurry you're in of a sudden! In Halifax you'd scarcely notice me after you up and married that vivacious little provincial. Now look at you! Ah, you men, you men! In town the country girl seems sweetest. But in the country air . . ." "Oh, come!" protested the fellow angrily. "This coyness don't sit well on you, Chloe. What's my marriage to do with it? After all, you've a husband yourself."

"And a very jealous one, darling! In Halifax you and I were well lost for an hour or two, and no one the wiser. But here . . . no. No! What with the regiment and its wives, the carpenters, the sutlers, and the rest, there's several hundred pairs of eyes in Fort Cumberland and nothing to watch but each other's behavior. D'you take me for a silly slut of a private's wife, to romp with a man in the shade within two musket shot of the fort? You're too bold a soldier, Jack, my dear!"

"Bah!" snapped the man irritably. I knew him then. It was Helyer, of course.

"Look here, Chloe," he burst out, "d'you mean to tell me you're going to play the virtuous wife all the time we're at Cumberland? We may be here till the end of this damned war; who knows? We'll certainly be here the coming winter—and have you any notion how deadly dull that will be? Four hundred people, counting the soldiers' wives and brats, cooped up together in that earth-and-timber dungeon behind us for six long months on end! Winter's a siege in these parts."

"La, Captain, but sieges can be broken. There's such a thing as a sortie, I think. A ride abroad on fine afternoons, for instance. And if I should chance to be driving alone on the Baie Verte Road and should stop at a discreet farmhouse for a sup of mulled cider and a chance to fling off my wraps and toast my toes by a private fire, and you should happen to be there, my Jack . . ."

"Where?" he cried eagerly. "Where?"

She sat up in the saddle and put on her blue hat, with its broad, shady brim and gallant feather, and her fingers began poking and patting at her curls and back hair; in short she began to show every sign of a woman about to fire a telling shot and be off.

"That's for you to discover—and arrange, my dear. Maneuvers are a soldier's business. You lay the ambuscade, and if it's tempting enough and well concealed, why, I'll probably walk into it, poor weak creature that I am."

"Ah!" said the man, brightening.

"But don't you take me for granted, Jack Helyer!"—tossing the yellow curls and turning her eyes to the marshes—"I'll not be taken for granted, by you or my husband or any man. You shall campaign for me, my bold captain."

"Observing the rules of war?" he asked.

She gave him a look and a gurgling laugh that would have set a hermit scampering after the village goose girls. "Variety's the spice of life, Jack darling. And where's the woman that don't like to be taken by storm once in a time? But mind, my palisades are sharp."

"Ah," returned Helyer gallantly. "But such charming ramparts . . ."

"Pouf!" she said, and gave her horse a lick of the crop at her wrist and was off at a gallop toward the fort. Helyer watched her out of sight around a bend and turned his horse purposefully toward the north.

"Damn!" I swore, as his hoofbeats died. "He'll spend the rest of the day laying his pretty ambush on the Baie Verte Road—your road, Allan. We'll have to watch our way back. That man knows me."

Allan's eyes blazed, and all his instinctive Scotch piety was in his harsh, "Och, what a lewd blight upon our decent countryside, lad! This garrison will be the ruin of all morals if it stays here long. The story's an old one here: first the French and then the English, the soldiers and their women depraving the countryside with their loose talk and ways. And when garrisons go they leave their dregs behind. Oh, some are good men, but most are broken subalterns, time-expired sergeants, corporals, and drummers, squatting in huts beside the roads, drunken, lazy, good-for-nought scoundrels, living on their half pay or God-knows-what—and whining to Halifax about their loyalty and their past services to the king, whenever there's a magistracy or some other petty post to be had. That's been one of our grievances in Cumberland ever since the French war."

"Who was that woman?"

"Mrs. Fanning. Mrs. Commissary Fanning. Husband's too busy

swindling his king on the garrison's fuel and supply contracts to keep a good eye on his wife. At least, that's what I'm told. Some say Fanning's well aware of his wife's gallant ways and that he condones it, ay, connives at it—so long as she spreads her favors in the right quarters. This Captain Helyer's got influence in England of some sort—or that's the tale—and a thieving commissary someday might stand in need of it. Knavery! Roguery! The army's rotten with it. No wonder the king's cause stinks!"

We returned to Inverma at a cautious amble, keeping a sharp watch ahead, but we did not see him.

That night Allan made ready for his journey. I was staying for supper and bed, planning to ride with him in the morning back to Sackville, where he could board a shallop going down the bay. But his dress was strange for a man going asea. When I saw the moccasins and the leather thigh leggings, the gray hunting shirt, the knapsack, powder horn, bullet pouch, and musket I exclaimed, "I thought you were going to join Eddy at Machias?"

"I am," he said calmly. "But I'm going through the woods. I want to sound the Indians between here and the St. John before Eddy undertakes a march around Fundy. I go to Baie Verte in the morning and I'll take a canoe there for the Indian camp at Cocagne River. From Cocagne I'll make my way through the tribes. By traveling light and pushing hard I can do it in ten days."

"Let me come with you," I urged suddenly. "There'll be nothing to do here till the Machias force arrives. That may be a month or more."

He considered. "No," he declared firmly. "I want you here, David, at Inverma, for a number of reasons. One's selfish—I want to feel that Mary and the children aren't left alone. The tenants are all right, of course; they worship Mary. But they're Acadians after all—while you're one of us. You see, if Eddy's failed to get the support that Massachusetts promised I intend to go on and have it out with the Congress or Washington or both. I've a sound plan for the campaign in Nova Scotia. It calls for three thousand men, well armed and equipped, and at least eight vessels to transport the siege train and supplies. We don't want another Quebec failure here. With a force that size we can rouse all Nova Scotia to the American flag, and together hold the province against any attack. Anything short of that will mean defeat and the ruin of every man who has put his faith in the Cause. I drew up my plan long ago, in all detail, and sent it to the General Court of Massachusetts and to the Congress. They've had good time to study it and to see to their side of the compact. I intend to see that they carry it out."

"And if they don't?"

"There will be no revolt if I can help it."

"Well, I'll stay," said I, reluctantly.

"There'll be plenty to do, David. The fort. Watch every move of Gorham's. See how far he carries the repair of his earthworks—never mind the barracks. My guess is that, being a fool and thinking of nothing but his winter's comfort, he'll spend all care on the buildings and let the ramparts and outworks go hang. See what stores he gets and what reinforcements. Study his men; there are plenty of American deserters amongst 'em, and there may be some who'd give us a hand from within. Well . . . all that, I leave it to you. You've got a smart head on your shoulders if you're a son of Matthew Strang's." He hesitated. "There's something else, David. I'm an outlaw with a price on my head from the moment that proclamation reaches Fort Cumberland. I'll be out of reach, so they'll confiscate Inverma and all that's mine. I wish you'd bear a hand in moving Mary and the bairns to her father's place. If our battle prospers all will come right. If it doesn't you must find some way to get my family to Machias. My neighbors won't be able to help, for they'll be proscribed, every one of 'em—their names and sympathies are too well known. You're a stranger in these parts and you'll have a chance to move about after—I mean if we're defeated."

"We're going to win," I said stubbornly.

CHAPTER 23

The Letter

CUMBERLAND WAS MARVELOUS to my eyes after a life on our rocky south shore, where the woods crowd down to the sea. Here was rich red earth and wide views over the marshlands, all shimmering green and gold under the August sun, the great tides rushing up the creeks into the heart of the land, the mighty cone of Shepody Mountain, blue and afar across the broad mouth of the Petitcodiac, the snug farms by the isthmus road, the screaming wild fowl of Tantramar. But chiefly it was the fort and the knowledge that I was treading in the footprints of my father and his rangers, walking upon history, ay, and knowing and exulting that history would be made here soon, and I should have a part in it.

I dressed like any laborer on Allan's farm, in hodden breeches with leather-patched knees, a linsey shirt and coarse country-wool stockings, and moccasins of ox hide. My black mane hung loose to my shoulders, and my face was soon dark as an Indian's, for I worked in the fields with Allan's tenants and got my hands as coarse and broken-nailed as theirs. Whenever one of Gorham's soldiers came sauntering along the dusty road, listless in the heat, I was ever ready with a hail and would fetch a drink of cold water from the spring down by the marsh and sit in the wayside grass to hear his tale. All had a tale. The Royal Americans hated this place and longed for Halifax, or better still their homes in Massachusetts, England, Switzerland, Germany, and the dozen other countries of their origin. From that point 'twas easy to steer their tongues to matters within the fort. I learned how to do it with a word—but never a question—dropped carelessly into a gloomy silence.

I saw Captain Helyer frequently riding past. Once or twice I gave him a bold Good Day and twitched my forelock respectfully, and he gave me a nod and a glance—no more. That gave me confidence. I knew from the soldiers that my brother was not on the garrison roll, and no one else in Fort Cumberland could recognize me but Fear. I saw her sometimes riding with one or two other ladies up the red road from the fort of an afternoon and got out of sight while they passed. I was amazed to find that I could look upon her with something close to indifference. The old sick yearning was dead. I could even look upon the affair of her husband and Mrs. Fanning with a cynical amusement. That gallant pair had found a rendezvous at the house of one Maultasch, a drunken old soldier left behind by Bragg's Regiment after the French war. He and his hag of a wife were glad enough to play pander to such well-paying lovers, and the house stood off the Baie Verte Road in woods and could be reached by two diverging lanes, admirable for the purpose. A guinea would seal the Maultasch lips as a penny seals a dead man's eye, and I think no one in the fort knew where the pair conducted their amours. But all the garrison saw the horns on Fanning's brow, and 'twas a common jest in the barracks that the money Helyer won from Fanning at whist went somehow to pay for Fanning's cuckoldry.

I kept a close watch on the fort from the thin woods by the old

north outworks. Nothing was being done to the ramparts and bastions.
After the buildings in the fort were made weatherproof, Gorham
turned his carpenters to those which flanked the parade ground outside—a couple of barracks, a canteen, and the quarters for married
officers; these and the parade ground were enclosed in a stout new
palisade, pierced for musketry. South of the palisades, where the ridge
sloped down to the Missaguash marshes, stood a number of wooden
houses built by the swarm of sutlers with Monckton's army in '55.
Some were in fair repair, and the Fannings lived in the best of them.
Two or three middle-aged officers and their families took up residence
there also and made gardens behind running down to the marsh edge.
Upon the southeast side, where the ground sloped down to the Aulac
marshes, were a number of huts put up by married soldiers in Monckton's time and occupied now by Gorham's married men. Altogether a
fair-sized village clustered on the slopes south of the fort, and it had a
busy air, with everyone getting ready for winter—as if winter were the
only foe to worry about!

I was tempted to venture into the fort with a load of firewood to
sell but put the notion aside. There was too much at stake to risk
recognition and capture now. Instead I sent François, with fish to
peddle or baskets such as the Indians made for the fort trade—and
with instructions to use his eyes. They were keen eyes, and afterward
François would squat on the beaten red clay by Inverma's well and
scratch little diagrams with a stick.

I made journeys afield, too, on foot, by horse, and often by canoe:
to Westkok, to Minudie, to Amherst, even to Point St. Mary over
Shepody Bay, and, compass in hand, I came to know every road and
path about the isthmus and the basin and made a map for future reference.

August passed quickly in these activities, and in the early September days I noticed a new coolness in the westerly wind, a reminder
that fall was here. Still, it was pleasant to lie on the green side of Camp
Hill and watch the little wind squalls bending the marsh grass like
cat's-paws on a sea and cloud shadows racing across the Tantramar
from Sackville, blue in the distance westward. The shadows ran over
the marshes lightly, crossed the Aulac stream at a bound, and swept
up the slope and over the ramparts of Fort Cumberland like a con-
quering army. I thought of the army now gathering at Machias. But
now came a pair of Indians, Passamaquoddies, in a canoe, with a letter
that shocked me out of my dreams for a time.

Machias, August 13, 1776

My dear David,

Please shew this scrawl to Mary. It will witness that I am safe and well, tho' much fatigued. I reached this place this morning, having seen and talked with the Micmacs, Malicetes and Passamaquoddies on the way. They will say nothing on which way they will fight. 'Tis a matter of gifts with them, and neither the English nor the Americans have given them enough to sway their judgement. We must remedy this, and quickly, for these tribes are masters of the whole country between Fundy and Quebec. I have felt this all along, and more than ever now that I have seen Eddy.

What a state of affairs here! Not a single Continental soldier, nor a Massachusetts soldier for that matter, in Machias, after all the hopes held out to us. Boston now promises a quantity of arms and ammunition, nothing more. Colonel Eddy has no force but a parcel of woodsmen and others, 25 or 30 at most, gathered here on the promise of plunder in Nova Scotia. I spent the whole afternoon in argument with him and his wild men, and could do nothing with them. We parted on harsh terms; their preacher, Mr. Lyon, called me the politest name and that was Faint Heart. They are bold and able men and I don't doubt will fight well in their fashion, but such an undisciplined handful can accomplish nothing but a destructive raid at best, and at the worst may persuade our people into arms and then leave them in the lurch, as Arnold left the Friends of America in Canada.

I can't express the agony of mind in which this leaves me; but my course is clear. I go on to Boston tomorrow to urge my plan upon the General Court, and if I have no success there I shall go on to the Congress and if possible General Washington.

Yours &c.,

JOHN ALLAN

P.S.

Shew this letter to Uniacke, and let him decide whether or not the Committee shall see it.

I found Uniacke swinging a scythe in his grain patch, stripped to the waist and dripping sweat, a tall, strong figure looking nothing like a Dublin lawyer, and his pretty child wife Martha standing at the rail fence watching him with pleasure in her eyes. He threw down the scythe and came to me wiping his brow with the back of a big brown hand.

"You're a stranger, Davy."

"I bring strange news," I said.

He read the thing, with his bold eyebrows going up and down, and he whistled at the end, staring off across the marshes.

"What'll we tell the committee?" I demanded.

"Nothing!"—promptly—"If we tell 'em the worst they'll probably receive Colonel Eddy with musket shots, and there's an end to everything. And now"—rather curtly—"I'll get back to my mowing."

All Cumberland was busy harvesting, and there was an air of anxious haste about the way men swung their scythes and reaping hooks. A sloop had come to Westkok from the St. John, with some wild tale of an American army on the march for Cumberland. All were eager to get their crops in, to free their hands for the fighting. Colonel Gorham heard the rumor, of course—the Yorkshire preacher John Eagleson hurried to the fort with it—and sent a party under a subaltern to establish a watch on the Shepody side.

Also Mr. Commissary Fanning began to buy cattle all over the district. He got none from our people, but the Yorkshiremen sold readily enough, and every day we saw men and boys driving bullocks down the red road to the fort. Some of our men stopped them along the road and tried to argue them out of "making blood money out of Nova Scotia's struggle for liberty," and some of the drovers turned back. But not many. To have stopped them by force of arms would have brought a column of troops out of the fort, and with our scant supply of powder we should have been swept into Gorham's custody like cattle ourselves.

All this went on in the peaceful autumn sunshine, with cranberries ripening in the marshes and new flocks of wild fowl coming out of the North to add their outcry to the din of Tantramar and apples hanging ripe in the orchards and the wild rosebushes laden with red hips and Michaelmas daisies and goldenrod blooming everywhere along the dikes and beside the lanes and thistledown blowing on the wind and flocks of sparrows busy in the grain stubble. Across each lovely evening sky flapped the crows in their ragged squadrons and the wild fowl in the marshes, settling after the day's clamor, talked to each other in queer half-human calls and mutterings; and after dark the northern lights burned all along the black horizon toward Baie Verte and the Gulf, flickering and sending long tongues to the very zenith and sometimes rolling along the treetops like a forest of bright spears in movement. Like an army on the march! Often, sleepless, I watched them from my chamber window. They were brighter here than I had ever seen them on the south shore, and there was more color; the flames were all hues like the flames of a driftwood fire. I was romantic still, for all the bitterness I had known and the disillusionment that was past and might yet come.

I saw in these wonderful wildfires a portent of victory.

CHAPTER 24

A Woman Scorned

BUT THE STRANGE and sinister calm in our affairs went on. Even the cool west wind stopped blowing for days on end, and the wide marshlands steamed under a sun that belonged to August, not September. An Indian, a Malicete this time, brought a curt note from Colonel Eddy. He had advanced as far as the St. John and lay at Maugerville, awaiting guns, flints, and ammunition from Boston. We were to be of good heart but lie low.

We were ready. The crops were in. Some of the Tory families had shut up their houses and removed to the hovels just south of the fort, and others were packed and ready to go as soon as the first shots were fired. And Gorham sat in the fort and did nothing. Nothing! To be sure he had, through Fanning's purchases, gathered a herd of beef cattle in the small fields south of the fort. And he had become anxious at last about his fuel supply. Hardwood is the only proper fuel for a Cumberland winter, cut and sledded the previous season and split and dried in a summer's sun. Gorham had arrived in June, and the Cumberland Ridge had long since been stripped of its hardwood as far back as the woods of Point de Bute, a long haul for green wood on wagon wheels. Fanning, driving about the countryside in gig, a slight, middle-aged, sunken-eyed, soft-talking image of avarice, had kept the garrison's cooking fires supplied through the summer, but now that the cool weather was here, windy Fort Cumberland needed brisk fires in all its clustered chimneys. Our Yankees refused Fanning's offers with contempt, and the Yorkshiremen he hired had to bring their wagons around the marshes and cut wood about the Jolicoeur lakes, dragging each log painfully over the bare ground to the road and mourning the cost in broken harness.

With these efforts Fanning managed to keep the fort supplied and to gather slowly a reserve in a field at the marsh edge south of the fort. But it was small; when December brought the real cold weather those meager piles would vanish like snow in May. I watched that field (Gorham dignified it with the title of Garrison Fuel Yard) with a growing exultation. Here was a sure key to Fort Cumberland, whether Eddy brought cannon or not. We could shut off the ridge to Gorham's woodcutters and ultimately freeze him out. Captain Helyer's words to naughty Mrs. Fanning rang in my mind like bells: "Winter's a siege in these parts."

This notion gave me patience for Eddy's long delays. October came, with the maples red and gold by the streams; the birches and beeches turned yellow, and then the poplars burned and shimmered like golden torches in the sun.

We heard that Howe had defeated General Washington on Long Island and now occupied New York, but all that was far away; bad-enough news, but news from another world. The fall gales came and stripped the leaves from the hardwoods with a swoop, and now all the countryside was brown bush and black, bare trees, and the marshland a dirty gold of withered grass; and there was ice in the pools of a morning, and dead leaves blew along the roads.

Now the nights were cold, and Gorham's people kept indoors, and I made ventures with François along the edge of the marshes past the fort, scouting amongst the ramshackle houses and barns to the south of it, peering and eavesdropping. Sometimes, bold against the stars, we saw the lone sentinel on the flagstaff bastion, wrapped in his blanket for want of a greatcoat and shuffling and stamping to keep the frost out of his broken shoes.

Sometimes amongst the houses people burst suddenly from one lit doorway to another, complaining loudly of the cold, and sent us diving into the shadows. We sheltered in a pigsty once, and once in a privy. 'Twas amusing and, I flattered myself, useful, for I came to know every nook and corner of that queer wooden slum below the fort and learned much regimental gossip outside the frosty candlelit panes. They were expecting a sloop with the garrison's winter stores and a few more troops. Half the officers were at odds, ay, at sword points, for there had been at least three duels in a lonely part of the marshes, and Captain Helyer had pinked an ensign over some matter involving Mrs. Fanning's name. On the subject of a rebel invasion the gossip was divided; most said it was a mare's-nest: the rebels had suffered too sharp a lesson at Quebec to venture another campaign on the verge of winter, and as for the local Yankees—pooh!—they hadn't enough powder to fill a snuffbox. Besides, they wouldn't dare!

Fortunately for our purpose the full-moon nights were cloudy, with specks of snow blowing, but on one of those nights I got a shock, at a time when all was quiet and the hour getting on for midnight. Most of the houses were dark and sleeping, with the wisps from dying fires blown from the lips of the chimneys by a cold west breeze. Here and there a pane was yellow, and up the slope inside the palisade gate I could see the candle guttering in the guard lantern.

As I slipped, silent in moccasins, past one of the houses the door was flung open, and in the lit rectangle of the doorway a stout woman called Good Night and added, "Run, my dear, it's bitter—Brrr!" The door closed, and I heard the bar being dropped for the night, and in that moment a swift person in a cloak ran full tilt into me. 'Twas a woman, with her capuchin's hood drawn forward against the cold, and I could not see her face. I stumbled aside, muttering some apology, sure that I was taken for one of the sutlers or some other camp follower.

But at that moment a prank of the night wind tore the clouds apart, and the full moon turned the whole place light as day.

The woman was Fear Helyer.

"Who are you?" she said imperiously.

I muttered something and began to edge away, but François had run up behind her, silent as a shadow, and I saw the moon gleam on the blade of a lifted tomahawk.

I cried out sharply to him, "*Jegulaase!* [Away with you!]" and caught the girl's cloak and dragged her aside. I expected her to scream, and so did François, for he stood his ground making little preparatory strokes in the air at her back.

Instead she gasped, "David! David Strang! What are you doing here?" I motioned fiercely to the Indian, and he slid away into the blue shadows.

A rule in my military studies had said that attack was the most satisfactory form of defense. I said rudely, "First, what are *you* doing abroad at this hour?"

She jerked her cloak aside and I saw a basket on her arm.

"Sitting up with a corporal's wife in childbirth—not that it's business of yours!"

"And does Captain Helyer know he married a midwife?"

"Captain Helyer"—her voice was level and cold as the night—"does not concern himself with his wife's comings and goings."

'Twas on the tip of my waspish tongue to ask, "Nor the goings of other men's wives?" but instead I said, moving off, "Well, it's nice to have seen ye, ma'am."

She raised her voice in a sudden "Stop!" I stopped and glanced uneasily uphill toward the palisade gate. I had a notion to bolt for safety, but my way lay along the narrow slope past the ramparts, and the moon had turned the marshes to a silver sea. "What do ye want?" I said roughly.

"You're here on some deviltry, David—you and that Indian. What is it? Tell me, or I'll call the guard. I can yell as loud as any Indian if I want. I could scream the whole garrison to arms, David Strang, and well you know it."

She could, too—and she would. I knew that. Captain Jack, whatever his behavior, had done nothing to that spirit of hers.

"What!" I said desperately, "and make yourself a laughingstock for the garrison wives? Think—think of your husband, ma'am. He knows I'm an old flame of yours. Here you are, and here am I, outside the palisades together, at midnight—and you with some cock-and-bull story about a corporal's wife in childbed. What," I added brutally, "would Mrs. Fanning say?"

She caught her breath at that. "What do you know about Mrs. Fanning?"

"Everything," I said.

She stared at me for a long time and swayed a little, or perhaps it was only the wind in her cloak. Her eyes were enormous, with great black pupils in the queer light. "You know everything," she said, "and you can talk to me like that, David?"

"I could say more and worse," I said harshly. I wanted to hurt her. I hated her. She was part of all the bitterness, the one and indivisible bitterness.

"Go!" she said, and went on saying Go, with her voice lifting and crying.

I went and in the blue moon shadows found François and crouched beside him watching the running figure, cloak blowing, up the path to the palisade gate. She knocked; a voice challenged, and the heavy wooden gate creaked open, and a most unmilitary sentry stood there with a lantern, his head and shoulders muffled in a shawl. A word, and she passed inside.

I pointed and said in Micmac, "There is a way we too can go when the time comes."

"Ayah!" said François.

Chapter 25

Colonel Eddy

Upon an afternoon late in that long October of '76 I rode over to see Uniacke. I had lost none of my old worship of him, though he had been pretty short with me lately.

"Where's Eddy?" he demanded at once.

I shrugged. "He must be drawing near. But there's no word."

"What's Gorham doing?"

"Warming his toes in the fort."

"Humph! An example to us all, Davy boy. I don't believe a word of Eddy's tall talk. A wild, hell-for-leather sort o' fella at the best o' times; and now, with this rebellion bee in his bonnet and his farm confiscated by His Majesty, he'll do or say anything to raise a dust."

"He's been made a colonel in the Continental army; the Congress must have some faith in him."

"The Congress!" He was straddling a chair, resting his forearms on the back of it and glooming at me with his chin on his big work-bitten hands. "I've so little faith in Colonel Eddy, the Congress, the General Court of Massachusetts, and the rest, including this so-called 'army' from Machias, that I've taken a contract to cut and deliver twenty thousand barrel hoops before the 20th of November. Hoops, my boy! There's money in 'em—thirty-seven pounds ten shillings, no less. I'll have to share it with my Tory father-in-law, of course—he's with me on the contract. But that's what I think of Eddy's army. Hoops, hoops—'good and sufficient hogshead hoops, twelve to fourteen feet long'—according to the contract, and a penalty recoverable in the Halifax courts if I fail to deliver. So there ye have it—hoops, hell, or Halifax, and hurrah for old Moneybags Uniacke!"

"I don't see how you can talk about money at a time like this," I said hotly.

He shut one blue Irish eye and regarded me with the other. "Davy, tell me, have ye ever earned an honest dollar in your life?"

That took me aback. "I never had to. My father . . ."

"Ah!"

"My father let me do pretty much as I liked—and I liked hunting. But look here, I studied navigation and would have been doing well in the codfishery if His Majesty's navy hadn't interfered. Since then I've been more hunted than hunting. Besides, I earned some kind of living in Malachi Salter's store."

"Ye mean Malachi hid ye in his store and gave ye pocket money. And why? Because ye aimed to be a rebel officer."

"Is that a disgrace?"

"No, no, Davy. That's ambition, a fine thing—like me wanting to be a lawyer. But I've noticed the military mind runs to a fine scorn of money and the people who have to dig for it. It's all right, no doubt. A soldier's mind should be on higher things. I've observed they like their pay and allowances paid promptly though—and what in hell would you fighting cocks live on, Davy Strang, if it wasn't for people like me?"

I was in such a rage that I would have struck him if he hadn't sat there, chin upon hands, regarding me with the one cool eye.

"Well," I blustered when I could find tongue, "I've done with idling, my friend. I'm off!"

"Where for?"

"Down the Bay to find Eddy."

"A wild-goose chase!"

"A hunter could ask no more. Good-by to ye—and your damned hoops!"

Some Micmacs were wintering west of Sackville in the little valley called Frosty Hollow, and François with the amiable Indian instinct for his kind had gone to stay with them. I rode there by a moccasin-worn trail and brought him on to Westkok, trotting at my stirrup. There we got a canoe and some scraps of food and set out. It was nearly sundown, the sky cloudy, with a chill breath of sea wind up the Bay, and soon after we passed Minudie it began to rain. François gazed wistfully toward the wooded shore, but I kept our bow to the lop, paddling fiercely. I had my anger at Uniacke and all these witless frustrated weeks to work off somehow. We kept on in the dark and rain until the rising sea forced me to seek the loom of the land. We got ashore somewhere about Cape Maringouin. There was no dry wood to be found in the dark. We turned the canoe over a couple of stumps and sat under it, knee to chin, through the long miserable night.

I was cramped in the morning, and the effort of lifting the canoe down to the water put a painful kink in my back that took a hard morning's paddling to work out. Dinner was a chunk of bread, gnawed as we went along. The rain had ceased, but a thick fog—what sailors call a Fundy feather bed—lay on the water and hid the land. This was awkward, for the heavy set of tide out of Shepody Bay carried us over to the Chignecto shore, which loomed suddenly on our left hand, a steep and forbidding mass that scared us both into a yell. The cliff gave back our voices in a hollow and immediate echo. François looked round at me uneasily.

This Chignecto country was a weird place to the Micmacs, the ancient haunt of Gluskap, the great god magician, who created Minas Basin to make a pond for his giant beavers and used Blomidon for his wigwam and made the first man out of an ash tree—ay, and changed certain men back to trees again when the whim struck. A god whose queer humor dragged the Fundy tide up forty or fifty feet twice daily, just to fill his fish weirs, and let it go again with a rush that scared even His Majesty's navy.

We turned away from that ominous shadow in the mist and fought our way across the ebb until the opposite shore loomed. It was then far into the afternoon. I knew we must have been carried well down the bay in our wanderings, so we went close in, exploring, while I tried to identify the land on a scrap of chart I had. We had no luck for two hours. Then the land curved away northward, and we knew the cape for Point Enrage and went ashore for the night. A pine stump yielded dry kindling, and we made a good fire, a white man's fire as the hunters say on our south shore—"An Injun makes a little fire and wraps hisself all round it; but a white man builds a big 'un and sets back a ways." We sat back comfortably from our big 'un while the salt pork boiled in the kettle. We cut some brush for dry lying and slept tolerably well while the fire burned; but toward morning a flood of rain descended upon us, and we crawled under the canoe, soaked to the hide, and waited grimly for daylight. The morning light was a sort of visible cold that penetrated to the bone. François wanted to make another fire and boil meat, but I would have none of it. I was too sore in mind and body now to care for anything but movement. Besides, an Indian would stop and boil kettle every two or three hours if you let him.

I was determined to keep along the coast to the St. John, to seek out Colonel Eddy and tell him what we thought of him; my head was primed with ironic remarks thought out in the long, sleepless hours. We launched the canoe and paddled stiffly northward along the foggy shore and found ourselves fetching a slow compass around Salisbury Bay, for the land trended westward and then south again. Toward evening there was a stir of air, and the mist began to thin overhead.

We held on in the teeth of an increasing westerly breeze, with the fog opening and shutting until at last it cleared in a sudden sweep, and we saw the sun low over a headland which I knew must be Point Wolf. But we had no eyes for sun or land just then. A small procession was coming around the shoals off the point, four canoes and four whaleboats under oars, all full of men. François called back to me, "Those are Malicete canoes."

Friends or foes? The gun of Louisburg lay empty in the bottom of our canoe; I had not loaded it for fear of wetting good powder in this weather. The presence of Malicetes argued that these were part of Colonel Eddy's force, recruited on the St. John. But Michael Francklin had been busy with offers of alliance to the Malicetes, and these whaleboats might contain a group of Tories from the St. John mouth, flying with some won-over Malicetes to warn Fort Cumberland of Eddy's approach.

They had seen us and came straight on, the canoes ahead. François looked longingly toward the woods, but I determined to let them come up with us and, if they were Tories, brazen it out. The canoes held four Indians each, and as they approached I recognized with a start the two chiefs I had seen at the feast of St. Aspinquid, old Ambroise and Pierre Tommo, sitting on skins in the bottom, with two young bucks paddling. All wore caribou-hide hunting shirts, buckskin leggings, and moose-hide moccasins, and as they drew near, Ambroise with great dignity put on the gold-laced hat I had seen Michael Francklin give him months before. He was warming his old bones with a blanket wrapped about him.

We greeted them in Micmac fashion: "Kway! Kway!" right hands uplifted in sign of good faith, and in answer the two older men fluttered lean brown hands like winter leaves. The young paddlers watched us warily. None of them were painted.

"Who are you?" Pierre Tommo demanded in Micmac, eying François.

I invoked the only name I knew that might impress him with our worth.

"A son of The Hawk."

It amused me to see the start it gave the younger men as well as the old. I had not realized how far the grim figure of my father had become a tribal legend.

"My name is Young Hawk," I added proudly.

They gabbled amongst themselves, all but Ambroise. The venerable old chief of the Malicetes, with all the world's wisdom in the lines of his leathery face, stared at me with bright, small eyes. Without lifting that gaze he muttered, "Here is indeed The Hawk as I knew him in the time long past. An evil omen. Blood flowed always where The Hawk came."

"This time it shall be the blood of thine enemies," I said boldly.

"An omen," he repeated, as if he had not heard.

The whaleboats were coming up. In the first I counted fifteen men. A man in a raccoon-skin cap stood at the bow, fumbling with a little mast or staff, and suddenly a bundle of bunting broke out and straightened, snapping in the evening breeze. 'Twas a flag I had never seen. There was some sort of device in the upper corner next the staff, and the rest was a series of horizontal stripes, red and white alternately, like nothing so much as a piece of striped bed ticking.

I looked at the men, a rough lot, some bareheaded, some in fur caps, some in red nightcaps, one or two in carelessly cocked hats; there were hunting shirts, some of gray hodden, some of buckskin, and three or four short blue jackets such as seamen wear. Most of them were bearded, and they were all ages from fifteen to fifty. From the midst a figure arose in white breeches and a blue coat faced with buff and wearing an empty sword belt. He was a man of middle size with a hard, blue-shaven jaw and a pair of reckless green eyes.

" 'Vast oars!" he snapped, looking at me very hard. The whaleboat came alongside under its own way, and two of the men reached over and caught the gunwale of our canoe.

"Who are you?" said Blue-and-buff. "And where from?"

"Japhet Moreton," I answered promptly, "late of Halifax, this province. This Indian's my servant. And you?"

He threw out his chest, and I saw his men winking to each other.

"Jonathan Eddy," he announced in a sonorous voice, "colonel of the Continental Line and at present commanding the army of liberation in Nova Scotia."

The other whaleboats drew up. I counted swiftly. There were sixteen Indians in the canoes and about sixty white men in the whaleboats.

"Where's the rest of the army?" said I.

"Why d'ye want to know?"

"Because," I snapped, "I'm just from Cumberland, where our people have waited the past several months for a sight of it. My name's rightly Strang—David Strang, a member of the Committee of Safety for Cumberland."

His small hard eyes bored into mine. "Ye lie. I'm a Cumberland man myself and never saw ye in my life."

"I arrived there in July, after you'd gone."

"Name the Cumberland committee, and tell me what each looks like."

I went through the catalogue, grinning like a schoolboy given a familiar verse to recite, but before I was finished there was a hail from one of the other boats and I lost all interest in Jonathan Eddy.

"Davy! Is that you, Davy boy?"

It was Mark—Mark in a greasy, raccoon cap and a checkered seaman's shirt and soiled duck trousers, with his big arms thrust through holes in a clumsy waistcoat of bearskin. His face—as much as I could see of it, for he was black-bearded to the cheekbones—was sunburned to the color of blackstrap molasses, and a pair of outlandish brass rings gleamed in his ears.

One of the oarsmen in Mark's boat passed me an oar tip, and I pulled our craft over to her gunwale, ignoring Colonel Eddy as if he had ceased to exist. I jumped into the boat, and we fell into a bear hug, laughing and cursing affectionately and thumping each other's backs. The other boats and the Indians watched this with great interest, and Colonel Eddy sat down on his thwart, a little glumly, it seemed to me. But he asserted himself in a powerful voice.

"Ye seem to be known in our company, young feller. Fall in with us then. And give way again, lads. I don't like the look o' this shore for the night's camp. We'll go back around the point."

CHAPTER 26

A *Council of War*

INSIDE POINT WOLF was a small cove, with a brook flowing into the head of it. There we cut brushwood for beds and bivouacked about half a dozen brisk fires, with a cold wind from Canada stirring the fir tops overhead. We made a good supper of lobscouse—potato and turnip and broken ship biscuit, with a few chunks of corned meat, all stirred up together in the pots over the fire—and washed it down with mugs of hot grog. The men pulled out pipes and lay beside the fires, smoking and talking. There was some singing later on, and a rawboned fellow with a fife rendered "Yankee Doodle" and "Green-sleeves," with great spirit, I thought. At one fire some sailorly fellows, English by their accents, danced a hornpipe and then got some of the Malicetes to war dancing. Well primed with rum, the savages shuffled and stamped and howled up at the stars, and the sailors sat back and clapped and hallooed as if the whole expedition were a show.

Eddy's landsmen—Maine woodsmen, if I know chalk from cheese—were not so amused, and there was some muttering around the other fires.

Mark and I drew aside into the shadows, with François crouching like a happy dog at our outstretched feet. I said at once, "Let's have your story—all of it."

" 'Twould take too long," Mark said, and took the short clay out of his bearded mouth and spat. "But I'll give ye the hang of it. After that night in Market Square I was put in a tender for Boston with some other pressed men and transferred to a frigate on the station there. They made me a topman, and I did my duty cheerfully enough, watching a chance to nip off. But none came till we went to Jamaica. We anchored in Kingston Roads, and our captain reckoned the sharks were guard enough, but I swam ashore in the dark for all that and got away into the country.

"A light brown woman gave me shelter and food and a share of her bed for a spell, but I got tired of it and made for the coast again, hoping to find passage home in a Nova Scotia fish trader. On the Spanish Town Road I walked right into my old lieutenant, driving into the country for a booze with some planters, and his niggers had me down afore I say Boo. I got two hundred at the gangway for that escapade; I'd ha' got more, but good topmen were scarce. We came north and cruised for a time along the Massachusetts coast to annoy the privateer nests east o' Boston.

"I was one of an armed party that landed near Gloucester one night, aiming to burn a schooner at a wharf. We ran into a swarm o' rebel minutemen; the lieutenant got a ball in the head, and most of us were killed or captured. The rebels offered us liberty if we'd join 'em, so we did—we were all pressed men with no love for His Majesty's service. Well, we shilly-shallied about for a time, playing at soldiers, country-style; then we heard a yarn about a force gathering at Machias 'for the liberation of Nova Scotia,' and I pulled foot. Those other English lads came with me. It's all a lark to them, o' course, and these Machias fellows talk o' high plunder up there when the fighting's done. A rough lot, but what d'you expect, with a leader like Eddy?"

"They're rough, all right."

"Rough! When we got to Machias, Eddy had twenty wild Maine woodsmen, no more. But he'd got some powder and flints and a few spare muskets from Boston and said he'd wait no longer for the Massachusetts troops. Said he was going to drive the English out o' Nova Scotia with what we had. I told him he was mad. But fool or not, the man can talk and, damme, he convinced me in half an hour. Said the Nova Scotia people were all for the Cause, and we'd roll up an army as we went along, like a snowball in March—specially after we took Fort Cumberland. So we started. Picked up seven men at Passamaquoddy and got another twenty-seven at Maugerville on the St. John. His talk of an army was bosh, o' course; he'd no supplies for an army, let alone arms. So he took the pick o' the men in each place, the daring fellows, the active hell-for-a-holiday sort that'll fight best on a hard lay. Eddy talked over the Injuns there too. I argued against it, for there's no knowing what'll happen when ye stir up those devils, and going into Nova Scotia along of a swarm o' Malicetes 'ud turn the people against us. But something else decided the matter. The Injuns were willing enough, but taking the warpath on the edge o' winter's a serious matter with them—who's to look after their families? In the end we brought only the two chiefs and fourteen picked warriors. Eddy figures to get 'em yelling about the fort at night, to put the fear o' God into the garrison afore he makes an offer o' protection by his 'American troops.' It may turn the trick, at that. Anyhow, here we are, seventy-two men and a Continental colonel that don't care a continental damn. How many can ye raise in Cumberland?"

"That depends," I said cautiously. "There's three hundred ready to fight if there's any chance o' success. But they're expecting an American army. D'ye mean to say this is all Eddy's got?"

"Oh, there's another lot o' Machias men to come along later with Captain Shaw. Maybe there is an American army to follow. I don't know. What d'ye think of our chances as they stand?"

"Offhand, I wouldn't give sixpence for 'em. But the garrison's a poor lot, badly clothed, and Gorham's an old woman. A bold stroke might do it. Hell, it's got to do it! I'll say this: if we can take Fort Cumberland with its garrison, the province is ours."

Mark looked over to Eddy's fire, a little apart from the others. "Come over and tell the colonel, Davy."

We went over, and I got my Cumberland map out of my knapsack. Eddy and a group of his leading spirits (all with the rank of captain, except that one was a major) gathered about while I spread the map in the firelight. I went over the principal points and described Gorham's preparations and the state of the garrison.

"You seem to have given this business a lot o' study," said the colonel.

"Why not?" I said acidly. "I spent the whole summer and fall there, waiting for you."

"What's your plan?" he said testily. "You must have a plan. All young men have plans."

"Well, to begin with, Gorham's got an outpost on the Shepody side, watching the Bay. We must surprise that post and not let a man get away. It can be done."

"And then?"

"Go up Shepody Bay to Memramcook."

"Why not up Cumberland Basin?"

"Because Gorham's expecting a vessel with winter supplies, and it's sure to have an escort. You can't risk being caught with these boats in the Basin. Besides, you might be seen from the fort, and then Gorham 'ud know what was afoot."

"Ah! But how do we get to Cumberland?" snapped Eddy.

"Cut a path through the Beech Hill woods from Memramcook to the upper Sackville settlement. It's not more than twelve miles in a straight line, and that'll bring us out to the marshes well up the Tantramar. There we'll take the road around the marshes through Mijik and reach the Cumberland Ridge at Point de Bute. We'll appear before Fort Cumberland out o' nowhere."

"And then?"

"Storm the fort that same night. Why wait? You've got no cannon."

"Phew!" said one of the captains. "You're a bold 'un."

"Aren't you?" I asked promptly. "It's storm the fort or sit down and wait for Gorham's fuel to give out. Ye could do that. He's short o' fuel."

"And s'pose he sallies out against us?" Eddy asked.

"He won't—the kind of man he is, with the kind of troops he's got. If he did, it'd be a little Bunker Hill anyhow. The ground slopes upwards northeast o' the fort, and we've got trenches ready-made— Monckton's old outworks. Gorham hasn't touched 'em; they're overgrown with bushes, and he's forgotten they exist or doesn't care."

"What are his chances o' help from outside?" one of the Machias captains asked.

"It'd have to come by sea if we send a party to Partridge Island to block the ferry landing from Windsor. And shipping's mighty chancy in the Bay at this time of year. But all that's assuming that Gorham gets word to Halifax. If we keep our eyes peeled we can catch any messengers out of the fort. And Halifax won't be expecting any communication from Fort Cumberland till spring. That gives us a free hand for the winter."

It is strange how a man arguing for the sake of argument will convince his own doubts, if not the doubts of his hearers. I know that I convinced myself there and then of our chances of success. And my conviction seemed infectious, for all the captains and the major thumped me on the back and swore we would be in Halifax for Christmas. Men came running from the other fires, and Colonel Eddy went down to his boat and brought back the queer flag. He bade me take a corner of it in my hand, and I obeyed, wondering.

"Count those stripes," he said.

I counted seven red and six white. "Thirteen," I declared.

"One for each colony represented at the Congress. This, Strang, is the American flag. We're going to add the fourteenth stripe and make the thing complete."

The men cheered, and the Indians, without knowing what it was all about, whooped and yowled. I looked at the flag again and saw the union jack in the upper left corner. I suppose my brows lifted, for Eddy laughed and said, "It's copied off the flag that Washin'ton flew at Cambridge. I got a couple o' Machias women to make it."

He threw a swift glance over all the faces, the faces that looked so fierce now in the light of the fire. "Course, since they declared Independence, this thing don't belong any more." He poked a finger at the crude union in the corner. " 'Tain't decided what's to go in its place. Stars, some think—one for each colony—but nobody seems to know. Should we rip it out, think you?"

I said, "Ye can rip it to hell for all I care. But"—I seemed to see Uniacke's face and Malachi Salter's—"maybe you'd better leave it in for a time. Till we're in Halifax, anyhow."

"Ah, Halifax! Fetch up another keg from the boat, lads, and let's drink. To Halifax. Christmas at Halifax!"

We filled our battered tin cups and drank that toast with a will and gave three cheers into the bargain. "And now," Colonel Eddy said, "take ahold o' the flag again, Mr. Strang. D'ye swear to uphold the cause o' Liberty, now and forever, foul or fair weather, good fortune or bad, so help ye God?"

It sounded like part of a marriage service, and I mumbled "I do" as sheepish as any bridegroom.

"To the death?"

"To the death!"

Colonel Eddy cleared his throat. "By virtue of the authority vested in me by the Congress of the United States of America, I confer upon you, David Strang, the rank of lootenant in the army of liberty in Nova Scotia. Shake hands with him, boys, and let's have another drink all round."

We shook and drank and shook again and drank again, till my finger bones ached and my head sang. We sought our blankets at last, and I was glad, for I was nigh dead for want of sleep. But sleep came only fitfully. The savages, livened by the raw liquor, whooped and danced in and out amongst the fires, brandishing guns and hatchets, far into the night. In the intervals of wakefulness I cursed them separately and together, with something of my father's spleen.

When we set off in the morning Mark brought his little canvas ditty bag and a musket and powder horn to our canoe, and we made three from that time on. The whaleboats hoisted their sails to the cold west wind and used their oars as well. In the clear weather we went up the Bay famously and could have made Shepody before dark. But there was Gorham's outpost to be taken first, so we went inshore a few miles past Cape Enrage and waited for sunset. The post was on a small hill looking out from St. Marys Point, with a good view up and down the sea approach to Cumberland. In the dusk, with muffled oars and thole pins well wrapped in rags, we crept past the tidal flats to the point. The Indians were eager to go on ahead and do the whole thing, but Eddy kept them in hand. The soldiers were keeping no night watch; in fact we found no one on the hill at all and discovered them all below in the house of a Tory named Peck. A yell and a rush, and we were inside, and a shot fired into the floor was enough to set them crying "Quarter!" They numbered thirteen, under a Lieutenant Walker. We made a jovial meal of their rations and lay there the night and at dawn set out along Shepody Bay, with the soldiers and Peck sitting sulkily in one of the whaleboats. It was the 30th of October, with a keen wind blowing out of the Petitcodiac Valley and snow squalls piling in black-and-white masses across the sky.

The *Acadien* village of Memramcook lay a good ten miles up the river of that name, and the people saw us coming a long way off and gathered curiously on the bank. Eddy's boat took the lead with the striped flag snapping from the bow staff and the colonel himself standing beside it wearing Lieutenant Walker's sword. The villagers spoke little English, and we had less French, so the two Malicete chiefs had to interpret for us, a comic state of affairs. I looked at the *Acadiens* with interest. These were the tough hard-fighting Frenchmen who had resisted and survived the great expulsion of '55, a very different lot from the docile folk of Grand Pré and elsewhere down the Bay. It was while fighting these men in '55 that my father received the wound which crippled him for life. They had the alert, springy step of woodsmen and, by the look of their farms, were more fond of the hunt than the plow, though they had very few guns amongst them.

Colonel Eddy announced that he had come to liberate Nova Scotia and invited them to join him in the taking of Fort Cumberland. Cunning old Ambroise interpreted, and I have often wondered what he said. It must have been something magnificent, for their faces lit; and from aftergossip I suspect that he told them what all the Malicetes and Micmacs then believed—that our small force was the forerunner of a great Yengee army, numerous as the leaves of the forest, which would drive the English out of Nova Scotia, out of all Canada, and turn the country back to the king of France. At any rate, the men and boys of Memramcook capered and yelled and demanded arms and a sight of the enemy. They would have made a fine reinforcement for our slender force, but again the lack of muskets obliged Eddy to select a few and bid the rest stay home.

We set out at once for Sackville through the woods, with our precious kegs of rum and powder and ball fastened securely to the backs of borrowed horses. Colonel Eddy had a chest and a tent. There was no other baggage but what we carried in our knapsacks. I had surveyed the route over the Beech Hills in September, and now there was no concern but to follow my old blazes and cut out a tree here and there to make way for the pack horses. I took charge of this work with a party of axmen, and we emerged upon the upper Tantramar marshes in late afternoon, with the meager winter sunshine casting long blurred shadows from the grass clumps over the gray ice of the pools.

Lest some of the Yorkshire folk try to get word to the fort, Colonel Eddy dispatched a small party to watch the Mijik Road and another to the mouth of the Tantramar. Then in the sunset light we marched down the long, straggling street of Sackville village, led by Colonel Eddy with the flag bearer and our grinning Negro drummer, and the rest of us following two-and-two to make the column as long as possible, with the Indians bringing up the rear. 'Tis a droll picture when I think of it now. Troops in small numbers are impressive enough when they wear bright uniforms and pipe-clayed crossbelts and carry their muskets at an exact slope, with all the gaitered legs moving together to a good march tune and all the boots crashing down on the road. We were a walking rag bag, with guns held anyhow or slung by a strap to the shoulder; our music was the one lone drum, whose skins had gone damp and flabby in the passage up the Bay, so that the busy Negro's sticks produced little more than a hollow whisper, and we marched all out of step with our moccasins—even the English deserters wore moccasins—padding dully on the hard red road. A sorry show, and I remember how the people ran out of their gray-weathered clapboard farmhouses and stood under the gnarled, bare apple trees by the road to watch us as we passed.

Most of them were silent, but some cried out, "Who are ye?" and we answered fiercely—lest anyone smile—"The army of liberty!"

That night was a stormy one in more ways than one. Snowflakes were specking the panes as we sat down to supper in our various billets, and afterward when we stumbled up the dark road to Sam Rogers' house for a meeting with the committee we had to fight our way through a wild snowstorm blowing across the marshes. In Rogers' big kitchen the hearth blazed cheerfully, and Ma'am Rogers had lit half a dozen candles, a great extravagance in frugal Cumberland. The place was half full of men, with more arriving, red-faced and snow-crusted, some by horseback from as far away as Point de Bute. Most of our meetings had been held in kitchens, and that seemed right. Where else should a revolt of the people be hatched? But there was a chill in this one that the bright hearth could not warm. Somehow, without reasoning, without a word spoken except in the way of greetings, we had ranged ourselves in two groups—Colonel Eddy, his officers, and the more ardent Friends of America on the one hand, and upon the other Richard Uniacke and a majority of the Cumberland committee.

Eddy in his headlong way came to the point at once. "Well, gentlemen, here we are—and there you are, warming your backsides at the fire. I hope it's not a chill in your spines? Who'll fight for the Cause?"

Everybody began to talk at once, each trying to outvoice the other, like a flock of crows in a pine wood at sundown. At last old Mr. Scott stood on a chair, and the angry voices made room for his.

"Gentlemen, this isn't a town meeting selecting a hog reeve; it's a council of war. For the Lord's sake, let's have some order and reason in a matter which affects the lives and properties of us all."

"Not to mention your freedom," put in Colonel Eddy loudly.

"Suppose, Mr. Eddy, ye tell us what ye hope to accomplish."

"In a word, Liberty." He paused, to let them taste the word fully, running his shrewd eyes over their faces. "Ye know how things stand in Nova Scotia as well as I do. The province is held under the tyrant's heel by nothing more than a corporal's guard at Halifax, a handful o' young Scotchmen playing at soldiers in Windsor and this force o' Gorham's at Fort Cumberland. Ye know Gorham; ye know what sort o' men he's got. Ye know the weakness o' the fort. One stiff attack by determined men and all's over. Then for Windsor and the Halifax Road."

He paused, and Uniacke spoke. "Jonathan, that's not the point. Weak as Gorham is, his garrison's got cannon and plenty of muskets and ammunition if nothing else, and they're sitting in a fortified position."

"Bah!" ejaculated the colonel.

"Don't bah me, Jonathan! I'm Irish and don't like the sound of it. And if ye think ye can bah down the ramparts of Fort Cumberland as Joshua did the walls o' Jericho, you're getting your tactics out o' the wrong book. That's what Montgomery tried to do at Quebec."

"He very nigh did it, Richard."

"He's under the grass roots just the same. Gage tried to do it at Bunker Hill too. I'm told the American earthworks there were a joke and defended by a squabbling mob of citizens—but they shot the hell out of a disciplined English army that attacked 'em." He raised his voice angrily. "Where's your siege train? Where are the American troops? Where are your supplies?"

"On the way," returned Eddy coolly. "Cap'n Francis Shaw's to bring 'em along in fifteen days' time. In short, we're an advance guard. But what are ye going to do—sit on your rumps and let Massachusetts men do your fighting for ye? That don't sound like my old Cumberland friends. That don't sound like men that wants freedom, men that's born and reared here in America. That don't sound like the men who signed the petition I took to the Congress. What's wrong? What's happened? Maybe I'm to the wrong meeting—ye *are* the Friends of America, ain't ye?—or is this one o' those Yorkshire immigrants' Methody love feasts?"

"Damme . . ." Uniacke began hotly.

"No bad language, Richard, please," cut in the colonel piously. "Besides, you ain't one of us, speaking strict, Richard. Let my old

Yankee friends, the pioneer settlers o' Cumberland, speak for 'em-selves."

"We've not changed our minds," Eben Gardner said. "Our mind's to fight, provided we get support. That's the question—the support. All we can see is a bunch of Machias woodsmen and Maugerville farm-ers and a handful o' French and Indians, with nothing more'n a mus-ket apiece and what they carry on their backs. Ye say the Massachusetts troops are on the way. All right. Suppose we wait for 'em?"

Colonel Eddy's eyes were bright and fierce. "Now, Eben, man, Eben! What way is that to talk? Freedom's a thing ye've got to fight for, not wait for. What'll the Massachusetts folk think of us? What'll the Congress say? What'll General Washin'ton say? Look . . . this is our chance to show we're worth support, ay, and fit to run our own affairs when fighting's done. Yonder's Fort Cumberland, the flint for your steel. Ye can strike a spark there that'll set the whole province aflame like a fire in dry slash. Men are waiting for it, praying for it, everywhere from Cape North to Cape Sable. Listen! We'll be in Hali-fax by Christmas. We're going to do away with the government o' the king—no more import duties on the things we need, no more Shipping Act, no more press gangs, no more bloodsucking Tory of-ficials, no more governor that we must kowtow to like a Chinaman, no more Church of England with a finger in our affairs, no more assembly stuffed with Halifax merchants—none o' that any more. We're going to govern ourselves with town meetings as we always did afore town meetings were forbidden—and a conference in Halifax once a year."

The man could talk. Some cynical little devil in my mind suggested that he must have had good practice with these arguments at Machias, at Passamaquoddy, and on the St. John. But practice or none, he knew how to play on these hardheaded Cumberland farmers and he made a convincing military figure in their eyes, with his Continental uniform and Lieutenant Walker's sword, with one foot on a chair, leaning for-ward, now open-handed, now shaking a brown fist, now dropping his voice to a whisper, now raising it to a yell—all in the nasal New Eng-land speech that was their mother tongue—the accent that made Uni-acke sound a foreigner.

"S'pose Gorham beats us off—what then?" asked a sober voice.

"Then we'll fall back on the—ah—main body."

"With our families? And there's our farms and things—all we have in the world."

Colonel Eddy straightened suddenly. There was a metallic gleam in his eyes. I had a notion that he had been waiting for that very remark.

"Ah!" cried he. "Got something to lose, ain't ye? I had a fam'ly too —I had to hustle it out o' the country! I had a good farm—I had to leave it to be confiscated! What was good enough for me ought to be fair enough for you! Bah! America's going to win this war. And when it's won, after all the struggle and suffering, things'll go hard with them that failed to play their part. Sooner or later the American army's going to throw the English out o' Nova Scotia—with your help or without it. If ye fail me now"—he filled his broad chest with a mighty breath—"I'm duty-bound, as an off'cer o' the Continental army, to report to my superiors"—stabbing a finger toward the west—"that Cumberland's hostile and giving aid and comfort to the enemy. When our army advances ye'll have to take the consequences, the kind that any Tory has to take."

He paused. Then, with all the deliberation in the world, "But sup-posin' our army decide not to advance, supposin' they withdraw till this district's come to its senses—there remains the Injuns."

The last word, softly spoken, fell on the men in the room like a thunderbolt. There was a silence that prickled the skin. I knew what these men were thinking. They were thinking of their empty pow-der horns and scattered, defenseless settlements, of the old bitter hate of the Malicetes and Micmacs, the memory of the old cruel frontier wars whose tales were still told in every farmhouse by the shores of Fundy. Suddenly I knew why Eddy had been at such pains to bring along the Malicete chiefs and their party of picked warriors and why he had arranged for Chief Charles and a group of Micmacs to join him here in Sackville. Their presence in the village gave his words the force of a war whoop. It was well known that Washington had been treating with the tribes.

"Who'll help ye then?" asked the soft, mocking voice. "Gorham —that timid old fool? Halifax—will Halifax send troops to keep the In-juns off a people who've refused to take the oath of allegiance to the king and openly sent representations to the Continental Congress?"

"Ye wouldn't set those red devils on us!" Mr. Foster gasped. "Not you, Jonathan, not you!"

Jonathan shrugged his buff lapels and looked sad. "'Tain't a matter o' setting 'em on, gentlemen. It's simply a matter o' withdrawing pro-tection—the protection o' my troops and influence, and I include the forces now in reserve to the westward. Why, the whole Malicete nation wanted to take the warpath with me! I let a handful come, for the sake o' their feelings. But not I nor any man can answer for the tribes if our army withdraws from Fundy Bay. All I know is, they've made a wampum to kill the enemies of America—and that includes all who won't fight for America."

Uniacke's voice was at my ear. "And this is your doctrine of Liberty, Davy?" I set my mouth and nodded, without taking my eyes off Eddy. I did not like his methods, but Liberty couldn't be finicky about her instruments—look at Sam Adams!—and Eddy's principle was right; we in Nova Scotia must show our faith by fighting as others had done. Anything short of that was shabby and dishonest.

The committeemen consulted together in low voices—all the voices were low now. The shadow of the tomahawk hung over the meeting. You could almost see it. Men spoke slowly and in turn. There were long, hard-breathing silences. We burned Mistress Rogers' candles far into the night, with the snowstorm swishing against the frosty panes and the fire, forgotten, sinking to coals and then to ashes, so that a chill crept through the kitchen and through our flesh to the bones. At last, with the hall clock striking four, the matter was put to a vote. To fight or not to fight? The Yeas carried it with twenty votes to twelve, and we uttered a cheer together that woke the house.

Uniacke's voice had been firm amongst the Nays. Colonel Eddy turned to him now. "Well, Richard, we've often talked of liberty, you and me, in times gone by. Are ye going to stand aside now and see your neighbors fight for it?"

"Not I!" said Uniacke. "I still think you're mad, and we should wait word from the shoemaker if not from John Allan—our proper leader, Jonathan, with all due respect to you. But let it go. Since it's fight, we'll fight together. That's our only salvation now. And now let's get to bed and sleep while we can."

CHAPTER 27

We Take a Prize

JONATHAN'S FAULTS did not include a lack of energy. On the very evening of our arrival at Sackville he had sent a party of the Machias men to Westkok to secure boats. And the following morning I was sent there with a reinforcement of Sackville men and the English sailors. The storm had blown itself out, but we made hard going of the eight miles down the west bank of the Tantramar and around its great bend to the little settlement of Westkok. There I found trouble.

The Machias men had seized a trading schooner from Annapolis and were busy helping themselves to cider and apples and to a quantity of English dry goods, which were strewn all over the deck. Her master, a tall man in a towering rage, came to me as I marched in at the head of my little troop.

"Who the devil are you?" he roared.

"Lieutenant Strang, of the army of liberty in Nova Scotia." It rolled off my tongue very easily. "And who are you?"

"John Hall's my name, and yonder's my schooner, with your damned army taking liberty with everything aboard. I'll have somebody's hide for this! I am a Friend of America, damme!"

I boarded the schooner and ordered the men to pile everything in the cabin and was told to go to hell. I sailed into them at once with musket butt and fists, with young 'Lije Ayer and some of the Sackville men at my back. The English deserters stood aloof, arguing that a prize was a prize very loudly. There was a merry scrimmage for a time, but we had the best of it at the cost of some black eyes and bloody noses, and in half an hour I was able to tell Friend Hall that his schooner and goods were intact. But it was a bad start for our enterprise. The men of Westkok, who had been strong in the Cause, now held aloof, and we had to keep a watch lest they take their boats and warn the fort of our presence.

The weather turned soft, and the snow went to water under a cold southeast rain, followed by a dank fog that lay over the whole Basin and shut off our view of everything. On the 5th of November Colonel Eddy arrived on horseback leading another troop of Cumberland men, amongst them Benoni Danks, the old ranger captain, whose farm lay in the very shadow of Fort Cumberland. Eddy was in high spirits, and we foregathered that evening in a Westkok farmhouse over a couple of candles and a keg of rum. Somebody remembered it was Guy Fawkes Night, and we all laughed, seeing how like a clutch of conspirators we were. Things went well, Eddy declared. "We've got two hundred men under arms—their own weapons, o' course, such as they are—and should have three hundred by the twelfth. I've marched the main body to Point de Bute. They're quartered in the houses and barns at Inverma."

"How is Mrs. Allan, and her family?" I asked quickly.

"All well. Colonel Gorham sent out a party to search for Allan, but the family weren't molested. The soldiers keep close to the fort."

"Does Gorham know we're here?"

"Only that a party of rebels is somewhere in the district. He sent a boat to Shepody with supplies for his post there, and o' course that Tory woman told what happened."

"What's Gorham doing?"

"Unloading stores. The supply schooner came in the morning after we took the post at Shepody. She must have passed us in the night, escorted by H.M.S. *Juno*—a narrow squeak for us. The *Juno's* gone, and now we must make sure that Gorham gets no word out to recall her or to warn Halifax."

I fished out my cherished map. "Then first we must send a party to seize and hold the ferry landing at Partridge Island. That'll cut Gorham's one sure communication with Windsor and Halifax. I'd send some of the Machias men. They'll be out of mischief there and will put up a stout fight if the need comes."

"Do that. And now there's the schooner. Tell him, Benoni."

Captain Danks thrust his sly old face forward. He had fought all over this region with a company of rangers in the old war, had wreaked some memorable slaughter on the *Acadiens* and Indians, and was at the siege of Quebec, and later at Havana. "Gorham's fatigue parties are makin' slow work of unloadin' that schooner. She's lyin' in Cumberland Crick, below the fort, and they have to tote the stuff along a dike through the marsh. They've taken out a four-month supply o' flour and peas but no pork or anything else. There's a sergeant and twelve men left aboard for a guard each night, and a fatigue party comes down from the fort the first thing every mornin'. Now if the weather holds thick—which it will—we've a chance to slip a party over there by boat in the early mornin' and take the schooner where she lays. She's out o' gunshot from the fort, and we could work her out o' the crick in the fog afore the garrison's proper awake."

"And there," said Eddy, eyes gleaming, "is a winter's provision for our army, and ha' done with these petty requisitions from the farms. There may even be powder aboard, though I doubt that. They'd take that out first, and anyhow Gorham brought enough to fill the fort magazine when he came."

"Let me take the party!" I begged.

Benoni looked at me doubtfully; then to Colonel Eddy, "Let him go if he wants. But put Zeb Rowe in charge. He knows his way about the flats in the dark."

We set off well before dawn, thirty men in all, in three boats under muffled oars, steering by Zeb's instinct and a few quick peeps at a compass by the light of a lantern under a tarpaulin. The tide was nearly out, but we had a stiff row against the last of the ebb, increased by the flood out of River Hebert after the rains. 'Twas a weird sensation in the fog and darkness. The boats kept in line, with each painter fastened to the stern ahead lest we get apart in the murk, and we seemed to be standing aground, with the ebb rippling past. But we moved right enough. The channel runs fairly close to the edge of the Tantramar marshes, and we got in to the rim of the marsh flats, disturbing the waterfowl, who rose in unseen flocks and filled the night with their clamor. We sheered off hastily and after much wandering came by good luck upon a tall stake rammed into the edge of a flat.

"This marks the channel up the crick," whispered Zeb. "We must foot it from here. The schooner's layin' high and dry further up."

"Hold on," said I. "If we take the schooner now, and there's a shot fired, we'll have the garrison down on us before there's water to float her. We must wait here till the tide's on the flow. It can't be long."

So we waited, in a dour silence, realizing suddenly how desperate was our enterprise. If we lost our way on the mucky flats in the fog and dark we should be overtaken and drowned like a basket of kittens by the forty-foot tide. And if the schooner's guard beat us off we should be caught between their muskets and the rising water, with no choice but surrender. It was still too dark to see the water. We had to feel for it with our bare hands, measuring its distance from the lip of the flat. 'Twas an eternity before we found it rising. Then it came quickly, and all about us and far behind us sounded the whisper and chuckle of the flow.

"Now!" Zeb called softly.

We set out, twenty of us, the rest staying to keep the boats in charge as the tide rose. At the first step I sank knee-deep in the muck, a bad beginning. We floundered on, Zeb in the lead. Sometimes the footing was fairly good, no more than ankle-deep, and we thought we were approaching the firm shelf of the creek; but this was followed always by a plunge that took us to our calves or to the knees, and there were little runnels and holes left full by the old tide, into which we plunged to the waist. The water was like ice, and as we wallowed along, holding our muskets high, it seemed to me the schooner's guard must hear the very rattling of our teeth. We must have covered three or four hundred yards like this. I think to this day that we'd have missed our way altogether and perished miserably, if the sentry on the schooner had not heard the splashing of our feet.

He challenged suddenly. The voice came from the darkness at our left, and we made for the sound at a blundering run, moved by fear of the tide as much as anything else. Of all danger give me the dangers of daylight, on land or sea; this affair betwixt earth and water in the clammy November dark gave me a chill at the heart that I do not like to think of, even now.

We could hear the fellow thumping on the cabin scuttle to arouse the guard. I suppose he did not like to fire his piece and arouse both guard and fort, lest it prove a false alarm. Zebulon Rowe and I reached the vessel thirty yards ahead of the others. She was sitting on her keel, wedged firmly between the wet clay cheeks of the creek, and loomed suddenly out of the fog, a high black shape against the first illusion of daylight. Zeb and I could reach out and touch her bilge with our musket muzzles. While we stood thus, staring up her sheer side and wondering how we should get aboard, a hand dangled a lantern over her bulwark, and the bulwark was lined with pale faces peering, not down at us but over and past us into the dark, where the rest of our party floundered.

Zeb and I put musket to shoulder, aiming at the face behind the lantern. We had to tip our heads well back to sight along the barrels.

"Halt!" the fellow bawled into the fog. "Halt or we fire!"

Zeb called up to him sharply, "Move a hair and ye're a dead man!"

'Twas comical to see that dim row of shimmering faces turn and stare downward, as if jerked by a string. They were more or less blinded by the fuzzy radiance cast by the lantern but they could see our musket muzzles well enough. The faces remained, open-mouthed, bewitched, and bodiless like a row of tobies on a dark shelf. Now our others were pattering up, and I could hear the click of their gun cocks behind and all about me. I doubt if a single pan was dry after that long wallow in the fog, but the face above the lantern said, "Don't fire, lads, for God's sake! Who are ye?"

"The Continental army."

"Well, you've got us—got us handsome."

The daylight was increasing now. So was the tide. It was nearly up to our knees. These fools of soldiers could have shot back at us or simply dropped behind the bulwark till the tide swept us off our feet. The schooner's side was like the wall of a house. But the lantern bearer said hastily, "Drop your guns, men." There was a convincing thump and clatter on the deck. My arms ached from holding that rigid aim, and the clutch of the cold water on my legs was painful.

"Chuck us down a rope," Zeb called up easily. "Not you," he added, looking along his barrel at the sergeant's pallid face. Down came a rope. I slung my gun and caught it and hoisted myself out of the water and mud with an effort that stretched my bones and after another breath I went up hand over hand, helping myself with the thrust of my knees against her side. On deck I found a dozen soldiers grouped about the sergeant and the lantern, some in green jackets, some in the nondescript coats and breeches I had seen the Royals wearing all summer. Two or three looked at me in a surly fashion, and their eyes slanted to the guns on the deck, but now Zeb was coming over the bulwark with a hatchet in his teeth, and Will Eddy's fur-capped head popped up behind. The soldiers stood back, hands in waistbands, and glumly watched the rest of us come aboard.

We ordered them below. The tide was coming with a rush now, and the fog thinned so that we could see both banks of the creek.

"There'll be a breeze in a few minutes," I said. "Let's get sail on her."

With twenty pairs of hands on the halyards it took little time, but we made a great noise, what with the stamp of feet and the dry screech of blocks and parrels, and we kept looking over our shoulders toward the fort, still hidden in the mist. By this time we could see our boats and beckoned them in. They came under the schooner's stern, and we passed a cable out to them for towing and were making the bitter end fast when we heard footsteps coming along the marsh dike from the fort.

"Down!" spat Zeb. We lay flat on the deck, listening. A voice hailed. I peered through one of the scuppers and saw three men standing on the edge of the clay berth. I recognized them; Captain Barron, the veteran of Bunker Hill who was now engineer of the fort, Mr. Eagleson, the S.P.G. missionary who was acting chaplain to the Royal Americans, and a green-jacketed corporal.

We rose and covered them with our muskets—as surprised a trio as I ever saw.

"What's this?" Barron snapped.

"You're prisoners of the Army of the United States of America— including Nova Scotia," said I magnificently. "Come aboard!"

They looked longingly over their shoulders into the mist, but there was no help there. We gathered them in.

Barron was on his way by boat to his father's manor at River Hebert, with Eagleson, intending to bring back the old gentleman to safe-keeping in the fort. The corporal was carrying a dispatch for Hali-fax. We opened it gleefully and found Gorham's agitated scrawl addressed to General Massey at Halifax:

"This is to inform you that a Rebel Army is now in Cumberland from Massachusetts, has captured my post at Shepody and lies now across the ridge on which this Fort stands, cutting my only communication by land. This latter information came to me by Mr. Moses Delesdernier a loyalist farmer, who came in with his cattle before the rebels closed the road. He is uncertain as to the rebel strength, but says the men of Cumberland are flocking to their standard, and that they mean to have the Fort and march upon Halifax. I sent word to the Yorkshire men in the district to come and join our defence, but only 8 or 10 have come, and they brought their entire families, a great drain on our provisions. Fortunately the provision vessel is here and I shall have her discharged in another day or so. I have armed 15 carpenters who were working on our buildings. This brings my force to 251 all ranks, less the 13 captured at Shepody. But I have many sick, and others of uncertain temper, and must pray you to get relief to me in the quickest manner.

Yours &c., &c.,
Jos. GORHAM, *Lt. Col.*"

Zeb read it aloud and laughed in Captain Barron's face, but the mention of Mr. Delesdernier saddened me. That good old man had cut himself away from his family for the sake of his Tory principles. His son-in-law Richard Uniacke was in the rebel ranks; so was Louis Deles-dernier, and young Frederic had gone to Massachusetts to act as John Allan's aide.

But now came another sound of feet along the dike. We drove the new prisoners below, and this time hastily reprimed our muskets. Again we lay behind the bulwark, and the men in the boats astern crouched below the gunwales. Again the puzzled hail, the sudden array of muskets held by wild muddy men, and again the "Don't shoot! For God's sake, don't shoot!" This time the chorus arose from a ser-geant and sixteen men without arms—the fatigue party coming to un-load stores.

We took them aboard and shoved them below with the rest. We were in high humor, and Zeb jested that we should lie here until we had the whole garrison, tolling them in as a fox on the shore tolls ducks. Humor aside, I had a warm feeling that this astounding luck was a forerunner, that all our plans would prosper. At one stroke we had the schooner, still half-laden with supplies, and we had taken off Gorham's muster roll thirty-five officers and men, including his chaplain and his only engineer.

The morning breeze came without warning, a damp draft that rolled up the mist as a housewife peels a quilt from a bed. The schooner shuddered and bumped gently. I sprang aft and yelled to the boatmen to start towing. All eyes were on the fort. 'Twas farther away than I had expected; there appeared to be a good mile of marsh between us and the palisade. No sign of alarm up there. The smoke of morning fires curled peacefully from the clustered chimneys; the flag stirred damply over the northwest bastion.

"They reckon the guard's just hoisted the sails to dry 'em," chuckled Zeb.

As he spoke there was a flash and a whiff of smoke from the Prince William bastion. We saw the ball splash harmlessly in the marshes and heard the delayed thud of the gun. It had not been aimed at us. Mark, in charge of one of the towing boats, shouted and pointed toward Westkok. In the offing were Hall's schooner and a number of boats coming straight for us. Alarmed, I thought Hall had turned Tory after all his protestations, but a shift of his helm showed Colonel Eddy's striped flag at the gaff. This the fort had seen.

Our prize was moving now, stern first, under the jerky efforts of the oarsmen. Now the fort gunners transferred their attention to us, a wicked waste of the king's powder and shot at such a range. We yelled and danced as each ball fell short in the marsh. But Gorham was thoroughly awake at last. The solid timber gate in the palisade swung wide, and out trotted fifty or sixty men with muskets at the trail, led by an officer. They poured down the slope all anyhow, a little scurry of ants, and then swung into a narrow column as the officer took the path along the dike. Zeb watched their approach coolly through a glass he had found in the cuddy. The fort gate remained open and gave birth to a nine-pounder mounted on wagon wheels— a contrivance of Barron's no doubt—and drawn by four horses. It came bumping and swaying along the dike behind the others, with two or three men in the blue jackets of the Royal Artillery hanging on.

Hall's schooner was very close now, luffing, in fact, to give us room and Colonel Eddy waving his hat in encouragement. Our boatmen were churning the red Fundy tide like madmen. We had no fear of the infantry; we should be out of musket shot by the time they reached the shore, but the nine-pounder was another matter. There were some anxious minutes.

But at last our bow was clear of the little creek, and we could let

our sails fill. We bore off southward under the breeze, with the Royal
Americans scattering along the dike and firing at us hopelessly. The
artillerymen slewed their cannon at the end of the dike and gave us
several shots. The first splashed under our stern. The second rico-
cheted and went droning over the Missaguash marsh. The rest were
a joke. Our small flotilla held on to the mouth of the La Planche
Creek, two miles along the marsh bank, where the tide now enabled
us to work up behind the low ridge of Fort Lawrence. The small
log-and-mud fort built by Lawrence in the old war had tumbled down
long since. A farmhouse stood on its site. But here was a strip of upland and a road that passed the marshes and connected with Point de
Bute. We unloaded our prisoners and the captured stores and looked
across the deep Missaguash River and the wide sweep of marshland
to lonely Fort Cumberland. This was the way that Monckton came in
'55; we took it as a good omen for our own attack.

CHAPTER 28

An Alarm and an Excursion

THE WIND blew hard from the north and turned the red-clay road to
stone. We put the captured stores in farmers' carts and took them
around to our main force on the Cumberland Ridge, leaving a guard
at Fort Lawrence in charge of the prisoners. I was in hopes of an attack
on the fort that night, but at Point de Bute we found affairs in an
uproar. The English sailors and some of the more unruly fellows from
Maine had demanded the plunder they were promised in Machias.
The Committee of Safety retorted that there was plenty in Fort Cumberland. But that was not so convenient to the malcontents as the
farms of the Yorkshire immigrants, who had refused to join us in
arms. In vain Mr. Foster pointed out that any mishandling of the
Yorkshiremen would drive them into arms against us. "Then," said
they, "we must disarm them." In this they were joined by certain wild
spirits of our own and they had gone from farm to farm, taking arms
and anything else they fancied. They drew no fine distinctions, either.
Several homes of our own Cumberland Yankees, serving with the
force on Cumberland Ridge, had been ransacked in their owners' absence, and Will Howe and some others had burst into the home of a

magistrate in Sackville and behaved like a party of drunken Indians. Uniacke and I went in a rage to Colonel Eddy and demanded discipline, and we rode together to Eben Gardner's house, where the Committee of Safety sat.

It was a cold and hostile gathering. These hardheaded Yankee farmers, like the folk of my own south shore, had strict notions of law and order. But Eddy fired the first gun, a sharp question which forced them to admit that they had granted an order to gather up the arms of the Yorkshiremen as a measure of precaution. They had given it under pressure, they added sourly.

"Ah well, a little petty pilfering," said Colonel Eddy easily.

"Petty be damned!" exploded Uniacke. "They're performing a systematic robbery everywhere. I've word that the party we sent over the Boar's Back to Partridge Island stopped in River Hebert and plundered Michael Francklin's manor and Mr. Barron's and the homes of their tenants—many of 'em Friends of America. And it's broken out behind us at Fort Lawrence. Obed Ayer and some of his fellows have robbed a Tory farmer there—even compelled him to carry a keg of his own rum down to their boat. You say our affair here will set an example to the Friends of America throughout the province. What kind of example d'ye call that?"

Colonel Eddy, sprawling in a chair, put his chin on his breast and looked under his thick eyebrows at the committee.

"Soldiers must be paid, gentlemen."

Uniacke snapped, "I thought these men were in the pay of Congress, or anyhow the pay of Massachusetts."

"Truth is, they ain't," Colonel Eddy said calmly. "They're all raised this side o' Massachusetts. Come to the fine point, Machias is part o' Nova Scotia, same as the St. John Valley, same as Cumberland. Ye ought to know that. Well—ye can't expect other colonies to pay the army o' Nova Scotia. They've got troops o' their own to pay."

"Like the Massachusetts soldiers now on the march to join us?" suggested Uniacke.

"Reckon so, yes."

"What are you driving at, Jonathan?" burst out Mr. Foster.

"Since the matter's come to a head, I'll tell ye, gentlemen. Ye've got to make arrangements to pay the men. And clothe 'em. We can feed 'em with the stuff we took from Gorham's schooner."

"And the supplies your men have taken from the farms!" Gardner said bitterly.

"My men! My men! Damme, they're your men. It's your army. I

merely command it. Your duty's to maintain it. And what have ye
done? Sat down and twiddled your thumbs. Now ye see the result—
the men maintain 'emselves, ay, and pay 'emselves. And ye whine
to me! Me! Damme, I won't be put upon like this! Not I, damme!
You're not talking to some sniveling committeeman now. You're talking to a colonel of the Continental Line, in command o' the army of
Nova Scotia. For two pins I'd dismiss the lot o' ye and rule by martial
law!"

The committee sat stunned. I could see the hot blood in Uniacke's
face, but his jaw was clamped tight.

Eddy dropped his voice again. It was cool; it was smooth as cream.
"Now, gentlemen, let's be sensible. Ye're all in this, the same as me.
Gorham knows who's in arms against him—knows every last one o'
ye. It's fight and win now or be hanged like dogs. Look at me—a
man that's got a price on his head and had his farm and goods confiscated by the king. Am I whining?"

"None of our Cumberland men want pay, barring a few irresponsi-
ble rascals," Mr. Foster said. "It boils down to your lot. Well, how
much do they want?"

"A suit of clothing now and eight dollars a month, hard money."

"There's not that much hard money in Cumberland," protested
Simeon Chester.

"There is if ye pay just the Machias men and the sailors, say, and
Obed and half a dozen o' the Cumberland lads. You're the civil
power; make a levy on the county for't; that's the easiest way and the
fairest." Having settled the matter, Colonel Eddy got up abruptly and
left, sword swinging, shoulders square, with a "Why bother me?" air
about him that drew a wry smile from Uniacke.

So Eddy's little band of originals were paid, together with a few
malcontents of our own, by a levy on the townships of Sackville and
Cumberland, most of whose men and boys were serving under arms
without pay of any kind.

Meanwhile our main force remained at Point de Bute sorting itself
out, miles from the fort, while Colonel Gorham, emboldened by our
failure to appear at his gates, advanced his outposts a mile up the
ridge to protect his fuel cutters and ordered near-by Yorkshire farmers
to slaughter their cattle and hogs and bring the meat to the fort. An
abler soldier would have marched his whole force up the ridge to our
weak position at Point de Bute and scattered us to the winds; for our
whole "army" numbered less than two hundred muskets, and apart
from its own dissensions it had been weakened by the party sent to

Partridge Island, the guard over the prisoners at Fort Lawrence, the outpost at Westkok, and a party of Acadians sent to seize an English vessel at Baie Verte.

Uniacke and I urged Eddy to advance to Camp Hill, which our small force could defend with ease, and at the same time menace Gorham's woodcutters and victualers.

This he did on November 9th, and I drew a sigh of relief, standing as we did in Monckton's old camp. We threw up some small works of logs and earth, but these were hardly necessary. The steep slope of the hill toward the marshes on both sides and its abrupt rise from the spur on which Fort Cumberland stood made it a natural citadel. The fort was a good mile or more away, hidden from view by the intervening woods, though we could see its smokes rising straight into the air on frosty mornings and evenings.

We took up quarters in farmhouses and barns around Camp Hill and erected some log huts and makeshift tents. The Indians made little brushwood bivouacs on the Missaguash side of the slope. Colonel Eddy placed his headquarters in the farmhouse of Eliphalet Reid, and there we officers gathered on the night of the 9th and watched him draw up a manifesto to Gorham, demanding the surrender of the fort.

"Before ye send that in," Benoni Danks said, "we ought to feel out Gorham's defenses. And we ought to do it now—tonight!"

"You took the words out of my mouth," said I joyously.

"Listen, Colonel—we'll slip along the ridge in small parties after dark, by both roads. Gorham keeps no outposts after dark—fear they'll desert. That gives us a free hand in the buildin's outside, and some o' them buildin's are right up ag'in the glacis o' the fort, specially on the southeast side. From the roofs there ye can shoot into the upper rooms o' the barracks."

"We'll give 'em a scare, if nothing else!" yelled Captain Sam Rogers.

"And pave the way for my manifesto in the morning!" beamed Colonel Eddy.

Mark came with my party, and François and half a dozen Cumberland farmers. It was cold, with a northeast wind whipping hard pellets of snow through the dark. We followed the road along the east side of the ridge to a point opposite the old British outworks, then took to the marsh edge and reached the first empty buildings about midnight, walking up the slope through what had been the garrison's gardens. As we climbed into position we heard the sentries on the fort's five log-and-earth bastions crying the hour and All's Well, and I remember Mark muttering that we would change their tune pretty soon. These old houses were mere weather-beaten shells swaying in the wind, robbed of doors and windows and in some cases even their flooring by thrifty Cumberland farmers in the empty years gone by. The one I chose was on the southeast side of the fort, facing directly toward the interior gate.

Perhaps I should explain that the fort proper was a five-pointed star with a bastion at each point, and the whole surrounded by a wide but shallow ditch and then a low counterscarp and glacis. The ditch was dry or at worst a little boggy. After the capture in '55 the English engineers had torn away the counterscarp on the southwest side and made a long earth fill extending southwesterly on the same level as the floor of the ditch. This was the outer parade ground, now flanked with additional barracks and officers' quarters and protected by a palisade twelve feet high and six inches thick, with loopholes cut through the wood every few feet. Thus the fort was really an entrenched camp, shaped like an angular tadpole. Gorham had repaired the palisade— the tadpole's tail—during the summer, but he had done little or nothing to the crumbling earthworks of the fort itself, and the inner gate, which connected the fort with the parade ground, remained a simple door of heavy oak.

'Twas bitter cold on the roof of our ruin, and the wind moaned through its empty windows and doors and amongst the naked joists in a mighty mournful way. We waited impatiently for the fun to begin. It came in half an hour or so, though it seemed half the night; someone in the party advancing along the fort's west side took a shot at the sentry on Duke's Bastion—the flagstaff bastion, a temptation I'd often resisted in my own nocturnal prowls. We saw the quick, bright flash of the sentry's piece in reply, followed by panicky shots into the dark from all the other bastions. In a moment there was uproar within. It came to us now loudly, now faintly, as the wind rose and fell: shouts, commands, a furious ruffling of drums. Before long the bastions, the sagged earth curtains between them, and all the loopholes in the palisade were spitting fire into the night over the marshes, and from the housetops and other points of vantage our fellows made sharp reply.

I had calculated that our roof commanded a view of the inner gate and hoped to work some mischief amongst the soldiers rushing out to man the palisade but now in the light of the musket flashes I saw that a small, dim building on the counterscarp effectually covered it— the garrison carpenter shop, someone said.

We opened fire anyhow and produced some howling within, probably from sheer surprise at finding the rebel army so close; we were within four hundred feet of the rampart, and much less than that from the counterscarp.

At first we lay on the southerly pitch of the roof firing over the ridgepole, but it was awkward to reload in that position, and as the frenzy grew we found ourselves standing boldly erect, shooting and loading and yelling like fiends.

Faintly across the wind and uproar we could hear the whoops of the Malicete warriors on the far side of the fort and nearer at hand the high yells of Chief Charles and his Micmacs, and to these and the shouts of our fighting farmers François and I added the old Mohawk yell of my father's rangers.

How long this lasted I don't know, but the fire of our skirmishers slackened as they emptied their powder horns, and they began to slip away to Camp Hill along the edge of the marshes. Our party were better provided, for I'd insisted on their making a supply of cartridges to supplement their powder horns, and our ears sang with our own shooting. We were sweating there in the cold night with sheer exertion and excitement, our voices gone harsh with yelling and the bitter taste of our own powder as we bit the cartridges, and the burnt fumes stung all eyes. I was weeping copiously and I suppose that is why I vaguely accepted the sudden glow on the ramparts and glacis as moonlight or sunrise or anything but what it was. Young Sam Fales jerked my sleeve and yelled in my ear, "Look! The Injuns have fired Mr. Harper's barn!"

So they had; a big barn at our left rear was blazing like a torch. It must have been full of marsh hay, for it threw a pillar of sparks into the sky that seemed to touch the stars—and it threw our lonely party on the roof into high relief. The soldiers in the Prince William and Prince Frederick bastions had a proper mark for the first time, and a number of men clambered upon the roof of the guardhouse inside the fort gate and shot hard at us. The air over our rooftop seemed to swarm with angry bees, and the sound of shot striking the crazy wooden walls of the house was like the spilling of dried peas on a drum.

We shot back defiantly. Then a cannon belched a stream of fire straight at us from the Prince Frederick bastion. We ducked as the ball went past and howled our opinion of their shooting. But the Prince William gunners let fly a blast of grapeshot that screamed all about us, and I found Mark shaking my shoulder with his big fist and yelling savagely, "Will ye come to hell out o' this, Davy, or must I kick ye down?"

I turned then and saw our party scrambling down through the holes in the roof. We made our way to earth with more haste than care, for shot were slapping clean through the pine boards and whining in by the gaping windows. We tumbled out at the rear and raced down the slope to the marshes. I fully expected to see the Royal Americans rushing out to cut off our retreat, but none came. We made our way carefully northeastward, squirming through the dead reeds and screened to some extent by the empty farmhouses and barns along the ridge road, and finally worked out of the last of the glare into the friendly dark. We heard the garrison still shooting hard into the darkness long after the burning barn had sunk to embers and when, in fact, our last straggler was being challenged by the outposts on Camp Hill. Whatever the result of our shooting, we had given Joe Gorham a scare.

We were a wild-looking crew in the light of the camp lanterns, with powder smudges streaked with sweat and the streams from our painful eyes, our clothing all torn from our scrambles in the dark. The marvel was that no one was seriously hurt, though many were bruised with falls and bleeding from bullet grazes. I found my hunting shirt torn in five places, and a ball had passed through the slack of my leather breeches and given me a painful graze where I sat—a jest in the camp for days. I blamed it on the grapeshot. I would not admit that soldiers could shoot so well.

CHAPTER 29

Into Battle

COLONEL EDDY'S SUMMONS to surrender went into the fort next morning by a Yorkshire boy. But I remember that morning for the unexpected yet simple incident which robbed us of Richard Uniacke. He and I were visiting rounds ahorseback, unarmed, and were talking to the picket on the southeast brow of Camp Hill when I noticed a little group on the road below, a quarter mile away, boldly headed for the fort with a loaded cart.

"That's Keillor the Yorkshireman," said a sharp-eyed boy in the picket. "Him and his boys."

"I know them," Uniacke said. "They'll turn back for me. Stay here,

Davy." He put spurs to his horse and rode down the hill, clearing stone walls like a hunter, and galloped along the lower road to them. We saw the cart pull up. There appeared to be an argument.

A farmer in the picket said, "That Keillor's a powerful man, and his three sons are strapping lads." There was something in the way he said it, and I asked, "What d'ye mean?"

"I don't reckon they'll turn back. Some o' Eddy's liberty boys ransacked Keillor's house t'other day. Keillor's blood is up."

I wondered if I should ride down and add my voice to Uniacke's persuasions, but I was still unconcerned for his safety. I remembered the fighting giant of Market Square. One of the sons strolled around Uniacke's horse idly, in the fashion of countrymen, who can never resist looking over a likely horse from all sides, and at Uniacke's back he stepped in close to the stirrup. In a flash they were on him, all four of them, dragging him out of the saddle.

I snatched a musket out of the nearest hand and put my nag down the steepest part of the hill. I lost sight of the struggle for a time—there were trees in the way—but I was confident that I could get there in time to put an end to their nonsense. They were not yet in sight of the fort, and six-feet-two of fighting Irishman is not easily subdued. But when I galloped into the straight of the fort road the cart was rattling off at a breakneck pace; Keillor was at the reins flogging the horse, while the three young men ran beside, and Uniacke was lying a senseless heap on top of their load. He could never remember afterward what happened, but they must have struck him over the head and bundled him into the cart.

The sheer audacity of the thing made my eyes pop—under the noses of our picket line, you might say. I rode at them, shouting and brandishing the musket. But now something else came into the game, something that the Keillors had seen and we had not. One of Gorham's fuel-cutting parties was in the woods not a hundred yards away, with an escort of green-jacketed Royals. The flurry in the road brought them out of the cover like ants from a kicked heap, sweating soldiers in shirt sleeves, clutching axes, and the wary escort covering both cart and me. The Keillors shouted something to them and held on at the same pace toward the fort with their prize. The soldiers gave all their attention to me, and I reined up. We looked at each other for a moment. I said nothing. They said nothing. I threw up the musket and fired, without aiming, simply to make them duck, and threw the thing away and wrenched my nag's head toward Camp Hill, raking her belly with the spurs. 'Tis an unpleasant sensation to have twenty muskets shooting at your back. I crouched low over the mare's neck and counted the shots aloud for the sake of hearing my own voice. She twitched her ears as if she understood, but I think 'twas the whine of the bullets that put the new spring in her legs. I was out of their range in a minute but I held on for another two or three before reining up. Standing in the stirrups, I could see the cart careering past the north scarp of the fort, just visible beyond the trees. The soldiers yelled and shook their fists for my benefit, and one or two knelt hopefully in the road and tried long shots.

I met our pickets soon after, sweating and winded after their run down the hill, and turned them back. 'Twas no fault of theirs, poor devils, but I cursed them for not seeing Keillor's cart until too late. The picture of proud Dick Uniacke carried triumphantly into Fort Cumberland upon a load of fresh-killed pork made me writhe for days —far more than my still smarting backside. I had a foreboding, vague and dismal, that our high enterprise might come to some such ludicrous end, our drama, so earnestly conceived, staged in the lonely and dramatic setting of these marshes, ruined by a troupe who did not know how to play their parts; that was the gloomy figure in my mind as I rode slowly up the hill to report the affair at headquarters.

Colonel Eddy received the news coolly. He had no use for Uniacke, and there were greater things toward. Surprisingly for so inert a man, Gorham had wasted no time in replying to our manifesto. Eddy read the answer aloud to us in Eliphalet Reid's parlor. It struck a note as bold as ours, brushed aside our demand for surrender, and in return demanded the submission of "all persons now in arms against His Majesty in Cumberland." Gorham's pen, it seemed to me, had been aimed at the committee rather than Colonel Eddy, for it declared that the king's troops had been sent to "protect" His Majesty's subjects and threatened us all with "the calamity of fire and sword" if we persisted in refusing that protection. There was something droll about that. Our committee replied in a vein quite as ironic and ended with a boldly written, "We had rather die like men than be hanged like dogs."

We sent it off by the Yorkshire boy, pleased and flustered with his own sudden importance. Sam Rogers was fingering Colonel Gorham's high-flown message. "This sounds pretty bold for Colonel Joe. Wonder who really wrote it?"

Josiah Throop said bluntly, "There's bold enough men in there. Major Batt's a fighter. So's the adjutant, Peter Clinch. Captain Gilfred Studholme's an Irishman with a long experience of war in

America. Burns and Grant are good men. Captain Helyer's a hard-drinking, hard-swearing hellion, the kind that'll fight as soon as eat. And there's a neighbor of mine in there, Lieutenant Dixson, a veteran of the rangers that knows this country like the palm of his hand —and knows how to fight in it."

"Well, we've got fighting men too," snapped Eddy, not liking the trend of Throop's talk. "Losing your courage, Josiah?"

"No—nor my memory," Throop said. "I was engineer officer at Fort Cumberland in the old days. I know how it can be defended and I know how it should be attacked. And I tell you right now that you can't take Fort Cumberland without cannon. Why, if we only had a couple of light field pieces 'twould be different. We could boat 'em around to Cumberland Creek in the night, run 'em up the path along the dike, shoot the outer gate to pieces, and rush the palisade."

"There'd still be the fort itself," I objected.

"If we can take and hold the barracks inside the palisade, the fort itself is finished. Here's why. Monckton made some important changes after he took the place in '55. He'd taken it by heaving bombshells into it from a battery further up the ridge and thought anyone else would have to do the same. So he built some elaborate outworks—they're gone to ruin now—to keep the enemy out of mortar range and then reckoned it safe to build a tail on the fort's backside. That's the part in the palisade. In there he built a new magazine of brick, several feet thick. And in there he dug the garrison wells—two of 'em, one at each foot of the Prince William bastion as it's now called. The French used to get their water from a well down by the marsh, sneaking it in at night."

"And once we've rushed the palisade, the magazine's ours?" Eddy asked eagerly.

"Not so fast. The magazine's covered from the fort by a stone curtain with loopholes. We couldn't get at the powder. But nor could they! And they couldn't get water, either."

"Nor fuel," I pointed out. "And it's cold weather."

"According to a deserter we picked up yesterday," Colonel Eddy said speculatively, "Gorham's got a reserve supply of water inside the fort. They keep it in fifteen hogsheads on the inner parade ground."

"We can make 'em use that in one stroke," said old Benoni Danks.

"How?"

"Pick a good night with the wind from the south'ard and put torch to the old houses and sheds outside. They're right up ag'in the fort— and the roofs o' the fort barracks stick up above the ramparts. They're bound to catch afire. Gorham'll have to chuck his reserve water supply on the flames or roast."

A question came to my tongue but I set my teeth against it.

Sam Wethered was thinking of the same thing, for he said uneasily, "What o' the women and children in there? Gorham's taken 'em all inside the fort."

Colonel Eddy broke in harshly, "Think what'd happen to your own women and children if the shoe was on the other foot. What'll happen to 'em anyhow—if we fail here?"

The following night soon after dark I took a party along the foot of the ridge by our old route and explored the buildings south of the fort. Danks was right. They were close enough to fire the buildings in the fort itself and they were deserted. Gorham had withdrawn the garrison's women and children together with the camp followers and their families inside the palisade. Even the horses and cattle were inside. Our night attack had accomplished that much, anyhow. By day soldiers and others strolled outside, and fatigue parties carried in wood from the well-nigh bare fuel yard, and they even drove their cattle and horses down to the marsh for water and a chance to crop the brown grass tops. But by night every foot of ground outside the fort and its palisade was ours. Colonel Gorham sat in his fort as if the very marshes were a rebel army.

We were out till the break of dawn; in fact we were seen as we withdrew along the marsh edge, and a sentry on the Prince William bastion turned out the guard, who shot hard at us. I went straight to headquarters at Eliphalet Reid's and found Colonel Eddy at breakfast with Captain Danks and Captain Rogers. Eddy was in high spirits. He had word from the outposts beyond the Basin. The Partridge Island party had picked up a corporal of the Royals, on his way to Windsor with a message from Gorham. Another messenger, a Yorkshire farmer named Douthwaite, had been nabbed at Westkok. We had Joe Gorham shut in as tight as a fly in a bottle.

I am no easygoing soul, and my temper is never improved by the loss of a night's sleep. The sight of Eddy comfortably at breakfast angered me, unreasonably perhaps. My clothes were the worse for several hours of crawling in the dark, and the night's frost had nipped my fingers and feet and made my bullet graze ache painfully.

"A good night's work and an excellent report," the colonel said to me, with a nod of dismissal.

"Well," I said sharply, "what are you going to do about it?"

He frowned. "What d'ye mean, Lieutenant?"

"I mean we should attack the fort tonight, before Gorham does any more work on his defenses. We'll never know what we can do till we try."

"Without waiting for reinforcements?"

"Reinforcements, hell! I don't believe in your fanciful army on the march from Massachusetts, Colonel Eddy. Nor does anyone else now."

"Well," he said, pursing his lips, "we should wait for the Cobequid men and the Truro men, anyhow. I've sent 'em word, Strang."

"Word! Word! Your word's not worth a tinker's damn, sir! Ye may get a handful of Cobequid farmers, but the Truro men'll sit tight. And why? Because the tales of your methods in Cumberland are too well known there. They'd just as soon fight you as the king—and they've damned small use for the king!"

"That's no way to talk to me," said Eddy, sitting up very straight. He would have looked majestic but for the fresh egg stains on his waistcoat.

"I know no better way. And while my tongue's on the wag, some of your Sons of Liberty went to Moses Delesdernier's house yesterday . . ."

"He went over to the enemy, Strang! Took his cattle into the fort!"

"He was never one of us and made no secret of it. On the other hand, the men of his family are all fighting for the Cause. Your fellows went there, ransacked the house from cellar to garret, destroyed what stuff they couldn't carry off, and left twelve women, children, and servants to get along any way they could. Then they sent word into the fort that unless Moses came out and gave himself up, they'd set the Indians on his family! That poor old man! Damn your soul, Eddy, you wouldn't ha' dared do that if Uniacke was here!"

Colonel Eddy seemed absorbed in brushing crumbs from the table. "You'll be interested to know, Lieutenant Strang, that Delesdernier came out last night. And he's signed a paper we're now circulating amongst the Yorkshiremen—renouncing King George and pledging allegiance to the United States."

"Under threat of murder! Giving the United States a fine name in these parts, aren't you?"

Eddy leaped from his chair—he would have leaped at my throat, I think, but the table was between.

"Hold hard!" Benoni Danks said sharply. "The place for bloodshed's down the ridge, my fighting cocks. What, are we goin' to quarrel amongst ourselves, like those hot-blooded officers o' Gorham's? Strang, you take a reef in your tongue. Colonel Eddy, there's somethin' in what he says. The township's buzzin' like a hornet's nest that's been whacked with a stick. There's ugly tales on the go; they've reached Truro already, and the first thing ye know they'll reach Michael Francklin's ears at Windsor. Then the cat'll be out o' the bag."

"Pooh! What's he got there? A handful of raw Scotchmen!"

"He's got a strong personal friendship with the Yankee farmers all along the Valley. Give him these tales to work on, and he'll have 'em fightin' tooth and nail ag'in us. Besides, Colonel, we can't stand still like this, doin' nothin' but mischief. The friends o' the Cause in Nova Scotia ain't goin' to march to join us at Cumberland, no more'n the snow in a field'll come to a snowball. We've got to roll and keep rollin' in a movement like this. Add to that, Gorham's improvin' his defenses every day that goes by. I say strike—strike tonight. If the fort can be taken by storm, now's the time. I think it can."

"Very well," growled Eddy, and breathed heavily through his nose. "Tonight it shall be."

All day we made plans and preparations, and I can say honestly that our differences were forgotten, or anyhow laid aside. The preparations were simple enough. We made scaling ladders of spruce poles and maple rungs, some twenty feet long for scaling the palisades, others thirty feet for the ramparts of the fort itself. Certain men were to carry axes and saws for hacking through the inner fort gate. The Indians were to creep up to the fort on the north side, making use of its drains and the brick kiln. At a signal they would start shooting at the Prince Edward bastion and the Prince Henry bastion to attract the garrison's attention there. A considerable party of our men were then to open fire on the flagstaff bastion, which jutted toward the marshes on the northwest side. The real attack was to be delivered by fifty men from the east, against the curtain which connected the Prince Frederick and Prince Henry bastions, now the weakest part of the ramparts.

Colonel Eddy, with an ironical smile, put me in charge of the scaling party "since Lieutenant Strang is most familiar with that aspect of the fort." Benoni Danks had charge of a party which was to attempt the palisade when things were at full pitch on the other sides.

There was some debate about the hour. The stroke of midnight seemed right by all the rules of romantic adventure. But shrewd old Benoni suggested four o'clock in the morning, when the garrison would be in deepest slumber and even the late-gaming officers had forsaken their whist cards for bed.

"In fact," said Benoni, "a leetle after four—half-past, say. That'll give the old guard time to get into their blankets, while the new guard's still rubbing the sleep out of its eyes."

There was a scarcity of timepieces amongst us, and the owners were dubious about taking them into a fight. It seems droll to look back on it—a man objecting to risking a precious toy in an affair which might cost him his life. But at the time it seemed natural and reasonable, and we had a long and grave discussion before we got the watch-keepers distributed amongst the various parties. The man who was to accompany the savages on the north side protested to the very last that "the damned Injuns'll steal my ticker, and where'll I get five guineas for another?"

I had now been two days and a night with little sleep or rest, and late that afternoon I threw myself on a couch in Eliphalet's house and tried to settle my thoughts for slumber. Absurd! As if any man facing a supreme adventure could sleep or even eat. I was never more awake in my life. The strange thing was that I felt I could go on like that for days and nights on end, a glorious illusion of strength beyond measure, the silly self-assurance of youth and hard health that the world and the devil beat out of a man at thirty and is only a sad and sheepish memory at forty-five. Youth! Youth! When I think now on Fort Cumberland and its bitter memories there is one last warm glow, the flicker of a time when I was young and strong and thought I could hack my way through hell with a tomahawk. That is the trick that life plays on all young men, I suspect, to make the disillusionment complete when it comes; for it is in the disillusioned thirties and forties that a man's best work is done.

But give me again that wild, sweet time between twenty and thirty, with all its illusions, its loves and loyalties, and death could have the rest.

CHAPTER 30

The Assault

IN SOME RESPECTS the weather was made for us, a cold night with a high scud drifting slowly across the stars and a low mist curling up from Cumberland Basin and from every stream in the marshes. But

I would have liked a whistle of wind and snow blowing to muffle our approach.

Our pickets advanced to the old fort outworks soon after dark, and at midnight the main force set out along both roads toward the fort. We left the Indians at the picket line, there to begin their crawl through the rough pastures to the north glacis. The rest of us took the now familiar routes along the marsh edge, both sides of the narrow tongue on which the fort stood. My party reached the hovels southeast of the fort in about an hour, walked up through the abandoned gardens as before, and settled ourselves in the gloom of the buildings. 'Twas a long wait in the dark, three cold mortal hours, and we cursed ourselves for starting so soon. The chilly marsh mists rose and thickened as the night went on, creeping up the slopes and over the fort like Noah's flood gone white and bodiless.

The point of our attack was an earth wall, grass-grown and gullied by the rains of years, supposed to be twelve feet high but known to be badly sagged. Inside, a high firing step enabled the defenders to shoot over the broad sentinel's walk along the top, and of course it was flanked by the fire of the two bastions it connected. Outside was the fort ditch, shallow and grass-grown, thirty feet wide, and beyond that rose the counterscarp with a grassy ledge which the fort engineers called the "covered way," covered by musketry from the curtain wall. Upon this ledge and immediately opposite the curtain stood an old hovel, formerly the garrison bakehouse, and the counterscarp at this point was pierced by a narrow passage intended for a sally port. My careful spying had shown me long ago that the old sally port, never used in all the fort's history, offered an approach for our attack. It opened into the ditch at an angle which screened it from the fire of the curtain and also the Prince Henry bastion. The fort's designers had intended to cover the sally port with fire from the Prince Frederick bastion, but during the long time of peace the bakehouse had been built exactly in the way—and neither Gorham nor his officers had recognized the fact.

My father, with his old ranger's instinct for the open, used to say that when a man shut himself up in a fort he shut up his mind at the same time. Here was proof.

I had explained all this to my party in the afternoon, scratching the fort's design in the hard earth of Camp Hill with a stick. As the night wore on I saw the silly side of our solemn wrangle over timepieces; we could not see them in the dark and dared not strike a light. Gorham's sentries, stiffly turning their sandglasses every half-hour by the light of their lanterns and crying the hour from bastion to bastion, told us all we needed to know.

At "Four o'clock and all's well!" with the subsequent clatter and murmur of the changing guard, we loaded and primed our muskets, taking great care to avoid a rattle of ramrod or powder horn, and covered the pans against the damp. The feet and voices of the guards had a curious effect of coming from a great height, as if Fort Cumberland had grown skyward like the beanstalk in the fairy tale. Whimsically I saw myself as Jack, about to mount the vine and kill the giant.

The affair broke suddenly. The Indians on the north side, cramped and half frozen in the fort drains and about the brick kiln, opened fire a few minutes after the change of guard, a ragged crackle of musketry followed by terrific war whoops. This was bad, for the old guard scarcely had its shoes off. The sentries on the bastions shot back wildly into the darkness, and then came the volley of Sam Rogers and his thirty muskets aimed at the flagstaff bastion and the cheering of his fellows—and a wild roll of drums within the fort.

"Now!" I said, and led off at a swift crouch, with Mark and François at my shoulders and the end of a scaling ladder nudging the small of my back. The glacis was steep but short, not more than twenty feet at this point. The old sally port was in a bad state. The fascines which supported the sides had rotted away long ago. We stumbled over heaped earth and sods all the way. The little wooden bakehouse loomed before me. Then I felt under my moccasins the stiff dead grass of the ditch. There were powder flashes from the Prince Frederick bastion to the left and the Prince Henry bastion to the right, but the soldiers were shooting blindly toward the dark rooftops of the abandoned settlement, out of sheer fright, remembering that other night attack. Their powder flashes glowed in the night mist like fireflies on a summer night, very useful to us now, for they marked the true height of the bastions and showed us the black wall between— which was the object we sought.

"Come on!" I said, and ran across the ditch toward the curtain. It appeared before me suddenly—I nearly ran slam into it—a steep earth bank covered with brass.

"Ladder! Ladder!" I hissed. I could hear the hard breathing of Mark and François and several other fellows behind and beside me. But there was no ladder. I ran back to the bakehouse and discovered several men struggling with a ladder there. The bakehouse and the angle of the sally port made it impossible to carry the thing forward. So much for well-laid plans! There was nothing for it but to carry the thing openly over the glacis and down into the ditch. But before I could make them understand what I wanted, the heave and thrust of the men behind shoved the ladder like a battering ram against the bakehouse wall. The empty hovel boomed in the dark like a big wooden drum. I heard a yell from the Prince Frederick bastion. By this time our impatient fellows were swarming up the glacis, dragging other ladders, and tumbling down the counterscarp into the ditch with such a clatter of dropped saws and axes and muskets as would waken the dead.

Soldiers in both bastions were yelling their heads off and letting fly at the sound of us. All that saved us then or thereafter was the tendency of men to overshoot when firing from a height. They sent enough lead over our heads to kill an army. By the time we got a ladder against the curtain we found its parapet lined with soldiers loosing off wildly into the dark. I mounted first, with Mark at my heels, and sensed rather than saw other ladders going up to right and left. We were all yelling now—cheers, oaths, war whoops, and shouts of "Liberty! Liberty!" I reached the edge of the parapet with the gun of Louisburg slung to my back and a tomahawk in my hand. At once the figure of a soldier bobbed up before me like a jack-in-the-box, lunging straight across the wide top at my face. His bayonet pierced my cheek, gritted between my teeth, and cut my tongue. Startled, I went backward, and with me the ladder and half a dozen men. We fell on the heads and shoulders of the men now crowding toward the foot of the wall, crashing upon them out of the dark like a thunderbolt. Some were hurt, and all yelled.

By the time I got to my feet, my mouth was full of blood, and I could see another ladder slowly toppling backward, its men outlined by the running flicker of musket flashes along the curtain top. The number of those flashes was ominous. The whole fire step of the curtain was manned, and behind it the wooden roof of the provision store was crowded with soldiers shooting hard. Plainly Gorham had scented the real attack.

There was now such a storm of bullets beating on the counterscarp and shattering the wooden walls of the bakehouse that some of our party remained penned in the sally port. The rest of us were in a queer position. At the foot of the curtain was comparative safety. To go back meant running through that storm of lead. To attempt the curtain further was sheer madness, though we persisted in our madness until several more ladders had been thrown down.

I stared blindly along the black hollow of the ditch. In a few moments some of the cooler soldiers in the bastions would slue a cannon and send a blast of grapeshot along the foot of the wall. Already musket balls were whizzing from both angles. After the first ladders fell we shot back at the musket flashes along the wall; now we held our fire lest we give the soldiers a mark to shoot at. Beyond question our assault was hopeless. It was a matter of getting away and hoping that our other parties had the better luck. Carefully in the inky mist, hugging the very foot of the curtain and the Prince Henry bastion, most of our own party were creeping along the ditch northward with the garrison making a leaden roof over their heads. The soldiers were pouring their fire at the top of the counterscarp, plainly expecting a mass assault and reckoning that the rebels in the ditch were merely an advance party. Eddy's bold talk of an army from Massachusetts had borne some unexpected fruit on this branch of His Majesty's service.

Cannon were firing now and blasts of grapeshot shrieking over the ditch in streams of red fire that must have scorched the dead grass on the counterscarp. I could hear the bakehouse going to flinders and hoped fervently that none of our lads had been caught on the open glacis. Those in the sally port could make a way to safety on their bellies, and the fellows now stealing north along the ditch would soon be past the worst of the fusillade. Somewhere around the corner of the Prince Henry bastion in the fog and gloom they could make a quick dash up the counterscarp and down the glacis to the shelter of the old zigzag trench which led to the abandoned outworks. Judging from the din, the greater part of Gorham's garrison was now crowded into the Prince Henry and Prince Frederick bastions and along the curtain top, too busy shooting into the fog over the east rim of the counterscarp to notice a scuffle in the ditch. The noise was terrific.

I found myself with Mark and faithful François hugging the frozen clay face of the Prince Frederick bastion and Mark growling into my ear, "Let's get out o' this!" He tugged my sleeve. He wanted to go north along the ditch after the others. But I hated to give it all up so easily. There was nothing to be done here, of course; but the stupidity of the Royal Rascals, pouring shot into their own counterscarp and over the Missaguash marshes, filled me with a wild contempt. My foot struck something in the brittle grass. I stooped and picked up an ax. I knew then what we might do. I jerked Mark's arm and François's to make them understand that we must go south along the ditch. We crept close along the foot of the curtain and around the angle of the Prince Frederick bastion. There the ditch turned sharply westward toward the fort gate and merged with the palisaded parade ground. The

gate wall and the Prince William bastion beyond were outlined in
the murk by the stabbing musket flashes. They were shooting at the
south counterscarp and the old carpenter shop as they had done in
our first night attack. I welcomed the sight and sound of it, a ceiling
over our heads to warrant a safe passage through the palisade where it
joined the fort wall. The palings here were poor things, hastily hewn
in the fort from odds and ends of timber, and in the thunder and
crackle and general uproar I hacked away without fear of discovery.
At last I got a paling off, and we squeezed through, crawling on our
bellies past the oak gate of the fort itself. I expected it to fly open
at any moment, pouring men forth for a sortie from the palisade, but
nothing happened. The gate guards were on their parapet shooting
like mad toward the south.

We kept along the foot of the Prince William bastion, whose defenders were shooting impartially toward the west and the east. Southwest from the angle of this bastion stretched the parade ground. The
barracks and other buildings along both sides of it were dark. The
palisades appeared to be well manned. We could not see the muzzle
flashes of course, but there was a regular flicker of musket pans inside,
and the noise was convincing.

The thing in my wild mind was the magazine at the head of the
parade ground. Surely three desperate men could overpower the sentry
there. I pictured myself broaching a powder keg and rolling it along
the floor and out over the doorsill, kicking the magazine lantern into
the spilled black grains and running like the devil. But when I peered
around the angle of the bastion I could see a shadow play of figures
in the lighted square of the magazine door. They were passing ammunition into the fort by a set of earth steps in the flank of the bastion,
just where it joined the stone curtain whose loopholes covered the
magazine. That explained the shut fort gate, but it ruined my romantic scheme. We hovered there uncertainly, on our knees. There was a
good deal of commotion within the palisade, officers bellowing orders,
feet pattering back and forth across the beaten earth of the parade
ground, doors opening and slamming in the barracks—all heard fitfully
as the storm of cannon and musketry rose and fell. I had a dismal
notion that I had led Mark and François into a worse trap than the
fort ditch, if that were possible.

I got to my feet. Mark cried at my ear, "What now?" I gave him a
savage dig in the ribs for silence—too late it seemed, for a soldier was
coming straight toward us from the magazine. He was carrying a
wooden bucket—of cartridges, I suppose—and grunted something at

us and went on into the darkness toward the east side of the palisade. My jaw dropped with sheer astonishment and the gashed tongue dribbled blood down my chin. And as we stood there another fellow trotted past us toward the magazine and called out to us, "I think we've beat the bastards off!"

"Listen," hissed Mark. "They don't know us from their own in the dark. That's our chance. We'll march straight down the parade and climb on one o' the fire steps o' the palisade, as if we'd a right to be there, d'ye see? We'll be over the top and gone afore anyone can stop us. It's only a few yards to the shelter o' the old houses outside—and anyhow these sogers can't shoot for beans!"

"Hell!" said I. "If we could do that, we could walk up to the palisade gate, knock down the men there, and have the thing open in two two's. Danks is outside there somewhere with his party. By God, we'll win this fight yet."

"No," grunted François solemnly.

"Yes! Come on!"

It is grotesque when I think of it now—François, Mark, and I trotting boldly down the length of the parade ground at Fort Cumberland, taking our bearings from the loom of the darkened barracks. Several times a scurrying figure nearly bumped into us, cried something, and vanished into the fog and dark.

The gate stood near the west corner of the palisade, a fact which I forgot in the excitement, and our advance brought us to a busy figure loading a musket on a wooden fire step several feet above ground level. We swerved aside and came to the gate. Three men were firing through loopholes in the stout oak, with three others below loading guns for them, and to either side on high fire steps, like the one we had seen, men were shooting through loopholes in the palisade itself.

We could see all this very clearly, for a lantern stood on the ground to give light for the gun loaders. There was no need—indeed there was no time—to make a plan of attack. We saw what was to be done and did it.

We cracked the three musket loaders over the head with our gun butts. One dropped without a sound; one squawked faintly like a hen on the chopping block, and the third uttered a scream that pierced the whole uproar. The three at the loopholes turned, yelled, and jumped at us. Fortunately their guns were empty, and more fortunately their bayonets were in the leather sheaths at their belts. But it was barrel and butt, fist and foot, and the three of them yelling blue murder. I engaged one of the soldiers in a game of quarterstaff, played with muskets, bruising to the fingers and knuckles, not to mention head and shoulders. But Mark had learned a thing or two about rough-and-tumble fighting in His Majesty's navy. He dropped his musket, seized the musket barrels of the other two, jerked the owners forward into his big arms, and yelled to François, "The gate! Open the gate!"

The gate had three stout oak bars. François slid two aside and was at the third and topmost when another man ran into the light of the lantern, a stocky gray-haired man, hatless, and wearing a sword belt over his waistcoat. The naked sword gleamed in his hand. I knew him. It was Dixson, the old ranger officer, retired on half pay in Cumberland after the French war. He struck at François without hesitation, a terrific sweep that cut the Indian's arm to the bone, and François fell off his perch, taking the bar with him and uttering a howl that was half war whoop and half agony. I dived at my opponent's feet and knocked him over. All this time Mark and his two were engaged in a rolling, thumping, gouging struggle on the ground. But Mark had managed to work the fight over to the gate, and now he threw his weight against it, with the two men clinging. The gate swung open, and we all rolled outside, squirming and clawing, with Dixson aiming cuts at my head and at Mark's whenever the chance offered.

Now from the darkness where the rickety sutlers' houses stood there came a splatter of musketry, and under the cover of it some of our fellows came running and whooping toward the gate. Dixson jumped back, catching at the gate and roaring to the soldiers. They scrambled clear and ran back with him, and as Mark and I got to our feet we heard the slam of the heavy oak and the hurried scrape and slither of the bars. I heard Benoni Danks's voice. "Quick! Throw yourselves ag'in the gate!" and the rush and thump of bodies flung against it.

It was too late, of course. There was a strange lull in the firing—I suppose every soldier in the palisade wondered what was afoot at the gate and held his fire—but we all knew the storm would break again in a moment.

Mark and I found François lying in the dark just outside the gate and picked him up. We made off toward the houses at an awkward trot. François uttered no sound, but a stream of blood from a severed artery squirted all over my shoulder and ran down my neck. He was bleeding to death. That was all I could think about—that and the distance to safety, which had seemed so short and was now so terribly long. The firing broke out behind us with all the sudden fury of summer thunder. I thanked God for the fog and the dark. Lacking a mark, the soldiers were overshooting as usual, but the balls sang mighty close to our heads at times, and as we gained the first wooden ruin we could hear the lead thwacking through its boards.

We held on toward the marsh and where the steep descent of the ground gave us shelter we dropped François on the frozen earth without ceremony and tore off his hunting shirt. Dixson's sword had cut clean through the hard muscles of the upper arm. We bound it with strips from our shirts, tighter and tighter until the bleeding stopped, but it took an awful time, and Mark and I were drenched with poor François's blood before it ceased. He was unconscious. I thought he was dead. Mark said not.

"He's dead," Benoni said in a matter-of-fact voice. Like all old rangers he considered an Indian no more than a dog. "Leave him, lads, and let's get out o' this while there's time."

"Time?" snapped Mark.

"If Gorham's any soldier he'll be sendin' out parties to cut off our retreat along the edge o' the ma'shes, now the attack's beat off. Come on!"

Off he went, and his men with him.

The firing was dying down in a ragged splutter of musketry all around the fort's defenses. But there was no shooting from outside. Our men were making their way back to Camp Hill in straggling groups along the marsh edge. We could mark their progress by the small flames which now began to flicker in the foggy dark along both sides of the ridge. They were firing the empty houses and barns and stores as they went. The flames rose and spread, and in the impressive silence after the night's tumult we could hear the crackle and snap of burning wood and the frantic crying of wildfowl over the marshes. We carried François down the dike track to Cumberland Creek, the longest mile I ever traveled. 'Twas our only chance to get him away. The old buildings on three sides of the fort were now well ablaze, making a huge glare in the fog that lit the slope clear down to the marshes. Mark cursed aloud the fools who had put fire to them.

" 'Twould have been done sooner or later," I muttered. "Gorham's been tearing some down for fuel the past few days."

A high tide had filled the little creek to the shoulder of the clay dike, and on the dike itself we found a pair of bark canoes and a whaleboat. We rejected the boat and felt over the canoes for holes. We chose the smaller one, laid François carefully in the bottom, and were about to get in ourselves when some fellows came trotting down the dike. We ran the canoe into some tall reeds and slid into the cold water up to our necks. Peering through the reeds I could make out

five men against the glare about the fort. One was Lieutenant Dixson
—I recognized his voice—and there were two soldiers and two inhabitants, Yorkshiremen by the sound of them. They launched the whaleboat after some grunting and squelching and rowed away into the
gloom over the Basin.

"There goes a message to Windsor," Mark said.

"Our fellows'll pick 'em up between River Hebert and Partridge
Island," I said confidently. Our teeth were rattling with cold. We
crawled out like sodden cats and got into the canoe.

"Why d'ye think he chose the whaleboat?" Mark demanded. "I'll
tell ye. They purpose sailin' the whole way round to Windsor."

"You think like a sailor."

"And you talk like a soger, Davy. That fellow's no fool—he was
smart enough to think of gettin' out o' the fort while our fellows were
still confused by the lost attack and he's smart enough to guess we've
seized the Partridge Island ferry. Well, it all comes o' followin' a lubber
like Eddy—him and his 'Avast oars!'—and not lookin' at the calendar."

"What's that to do with it?"

"This day's the thirteenth o' November. Thank God it ain't a Friday
or we'd ha' fixed our flint for keeps. Why, it's worse'n that fella
Montgomery attackin' Quebec on New Year's Eve."

"Oh, take your paddle, man, and dig," growled I. My cheek had
stopped bleeding and was stiff as wood, but my teeth ached, and my
gashed tongue ran a steady stream of blood that I had to swallow
continually lest I lose it—"lost blood, lost life." "The trouble with
you, Mark," I bubbled at him, "is that you are too damned supersti-
tious."

CHAPTER 31

Recriminations

IT WAS BROAD DAYLIGHT when we reached Sackville. Our wet clothes
had gone stiff with frost. Somehow we got François to a house above
the Tantramar. I was weary to death, and my face and tongue so
swollen that I could not speak. The good wife recognized me—the
Lord knows how—and she and her tall daughters stripped me naked
as a babe newborn and laid me in blankets that one of them had

been chafing furiously with a warming pan. I was only half conscious. I heard them exclaiming over my bullet grazes—there were two or three new ones, as I discovered painfully when I awakened in the night—and they bathed my stabbed cheek and plastered a homemade salve in the cut and wound my face and head with soft, old-linen bandages. I lay sleeping fitfully all that day and the night.

On the morning of the 14th Mark came, fresh from a council of war at Camp Hill. One of the girls had brought me a slate and pencil so I could make known my wants. What I wanted most was news—and of François, first.

"François is all right," Mark said with a flash of white teeth in the black beard. His long black hair, naturally oily, shone as if greased like an Indian's. It hung to his big shoulders and the brass earrings glinted through. The housewife thought he was "one of them wild fellers from Machias."

"She didn't want to have anything to do with an Injun first," Mark said. "But I told her he was son to a Malicete chief, and the savages 'ud be touchy if he died on her doorstep. I've had two men in that know somethin' o' surgery, and they say he'll live. But he'll never use that arm again, Davy."

"Cumberland?" my shrieking pencil demanded next.

Mark sat back against the bed foot and clasped one of his leather-patched knees. "The devil to pay. Our whole attack was beaten off—you know that. Good thing Gorham didn't come out after us. The men straggled back to Camp Hill all anyhow. A lot had left their guns in the ditch, along o' the axes and ladders, a pretty how-d'ye-do with arms so scarce amongst us. Eddy wants to treat the whole thing as a joke. Says there's nobody killed and only one wounded—François. Anyone that can hobble around in a day or two—like you—don't count. Swears if the Injuns hadn't bungled their part of it we'd ha' taken the fort afore the garrison could roll out o' their blankets. Maybe so. But we had a hot meetin' at Reid's house. Sam Rogers was there, and Throop and Howe and Benoni Danks and all the committee— a new Committee o' Safety by the way.

"Eddy heard some pretty plain talk. Two things were clear to all: the Royal Americans can fight when they're pinched, and Fort Cumberland can't be taken by storm—not by a parcel o' farmers and sailors and woodsmen, anyhow. Those ramparts look easy from a distance, but when you're down in the ditch, lookin' up at the musket flashes, it's a different matter. Comes home to ye, then, that a hundred and fifty poorly armed men attackin' two or three hundred sogers in a fort just don't make sense. The committee went at Eddy fierce about the 'army from Massachusetts'—and Eddy admitted, cool as a cucumber, that he'd lied and the only reinforcement on the way was a party o' fifty Machias men under a fella named Prescott. That caused an uproar, I tell ye! Well, the question was, what to do? Everybody's still full o' fight, but there's several minds on how to go about it. Benoni declares we must get some cannon from Pictou, off o' some o' the merchant ships there, land 'em at Baie Verte, and sled 'em across the is'mus on the first good snow. Eddy's jumped at the notion and sent off a party to Pictou—another fritterin' of our force. They're promised help at Pictou from friends o' the Cause—Dr. Harris, and Waugh the Scotch Covenanter, and some others. But Jo Throop and some more say there's naught to be got at Pictou but trouble, and our proper plan's to sit tight on Camp Hill and freeze Gorham out. If he comes out into the open to attack us we can beat him off, and in the meantime we'll send another petition to Boston for help. Eddy agreed to that too—he's mighty agreeable to anybody just now, is Jonathan. Throop's gone off to Boston with the petition, in the sloop we captured from Gorham, together with a few more of our men and the prisoners we've taken. The petition asks that this part o' Nova Scotia anyhow be taken under the protection o' the state o' Massachusetts, that our army be considered part o' the Continental Army and our officers given Continental commissions, that Machias be fortified and garrisoned for a retreat for our women and children if need be, and . . . let me see . . . that cannon and stores be sent to Machias this winter so we can get 'em in the early spring, that two or three armed vessels be sent . . . and the rest don't matter much . . . except the bit at the end. I memorized that for you, Davy, my fine old Whig . . . 'By the Divine blessing and your friendly assistance we shall soon add another stripe to the American flag and another colony to the United States.' How's that? But . . . I don't know, Davy. John Allan's been after our American brethren a long time for somethin' like that, and what's he got? A first-rate knowledge o' roads 'tween Boston and Philadelphia! Jo Throop'll find himself shuttlin' back and forth in the same coach with Allan, like as not. It's a queer mess, and I'm hanged if I know what to make of it."

Furiously, I scratched on the slate, "We'll all be hanged if Halifax knows what to make of it."

I was up the next day and took my sore head and bones around the marshes to Inverma on a borrowed horse. Mary Allan greeted me anxiously. She had heard that I was bayoneted in the head and left in the fort ditch for dead. I assured her—on the slate, for I had to carry the thing about with me like a mute—that I was very much alive and purposed riding on to Camp Hill. She would not hear of that, and to satisfy her (and my sore bones) I dismounted and stopped that day and the night.

At Camp Hill I found less than seventy men on duty, and these humorously indifferent to any danger from the fort. It may sound strange, but Gorham's lack of soldierly energy was the ruin of us, first and last. 'Twas impossible to make our fellows take him seriously. I found half our outposts empty and the others held by twos and threes of homespun-clad men and boys, squatting over a fire out of the November wind and playing knuckle bones.

In my tongueless state I was fit to be tied, and the violent scratchings on my slate only made them grin.

"Why should we keep a close watch?" said one fellow to me. "Gorham's scared to come out. And if he *did* come, why, he'd march 'em up the road in fours, with half a dozen drums to keep their courage up, and we'd hear 'em a mile off."

"Let him come out!" said more than one. "That's what we want, Lieutenant. Give us a crack at those damned sogers in the open, and we'll have the whole thing over in half an hour."

I rode back to camp in a rage and inquired for the officer of the day.

"Sam?" the headquarters orderly said, lounging against Reid's doorpost, hands in waistband. "Why, Sam's off moose huntin' with some o' the boys—over Jolicoeur way, I guess."

I know now that such evils must beset any irregular army in days of inaction. There was no discipline. When a man and his sons wanted to go home and cut a supply of firewood for the farm they went. They might or might not say a word about it to their officer. And when it wasn't firewood, 'twas a sick cow to beef or new moccasins to make or a bad leak in the barn roof to be shingled—all the hundred-and-one things that loom so large to a farmer and make him unfit for anything but hit-and-run soldiering. The Indians wandered off to hunt, out of sheer boredom, though they appeared regularly at Camp Hill for their issue of rum. As for the outlanders amongst us, the Machias woodsmen, the English sailors, the Royal American deserters who had crept out into our lines and forsworn the king and signed Eddy's "Association," these roamed the countryside on errands of their own. "Foraging," Eddy called it. The countryfolk had another word. We kept no muster rolls except for Eddy's little band of mercenaries. I suppose from first to last we must have had three or four hundred men and boys under arms, but never more than two hundred on duty at a time, and these scattered on various posts and expeditions all the way from Partridge Island to Pictou. The force at Camp Hill, the vital point, was usually less than a hundred.

For firearms we had muskets of all ages, kinds, and calibers. Each man carried his own mold and melted and poured his own bullets—which seldom fitted the gun of the fellow to his right or left. Lead was scarce, and in our search for powder we had tapped every powder horn in the countryside and scraped the kegs in the captured sloop. As for our commander, we could admire Colonel Eddy's faith in the Cause, his ruthless hatred of King George and all the royal followers, but we despised him for his glib lying, his almost frantic eagerness to get every man's head inside the noose that hung about his own neck.

And this was the force upon whose success or failure hung the fate of the Cause in Nova Scotia!

The weather continued bleak, with morning mists and yellow sunsets and a sad, small air across the marshes. But on the night of November 21st we found a strong wind blowing from the south and put torch to the few old buildings that remained standing south of the fort. Embers and blazing shingles sailed on the wind over the ramparts. As usual the garrison stood to arms and shot wildly at nothing, but soon they had to lay their guns aside and take buckets, for the barrack roofs took fire under that burning shower and then the roof of the provision store, the officers' quarters, and the guardhouse. The thing succeeded so far beyond our hopes (for the weather had been alternately frosty and damp) that we were quite as surprised as the garrison and so missed a supreme chance to take the fort. Gorham had to put most of his men at fighting the flames inside the ramparts. We shot hard from our cover at the men on the roofs but we were too few to accomplish much, and by the time Eddy had hustled the main force down from Camp Hill the wind had shifted and the chance was past.

Next day Gorham had the roofs torn off every building within the ramparts, so that nothing wooden remained exposed to us. A wise move. But it forced his women and children to shelter in the damp casemates under the ramparts. I was pleased to find that I could think of Fear Helyer with a cold detachment then. She was one of them. Very well. She should suffer with the rest. The more they suffered, the quicker it would be over. They could not hold out long in such a state. A deserter told us that half the garrison was down with colds and pleurisies and rheumatic fevers of one kind or another. Our confidence grew as the weather sharpened. Gorham's desperation for fuel became apparent soon afterward, when one day we observed fatigue parties tearing down the buildings southeast of the fort—the last of the village that had grown there in the peaceful years after '55. That night we set fire to them all—twelve houses, a barn, and a large building used in time of peace as the garrison hospital. They made a fine blaze in the frosty night, and in the morning Fort Cumberland stood alone.

We all felt that the garrison's end was near. The following morning, taking advantage of the mist, Benoni and I took a force along the marsh edge by daylight, hoping to catch the garrison's cattle abroad. We came upon the herd suddenly and some greencoats pulling at a haystack to give them feed. We opened fire at once—and got a shocking surprise. Musket flashes stabbed at us out of the mist from three sides and in considerable number. We beat a retreat at once, and the troops followed us, led by some brisk officer defying Gorham's orders.

'Twas a queer fight in the fog, with groups of ours and theirs blundering into each other and little to fire at but the sound of feet in the marsh and the fort guns booming encouragement—or more likely a recall—to the soldiers.

They snapped at our heels all the way back to our outpost line, which was only half manned as usual. But the pickets joined their fire to ours and the troops withdrew. We had hit a number of them and saw the sagging forms carried off dimly in the mist. And they had hit a number of us, six badly, and some were missing. We never knew, after a fight, whether missing men had run away or were dead or had taken their wounds home, vanishing into the countryside. The Royals boasted afterward of the rebels they killed in this affair. How many, only God and the marshes know.

Chapter 32

In Which I Meet a Brother

A RUNNER from Partridge Island brought us news. Michael Francklin, at Windsor, had learned of the presence of rebels at the ferry landing and ordered the militia of Cornwallis to cross Minas Basin and re-establish the ferry. They had refused, to a man. We cheered at that. But there was something else, not so cheerful. Dixson had reached Windsor safely and pushed on overland to Halifax with his message from Gorham. So the cat was out of the bag at last!

We discussed all this in a council of war at Eliphalet Reid's. Eddy was confident as ever. Pooh! General Massey wasn't likely to stir from his snug fireside in Halifax. Cumberland was Gorham's nut, and he'd be left to crack it. Massey hadn't any troops at Halifax anyhow; and as for the Royal Highlanders at Windsor, how would they get to Cumberland? Bring transports around from Halifax? Pooh! His Majesty's naval commanders would turn purple at the thought. The Bay of Fundy was dangerous at the best of times; after mid-November 'twas a death trap, with snowstorms added to tides and fogs and the chance of a sudden freeze-up. Nunno! But suppose the Highlanders marched around Minas Basin? That 'ud mean one hundred and fifty miles, most of it through woods, and then they must come by way of the Boar's Back, where we could ambush them easily.

We added up these items, and the sum came right. We parted in high confidence, and when, on the morning of November 28th, a half-witted drummer deserted from the fort, babbling that a man-of-war had lain in the fog off Cumberland Creek all night, we roared with laughter.

That evening I went on picket duty in the woods between Camp Hill and the old fort outworks, and in the first dusk a man came to me crying, "Just nabbed a woman comin' up the road ahorseback. A pretty piece—one o' the off'cers' ladies by the style o' her." I followed him through the trees, guessing at once that our prize was Mrs. Fanning. I had wondered how long she and Captain Jack could restrain their amours in the confinement of the fort. Evidently she had slipped out at sundown—Helyer would see that the sentries opened the gate and shut their mouths—and was on her way to the Maultasch house, trusting to the darkness for a passage through our lines. Now we had her and with patience and a good watch we should nab Helyer too. But all these fine expectations went aglimmering when I came to the lady, still sitting her horse, with a disdainful curve to her back, surrounded by half a dozen shaggy-haired farm lads with muskets and fowling pieces. It was Fear.

"What are you doing here?" I mouthed at her. The wound in my cheek had healed to a big, indented scab, red and shiny-hard, and I had thrown the bandage away. I was an ugly object for I was still unable to shave. I could talk, thickly and painfully, though I still could eat nothing but soup, and that cold. My own mother would not have known me in the twilight, what with the impediment in my speech, the scarred black-stubbled jaws, the battered blue hat, the linsey-woolsey shirt, the leather-patched breeches all blotched with powder smudges and old bloodstains.

"Are you in charge of these men?" she demanded imperiously.

"I am."

"I wish to speak to you alone."

I waved the men back to the woods, with a caution, "If she makes off, shoot the horse." I could hear the click of their hammers cocking. I stood a foot or two from the nag's head, ready to dive at the bridle.

"Well?"

"I am on an errand of mercy," she said coldly. "I beg you to let me go."

I was silent. She read my suspicions.

"I swear it has nothing to do with military matters. You may come with me if you wish."

"What's up?" I mumbled stubbornly.

"A private of the Royal Americans, wounded in the marsh fight. He fell near your lines, and some Yorkshire people got him away across the Missaguash by a firm track they know. He's dying and wishes to see me."

"I'll go with you," I said after some hesitation. I smelled a trick but wanted to see what it was. I called to the picket, "Send word to Captain Ayer to come and take charge here. And keep your eyes peeled."

I caught her bridle and led the horse up the road. "You'll need a horse," she called down to me. "The boy's at a farm over on the Fort Lawrence Ridge."

That meant a three-mile ride up the Cumberland Ridge to Point de Bute, where a bridge crossed the Missaguash and probably four or more down the Lawrence Ridge. In these marshlands you were forever traveling three sides of a square to get anywhere.

The road wound up Camp Hill in an easy curve, and I got a horse at Eben Gardner's. Weatherhead's Tavern was lit from cellar to garret and full of the sounds of good company. Reid's house the same, and Gardner's. The fires of the camp made yellow halos in the night mist, on which the thrown shadows of the men stalked like giants. We could hear scraps of song and talk from the fires, and a yammer of drunken argument from the Indians in their bivouacs on the slope toward the Missaguash. No one challenged us. One or two figures going from

camp to tavern or fire to fire called out a Good Night, without knowing nor caring who we were. 'Twas so typical of the army of Cumberland that my lips twisted in a sardonic grin. I hoped that Captain
Helyer's wife would see in this damned carelessness the contempt we
had for her husband's men.

We met no one on the road. The farm folk supped and went to
bed soon after on these early winter nights. As we crossed the Missaguash bridge, its logs booming under our hoofbeats, a single dog
barked in the village of Point de Bute, that was all. The road along
the Lawrence Ridge was greasy, and the horses slithered and splashed
in the mud holes, but we made fair time, all things considered.

As we dismounted and Fear rapped at a farmhouse door I heard
a clock striking eight within. There was a whisper and a fumbling,
and the door was thrown open suddenly by a yellow-bearded Yorkshireman, who thrust a lantern into our faces with one hand and
cocked a pistol in the other.

"I'm Mrs. Helyer," Fear said.

"Who's yon? He looks like rebel!"

"He's escorted me through the rebel lines," she said quickly.
"Where is the boy?"

A tall woman appeared with a candle, which she passed to Fear.
"Go up, my dear," she said in the broad Yorkshire dialect. "The lad's
afever to see you and won't live another strike o' clock, I'm 'fraid."

I followed Fear up the narrow, creaking stairs. On the landing she
paused and drew in a great breath, as if to brace herself before passing
the chamber door, which stood ajar. She turned to me, whispering,
"Swear you'll not molest the boy or these people. . . ." Her voice
trailed off. The candlelight was full on my face. I saw her eyes wid-
ening, dark and enormous. "David!" she gasped. "Oh, my God!"

"Go in!" said I roughly, "and get it over with. I want to get back
to my post."

She kept whispering, "You! You!" with a sort of shuddering breath,
and her breast heaving under the trim green riding coat. She wore a
woolen tammy, a small thing that covered only part of her brown
head, and the night mist sparkled in her hair. A riper Fear than I
remembered, and the lovelier for it, despite the blue shadows under
the large eyes and the smooth skin blanched and transparent from
confinement in the dismal casemates of the fort.

"Go in yourself!" she choked. "Go in, David."

I still suspected a trap and entered warily, soundless in my moccasins. By the dim flicker of a night dip that stood in a saucer of water

upon a chest of drawers I perceived a young man lying in the good wife's best bed, staring wide-eyed at the shadowy half-tester overhead. His long hair, untied, lay on the pillow like a girl's. His face was the hue of the yellowy country-linen sheets, with a dark stubble on the clenched jaws. There was no such thing as a fireplace or a stove in these farm bedchambers; the room was chill as a tomb, yet the boy's forehead shone with sweat. I came a reluctant step or two nearer, and he turned his head and looked at me. My bones went to water then. It was John, my brother.

His sunken blue eyes stared at me in a mild, puzzled way, as a very small baby stares at people hanging over it. I heard the door closing softly behind.

I stooped over him, blurting, "John!" and forgetting how ill-favored a visage mine was. He uttered a low cry of fear, of pain, of shock—I don't know what—and turned his head away and back again, staring.

"It's me—David."

"David?" he whispered. Then in a stronger voice, "David?" His eyes seemed to clear.

"David, how did you get here?"

"I just—came." My frantic mind was turning over its memories of the marsh fight and finding nothing but dim figures in the mist and powder flashes and the splash of feet and God knowing who was friend or foe. His eyes seemed to accuse me, and I wanted to cry out against the injustice of it.

"I thought you'd gone to Connecticut with Luke," he said.

"Luke? I've heard nothing of Luke."

"He's joined the rebels, went with Seth Harding. Seth commands a Connecticut ship of war. The *Oliver Cromwell*, I think. Father . . . Mother . . . everyone thought you'd gone to join them."

"No."

"You're with Eddy?"

"Yes."

He closed his eyes. And after a long time, "David!"

"Yes, John."

"Don't go away, will you? Fear's coming—Fear Bingay, remember? You used to like her a little, didn't you? She's my officer's wife now. You must see her safe through the lines again, David. Promise me that."

"I will."

His tongue ran on feverishly, as if he knew his time was short. "I'm so glad you came, David. There's been something on my mind. It's

nigh driven me crazy lately . . . shut up in the fort with nought but
my sins to think about."

"How did you come to Fort Cumberland?" I asked, to shift the
subject.

"In the supply sloop. I'd been away on a recruiting party; we were
Colonel Gorham's last reinforcement before the rebels came. David
. . . I've got a bad wound . . . shot through the body . . . can't
last long. . . ."

"Don't say that!"

"Something I've got to tell you . . . or Fear . . . someone from
home . . . message for Mark . . . you know where Mark is?"

"Yes."

"Tell him Joanna . . . my fault . . . I was mad for her . . . she
wouldn't have me . . . in love with Mark."

"Talk about something else," I said.

"One night . . . when the whole house was asleep . . . I crept up to
her garret . . . door wasn't barred . . . she was asleep . . . woke up
and fought . . . like a wildcat . . . but in silence, that was the terrible
part of it. . . . David, she made no sound . . . afraid to cry out lest
Mother hear . . . or Father . . . or Mark. . . . I was possessed of the
devil, David . . . mad . . . mad . . ." He talked in gasps, like that,
with the cold sweat trickling down his tallow cheeks and staring at
me with eyes that seemed about to burst out of his head. It was terrible.
He was dying, and it was awful to hear him talking about a thing like
that.

"She was strong . . . we struggled a long time . . . and then . . .
and then she was lying there weeping into her pillow . . . and I with
all the lust gone out of me . . . nothing left but shame and wretchedness . . . and wishing I could undo it. O God, I felt rotten . . .
rotten. I crept away like a thief . . . I couldn't meet her eyes for days
. . . nor Mark's . . . nor Mother's. One night the devil came back
. . . but her door was barred . . . it was always barred after that.
Sometimes I cursed her in whispers through the door . . . sometimes
I slunk back to my bed and prayed God to have mercy on her . . .
but that was too much to expect . . . God don't have much mercy
on the helpless, Davy, does He? . . . I think God's somebody like
Father. 'Twas about the time that Mark had begun to make love to
her. . . . I got a devilish amusement out of it sometimes . . . knowing what I knew. When she couldn't conceal it any longer, and Mother
found out . . . but you know the rest . . . Mark suspecting Luke
. . . and I hating Mark . . . Mother's faith in all of us destroyed . . .

all of us scattered . . . like a judgment. O God, it's not fair! . . . so much affliction for one bit of sin. But I'd not care, Davy . . . if I could feel that . . . this . . . paid for everything. It should, shouldn't it? . . . That's fair, isn't it? God! . . . You know, Davy, once . . . after it happened . . . I went down to the wharf in the night . . . to drown myself . . . but I hadn't the courage. Pity, wasn't it? . . . I might have wiped the score from the slate . . . and saved our troubles since. O God, let me wipe the score. . . . O God, let me . . ."

"Stop it!" I said through my teeth. He sank back on the pillow. The door opened and closed softly behind me, and Fear tiptoed across the chamber and fell on her knees beside the bed. "Try to get some rest, John. Go to sleep. Please!"

"Do you think," he said to her, "a fellow's dying . . . a sinful wretch like me . . . could accomplish anything?"

I tried to harden myself with the notion that too much pain had made him maudlin, like too much drink, but it made me wretched to hear him talk so.

She lifted her head proudly and said—for my benefit, I think, as much as his—"You're a soldier of the king, John. To suffer for your king and country and to be loyal to the end—that is a very great accomplishment."

His eyes seemed to shine. "You think so? I was a good soldier, wasn't I?"

She bowed her brown head, weeping. He closed his eyes and shuddered, and I felt a miserable weight in my stomach, thinking he was dead. But he fell into a slumber, breathing with the hard snuffle of the badly wounded—a sound that, once heard, you can never forget. Fear remained kneeling, praying I think, and I sat in the chair till the clock below struck three.

"I must get back to my post," I said to her in a low voice. "I'll come again in the forenoon."

She stood up and lit a new dip from the sputtering shred of the old. She looked like a ghost, regarding me with grave, round eyes over the candle's glow.

"You can't go, David."

"He's all right till morning, I think."

"Perhaps. But I'm thinking about you now. You mustn't go back to your post."

"Why?"

She stood very straight, like the soldier's wife she was. "David, if I tell you something will you promise on your honor to stay here?"

"If it's important enough, yes."

"David, Colonel Gorham managed to get a message to General Massey at Halifax."

"I know that. And I know Massey's got no troops to send here."

"He's gathered some marines from the *Amazon* and *Savage*, David, and sent them by road to join the Highlanders at Windsor. A man-of-war, the *Vulture*, took the marines on board at Windsor, and the Highlanders sailed in a couple of sloops. The Scotchmen got blown down the bay in a storm—but the *Vulture's* here, David, and she's landed the marines."

"Pooh! Sea soldiers!"

"One of their officers is a man named Pitcairn, David. Wasn't it a marine officer of that name who led the march to Lexington, whose pistols fired the first British shots in this war? That's what they say in the fort, anyhow. But make no mistake, David, the marines are fighters. They've old scores to settle with the rebels."

"How many of 'em?"

"Two companies—ninety officers and men."

"Just enough to replace Gorham's sick and wounded and the prisoners we've taken."

"That's what Colonel Gorham said too. But Pitcairn and the other marine officer, Branson, thought differently. They'd come here to fight, they said, not to mount guard in a fort. The gossip is that Colonel Gorham's got too much influence to be removed, but General Massey's brushed his authority aside for the time being, and Major Batt of the Royal Americans is to take charge of the sortie."

"The what?"

"Sortie—Major Batt's taking the marines and a picked force of the Royal Americans, and they're marching out against the rebels, without even waiting for the Highlanders."

I considered that, astonished. "They'll be shot down like sheep," I declared. "Pitcairn'll think he's back at Lexington when our marksmen get sight of his lobsterbacks. We've got a strong position on Camp Hill and pickets watching both roads and the woods between."

She shrugged and said a little impatiently, "You don't understand, David. Batt knows where your pickets are and all about your lines on Camp Hill. He's done a lot of reconnoitering—it was he who led the soldiers in the marsh fight. Batt is taking his force up the Missaguash marsh, before sunrise, to the rear of Camp Hill. Your rebels won't know a thing till the bayonets are amongst them. By noon their whole silly dream will be over—they'll all be dead or prisoners

—and the hang ropes waiting in Halifax. Oh, David, don't you see? That's why you must stay here, keep out of sight, and make your way out of the country when things have blown over."

"What time does Batt start from the fort?"

"At half-past five, so as to get well up the marsh before daylight. David!" she cried sharply, "where are you going?"

"To my post!" I snapped from the doorway.

"But you promised, Davy. On your honor!"

"Duty comes before honor, ma'am."

"And before your brother?"

"And my brother."

CHAPTER 33

In Which a Farce Comes to a Bad End

THE HOUSEHOLD had gone to bed, but the candle they left on the shelf by the stair foot had guttered out not long since, for the greasy reek of it hung in the darkness there. I made my way out and found my nag by her friendly whicker in the gloom of the stable. The night was still foggy and black. I tried to flog the mare into a gallop, but she did not like the greasy feel of the clay road nor the night nor anything about the journey and granted me no more than an uneasy amble. At that she slithered and stumbled continually and kept snorting her disgust. After about a mile she checked suddenly, and a voice challenged from the dark in front. The voice had a Yankee twang, but that meant nothing; there were New England Tories in the ranks of the Royal Americans.

"Friend!" I answered, hoping to brazen it out.

"Come for'ard and let's get a look at ye!" I could hear men moving on the road ahead and through the wet grass on both sides of me. I clucked to the mare, and she moved reluctantly. Several dark shapes appeared at her head, and one seized the bridle. I looked for the white gleam of crossbelts and saw none.

"I'm a Friend of Liberty!" said I boldly.

"Where bound?"

"For the camp. I have urgent news for Colonel Eddy."

A silence. The whole fog about me prickled with suspicion. I think they would have shot me out of the saddle in another moment, but there was a sound of hoofs ahead, and three riders made their way through the men. Fortunately one was Dr. Parker Clarke, of Fort Lawrence Ridge, whom I knew. Explanations followed. The party consisted of twenty or thirty Cobequid men, led by Captain Tom Falconer and James Avery, coming in response to Colonel Eddy's summons. They had marched nigh seventy miles, by way of the Boar's Back and River Hebert to Fort Lawrence, where Dr. Clarke had offered to guide them. This was cheering news. If the scattered farms of Cobequid could send so resolute a company, surely we might expect a large force from the stout Whigs of Truro. I told them my mission, and Falconer and Avery rode on with me, leaving Dr. Clarke to bring up the men.

'Twas an age before we clattered over the Missaguash bridge, and all the way down the Cumberland Road my ears were pricked for the first shots. Daylight was not far off. Approaching Camp Hill, I told the others to ride on and warn Colonel Eddy at Reid's, while I swung off to the left to arouse the Indians. I was hoping desperately that Major Batt had found hard going in the marshes. I left the mare at a snake fence on the brow of the ridge and plunged on afoot through the pastures and thickets of scrub spruce and fir. The Indians' drunken conference must have lasted through the night, for as I approached the first of their brushwood bivouacs I could hear loud scraps of speech in Micmac and Malicete. But before I could summon my panting breath for a shout there was a single shot, quickly followed by a fusillade, a bellowed "Huzza!" that seemed to come from every side, and the sound of boots crashing through the undergrowth at an eager run. It occurred to me that I was unarmed, and I turned and ran for the camp. Dawn was just breaking on the summit. No real light yet but a dilution of the night's darkness, or as if the thick fog had in some way turned luminous.

I tripped over a tent rope before I realized I was in the camp—an accident which saved my life, for some fellow of ours shot at my head from the door of a hut not fifteen feet away. From my hands and knees I cursed him for a fool. Then came a rush of gaitered legs past my face. A redcoat lunged at the fellow in the doorway and stabbed him through. The point of the long bayonet stuck firm in the doorpost, and the poor devil hung there, pinned and screaming and plucking at the unyielding socket of the thing. The marine put a big foot against his belly, jerked the weapon clear, and went on. I crawled away into the bushes for a distance and then ran hard for headquarters.

There, in the growing light, I saw several green-jacketed Royal Americans shooting the glass out of Eliphalet Reid's windows from the edge of the road. There were one or two answering flashes from the house, and suddenly the door flew open and out burst a little group of ours, shooting as they came, with our Negro drummer rattling bravely just behind.

One of the greenjackets dropped to his knees, put his musket carefully aside, as if he might want it again soon, and fell forward on his face. The rest stood their ground, some firing, some reloading swiftly. 'Tis a quaint fact, I have observed, that men with a choice of targets always fire upon the most conspicuous. In this case 'twas the drummer who drew the attention, and more particularly his drum which must have been pierced by several balls. He uttered a scream and threw the wreck away and ran howling into the woods, closely followed by his companions. But they had succeeded in their object—a diversion to enable Colonel Eddy and his captains to get away by the rear. I saw more than one dim rider slipping from the shadows of the stable into the mist.

The soldiers ran into the house and in a moment came out again, with smoke curling behind them. Then they were gone. There was no sign of Eliphalet or his family. I crept over to the dead soldier and took his gun and cartridge box. All about me in the fog I could hear shouts and calls and scattered shots. Reid's house was well alight now, and the fog glowed in other directions. The marines had fired the camp and Jo Throop's house and Eben Gardner's.

The sounds of the running fight drew away northward, and I tried to catch up with it through the woods and pastures along the east slope of the ridge. Our fellows shot at the soldiers from each farmhouse along the road, and the progress of the fight was marked by the burning houses—Will Chapman's, Jo Cuzen's, Richard Jones', Haggard's, Gooden's, Wells', Dan Maguire's, and a number of *Acadien* homes. His Majesty's marines were a tough crew; they had been fighting up and down the coast of America ever since Lexington and had learned the ins and outs of American warfare remarkably well. They advanced in small, scattered rushes, using every bit of cover, and they could shoot; I saw one of them put a ball through the head of a running Indian—one of Chief Charles' Micmacs—at a hundred and fifty yards. Our fellows fell back from farm to farm, and at each new capture the redcoats went to the kitchen for brands and scattered them through the rooms and in the stables and barns. Fire licked out of every door and window until a single flame was burning a great hole in the mist and a column of black smoke rolling up to the invisible sky. Our men made a last stand at Inverma Farm; then they broke and fled toward Baie Verte with the marines at their heels. The redcoats burned farm after farm along the road as far as Jolicoeur, where they stopped out of sheer weariness.

I reached the skirts of Inverma just as the last few shots were fired. The bitter-smelling powder fumes hung in little pockets in the mist. A man could have snuffed his way along the fighting line by those alone. I came upon two dead rebels in the lane that ran down to the marsh—the old French road to Bloody Bridge. One was an Acadian tenant of John Allan's. Then I noticed a significant glow in the fog where Inverma reared its hospitable walls. I ran there calling out, "Mrs. Allan! Mrs. Allan!" with my sore and awkward tongue. A couple of marines came at me out of the fog. One fired, and the ball sang past my neck. I threw up the English gun and let him have it, a straight, quick shot that took him full in the breast of his red coat just above his crossbelt plate. The other came on, bayonet leveled, a tall, leather-faced man with a stride like a coach horse. I ran back to the woods for a chance to reload. He stopped and fired. I was scurrying along, bent nearly double, knowing what was coming, and the ball glanced along my back ribs and stopped in the flesh at the back of my shoulder. The blow knocked me down, and I lay under a thick bush of juniper while Leather-Face tramped slowly through the thicket, poking here and there with his bayonet.

Some others came up—Royal Americans by their accent—and Leather-Face said vexedly in a broad Lancashire dialect, "Thought Ah'd got another o' the boogers. Roonin', 'e was. Moost 'a missed 'im, though."

I lay there with the blood running down my side and gathering in a pool in the breast of my shirt, expecting to be dragged out and bayoneted any moment.

But one of the Royals suggested, "That's John Allan's place—Rebel John. He was pretty rich for a farmer. Ought to be good pickings in there. Let's have a look before the fire gets further." And off they went.

Painfully I crawled away down the shallow ravine toward the Aulac stream. Behind me the fog flickered red and yellow as Inverma, its six barns and the seven tenant houses went up in one flame together. Horses and cattle screamed and bellowed in the burning stalls and stables, a horrible sound, and somewhere a lone dog howled.

I had a notion that Mary Allan might have taken her children down the ravine to the marshes when the fight approached Inverma. The old French bridge had long since rotted away, but it was possible to get across the little branch of the Aulac stream in a strip of swamp below and thus reach the upland of Jolicoeur, where the road crossed on its way around the great marsh of Tantramar.

My back and right shoulder felt as if I had been smitten with a sledge hammer, but there was no sharp pain, only a dull, throbbing ache. My right arm hung numb, and blood was seeping down into my breeches. As I stood looking across the marshy stream a man came out of the woods on the nigh side, holding a musket warily. He wore a fur cap and a caribou hunting shirt—one of Allan's Acadians. I hailed him in a croaking voice, and he called something over his shoulder and ran toward me, followed by Mrs. Allan and a little flock of Acadian women and children. All were weeping—all but Mary Allan. She was dry-eyed, mistress of herself and of them all. There was no talk. They saw my bloody shirt and led me to their nook in the woods, where the women tore strips from their petticoats to bind my wound, and the man brought water from the stream, and the children stared.

'Twas not a bad wound. The ball had slit the thin flesh over my ribs and come to a stop at the shoulder, half exposed. When the women cut my shirt away the battered chunk of lead fell to the ground. In the hurry of the fight, Leather-Face must have charged his musket lightly. The women had snatched up a couple of kettles and some quilts before they fled Inverma, and the man Jean had a tinder box and an ax besides the gun. I looked around anxiously for Mary's children and found them sitting in a row upon a log, obedient to her orders.

"Thank God you're all safe," I said. "I wasn't here when you needed me—after all my promises to John!"

"What's happened?" she asked quietly, and the other women crowded about, watching my face.

"Everything. Our force is broken, and half must be prisoners. Colonel Eddy may be able to rally a few at Sackville, but I doubt if he gets the chance. Even that fool Gorham can't fail to send the garrison in pursuit."

"But the Massachusetts troops—they must be very near now?"

"There aren't any. We've been on our own from the first."

"What's to become of us?" Mary Allan said.

I shook my head. "God knows. The soldiers are in a wild mood. I reckon the marines are pretty tired and satisfied with the day's work. But the Royals must be in a sour humor, seeing how small a force had kept them shut up so long. They'll take it out on the people—and probably the Yorkshiremen'll give 'em a hand at it. I think you'll be well advised to stay in the woods a few days, till the fury of the soldiers has spent itself."

" 'The calamity of fire and sword,' " she murmured. "That was what Gorham promised us, wasn't it?"

I said, "It's the calamity of weather and hunger we've got to face just now. That air from the southeast spells rain to me. We must put up some shelters of brushwood and do some foraging."

I was not much help, but Jean was a good axman like all the *Acadiens* and the countrywomen were strong and quick-witted. By dark we had bivouacs of the Indian sort for all. There were fifteen women and girls and twenty-eight children of all ages. The rain began soon after, cold as charity, and fell all night. The wind rose and lashed the treetops in the full fury of a November storm and toward morning blew all our pitiful shelters down. The women and children huddled under sodden quilts and blankets. I heard no whimpering. The fate of their absent men weighed on the womenfolk too heavily for tears, and the children endured in silence, wondering, I suppose, why they were out of their warm beds this miserable night.

In the morning Jean and I prowled cautiously toward Inverma. We buried the two dead rebels in a shallow grave at the side of the lane. There was no sign of the redcoat I shot except a wide bloodstain on the dead grass, washed thin by rain. We poked with long sticks in the ashes of the big house, all hot and hissing under the rain, and found a treasure in the root cellar—a heap of potatoes roasted in their jackets. I sent Jean back for the women, to come and fill their skirts, and while we were all busy there I heard one of the Acadian girls gasp, "*Soldats! Soldats!*"

I looked up and saw a mounted officer and half a dozen Royal Americans coming toward us from the road. 'Twas too late to run. We stood about the ashes of Inverma and let them come up to us. No one uttered a word. There was nothing to say. The officer was the gray man Dixson, who had beaten our attempt to open the palisade gate and later made his hazardous way to Halifax with the word that brought relief to the fort. We kept our eyes on him, ignoring the soldiers. He was an old neighbor of these people, with a reputation for good sense and kindliness. He saluted Mary gravely and got off his horse.

"Mrs. Allan, ma'am, I'm sorry to say I have orders to put you under arrest."

"My children . . ." she said quickly. She had the baby, George

Washington, in her arms; the rest were back in the woods with the Acadian youngsters.

He hardened his face. "My orders are to bring you, and you alone. But you may take the baby. These women can look after the others."

He helped her to mount the horse and passed the baby up to her. He dismissed Jean with a diffident wave of his hand, but when he noticed my bandaged shoulder and the English musket slung to my back his eyes widened.

"Who are you?"

"My name is Strang."

"A rebel, or I'm a Dutchman. Fall in about him, lads."

The soldiers shouldered arms and formed a small double file with myself in the middle and the horse ahead. As we moved off Mary called out in French to the women, "For the love of God, take care of my children!"

The wailing of the women sounded behind us, fainter and fainter, all the way out to the road. We bent our heads against the rain that slanted down on the gusty wind. The soldiers cursed the weather and held their hats over the gun pans to keep the powder dry. But they found humor in each smoking heap of ruins that we passed, and I could almost feel the stares of the refugees watching us from the woods beyond the fields. A miserable feeling of weariness and emptiness came upon me as we climbed over the shoulder of Camp Hill, and Dixson, seeing me stagger, told me gruffly to put my good hand on his shoulder. The marshes looked gray under the rain, and when we reached the end of the ridge, Fort Cumberland with its fringe of burned-out structures was shabby and sordid. I dropped my hand from Dixson's steady shoulder and jerked up my head for the entry into the fort.

We went in by the palisade gate, and a crowd of soldiers' women and brats ran out of the barracks to greet us. We marched up the parade ground in a hullabaloo of shrill insult. The women were already wearing clothing pillaged from the farms, some of it Mary Allan's, the finery of her happier days, a bitter sight for her. Inside the ramparts we were separated, and I was marched to one of the casemates, where an armorer sergeant, after a glance at my stiff shoulder, decided to put the irons on my ankles. I was pushed into a dark cave full of men, who jostled about me, demanding my name and news; and one at the sound of my voice thrust his way to me in the foul darkness, threw his shackled wrists over my head, and hugged me painfully.

"Davy! Davy!" cried Richard Uniacke. "Devil a bit can I see of ye but, oh, man, man, it's good to have the feel o' ye!"

CHAPTER 34

Which Endeth the First Lesson

THE CASEMATE was one of the fort bombproofs, about twelve feet wide and perhaps twenty long, with a floor of stone flags and brick walls that arched and met overhead. The only light and air came from a foot-square, barred hole in the thick oak door. The bricks sweated coldly under the sodden earth of the ramparts, and the moisture trickled down and kept the flagstones wet. Twenty-five men were huddled in there when I came, and others were flung in as the hours went by until nigh forty of us stood in the all but utter darkness. The crowded bodies and our breathings made a smelly warmth. Less than half of us could lie down at a time. Few did.

We were marched out in sixes to a latrine in the palisade enclosure once a day, which was not enough. The casemate stank of urine. We were fed twice a day—biscuit and salt pork and for water a couple of wooden buckets with a piggin which passed from mouth to mouth. Once, on our way back from the latrine, Uniacke complained of the closeness of our confinement.

"Now ye know what we put up with, and our women and kids, the past three weeks," said the surly sergeant of the guard.

The supply of irons was limited, and only the prisoners considered dangerous were shackled. That, said Uniacke, rattling his short chain, was a compliment indeed.

Dr. Clarke was there and Captain Tom Falconer and Jim Avery. The Cobequid party had been caught without a chance, surrounded by a rush of marines as they marched up the road at the end of their long journey.

From the others, piece by piece, we put the tale together. The surprise had been complete. The camp was overrun before most our men were out of their blankets, and only the fog had saved a massacre. With Camp Hill taken, the men in the lines and on picket duty in the woods toward the fort had no choice but surrender, though some desperate fellows broke away and swam the Missaguash.

Colonel Eddy had rallied a considerable number at Inverma, but half were without arms, and the scarcity of powder—the bane of all our operations—made the end certain. Batt had led the soldiers with skill, and his picked force of Royal Americans had fought surprisingly well, though the marines decided the affair and exhausted themselves in the pursuit. Batt had begged Gorham to send the rest of his regiment over to Westkok and the Petitcodiac to cut off Eddy's retreat and destroy all boats and canoes. And Gorham, irresolute to the last, wrote the order and then canceled it, on grounds that it was raining and his men well-nigh barefoot.

'Twas hotly whispered in the garrison that Gorham should be relieved of his command. The women talked it in the barrack square, and his officers stood aloof when he made his rounds—the loneliest man in Cumberland. I have called him a fool, and most men called him coward. But let me say this of Joseph Gorham. He had the great virtue of mercy. Most men in his sorry position would have revenged themselves on the people who brought it about. Gorham forestalled a massacre by promptly making a proclamation offering pardon to all rebels who surrendered themselves and their arms within four days. About a hundred men and boys came out of the woods and surrendered, were disarmed, and sent to their homes. The rest were prisoners taken in the fight or had fled the country with Eddy. The subsequent persecution of the Yankees of Cumberland, which drove so many into exile, was none of Joe Gorham's work.

After the four-day limit expired Batt and his soldiers conducted an eager rebel hunt through the district. Some were brought in, and we heard their news. The burning of homes of fugitive rebels was still going on—Obed Ayer's by a party of vengeful Yorkshiremen. Colonel Eddy's brother Will, hidden in an oat bin in his barn, had the chilling experience of a sword run through and through the oats, one thrust piercing his coat, while his white-faced wife stood by. But it was the Yorkshiremen whose protests finally stopped the man hunt and the burnings. Perhaps they feared a rebel revenge if the Americans marched that way. Eddy had left that threat behind as he fled for the St. John with Howe and Rogers, the Machias men, the English deserters, and seventy or eighty Cumberlanders. They had a terrible journey through the wintry wilderness and did not reach Maugerville till after Christmas. Eddy himself did not stop till he got to Machias. By the irony of fortune he missed the slim "reinforcement from Massachusetts" on which he had built our airy castle. Lieutenant Prescott reached Shepody with fifty Machias men in whaleboats on December 9th, heard the tale of disaster, and turned back.

Of Mark and François I could find no word. They had vanished like many another.

The morning after Prescott made his appearance and hasty retreat Colonel Gorham released most of our caged birds. He had orders to send the leading spirits from each district to Halifax for trial and was in a pretty dilemma. From Fort Lawrence he had Dr. Clarke and Falconer and Avery from Cobequid, but the leaders of Cumberland and Sackville had escaped with Eddy. At last in their place he chose Uniacke and me, and old Benoni Danks, who was lying half dead from a wound, in the garrison hospital.

"Och, how often I've wished to represent Cumberland in Halifax!" cried the irrepressible Uniacke. "Davy, dreams do come true!"

We were to sail in the *Vulture* as far as Windsor and were awaiting the guard to take us down to her when Mary Allan came to the barred hole in our door. She had been released at last, and Mark Patton, her father, was waiting with a cart outside the fort to take her to his home. The sentry stood aside and let her speak.

"God be with you, David, and you, too, Mr. Uniacke. You're both so young! Surely He will grant us some little prayer for all the suffering."

The marines were returning to Windsor in the man-of-war. We marched before them down the dike, carrying Danks on a litter. The old man was pale and well-nigh speechless. Pans of ice were drifting about the Basin on the red Fundy tide. The marshlands glistened white with snow wherever the grass hummocks rose above the mud, and all the countryside was white and stark. The smoke of the fort's chimneys rose blue in the frosty air. It looked peaceful enough now, but off Cumberland Creek the *Vulture* lay dark and ominous—worthy of her name. In the time to come she lived up to it, what with her part in the affair of General Arnold and Major André and many another sinister excursion into the coast of America.

On the slope down to the marsh we passed the burial ground of the fort, with a number of new high mounds under the snow that covered the graves. One had a stake thrust into the snow at its head. Upon it, burned into the wood with a hot iron, was a simple

JOHN STRANG, *private, R.F.A.*
November 1776

It brought a lump to my throat, but I had no tears. God knows there was weeping enough in that sorrowful countryside. How many men were dead on either side we never knew. Both Gorham and Eddy, for their own ends, were anxious to minimize the whole affair. For instance, Gorham, who sat supinely behind his ramparts till the very last shot had been fired, put the loss of his Royals in the last rush on Camp Hill at two killed and one wounded. And his was the official report! Of the killed and wounded amongst the marines, who had done practically all the fighting, he mentioned not a word. They had rescued him—marines, of all people!—and put a seal upon his failure. That he could not forgive.

And in the same way Colonel Eddy, that rash adventurer who had bungled the whole affair and scuttled off to Machias without waiting to see the end, had the impudence to write Congress that "our" loss was one man killed. Meaning his little band of originals, I suppose, for they mostly saved their skins.

But the truth? When rebellions fail it is the fate of the uncomplaining dead to be buried in secret, lest vengeance fall upon their families. How many decent men and boys lie buried in the woods, in the marshes which tell no tales, in the orchards and pasture corners of Cumberland; how many others crawled bleeding to their homes, to be nursed in secret and hidden like lepers whenever the soldiers passed, no one will ever know. If earth could speak, those quiet Cumberland farms could tell a winter's tale.

God rest all those poor bones! Ill led, half armed, undisciplined and wholly unsupported, except by a vague faith that somehow they would win for their colony a freedom that the king denied, they had kept a superior force of the royal troops shut up in a fort for four-and-twenty days, had attacked that fort with nothing but the muskets in their hands, and come within an ace of victory.

A small affair, a skirmish lost in the thunders of a great war, a drama played at the wrong end of the spyglass. In the time to come our smug historians will ignore it if they can. Already I have seen them scraping their minds for pious excuses to explain the "seditious" attitude of Nova Scotia in '76.

I am an old man now and have seen great changes in government and in the minds of men. Let me write here then, with a firm pen and a clear memory, that to our small and scattered population of Nova Scotia in '76 the affair at Fort Cumberland had the proportions and significance of a Saratoga in reverse. Had it succeeded where it failed, had it been better planned and better led, had it received even a vestige of support from Massachusetts, we should have rolled on, gather-

ing strength from every town and village and planted the striped flag
on the citadel of Halifax.

CHAPTER 35

Prison Walls

IN THE *Vulture* we were taken below to some dark cubbyhole lit with
a solitary purser's dip. There was a reek of bilge and an eternal scurry
of rats behind the bulkhead. There was a fair wind down Chignecto
Bay when we left the deck, and ten hours later we knew by the motion
of the ship and the intermittent rush of feet on the upper deck that
the *Vulture* had rounded Cape Chignecto and was tacking to weather
Cape Split. A pair of feet clattered down a ladder and halted at our
door. Our dip had burned out long since, and we blinked in the light
of a lantern held by a midshipman in soiled white long togs.

"The old bloke's dropped off the hooks," he announced cheerfully.
"The captain says you may come on deck if you want to see the last
of him."

We scrambled upward at his heels and at a gun port in the waist
found a group of seamen grinning about the stiff form of Benoni
Danks. They had not bothered to sew him up in canvas but a pair
of heavy bar shot were lashed to his feet—"to carry him down all
standin'" as the boatswain said. A couple of officers stood by, and the
captain was leaning, bored, against the taffrail aft.

"Ye can't chuck him into the Bay like a dead dog!" protested Uniacke violently.

"Why not?" one of the officers demanded humorously.

"The man's entitled to a decent burial ashore; ye'll be in Windsor
in a few hours."

The officer turned away muttering something about "the rebel
bastard," but the captain came along the deck to know the trouble.

"This man," said Uniacke passionately, "served the king faithfully
in his time—in Nova Scotia, in Cuba, with Wolfe at Quebec . . ."

"Very well! We'll hold a burial somewhere. If this wind holds we
may not be able to weather Cape Split, and if it snows as I expect,
we'll have to go about and shelter inside Cape D'Or. You may remain
on deck if you wish."

The wind held cold from the northeast, and soon specks of snow were blowing, proving the captain's weather eye. The *Vulture* put back and rounded to under the lee of Cape D'Or. We were not permitted to go ashore with the corpse. A midshipman and half a dozen seamen took it off in a boat, with a couple of spades and instructions to "plant him high and dry as nigh the shore as ye can, and be lively about it." There was a bit of sea running around the cape, and the shore was steep. We watched them shovel a hole in the red-clay slope and thrust the dead man in. So ended Captain Benoni Danks, onetime commandant of Danks's Rangers, a veteran of four campaigns, a Nova Scotia pioneer, buried like a thief between high water and low. Not a lovable man, perhaps. They told some bloody tales of his ranger days at Beausejour. But he had fought bravely in his fashion in his time and might have spent his last days comfortably at the fireside of his Cumberland farm if his old gray head had not been fired with the notion of liberty.

At Windsor we tarried in the "fort"—Windsor fort was a pineboard barrack, a blockhouse, and a few old guns in a miserable earthwork— while horses and escort were arranged for the journey to Halifax. We set off holding the reins in manacled hands, and a chain was shackled from ankle to ankle under the horse's belly. Half a dozen soldiers and a corporal made the escort. The snow was fairly deep, but the traffic of supplies to Halifax had made a fair sled track of that abominable road. Avery, Falconer, and Dr. Clarke were bitter against Eddy for his mismanagement and for running away in the moment of failure; they were glum and said little. Uniacke was blithe enough, and I tried to keep my spirits up to his. When we stopped for the night at the place where I had searched and robbed the king's messenger, the woman of the inn had nothing to say to us and met my eyes with a cold, blank stare.

In the morning soon after leaving the inn we rode past the shore of a frozen lake, surrounded by snow-mantled trees, beautiful in the winter sunlight. "Here's a lovely place!" said Uniacke, pulling up his horse and halting the whole procession. "I've marked it before, though never in winter. In summer it's glorious. A man could live content here by the road and watch the world go by. Someday I'll do that, if God so wills. I'll call it Mount Uniacke after my old home in Ireland— you're Irish, aren't you, Corporal?"

The corporal nodded cheerfully.

"Look here," said Dick. "Take these things off our wrists and ankles, will ye—like a good fella? I give ye my solemn oath not to escape."

The corporal scraped his chin.

" 'Pon me honor as an Irishman!" added Dick in his best brogue.

The corporal shrugged and unlocked the shackles—but only Uniacke's and mine.

"Thim sour-faced divils"—jerking a thumb at Falconer and Avery and the doctor—"I can't trust and won't."

'Twas wonderful to have the irons off, but afterward I was sorry, for the incident put a gulf between us and the others. Uniacke waved a gay hand toward the white lake and the curving shore. "Mount Uniacke!"

Corporal Lawson twisted his mouth. "The damned lake's shaped like a hang rope!"

It was snowing briskly as we entered the streets of Halifax, and we bent low over the horses' heads against the sweep and bite of it. I was glad when we reached the old jail on Hollis Street, for I was half frozen and my shoulder ached. The jail was overcrowded. The shuffling jailer made space for Uniacke and me in a barred room with a dozen other men. Clarke, Falconer, and Avery were taken to another part. There were several hundred American prisoners in Halifax, mostly seamen. The town jail was full of them, and many others were confined aboard hulks off the dockyard. A roaring, happy-go-lucky crowd, men of all sorts, from militia taken at Bunker Hill to the crew of the latest privateer wrecked on the wintry coast. Every colony on the seaboard was represented, but most of the men were New Englanders, and their whimsical, nasal accents filled the rooms from morn to late at night. The prison fare was coarse and meager; no candles were provided, and no bedding but straw, so that a man needed money to sustain life within its walls. For that reason most of the prisoners were allowed to roam the town on parole during certain hours of the day, begging pence and castoff clothes from the inhabitants and working at odd jobs. They were men of all trades and would turn their hands to anything from blacksmithing to scrubbing floors, and some sat in their rooms whittling ship models and the like, which they peddled abroad on market days.

This loose confinement astonished me at first. The place was more like a seamen's lodginghouse than anything else, especially when they returned to their rooms of an evening, and various smells of cooking stole along the corridor, and their rum-tuned voices broke into song. There were iron bars over the windows, but the oak sills were old and rotten, and the great door was guarded only by the jailer, an old man with a high, whispering voice, and his slatternly wife. To be sure there was the guard at the governor's mansion, not far along Hollis Street, and little knots of marines and Colonel Small's Highlanders wandered about the town, as poor, as alien as the prisoners themselves. However our real guardian was the Nova Scotia winter. The only vessels moving out of the port were transports taking forage and lumber and such stuff to Howe at New York. And the path along the south shore to Yarmouth, where a fugitive might slip across to Massachusetts with a friendly Nova Scotia smuggler, was one long wilderness of snow. Come spring, said many a man from the side of his mouth, 'twould be a different matter.

I quickly discovered that our Nova Scotia rebels were on a different footing from the rest and were not permitted to roam the town. There were others besides our Cumberland group. Amongst them I discovered Parson Seccombe of Chester, that fiery preacher of the rights of man. And from Colonel Simpson, of the St. John River, charged with supplying the rebels with food and shelter, I learned that John Allan was at Maugerville, trying to gather up the threads that Eddy had dropped. This set me afire to escape and join him. I had made one winter journey along the coast and could make another. My wound was well-nigh healed. I pointed out the rotten window sills to Uniacke, but he was cold. "What! Leave the others to face the music, Davy? Not I—nor you. We'll stay and face our fortune with the rest."

Mysteriously, quilts, candles, books, and daily gifts of food came to us through the jailer. We needed some such bounty, for we were penniless, and on New Year's Day, the dreary New Year of 1777, the weather turned bitter, and the cold crept through our walls and set us huddling around the few stoves.

The jailer was mum to all questions, but I suspected that our benefactor was Malachi Salter. When, therefore, on a day in late January, Uniacke and I were taken to a small room in the jailer's quarters to meet a nameless visitor I expected to see that good old man. Instead we found a handsome, black-browed man in boots and a fear-nought coat and a beaver hat, standing with his back to a brisk fire.

It was Michael Francklin. He gave me a curt nod and said to Dick, "Well, Uniacke, strange things have happened since last we shoved our knees under the table at Francklin Manor."

Uniacke's face lit with his cheerful Irish smile. "Ah! We talked horses, I remember, and you said the Fundy settlements could be the Ireland of America."

"True. They raise good horses in Ireland—and good men. Too full of spirit though, Uniacke."

Uniacke's face went dark. "If ye've come to preach, sir, save your breath. You're a king's man; I'm a rebel. Let it go at that."

He turned to leave the room, and Francklin said, "One moment! You omit what we have in common. Forget I'm a king's man as you call it, and forget you're a rebel. Forget I'm an Englishman and you're an Irishman. Forget—if you can—that we both married American women. A man's true country is the place he makes his home, and our home's this queer, raw wilderness that men call Nova Scotia. Whatever you did in Cumberland, Uniacke, was done for what you considered the good of this province. Believe me then when I say that I chose my course long ago for the same end."

"Ye tried to get the Nova Scotia Yankees to take up arms for the king!" Uniacke accused.

"For the defense of the province only."

"Against their fellow Americans!"

"Against certain Americans—Jonathan Eddy, for instance."

'Twas a shrewd thrust, that, and Uniacke was silent.

"Suppose we forget the larger issues of this war, Uniacke. They will be decided without reference to what Nova Scotia thinks or does. A man's first interest is the defense of his home and family. It comes down to that, doesn't it? And who endangers the homes and families of Nova Scotia? King George? You know—none better—that the king hasn't enough troops in this province to make a show for a Halifax holiday. Why, barring a corporal's guard at Annapolis there's not a single soldier in all the western half of the peninsula, from Halifax around to Windsor—and that in a region populated largely by New Englanders!"

"There are no American soldiers either," Dick said ironically.

"Ah! True! I understand General Washington has set his face firmly against any invasion of the province. But General Washington unfortunately has no control over certain of his countrymen, particularly those who live in the ports of New England. Nor has the Congress, nor for that matter has the General Court of Massachusetts. All these have tried to establish law and order, and so far they have failed. The result is that every petty sea thief from Machias around to New Haven is out for plunder wherever he can get it—and the handiest place is just across the Bay of Fundy, in Nova Scotia."

I broke in, "What d'you mean?"

"I mean that every settlement on this coast, including your own home, young man—you're a Strang from Liverpool, aren't you?—is now under a reign of pillage and murder conducted by the lowest ruffians of New England. They come in fishing schooners for the most part, but also in sloops, jiggers, whaleboats—anything that will float. A few carry letters of marque issued by obscure committees in their home ports; some have papers openly forged in the name of the General Court or the Congress; most have no warrant at all and make no secret of it. It is mass piracy such as you cannot find in the world today except upon the coast of Barbary. They began by seizing Nova Scotia vessels at sea. Then they began to enter our creeks and harbors. Whole settlements have been plundered, whole towns held to ransom. And what they can't carry off, they destroy. All in the name of Liberty."

"Why don't you arm our people then?" I sneered.

He regarded me somberly. "I am not the governor. I can only suggest. And no suggestion is worth my breath so long as our people submit to robbery right and left in the hope that General Washington or the Congress or the General Court of Massachusetts will take notice of their plight. It's to Boston that they send their petitions, not to Halifax. How long will they persist in this folly?"

"So long as the king keeps a foot in Nova Scotia!" I said hotly.

"I'm afraid you were born to be hanged, young man." He turned from me abruptly and addressed himself to Uniacke.

"Richard, these are pressing times, and I'll waste no words. I want your help."

"For what?"

"For the freedom of Nova Scotia!"

"That's treason!" Dick scoffed, but he looked astonished.

"Reason," snapped Michael Francklin. "Rebellion's hopeless; you've seen that. There remains the other way—debate and compromise."

"Politics!"

"Why not? This war will bring a change in British colonial policy. Our people will be heard. But they must have a voice."

"What's wrong with yours, Francklin?"

"I am too old, and the struggle will be hard and very long. It needs a young man, one who understands the people and will fight for them with every art he knows. It will be a battle of wits, Richard, and using your enemy's weapons—privilege and influence. I think you'd enjoy it."

"And who will be my enemies?"

"The Council in Halifax to begin with. But that's only the begin-

ning. The Americans have written the northern colonies—Quebec and
Nova Scotia—off their books. They will win their war, and at the end
a boundary will be drawn, and across it will pour the refugees, the
American Tories, for there will be no room for them in the victorious
states. There will be thousands, people from all walks of life, and
amongst them the men whose greed and mismanagement have brought
about this war. They will try to establish privilege for themselves again,
here in Nova Scotia, and there will be a long struggle between them
and their Nova Scotia counterpart—the Council and their friends."

"And the people will lose, whichever wins," said Uniacke disdain-
fully. But his interest was caught. There was a gleam in his Irish eyes.

"Not if you play your cards well, Richard. Most of the refugees will
be plain people, and their interests as plain as ours. Keep your eyes on
the Council and on the newcomers who seek privilege. Play one
against the other. Get yourself into a position where you can lean
your weight towards the Council, for they will be the weaker, but keep
your balance always."

Uniacke uttered an amazed laugh. "Begob, you're a spellbinder,
Francklin. D'ye realize who you're talking to? Plain Dick Uniacke,
twenty-three, with just enough education to make him a poor farmer
—and now under arrest for treason. D'ye take me for Dick Whitting-
ton? This isn't the London Road."

"I take you for a young man of sense and spirit, with powerful Irish
friends in Halifax and in Britain if you choose to use them—Baron
George of Dublin, for instance. You see, I know a lot more about
you than you think. A friend at court is worth a seat on the Council
any time, and you can go on from there.

"Look at me, Richard. I came to Nova Scotia like you, a young man
with little but an education. Halifax was an outpost in a savage-
haunted wilderness. The business of half its people was to sell rum and
the other half to drink it. I began by selling rum in a shed on George
Street. In two years I had a pair of shops and a trucking business. I
shifted from rum to breadstuffs and fine wines and as time went on
I got into the fish-exporting trade with the Mediterranean and made
a small fortune operating ships between Halifax and Naples. That
gave me influence in the Council—guineas talk, with the king's voice!
—and I made another fortune in army and navy contracts. When
Wolfe went to Quebec it was I who supplied his fleet and army. I was
elected to the assembly, but they had no power. I got a seat on the
Council. For ten years I was lieutenant governor of the province.

"I was displaced last year—but I still am president of the Council, and all my influence, all these years, has been directed quietly towards the end I now propose to you. I am no rebel, though Governor Legge called me so. I have taken things as they are and made them my tools. I've not succeeded in all I undertook but I thank God I've kept our people from flying at each other's throats since '65. There remains a great work to be done; but in the meantime I must struggle merely to keep our people together, to defend our shores, to maintain law and order, and to see that our boundaries and interests are not sacrificed by those muddling men in England when the peace is made. The great work afterward must be undertaken by some other, some younger man, with a true love for this country alone and a willingness to work with knaves and fools and money-grubbing officials for the good of it. But mark this, Richard: he must be loyal to the British flag. No other road is possible now. Forget the king—kings come and go. It's the British people you must think about, not only in Britain but over the world."

That dark and handsome face of Francklin's was alight. He really believed these things. The words poured out of him. And when he was finished, Uniacke said slowly, "How am I to be freed? And what becomes of the others?"

"The others will be permitted to 'escape.' But you must be cleared, for the sake of your future. You have been arrested; your arrest is known, and there must be a charge. Providence works in mysterious ways. As it happens there is a charge at hand—a charge of debt. It appears that last autumn you made a contract with a merchant of Windsor for a supply of wooden hoops, on which there was an advance payment of thirty or forty pounds. You were so busy with—ah—other matters in Cumberland that your covenant lies broken and the merchant has taken a capias against you for debt. The case is to be tried at the Easter term, here in Halifax. It is all arranged. Your friends here have provided money to discharge the suit when the time comes— and there will be money to take you to Ireland to finish your studies at law."

"What? That'll take four years!"

"And what's that in a lifetime, Uniacke? The secret of success in life is to lay long plans and follow them through. In four years the affair in Cumberland will be forgotten in bigger things—the end of the war for one, I hope. You'll come back with your law degree and a fat appointment in your pocket—Baron George will see to that."

"Why are you doing all this for me?" demanded Uniacke in sudden suspicion.

"I've told you"—patiently. "But there are other reasons. One's that I'm anxious to see no hangings for the Cumberland affair—and certain members of the Council are determined to hang you all, for an example. But my chief reason, Uniacke, is that in you I see myself when young, with the long road ahead and the work to be done."

"Suppose I refuse?"

Francklin's dark eyes blazed. "Would you see your friends hang?"

"I must have time to think it over."

"Time! Time! The trials will take their course in time—young Strang's in two days or so. I can open jail doors but I can't tamper with the courts—nor the gallows. Understand this—if your friend Strang sets a foot inside the courtroom, he will hang! The case is clear against him. A foot inside! A foot!"

"I must have time," answered Uniacke stubbornly.

CHAPTER 36

The Scales of Justice

THE MORNING of my trial was sunny in the thin, gilt January fashion that serves only to emphasize the cold. A north wind whirled old snow along the barren streets, snow powdered by the traffic of horses and sleds and the hurrying feet of the frostbitten townsmen, snow sooty and stained by flung slops and the droppings of horses and oxen. Halifax was at its wintriest and worst. I was shaved by a barber for the first time in my life—he devoted especial care to my throat—and the deputy provost marshal sent four marines under a corporal to escort me to the courthouse. Hardly a soul was astir in the bleak morning air, and our small troop marched without notice along Hollis Street past the smoking chimneys and frosty panes of Government House, up George Street and across the Parade to Argyle Street and along Argyle to the corner of Buckingham Street. The courthouse stood on the northeast corner, a gloomy, wooden barn of a place built when the town was young, with its main portico facing Buckingham Street. A pair of marine sentries shivered in greatcoats outside the door, and along Argyle Street stood a number of sleighs, with horses steaming under furs and coachmen stamping up and down in the grimy snow.

I was in my old leather breeches and gray country stockings but I had a pair of pewter-buckled shoes on my feet, and Uniacke had given me a linen shirt and a decent blue coat whose full skirts fell to my knees. The barber had arranged my long black hair in a tight queue, town-fashion, but I had no hat and wanted none, having lived bareheaded in all weathers for so many months. In the barber's small looking glass my face was lean and dark as an Indian's, except for the hard, pale scar of the bayonet wound. My tongue was wholly healed, and so was the bullet score on my back and shoulder, though it itched intolerably at times. On the whole I felt presentable as a specimen Nova Scotia rebel and resolved in a queer lightheaded way to carry the thing off with bravado. I was even a little disappointed to find the space for the public occupied by a knot of townsfolk of the poorer sort, mostly women, huddling together in a corner as if for warmth.

The place was dark after the glitter of the street. The windows were too few and too small for the size of it and the panes crusted with frost. I was conducted to a hard little bench in the prisoner's box, with an armed marine on either side, and as my eyes became accustomed to the dim light I looked about me curiously. 'Twas typical of our poor province that this drafty box on the slope of Citadel Hill was also the home of our legislature. In this place Simeon Perkins and Seth Harding and William Smith had represented Queens County before the troubles came, and here, too, Jonathan Eddy and Will Scurr and poor Benoni Danks had spoken for Cumberland. My lip curled when I thought of the assembly now, with every friend of America unseated, and the province "represented" by chosen friends of the government—Nova Scotia's long parliament, which sat fourteen years without once going to the people.

The jurymen had been sworn and were on their benches, twelve men of all ages, clerks and petty merchants by the look of them. I recognized no face in the court but that of William Nesbit, the attorney general, the wizened sharp-tongued old man who had suppressed the letter from Congress to our legislature and sent it off to England instead. A rebel could look for no mercy from that quarter.

There was but one stove in the courtroom, set behind the judge's dais for his benefit and lit only an hour or two before by the feel of the air. Every man's breath hung in little cold wisps when he spoke. The attorney general and his clerk and the clerk of the crown sat at a long oak table before me, huddled in their black robes, putting their three wigs together from time to time and shuffling the papers before them. The crier, an old soldier by the look of him, stood at the table's end, holding his bell by the clapper. At the other end stood the deputy provost marshal, consulting a large silver watch from time to time and watching the door behind the dais. I knew who would come through that door: old Jonathan Belcher, the chief justice of the province, himself a native of Massachusetts.

But when the door opened, and everybody jumped up respectfully at the deputy provost's fierce gesture, the figure in the flowing scarlet robe and the big full-bottomed wig was nothing like the venerable Belcher's.

"His lordship Justice Morris!" bawled the deputy provost. I felt a twinge of disappointment. I had expected to be condemned by one of our own Yankees, anyhow. This man Charles Morris was an Englishman, surveyor general of the province for many years and now a justice of the Supreme Court. Evidently the chief justice did not consider my case worthy of his attention. I was a little indignant. (I laugh now to think how smug and self-important a martyr to Liberty stood in the prisoner's box that frosty morning.)

The crier rang his bell and uttered a long and unintelligible howl that began with "Oyez! Oyez! Oyez!" and ended with a sonorous "Gawd save the King!" His lordship's body servant appeared with a tin box of hot charcoal which he placed reverently before his lordship's feet, and he draped a small quilt over feet and box before withdrawing. I noticed, then, that foot warmers were in fashion at the winter courts, for the bewigged gentlemen at the long table had boxes of hot bricks nestling in straw beneath the board.

Evidently Justice, though blind, did not intend her toes to freeze.

His lordship rapped the desk with the gavel and without looking at me asked in an austere voice, "Has the prisoner an attorney?"

In the enormous silence I felt one of the marines nudging me and answered, "No!"

The deputy provost barked at me, "No, your lordship!"

"No, your lordship."

"Ah!" His lordship's hard eyes looked past me into the public area. From jail gossip I knew a little of court routine and guessed that he was about to appoint an attorney for my defense from amongst the hangers-on beyond the rail. The notion filled me with fury. His Majesty was determined to hang me—very well!—but ha' done with these smug rites beforehand! Putting a righteous face on murder-by-act-of-parliament! Hypocrisy! My head buzzed, but before any of these scornful and magnificent things could reach my tongue I heard a high voice behind me crying, "M'lord, I am prepared to act for the prisoner if it so please the court!" Not a sign of emotion crossed his lordship's grim features, but there was vinegar in the voice with which he said, "Very well, sir. You may consult with the prisoner."

There came into my view a thin young man in a too-small wig that sat on the top of his head and permitted a bristle of carroty hair to escape below and a stained blue coat with heavy, old-fashioned square skirts and a green waistcoat and black smallclothes and stockings. He unrolled a black gown from a bundle under his arm and covered this shabby apparel but he still had a threadbare look and peered at me sharply over a pair of small spectacles which I suspect he wore for effect.

"M'lord, I chance to be familiar with the prisoner's case and am prepared to proceed at once." He stepped forward to the table and sat apart from the others. They sniffed and had the air of well-bred dogs in the presence of a mongrel who has found a none-too-savory bone.

The crier howled, "His Majesty the King against David Strang! The charge, High Treason!"

The clerk of the Crown popped up and began to read in a singsong voice the indictment, a long document couched in the most ridiculous terms and typical of the pompous humbug which in those days choked our courts.

It nearly choked the clerk, at any rate, and he was forced to break his chant from time to time to suck in a long, whistling breath.

"'. . . David Strang, late of Liverpool, this province, seaman, being a subject of our present most serene sovereign lord George the Third, by the grace of God of Great Britain, France, and Ireland king, and not having the fear of God in his heart, nor having any regard for his duty and allegiance, but being moved and seduced by instigators of the Devil as a false traitor and rebel against his supreme, true, natural, lawful and undoubted sovereign, and also devising as much as in him lay, most wickedly and traitorously intending to change and subvert the rule and government of His Majesty's Province of Nova Scotia . . .'"

There was a good deal more of this rigmarole, with the clerk growing more and more purple in the face and gasping more and more frequently for breath; and then "'. . . in the month of November in the year of our Lord 1776, at and in the township of Cumberland with a great number of traitors and rebels against our sovereign lord the King, to wit, to the number of three hundred persons whose names are at present unknown to the jurors, being armed in a warlike and hostile manner, with drums beating and with guns, swords, pistols, pikes, clubs and other weapons offensive and defensive, falsely and traitorously assembled and formed themselves against our sovereign lord the King, and with force of arms did treacherously prepare, order, wage and levy a public and cruel war against our lord the King to the great terror and dread of His Majesty's loyal subjects, until dispersed by His Majesty's troops. All which is against the duty of his allegiance and against the peace of our lord the King, his crown and dignity, and against the form of the statute in that case made and provided, and against the laws of this province.'"

The poor devil sat down panting like a spent hound. His lordship looked at me severely. "The prisoner will stand!"

I stood.

"David Strang, you have heard the charge against you. Plead you guilty or not guilty?"

"Guilty!"

My threadbare attorney turned and favored me with a long, sad stare, and 'twas a temptation to stick my tongue out at him, schoolboy-fashion. For that matter I had a wild longing to whistle my contempt for the whole pompous lot of them, to hoot and howl, to raise all those solemn wigs with a war whoop. They knew my guilt; they were there to prove it and presently see me hanged for it, and because I had saved all their righteous humbug with a single word they gazed on me with shocked and disapproving faces, as if I had blasphemed. I smiled; I was about to laugh aloud, but a remembered bit of prison gossip froze the smile on my lips. Someone in the Hollis Street jail had mentioned that a prisoner pleading guilty to a capital offense might be assumed mad. "Better a dance on the rope and an end," that voice had said, "than a madman's cell in the workhouse all the days of your life."

All the besieging cold of the courtroom entered my body then. I was frozen with sheer horror. It was a blessed relief when his lordship rasped, with his eyes on Nesbit, "Call your witnesses."

The attorney general arose and cleared his lean old throat. "M'lord, my witnesses are all engaged upon His Majesty's service in far parts of the province. I have their depositions. Some of them are very long, and I know the court's time is precious; also the temperature of this courtroom is not—ah—conducive to long sitting. In view of these things and of the prisoner's plea, it seems clear to me that one deposition will be sufficient to serve the ends of justice; I shall rest my case on that." He passed a paper to the clerk of the Crown, who began to read again in that irritating singsong, gabbling the words.

" 'Deposition of Lieutenant Thomas Dixson, late Gorham's Rangers and at present attached to the garrison of Fort Cumberland, this province.

" 'This deponent declares that being with a detachment of the Royal Fencible American Regiment, a few miles from Fort Cumberland, on the morning of November 30th 1776, and approaching the farm Inverma, the home of the rebel John Allan, where fighting had occurred on the previous day, this deponent came upon David Strang in the company of Allan's wife and some other women of the refugee rebels. Deponent saith further that the said David Strang had a fresh bullet wound in his back, and carried a musket belonging to His Majesty, identified by the number 60, the said regiment's numeral in the Army List, being burned upon the butt of the said musket. Upon being challenged as a rebel, the said Strang gave himself up and was taken to Fort Cumberland and there confined awaiting His Majesty's pleasure.' "

The clerk sat down as if jerked by a string. The attorney general gave the least suggestion of a bow to the threadbare young man and sat down also. Up jumped Threadbare. "The learned attorney general's deponent relates this occurrence as of November 30th, the day after the rebel defeat. I put it to the court that on the 30th of November Colonel Gorham, commanding His Majesty's forces at Fort Cumberland, offered by proclamation in the King's name a pardon to all rebels who gave up their arms within four days."

Up jumped Nesbit. "If my learned young friend will examine Colonel Gorham's proclamation he will find that it was made on the afternoon of the 30th. The prisoner Strang was taken in the morning. Taken in arms!"

"I suggest that my learned friend is splitting hairs," barked Threadbare.

"I suggest that the learned attorney for the defense confine his attention to the facts!" snapped old Nesbit. "The facts"—he turned his head a little for the benefit of the jury—"are that His Majesty's peace and justice require a severe example, for the good of all. The facts are that the penalty can only fall on those rebels taken in arms before noon on November 30th; for by a piece of extraordinary—and if I may say so, unwise—leniency, the commander of His Majesty's forces at Fort Cumberland saw fit to pardon nearly the whole of the rebel army, thereby making loyalty a mockery throughout the district, to the great detriment of His Majesty's liege subjects."

His lordship spoke coldly. "It is not the function of this court to criticize the decisions of His Majesty's officers in the field. But I grant your point. The prisoner does not come within the terms of the pardon offered by Colonel Gorham. Proceed, please."

The wizened little bird man Nesbit ruffled his black plumage, and his lean claws picked meaningly over the little heap of depositions on the table before him. "I have no wish to take up the court's time unnecessarily. The case is clear. There is other evidence—much further evidence. But I shall not—ah—pile Pelion upon Ossa, in view of the prisoner's plea. The Crown rests its case upon the deposition of Lieutenant Thomas Dixson."

He sat down and again for the benefit of the jury caught up the pile of depositions, turned them on edge, and struck them sharply on the table to bring their edges even. Threadbare got up and looked over the jury. They were a very ordinary crew, now that I had studied them a bit, and my light mind went back to my childhood, when boys and girls used to pluck dandelions gone to seed and let the downy seedlings blow away on the wind, chanting "tinker, tailor . . . butcher, baker, candlestick maker . . ." I forget how it goes now.

The jurymen looked cold, and no wonder in that tomblike atmosphere. The older fellows had their hands tucked into their sleeves for warmth, and their noses were pinched blue. The clerk of the Crown crept on tiptoe behind the judge's dais to warm his hands at the stove, on pretense of thawing the gelid ink in his pewter well, and from the public behind me I could hear a great sniffing and blowing of cold noses and the restless shuffle of chilled feet on the worn plank floor.

I looked at Threadbare and wondered who had sent him here, this cold morning, to be my champion. Michael Francklin? Absurd! Francklin's queer half-Tory, half-Whig ideals were too lofty for so poor an instrument as myself. Malachi Salter, then! No doubt this young pettifogger, one of the swarm who hung upon the fringes of the Halifax courts, was the best he could afford. I wondered what Threadbare would say. What *could* he say? The case against me was complete and inescapable like the hang rope itself. Not that I feared the gallows now. I saw it as a release, a boon, a gift from God. For my mind was flooded with a horrible suspicion that Threadbare would plead insanity. I saw myself locked up with the other lunatics in the workhouse, moping and mowing through the bars at passers-by, as I had seen them many a time in that dismal wooden hell on Spring Garden Road. A month in there would turn a man as mad as the rest. The notion set me in a perspiration that soaked my clothes and turned them cold as ice against my hot skin. I had been afraid in other times and places but I had never known a fear like this. The worst of it was that anything I said in protest, in my present feverish state, would support his argument. A voice in my head said over and over again monotonously, "Say nothing! Nothing! Nothing!" and I locked my teeth obediently.

I prayed devoutly, ay, passionately, to God to let me hang. I fixed my mind on the hang rope until I could see it and I stared at the jury, from face to face, as if by an effort of will I could make them see it too.

"M'lord," said Threadbare diffidently, "I propose to call one witness only."

He turned to the crier and mumbled a name I could not catch.

The crier straightened his veteran shoulders and roared suddenly, "Mistress Fear Helyer! Mistress Fear Helyer!"

The name fell upon my ears like a thunderbolt. I must have looked a lunatic then, for my mouth dropped open, and my eyes seemed to start out of my head. But no one was looking at me; they were all gazing past the high wooden sides of the dock. There was a stir behind me, and then Fear came into my astounded view, walking with a firm step toward the witness stand. Her face was very pale, and her eyes looked bigger and darker than I had known them. She wore a fashionable blue cloak with a fur collar, and a small, dark tricorne hat was pinned to her mass of brown hair. She seemed rigid and composed, a figure of marble, but I noticed the slim hands trembling in her fur-trimmed gloves. The clerk of the Crown advanced, gabbling something about an oath on the holy evangelists and proffering a grubby Testament which she put without hesitation to her lips.

Why had she come? At whose request? And what could she say? Something good of my character in Liverpool, I supposed; as if that— or anything else—could change the course of His Majesty's justice! What utter folly! Under my breath I damned Threadbare and his mysterious sponsor for bringing her here and Helyer for letting her come. There was a touch of charity about this indulgence of Fear's husband that set my teeth agrinding. And I was angry with Fear herself. Damn her sympathy! I fixed what I hoped was a cynical gaze on her face. Outwardly she was calm, mistress of herself, ay, and of that cold and curious court, with the unmistakable air of a lady who has stepped into a hovel on some charitable errand and wishes no one to presume upon the fact. But she would not meet my eyes. There was something almost desperate about the way she looked at everyone but me. Threadbare addressed her in a gentle and respectful voice.

"Mrs. Helyer, you are the wife of an officer of the Royal Fencible Americans?"

"Yes."

"Were you present at Fort Cumberland throughout the late—ah—uprising?"

"Yes."

"Do you know the prisoner?"

Involuntarily her eyes went toward me, but they stared past my shoulder somewhere.

"I have known him since childhood."

"Were you fond of him?"

"We were sweethearts," she said clearly.

"But you married an officer in His Majesty's forces?"

"Yes."

"In a moment of infatuation?"

She turned a dark and disapproving glance. "That is not a fair question, sir."

"In any case," snapped the attorney general, bouncing to his feet, "I fail to see what the lady's conjugal feelings have to do with the charge against the prisoner, m'lord!"

His lordship was making a note, and his quill scratched the paper and every taut nerve in me. He pointed the end of the feather at Threadbare.

"Proceed!"

"Let me put it another way, Mrs. Helyer," Threadbare said earnestly. "In spite of this marriage you retained your old affection for the prisoner?"

"Yes."

Threadbare shoved his bony hands under his gown and coat skirts and teetered on heels and toes. I wondered what was coming next, and so did the court. There was a rigid silence. Even the coughing and snuffling had stopped.

"Did you see him again?"

"Yes."

"Where? Be exact, please, about the time and place."

Her round chin went up. She gazed over the heads of everybody, scornfully, as if she suspected the cleanliness of the minds beneath.

"One night last October, between eleven o'clock and midnight. Outside the palisades of Fort Cumberland."

"You were alone?"

"Yes."

"Was your husband aware of this meeting?"

"No."

A little chorus of "Ah's" from the public behind me. His lordship gave them a sour glance and fingered his gavel. The side pieces of his full-bottomed wig, hanging like enormous jowls, gave him the face of a great, gloomy bloodhound.

"Hem!" coughed Threadbare. "Mrs. Helyer, did you leave the fort that night for any seditious or traitorous purpose?"

"No. It was a—a personal matter."

"Did you discuss the fort or its garrison or any military matter with the prisoner?"

"No."

"What were your sentiments towards the war between His Majesty's government and His Majesty's rebellious subjects in America?"

She replied promptly, "I believed and still believe that the war was brought about by wicked men on both sides, for their own ends, without regard for the innocent lives that would be involved."

His lordship nodded vigorously and then, realizing what he was doing, checked himself and scowled at the court. He fumbled under his robe and consulted a large gold watch. He addressed himself to Threadbare. "The morning is well advanced. If the attorney for the defense has much more evidence to produce, it will be necessary to adjourn the court within an hour, and in that case the deputy provost marshal should send out now to arrange refreshments for the jury from a pastry cook's."

The jury brightened.

"M'lord!" cried Threadbare. "That should not be necessary. The innocence of my client can be proven within a turn of the glass. In less!"

In half an hour! The faces of the jurymen fell comically. I suppose the notion of refreshments—free—had been the one bright spot in a dull day.

"Proceed!" his lordship grunted, and his face conveyed his opinion of a lawyer's half-hour. Doubtless the coals in his foot warmer had lost their heat.

Threadbare turned to Fear eagerly. "To save the court's time, ma'am, I shall pass over the period of the siege of Fort Cumberland and come to the point—to the evening of Thursday, November 28th, the last night of the siege. Will you tell the court briefly, please, where you spent that night."

"And kindly remember, madam," thundered the attorney general, "that you are under oath!"

Fear spoke calmly, choosing her words. "I left the fort, alone, soon after sunsetting, with my horse and rode through the rebel lines . . . to a farmhouse . . . on the east side of the Missaguash marshes . . . in the settlement called Fort Lawrence. I . . . spent the night . . . in an upper chamber."

"A bedchamber?"

"Yes."

In a prickling silence Threadbare asked gently, "Was the prisoner with you?"

"He was."

CHAPTER 37

His Majesty's Jury

THE JURY, the people, the whole court broke into a hubbub, and in the midst of it I jumped to my feet, rattling my handcuff chain and yelling hoarsely, "No! No!"

The marines thrust me down on my hard little bench so that my teeth rattled. His lordship was pounding his desk angrily and glaring from side to side, with his gray wattles rippling and flapping.

"Order!" bellowed the deputy provost. "Order in the court!"

In the heavy hush that followed, the attorney general barked suddenly at me, "Do you suggest that the witness lies, sir?"

"I say she's telling a half-truth! She's trying . . ."

Down came his lordship's gavel with a whack that made everybody jump. He roared "Silence!" as in his earlier Crown survey days he must have many times set the woods ringing with a cry of "Chain!"

And silence fell so quickly that his voice still lingered faintly in the outer chambers of the court. He had harsh words for us all, beginning with the attorney general and ending with the people outside the stout oak rail. Threadbare accepted meekly some stern advice upon the behavior of his client, and presently the attorney general arose to question Fear. That man could put more cold contempt into the fall of a word than any man or woman I ever heard.

"You have the temerity, madam, to come into His Majesty's court and brazenly confess that you, the wife of a British officer, were engaged in a guilty intrigue with this vagabond in the dock—his calling is given as 'seaman' but he seems more familiar with pillows than billows—at a time when your husband was risking life and limb in the performance of duty?"

Fear's eyes were very bright, with tears I think, though it might have been anger.

She bowed her head for a moment and said nothing.

"Answer my question!" snapped Nesbit.

"Why should she?" I cried, jumping to my feet. The redcoats grabbed me again, but I struggled to keep my feet, shouting at the top of my voice, "She's only trying to shield me for old friendship's sake! I won't have it! I won't have it, I tell you! I'm a rebel! A lieutenant in Eddy's army! Hear me now! Down with King George and tyranny! Long live Liberty in Nova Scotia!"

And while I shouted, the angry judge hammered his desk; Threadbare rushed to me crying something in his high voice; the marines bellowed, "Siddown! Siddown!"; the deputy provost, the attorney general added their cries to the din; the jurymen jumped to their feet for a better view of my struggle with the redcoats, and behind me the people surged and muttered at the rail.

I was thumped upon my bench as before, with a hand over my mouth that smelled partly of gun grease and mostly of redcoat's salt-herring breakfast.

Everyone fell silent together, except his lordship, who went on banging the gavel down monotonously in the hush, and we all looked at Fear. She was standing with her face bowed in her gloved hands, weeping.

His lordship was speechless. I have to smile now, after all these years, when I think of him. He had been brought up, you might say, with compass in hand and a surveyor's chain hooked to his belt, and his later career as surveyor general of the province had to do with maps for the most part, where everything was laid off on precise lines, with exact angles, courses, and distances. Now that old Jonathan Belcher's failing health had settled the red robe of the chief justice upon Morris' shoulders, he expected the course of the law to follow just such lines and was outraged to find that it did not. I doubt if Charles Morris had a profound knowledge of law; he had spent too much of his life at other things, but he still believed in the compass and now he determined to hack and blaze a straight line through this thicket of conflicting evidence to a decision. He pointed the gavel at old Nesbit as if it were a tomahawk.

"The witness may stand down. Sum your case, sir! And be brief—if you can!"

The attorney general ventured a disapproving sniff and turned and ran his eyes over the jurymen. They were all watching Fear's departure. Her back was straight as a ramrod, her head high, with a small red spot in each pale cheek. She looked straight before her until she was about to pass the dock; then she met my bewildered and angry eyes with a look, mysterious and unfathomable, that shook me as a poplar shivers in the fall when no wind stirs the trees.

She passed beyond my sight, and I waited to hear the great door open and close, but it did not. She was waiting, then, somewhere amongst the people, to hear the end.

"Gentlemen of the jury," the attorney general's dry voice began, "you have heard some extraordinary evidence. Not much of it, but more than enough to enable you to decide this case upon its merits. In November last year a rebel army besieged His Majesty's troops in Fort Cumberland many days. The rebels counted in their ranks a few men from the vague border between Nova Scotia and Maine—or as I should say properly, the province of Massachusetts—but nearly all were residents of the county of Cumberland, this province, and they were led by the renegade Eddy, himself a former resident of Cumberland, indeed a former member of the assembly which meets within these walls. All were subjects of His Majesty. All were assembled for the purpose of treason and rebellion. Had they succeeded in their rash and diabolical enterprise, this whole province must have fallen under rebel rule, for it was well-nigh emptied of troops and it includes in its population a large faction ill-disposed towards His Majesty and sympathetic towards the rebel Congress. By the grace of God this fierce and licentious band of men was defeated and dispersed. On the morning after the battle, the prisoner, David Strang, was found at Inverma Farm, a scene of bloodshed on the previous day, and in the company of a number of rebel sympathizers including the wife of the notorious John Allan, who is at this moment on the St. John River attempting to rouse the Indians against His Majesty's peaceful subjects. The prisoner was suffering from a bullet wound recently inflicted and had in his possession a musket belonging to His Majesty's Royal Fencible American Regiment. I leave it to your good judgment, as loyal subjects and as men of the world, to decide how he came by that wound and that musket. He was challenged as a rebel by a party of Royal Americans—who were surely in a position to judge—and he submitted to arrest without a word. You must decide if his silence and submission were those of an innocent man. The learned young attorney for the defense has mentioned Colonel Gorham's conditional pardon to the rebels; but it has been established that the prisoner did not come within the terms of that pardon. If further proof were needed, you have it in his presence here, for he was sent to Halifax for trial—by Colonel Gorham himself."

The dry voice went on, buzzing and biting like a saw in a log. I felt giddy and exhausted. Fear's strange appearance and testimony had robbed me of all my bravado, though I can say honestly that I had no tremors for myself, only a sick longing to get it over with.

The voice paused and bit into another log. "The young but learned attorney for the defense"—with an ironical bow to Threadbare—"whose fortuitous presence in this court has provided him, not only with a dock brief but with an intimate and indeed miraculous knowledge of the prisoner's case, has seen fit to put his client upon the stand in his own defense. I leave it to you, who have seen the prisoner's behavior and heard his plea—and something of his sentiments . . ."

"M'lord!" cried Threadbare, rising like a jack-in-the-box. "I protest . . ."

"Sustained!" his lordship barked.

"Hum! The attorney for the defense"—another stiff little bow—"has placed his whole case upon the testimony of one witness"—Nesbit's voice rose to a higher pitch—"the confessed adulteress who occupied the witness stand a few moments ago. I ask you as godly and law-abiding men, how far you can trust the testimony of such a woman. To what lengths would she not go to save the life of her paramour? Indeed, what proof is there that on the night our troops marched out of Fort Cumberland to attack the rebels she was so many miles from her husband's bed and in the company of her lover?"

"M'lord," protested Threadbare, waving a paper. "I have here a deposition of John Southwaite, yeoman, and his wife Martha, of Fort Lawrence in the county of Cumberland, testifying that Captain Helyer's wife and the young man now in the dock were together in a bedchamber of their house on the night . . ."

"M'lord!" cried old Nesbit. "I object most strenuously—the defense cannot introduce new evidence at this stage . . ."

"Sustained! The jury will disregard the statement just made by the attorney for the defense."

Nesbit hitched his shoulders several times under his gown, like a little black hen ruffling her feathers in a shower.

"Gentlemen of the jury, we live in a perilous time. Only the grace of God has kept our fair province free of the blight of rebel corruption and disorder. There are many ill-disposed persons, in all parts of Nova Scotia, who await an opportunity to bring that blight upon us. Sedition is rampant. And, gentlemen, beyond the sea at this very moment rebel emissaries are bending every effort to bring France into this war against His Majesty and His Majesty's loyal subjects in every part of the world. What inducement are they offering to the French? Ay, what inducement can they offer but the return of Nova Scotia and the Canadas to the accursed French rule against which you and your fathers fought so many years? Some of you—perhaps all of you— are of New England birth. But you are Nova Scotians now, and what concerns you now is not New England nor the so-called United States —it is the future ownership of this province. British or French? That is the sole issue for Nova Scotia in this war. And, gentlemen, that is the issue which looms behind this trial today!" He paused a moment to let that sink like a flung stone into the pond of their minds. Then, rapidly, "This is the trial of a traitor! See him! See how sullen and desperate a creature sits there! Is that the face of an innocent man? Ask yourselves that question. Consider his plea. Consider the evidence —the testimony of a loyal officer of His Majesty's forces against the word of an adulteress. Consider the larger issue. And do your duty fearlessly as loyal subjects of His Majesty!" He dropped into his chair, panting after so much effort and looking shriveled with his own heat.

The courtroom buzzed and fell into a dead silence again as Threadbare got up, the forbidden deposition in his hand. He did not once refer to it, but throughout his address he kept waving it before them like a flag of truce. His tone was easy and conversational. "M'lord, and gentlemen of the jury, the prisoner is tall and big of bone; he bears the marks of a tempestuous life and looks older than his years. But he is barely turned twenty, the beloved youngest son of a loyal and veteran soldier of His Majesty—Captain Matthew Strang of Liverpool, this province."

I saw his lordship throw up his brooding head with a jerk that set the wig flaps dancing. He stared from Threadbare to me.

"Gentlemen, Captain Strang was a native of Massachusetts like so many of the men who came to Nova Scotia in the early days and carved a province out of a wilderness. His lordship knows what sort of men they were—for I believe his lordship served with them as a captain of rangers in the wild days of '45, with Noble in the Annapolis Valley in '47, and in the establishment and subsequent defense of Halifax. His lordship could bear me witness that no abler men, no braver men, no men more loyal ever served His Majesty than the Massachusetts rangers who fought the French and Indians up and down the length of Nova Scotia during fourteen bitter years and made it possible for settlement.

"The father of the prisoner, I say, was one of those devoted men. Like many another—like his lordship himself—he settled in Nova Scotia and brought up his sons here. The father is crippled as a result of wounds sustained long ago in His Majesty's service. One of the sons, when last heard of, was serving in His Majesty's navy. Another son, a private of the Royal Fencible Americans, was killed in the defense of Fort Cumberland!"

He paused impressively. Then, loudly, "And you are asked to believe that the youngest son—the young man in the dock—took up arms, not merely against His Majesty, but against his own brothers!"

Another pause, while the jurymen put their heads together, whispering in twos and threes, a sound that rustled across the still court like autumn leaves.

"Gentlemen, you have all been twenty. It is a wonderful age. The feelings then, and especially love for a woman, are new and keen and of an importance far beyond all common reason. This young man had a boyhood sweetheart. She married another. He followed her, and she discovered the old love still warm in her heart. There were meetings and assignations, guilty perhaps; but this is not a court of morals. They were together, on the far side of the great marshes from the rebel lines, on the night of the attack by His Majesty's troops. By early dawn, as you know, the rebel force had been defeated and dispersed. The sounds of the conflict carried across the marshes. It was morning, and the lovers were in great danger of discovery. It was impossible for the woman to return to the fort while the soldiers were on the road. Yet they must not be found together. So the young man left her, intending no doubt to reach Sackville settlement, where he had friends. The road to Sackville lay around the marshes and crossed the Cumberland Ridge. It was early morning, I say, and foggy, and the light was dim. There was still some scattered shooting from the woods along the road, where the rebels had dispersed, and a stray shot struck the young man in the shoulder. The wound was painful, and he lay the night in the woods. In the morning he made his way towards Inverma Farm, to have his shoulder attended. He found the place in ruins, with arms and accouterments lying about the fields and the dead unburied. He picked up one of the guns. He was almost immediately found with it in his possession and was put under arrest as a rebel. He said nothing. What could he say? Any attempt to establish his innocence must involve the lady herself. So, chivalrously—foolishly, if you like—he submitted to the charge; he has even pleaded guilty in this court, and he would stand condemned at this moment if the lady had not come to tell the truth."

The jurymen were looking past me—staring at Fear, in the back of the court. Their faces swam in a great and engulfing wave of sickness that set me sweating coldly all over, and his lordship's gaze was fixed on my face, stern and piercing, as if in a stroke of magic he had become nothing but a pair of eyes and a wig.

"The woman is very young, married to an army officer considerably older than herself, a man of the world, an Englishman of a titled family. She had no background but a country town. But let me tell you that only a woman of great moral courage would have thrown her position to the winds, bared her breast to the cruel daggers of gossip from Halifax to Cumberland, cast off forever the regard of her friends and family—as she has—in order to save this young man from a traitor's death. I say that such a woman's testimony is not to be regarded lightly. She has sacrificed too much."

Another pause, a final flap of the paper in his hand. "She sinned, perhaps. The young man sinned, perhaps. But that is a matter for Heaven's own judgment, not yours. Before this court he faces the charge of high treason—and on that an alibi has been proven. In the name of justice—British justice, gentlemen—I ask that you release this young man from the terrible and disgraceful charge against him, release him to the arms of his aged parent, that good and faithful servant of the king!" He uttered the final words at the pitch of his high voice and turned, stabbing a long finger toward the public rail, and every head in the courtroom followed it. I peered around the corner of the dock. There stood my father, holding himself rigidly erect, with his hard eyes fixed on his lordship's face. I knew he must be snorting within at Threadbare's "aged parent" with its suggestion of senility, but there was no emotion in his face. I did not know that the introduction of an "aged parent" or some such pitiful figure was the common resort of counsel with a weak case, a device as old as law and lawyers. In my great ignorance I marveled at this stroke of devilish cunning. I could see the jury staring at him. A good half of them must have known The Hawk in early days; I could see that in their taut faces and wide eyes, filled with sudden memories of the old, wild time when my father had been something of a god in Halifax.

Threadbare got back to his chair adroitly. He seemed to slide out from under their fascinated gaze, leaving it fixed where he wanted it.

His lordship turned to address the jury, and their heads swung back to him reluctantly. "You have heard the case for the Crown and you have heard the case for the defense," he told them grimly. "The learned counsel have wisely kept the evidence short and to the point, and I shall be brief myself. It cannot be denied that the prisoner was found in suspicious circumstances. On the other hand, there is the strong evidence of the woman witness that the prisoner was with her, far beyond the Missaguash marshes, on the very night that His Majesty's forces made their secret march to attack the rebel positions at Fort Cumberland. It is the woman's word against a circumstance. If you believe the woman, then you must find the prisoner not guilty of the charge against him. If you prefer the circumstance, then you must consider deeply whether or not it is sufficient to prove guilt. The charge of high treason is the most serious in the calendar. Therefore weigh it well. I find myself at odds with the suggestion of the learned counsel for the Crown that your duty is to make an example of this prisoner for the terror of all seditious persons in this province. Your duty as jurors in a British court—and therefore your duty to His Majesty—is to render a verdict according to the evidence regardless of the nature of the case."

His lordship hesitated, playing with the quill in his fingers, his lips twitching as if under stress of many things he wanted to say and could not—or would not. Abruptly he snapped, "You will now withdraw and come to a decision. Mr. Wood! Mr. Wood, kindly hand the indictment to the foreman of the jury. Mr. Foreman, you will write your verdict on the back of the indictment before you come forth—you can write, I take it? Good!" He waved them away with his quill.

The jury shuffled off into a chamber at the rear of the court. His lordship arose stiffly, turned, and stepped through the doorway of his own robing room while the court stood respectfully. Through the open door I could see his lordship's servant pouring something dark and steaming from a jug. The door closed.

The candles on the attorneys' table, lit to augment the meager daylight through the frosty panes, were down to their last inch and guttering in the drafts. There was something grimly symbolic about them. I was in a curious state. Sights and sounds were acutely clear, but they floated on a whirlpool of delirium like bright new chips on a roiled puddle.

The crier stood guardian at the jury-chamber door, and after a time there was a knock from within, thunderous in the silence. The crier unfastened the door; a hoarse whisper, and bang went the door again. The crier tiptoed across to the judge's door, as if in the presence of death. A discreet knock, a murmur within, the crier's head in the door, and a grave-side whisper to the unseen presence. His lordship emerged with slow and stately step, and once more the deputy provost marshal made his imperative gesture to bring the court to its feet. The marines lifted me, and I hung between them swaying on boneless legs, trying to hold my head up. The court seemed to be lurching to and fro like our old schooner in a seaway.

His lordship sat; the court sat—those who had chairs and benches anyhow—and the crier released the jurymen. They shuffled in, some looking at his lordship, some at the attorney general. None looked at me. The foreman passed the folded indictment to the austere man in the full-bottomed wig, who read the verdict written on its back with a face like stone.

"Not guilty?" he asked the solemn jury. "That is your verdict? You all agree?"

They answered in a running chorus of "Ayes" and "Yes, my lord."

Darting from behind the attorney's table like a little sparrow hawk from a thicket, old Nesbit stepped up to the dais, asking sharply, "May I examine the written verdict, m'lord?"

The judge pushed it at him testily, and the Crown's counsel scanned it with beady eyes.

"The Crown is satisfied?" his lordship asked.

"The Crown," uttered the prosecutor in a thin-edged voice, "can only accept what the jury in its inscrutable wisdom has seen fit to decide."

The dark mists rolled down. I caught only his lordship's final word, ". . . discharged!" which was barked at me like the discharge of a musket. But outside, the keen wind off the harbor revived me a little, and I found myself supported on one side by Threadbare and on the other by my old friend and benefactor Hart the Jew. My father, leaning on his familiar stick, was giving instructions to the driver of a waiting sleigh whose seat was piled high with furs, and as Aaron Hart helped me into it my father turned and counted a number of coins into Threadbare's ready hand.

"Sir," said my father in his strong voice, "that was a pretty piece of work."

Threadbare thrust his tongue in his cheek and the money into his shabby pocket. "Sir," he declared, shutting one eye, "I merely spoke from memory the lines that had been prepared for me. What a lawyer that fellow Uniacke would make! As for me, I have a notion to go in for play-acting as a career. I seem to have a flair."

And off he went on his thin, ridiculous legs toward the tavern across the street.

"Now," said my father rapidly, "we must get the boy away and keep him out o' sight till all's blown over. That woman's run away from her husband, and when he hears o' her testimony this morning he'll be after David's blood."

"I think not," murmured Aaron Hart sagely. "Captain Helyer can't leave his post at Fort Cumberland while the rebel force remains on the St. John. After that . . ."

I heard Fear's voice indistinctly behind me somewhere in the blood-shot fog that seemed to fill the world, crying that Davy was ill—couldn't they see?—and that they must get him a bed and a doctor—and, please, could she take care of him?

"Fear," I muttered. "Fear . . ."

My father's voice, snarling at her, "Begone, ye slut! Ye've got him in trouble enough!"

I felt myself being pushed helplessly amongst the furs and heard a confused outcry from the people outside the courthouse. They were calling somebody a whore, and as the driver whipped up his horse and we jerked away I had a dim glimpse of Aaron Hart shielding that someone with his arm and cloak against a shower of snowballs.

CHAPTER 38

The Unprodigal Son

JAIL FEVER is in itself a violent and unpleasant malady, but I was smitten by more than a mere infection caught in prison air. All the pains and exposures, the failures and disappointments of the past two years seemed to have gathered like a mighty burden on my frame and now crushed me deep down into the bed. There were fearful dreams.

I found myself back in the ditch at Fort Cumberland, seeking Mark in the light of the musket flashes and never finding him. Or I was on the rickety scaling ladder with the bayonet coming straight at my face —and I unable to move. Or I was carrying poor François away from the palisade gate, staggering under his burden for miles and miles in an endless night, with the warm gush of his blood upon me. Indeed I lived every incident of my strange life in '75 and '76 in slow and anguished detail. Sometimes I drifted to consciousness, but the taste of life seemed bitter, and I shrank back from it. The good Hart afterward assured me this was merely the bitterness of Dr. Jeffries' medicines, thrust with an iron spoon into my gaping mouth. I can recall vague but persistent shapes hovering over me and somehow trying to drag me out of the darkness, when all I wanted was to be left in peace.

Gradually these faces became clear. My father once or twice. The doctor and kindly old Aaron Hart and the women of his household. One day I wakened to find the March sun streaming warm through the diamond panes of the lattice and all the darkness gone from my mind. Mr. Hart was there, and the doctor stood beyond the dazzling sunbeam putting his medicines away. I had seen Dr. Jeffries at Malachi Salter's and supposed I was in a chamber of that good man's house.

I said, "Mr. Salter? . . . Malachi?"

The doctor cleared his throat noisily without saying anything, and I saw Mr. Hart behind him, finger at lips. As soon as the dour surgeon was gone Mr. Hart said quickly, "My son, you are in my house. And you must be careful what you say in Dr. Jeffries' presence. He is the Tory refugee who betrayed Malachi Salter to the courts."

"Courts?"

"My son, a great rebel hunt is in progress. Every man of New England birth is suspect, and when he happens to be a merchant with many in his debt, there are sure to be certain ones eager to denounce him, truly or falsely, to bring about his ruin. Halifax is ringing with accusations and denunciations. The Tories are scandalized by the failure to prosecute the Cumberland rebels, and the Halifax jail keeper has been dismissed for letting Clarke, Avery, and Falconer escape."

"Ah! And Uniacke? Where's Uniacke?"

Mr. Hart smiled. "On St. Patrick's Day? Where else but with his Irish friends at a tavern, toasting the memory of the good saint? I fancy they'll drink a bumper to Uniacke's arrest."

"What?"

"Tomorrow he is to be taken into formal custody for a debt in a matter of cask hoops."

"I see."

Mr. Hart stroked his little gray beard and regarded me gravely. "David, you said some harsh things of Mr. Uniacke when you were out of your head."

Angrily I burst out, "I can say more now that my head's clear. He's gone over to the Tories to save his own neck—on the pretense of saving mine. That was the Satan's bargain that Michael Francklin made with him."

"That is not true, my son."

"The truth then! About my trial—everything!"

"I do not know everything, David. I know that Uniacke sent a message to Francklin a few minutes after you were removed to a separate cell, just before the trial. But matters had gone too far to stop it then —and Francklin could not influence the courts. We were at our wits' end when the young woman came to the prison to see Uniacke and told him she could save your life. There was little time. Together we went over her story, and Uniacke worked out the defense which she and that young lawyer so skillfully presented in court. Your father appeared—he and Justice Morris had been companions in arms in the old days—and the rest you know. Frankly, I think the governor was glad to see the matter dropped. The Cumberland affair reflects no credit on His Majesty's officers in Nova Scotia. Besides, even the Council could see the folly of hanging the lesser leaders while Allan and Eddy and the others are still in arms on the St. John."

"Where is she—Fear?"

"Gone to New York."

"New York!"

"She has an aunt there, I believe, a Mrs. Shaddock. Her own parents will have nothing to do with her. Mr. Bingay removed from Liverpool to Halifax some time ago for the extension of his business and was extremely mortified at this affair. As for her husband . . ."

I turned my face to the pillow and wept out of sheer rage and weakness. I had always loved her; I knew that now and wanted her more than ever, though love was warped and wracked by the knowledge that Captain Jack Helyer was still the owner of her loveliness in the sight of God and man. One course was clear for me. I must get well, get out of this dismal town and its miserable memories. I must get away to the St. John and rejoin the rebels under Allan.

On the day I made my first tottering steps about the chamber Richard Uniacke came to see me. It irked me to see him so healthy and cheerful when I felt like a wet dish clout, and I refused to see his outstretched hand.

"So you've turned Tory!" I said bitterly.

"I'm just poor Dick Uniacke as ever was," he answered promptly. "But I'm going through with the career I've mapped out for myself. I'm off for Dublin as soon as I can straighten my affairs."

"And I'm for the St. John," I said stonily.

"Better go home, Davy."

"Is that all you've come to say?"

He hesitated, and all his quick Irish temper was in his eyes. "Not quite. I want to tell you what an ungrateful devil you are. A fine girl ruins her reputation to save your stubborn neck, and your notion of gratitude is to stick your head back into the noose. For what?"

"For the Cause!"

"If ye mean the cause of self-government in Nova Scotia, you're a menace to it—you and the rest of those poor, blind fools on the St. John. Freedom won't come that way. It'll come my way. Good-by, David."

"Good-by."

He was going to say something more, but his strong mouth closed angrily. Out he went, and I was sorry. It seemed to me then in a twinge of self-pity that one by one the Cause was cutting every tie of love and friendship I had known. The face of Liberty was not less beautiful, but she seemed to have grown jealous.

In May I bade farewell to that gentle and peaceful household in the heart of turbulent Halifax and took passage down the coast to Liverpool in a brig of Malachi Salter's, sailed by the sturdy old man himself. The Tory clique in Halifax was determined on his ruin. Jury after jury had refused to convict him, but the repeated arrests and investigations had reduced him to a point where he must captain his own vessel.

"I'm back where I started," he told me cheerfully.

"Why don't you go home to New England?"

"Home?" he uttered, astonished. "This is my home, David."

I had been away from home nigh fifteen months and confess I had thought little of it in that time. Oh, a queer, sick longing had come upon me once or twice in the weary waiting before Cumberland and in the prison since, but it never lasted long. My Strang blood was too stiff, I suppose, for much green-sickness of that kind. I doubt if any young man in hard health, with his feet toward the world's adventures, wastes much time looking back. I was not looking back, even now. There were two ways to the St. John. The Cumberland Road was a poor one now for a rebel so conspicuous as I. The sea way was the quicker and safer—and it led by Liverpool.

I looked at the shore of Dipper Creek as we swept up the narrow bay. In a few weeks boys and girls would go astrawberrying there. With a rush all the old longing for Fear came back to me, and I was seeing her uptilted face and the teasing cider eyes and hearing her soft laughter and tasting again the white skin under my lips. Like everything else in our Nova Scotia, that seemed to belong to an ancient time, an age of peace and happiness that was gone forever.

Malachi anchored his *Rising Sun* in Ballast Cove, since the tide did not serve to get over the bar, and I went ashore with him in the jolly boat. He had business with Colonel Perkins, and I walked along the water front hailing the men I knew. They stared, as if at a ghost, knowing nothing of my part in the Cumberland affair, thinking I had perished in the woods after killing the *Senegal's* seaman.

Several asked me if I thought it wise to return so soon.

At the town's end, on my father's wharf, a number of men were busy unloading Turk's Island salt from a shabby little brigantine, swinging it out of the hold in a big wooden tub by a tackle rigged aloft and under the direction of a man with a most familiar back. When he turned I shouted, "Mark!" and ran at him, and for the next minute we entertained the whole crew to a mad, thumping, hugging, laughing bear dance. Abruptly Mark swung on the gaping men with a roar that sent them jumping back to their tasks. In the gloom of the shed we sat on a heap of the coarse dull-colored island salt, and I cried, "How did you get away? Have you seen anything of François? What became of . . ."

"Belay!" he cried. "Ye sound like a damned tide waiter that smells a smuggled keg. I got away on my two feet—how did ye suppose? At Sackville I picked up François; he was still pretty sick—his arm is crippled forever, Davy. But his legs were all right, and he made good use of 'em. Those sogers would ha' shot a wounded Injun like a dog. We hid in the woods for a time, sneakin' out to a farmhouse now and again for a bite to eat. Scores of men and boys were doin' the same. It snowed, and the weather turned bitter cold. Some set off across country for the St. John to join Eddy again; but most had seen enough of him and gave 'emselves up to Gorham's offer o' pardon—and how the sogers cursed Gorham for that! But some o' the Yorkshire folk were out for revenge and made life a misery to the families o' the rebels. After the *Vulture* left with the marines I made up my mind to try for home. There was no chance of a sloop down the Bay at that season. 'Twas by Halifax or nothin'."

"But the Windsor troops were watching the Halifax road!"

"Ay! But François suggested the old Injun way across the country, by canoe through Minas Basin and Cobequid Bay, then up the Shubenacadie River, which takes ye clean over to within a short portage o' the Dartmouth lakes. The Micmac war parties used it a lot in the old days, raidin' the Halifax outposts. 'Twas the devil's own journey, a race with the weather—for a freeze-up would ha' caught us in the middle o' nowhere—and all upstream. François couldn't do much in the way o' paddlin'—and of all the damned, cranky things on the face o' the waters I give ye a bark canoe. I'd as soon go to sea on a log. I was like a wrung rag when we got to the lake the Injuns call Banook, just above Halifax Harbor, and the pair of us nigh famished. François was ill and out of his head, and we'd ha' died like starved rats if we hadn't tumbled on some Micmacs winterin' there. One of 'em was a young squaw that knew François—a bit too well, I reckon, by the look o' the younker she had—and she took care o' the pair of us. In January, when I begged passage in a coaster for home, she and the kid and François came along—they're livin' with old Molly now, back o' home."

"Home," I said, starting up.

"One moment, Davy, Mother . . ."

"Yes?"

"She thinks you've been hidin' from the *Senegal* all this time. Let her think that."

"I've done nothing to be ashamed of," I said angrily.

"Would she care if ye had? It's the worry I'm thinkin' of. She's had enough—all of us scattered—John dead—John's dead, did ye know that?—and Luke gone the Lord knows where."

I ran up the stony lane to the house and found nobody in the kitchen but a small-scale model of Joanna, a pretty little flaxen-haired toddler regarding me with round blue eyes. I picked her up and said, "Hello, what's your name?" I heard the swift clatter of Joanna's wooden shoes, and then she was in the doorway, wide-eyed, and crying over her shoulder, "David! It's David, home again!" My mother came in a rush of skirts. She looked worn, and I was sorry to see so much gray in her dark hair, but her eyes were young and glowing, and she was laughing and crying as I swept her against my chest.

Then the tap of my father's stick and his lame, dragging step and his great voice roaring, "Let the boy breathe! All this bussing and hugging!"

"You're jealous!" I grinned and kissed them all soundly, Mother, the baby, and then Joanna. Joanna blushed to the roots of her yellow hair, but there was a cloud in her eyes, and I turned and saw Mark watching us gloomily from the kitchen door.

Nevertheless we were a merry crew at supper that night, and I was pleased to see Joanna take her place beside Mother at the table as a daughter of the house. But when it came time for bed and we all marched out toward the stairs with our candles like a little Popish procession, I was astonished to see Mark turn into his old chamber and slam the door, while Joanna went on up the garret stairs as if she were a bound-girl still. I dropped back and muttered to Mother, "That's no place for Joanna's baby. Like an oven in summer and cold as Greenland in the winter."

She gave me the dark, unfathomable look that I remembered of old. "The child sleeps in my chamber—I insisted on that. As for Joanna and Mark, there seems some unhappy secret between them. Mark is scarcely civil to the girl, and Joanna keeps her distance. I feel like shaking him sometimes."

She changed the subject abruptly. "Davy, I had such a kind letter from Fear Helyer—Fear Bingay that was. You used to be rather fond of her, didn't you? Her husband was John's officer, and she was with our poor boy when he died. It's such a comfort to know he didn't die amongst strangers altogether."

My face seemed to freeze. How much had Fear told her?

But she went on, "Tomorrow you must tell me your adventures, Davy. You're home for good now, aren't you?"

I was not, and the pleading in her eyes made me feel a wretch, but Father saved me, hitching himself up the stairs with all the liveliness of a hot rum-and-butter nightcap. "Aha! What's this? Be off, young feller! I won't have my wife lally-gagging with strangers on the stairs!"

I wondered if Mark heard.

CHAPTER 39

Envy

THE LAST OF MAY was a hot still night. Father had retired early suffering pain in his old wound, and Mother had gone upstairs to rub it with opodeldoc salve. Joanna was busy in the kitchen with needle and thread, making a new dress for young Nancy—for so she had named her small daughter, after my mother.

In the warm dark Mark and François and I lay comfortably against a pile of herring net at the end of Father's wharf, smoking to keep off the black flies.

"Mark," I said, "what's wrong with the town? The men shut up like clams when I come around and look glum as a parcel o' boys caught whispering in prayer meeting. Even the women have a sullen look."

Mark took a long pull at his clay and blew out the pale smoke slowly. "I reckon it's because you're a Strang, that's all. Ah, they've been through hell this past two years, what with the king's ships and their highhanded ways and the rebel privateers harryin' the coast. It's no frolic to be caught between two fires, and they're blamin' it more and more on Simeon Perkins and his tryin' to keep at peace with both sides. That means they're blamin' Father, for everyone knows Simeon's just a figgerhead for Father and his 'Sit tight! Sit tight!'—you know the policy he laid down that night in our kitchen. Liverpool's a Whig town. Every American prisoner that escapes from Halifax—and there's a steady stream of 'em—makes for here, where they're sure of a refuge till there's a chance to get down the coast to Yarmouth. A lot of 'em just wait for a rebel privateer to put in hereabouts and then join her, same as if they were home. Ye can walk the town street any day and see a dozen or more strange faces—all runaway prisoners. Colonel Perkins just looks down his nose and don't see 'em. Same way, more than one rebel privateer's got provisions here when there was any to spare. And what's our reward for all this? The Congress won't allow any truck with us. The embargos killed our old trade with New England. What ships ye see are drogin' fish and timber to the West Indies, and every last one of 'em open to attack from American privateers on the score o' 'tradin' with the British.' Worse'n that, there's pirates out o' New England swarmin' all along our shore, flyin' the rebel colors and callin' 'emselves privateers. So far they've let our town alone. But they make a reg'lar rendyvoo o' Port Mouton—which is only ten miles to the west of us—and snap up every ship headin' in or out o' our harbor that looks like fat pickin's. That's killin' the last trade we've got. When some poor devil of a shipmaster complains they snap their fingers under his nose and tell him to snivel to King George, not them."

"Then," I said vigorously, "let Liverpool come out openly for the Cause and make an end of it. Every Yankee settlement around the coast from Halifax to Windsor is waiting to see what Liverpool does. Well, hoist the American flag on the Point and keep it flying there!"

"And bring another hell ship like the *Senegal* down on us! Ye've got a damned short memory, Davy. Ye can't find His Majesty's ships when their protection's needed, but they come in whenever they've mischief o' their own to brew—some hands to be pressed, a search for contraband, or some beef to be 'bought' at pursers' prices. Ah, we're between the devil and the deep sea, I tell ye, and God knows what'll come of it. Listen, back in March some o' the hot Whigs in town—Cap'n Eph Dean was the leader—stole both the old cannon from the Point and carried 'em off to Port Mouton to help arm a rebel privateer there. Father got wind of it and prodded Colonel Perkins, and Simeon sent a party o' his militiamen in a shallop to bring the guns back. Which they did. We needed those guns for our own defense. Colonel Perkins wrote to Halifax, pleased with himself, and pointed it out as a proof that he was keepin' law and order. The governor's answer was a man-o'-war to arrest Cap'n Dean and carry the guns to Halifax—said we couldn't be trusted with 'em. Now we've got nothin' bigger'n a musket to defend the channel over the bar—and what'll the rebel privateers do about that, think you? I expect 'em in here any night now, robbin' us bare and talkin' very high about liberty."

"You begin to sound like a Tory," I accused.

"The privateers are goin' to make a red-hot Tory out of every Yankee in Nova Scotia if they keep it up, Davy."

"What!" I scoffed. "Can you see our people fighting for the king?"

"Hell, no. But I can see 'em fightin' for 'emselves. It comes down to that, Davy—self-defense, the first law o' nature."

François, dismayed at our heat, slipped away wordless into the dark toward his hut.

"Listen, Mark. The trouble with our people is that they've lost patience with Simeon and his do-nothing policy. They're ready to fight—and don't care very much who they fight, if what you say is right.

Well, they've got to fight the king. King George is our natural enemy, and the Americans are our natural friends. Damn it, we *are* Americans! Look—John Allan's collecting a force on the St. John. I don't know his plan but I know what it ought to be—to cross the Bay of Fundy, seize Annapolis, and march through the Valley to Windsor, gathering the Yankee farmers as he goes. At the same time our people along the south shore should rise and march on Halifax."

"And if we don't?"

"It'll be another Cumberland."

Mark took the pipe from his mouth and spat into the dark. "Then ye'd best forget the whole thing, Davy. Us south-shore men ain't goin' to leave our homes while this swarm o' sea thieves out o' New England is hoverin' off the coast. That's flat."

"So you'll stay home, pottering about Father's wharf, when there's fighting to be done!"

"Damn ye, Davy," he growled, "don't take that tone with me. Where were you when there was fightin' to be done at Camp Hill? You were in charge o' the picket on the fort road that night, if I remember."

There it was, thrown in my face, the thing that had gnawed the soul out of me all the time I lay in prison! Was this what Uniacke thought—and the others?

In a burst of rage and despair I poured out all the story of that night, and because I wanted to hurt, I told him, word for word, the thing that John had confessed to me as he lay dying. I expected him to leap at my throat; I was ready for it—eager for it. But he sat hunched and silent, and I heard the little clay snap in his teeth. At last he said in a shaking voice, "Ye swear to that, Davy? It's true—every word?"

"Every word!" I snarled at him.

"Then for God's sake, why didn't ye tell me before?" He was up, and running for the house like a madman. In the candlelit kitchen window I could see the shadow of Joanna's round arm going back and forth as she stitched. I started after him, thinking of his big hands and his high Strang temper, but I stopped. My own mood was quite as savage as his, and some sneering devil within me insisted that Joanna by her very presence in our house had been the cause of the trouble between us; we had all suffered—why shouldn't she? A husband had a right to beat his wife. I waited, expecting to hear her cry out. But no sound came except the chuckle of the tide against the wharf spiles. That silence was terrible. My mood cooled, there in the May night. Perhaps Mark had killed the girl, strangled her there in the kitchen with his powerful hands, while Father and Mother and the baby slept on upstairs.

In a gust of remorse I ran to the kitchen door and entered softly. The place was empty. There was no sign of a struggle. One of the candlesticks was gone. I tiptoed into the hall and heard a soft creaking on the stairs and saw a grotesque shadow marching slowly up the staircase wall. Mark and Joanna were going up the stairs together, shoes in hand, Mark carrying the candle. One big arm was about Joanna's waist, and her head was against his shoulder with her bright hair catching the candle gleams softly. Something about the way they clung to each other, their restrained yet eager steps, the air of happy stealth about them, caught me by the throat and made me gulp. It was envy.

CHAPTER 40

March to Glory

THE TOWN WAS DARK and asleep, but I found a chink of light at the back of Mrs. Tabitha Pratt's tavern and hammered lustily on the door. Out went the light, and presently a chamber window flew open overhead, and Tabby herself bawled down to me, "Go away! Mine's a respectable house that keeps respectable hours!"

The window closed with a snap. I hammered again, and Tabby's head again popped out, like a wooden cuckoo from a German clock.

"What d'ye want, down there?"

"A word with your lodgers, ma'am."

"They're asleep in their beds like decent men," she shrilled. "Now begone, or I'll send for the walking constable."

"Not you!" I said merrily and began to sing "Yankee Doodle" at the top of my voice. There is not much music in me, but I can make a lot of sound when I choose. The window slammed as if to shut out that rollicking rebel tune, but in a moment the back door flew open, and from the black cave of the doorway a man's voice said, "Come in!" The muzzle of a pistol protruded into the starlight.

I stepped inside and was promptly seized and thrust into the midst of the kitchen, where I made out a number of dim, human shapes against the last glow of the coals in the hearth. Somebody blew on a

brand and lit a candle. There were nine or ten men in the room. Two
held my arms, and the fellow with the pistol stood before me pointing
the thing at my breast. They wore the dress of seamen, and their hard
faces had the sallow, waxy look that comes of a winter's confinement
in the hulks.

"Who are ye, and what d'ye want?" demanded the pistol.

"My name is Strang, and I want good rebel company to the St.
John River."

They looked at each other and back to me warily.

"What makes ye think ye're in rebel company?"

"Oh, come!" I said easily. "You're all runaways from the Halifax
jail or the hulks and you're waiting a chance for home. Here 'tis."

"What way?"

"The one way that's not watched by His Majesty's navy—across the
land to Fundy Bay, by canoe up the river. One man can't manage a
canoe upstream. Who'll go?"

"None of us. We're for Massachusetts by the shortest road."

I looked around the room. "You don't understand. This is a chance
to get over to the mainland and strike a blow for liberty. There's a
force of patriots on the St. John, where I'm bound. They're going to
liberate Nova Scotia from the king's fist."

He of the pistol said curtly, "That's no business of ours."

"No?" I said coldly. "Then what's your business? Don't tell me—I
know. You're privateersmen, and your trade's to rob and burn—and
risk your hides as little as possible. You can hardly wait to get back
at it."

"Ye talk pretty big, my fightin' cock," their spokesman muttered.
He lifted the pistol and stepped close, as if to strike me down with the
heavy barrel.

"No vi'lence in there!" cried Tabitha's voice through the door. "I'll
have no vi'lence. Mind now, Ab! He's one o' them wild Strangs from
uptown, and we'll have the whole pack about our ears."

A lean dark fellow of about my own age stepped into the light. "I'm
from Machias—name o' Crabtree. Fundy's the best road home for me.
I'll go."

The men broke into a chorus, trying to persuade him out of it, with
Tabby squalling outside, "No vi'lence! Ab, I'll hold ye 'sponsible if
there's vi'lence!"

In the end they let us go—"Ab" of the pistol assuring Crabtree that
he was a fool and all of them swearing that no good would come of it.

Crabtree and I stumbled up the river road to the Falls and wakened the Micmacs there to borrow a canoe. The river was swollen with the spring rains, and Crabtree was for waiting till daylight, not liking the sound of it in the dark, but I insisted, and we paddled off into the night.

Our Liverpool River, which some now call Mersey, is the old Indian canoe trail across the peninsula from Fort Anne to Uk-che-gum, the Big Water, seventy miles as the crow flies and—at a guess—a good hundred as the river winds. None of our seafaring townsmen had ever troubled to ascend it farther than the first lake, but I knew the general course of it from the Indian tales. Black flies were troublesome, but we smeared our hands and faces with rancid bear fat got from the abandoned winter wigwams at Panook—First Lake—and so saved our skins after the Indian fashion.

The journey took us through a second lake, and then to Uk-che-ko-spem—the Big Lake—where we were held up by a storm. Then up the rushing Kejimkujik stream, where we poled the canoe up the easier runs but had to make several portages. Then Kejimkujik Lake, a beautiful sheet of water scattered with wooded islands which the Micmacs hold to be the abode of spirits. From time to time we had to stop and forage for food. We had no weapons and existed on trout and the flesh of porcupines, roasted on a spit. We drove ourselves hard on this poor fare; nevertheless 'twas five days before we reached the small lake in the skirt of the South Mountain hills where our river takes its rise, not more than a dozen miles by crow flight over the hills from Annapolis.

The portage over the height of land was steep and long, and the sun poured down, and the flies were a pestilence. We reached the head of the brawling Lequille stream staggering with exhaustion. Our weariness made us careless—and the Lequille is not to be attempted carelessly in a bark canoe, pouring as it does through a narrow defile in the hills and shallow even with a spring flood. We came to grief on a rock after two or three wild miles; the canoe went to sticks and rags of bark in an instant, and we were pitched into the torrent. The Lequille bruised us sorely before it had done with its sport and then spurned us aside like bits of driftwood on a shoal at one of the bends. We were half drowned and nigh beaten to death and lay there a day and a night under a swarm of flies before we recovered life enough to go on. By God's good grace, after staggering a few miles down the gorge, we came upon a camp of the Annapolis tribe of Micmacs, and I croaked a greeting in their own tongue. They took us in, much astonished. One or two French adventurers had gone over the hills and down the river to the Big Water in the old days, but I think we were the first white men ever to make the upstream passage.

We lay there three days. I had in my pockets a good English clasp knife and two soggy sticks of tobacco, and for these we got another canoe, an old patched thing, though I think we had the best of the bargain. The Lequille wound sluggishly through rich water meadows to Annapolis Basin, as if exhausted by the rush down the South Mountain. The green ramparts of Fort Anne were just showing above the morning mist. There was no flag on the staff, no smoke in the barrack chimneys. A drift of sheep wandered over the glacis, nibbling the fresh spring grass. The place was empty. Once more I marveled at our opportunities. Here was the place for Allan to strike.

We had smooth paddling along the Basin in the shelter of North Mountain but found a nasty sea running in through the Gut, driven by a brisk north wind, so we landed and spent the rest of that day and the night in a cove where Tory refugees afterward built the town of Digby. When finally we got out through the Gut and found ourselves on the long smooth swell of Fundy I lost some of my confidence. The canoe seemed very frail and small in that watery wilderness, and by the closest possible steering it was forty miles across. I had the stern paddle and kept looking over my shoulder like Lot's wife, to keep a bearing from the steep scarp of the Gut. The North Mountain laid a long green finger on the sea behind, slowly turning to blue and sinking all the time, and I confess my heart sank with it. But Crabtree was in high spirits, whistling and singing at his paddle, and once he said, "At Machias there's a girl named Prue Adams, and if I ever leave her again you can call me King George and kick me."

I had hoped to reach the other shore before night, but in the afternoon a thick fog came rolling up from the west, and once again I found myself at the mercy of the strong Bay tide without a steering mark. But matters were far worse than when François and I were seeking Eddy's army. Crabtree and I were out on the broad belly of the Bay, and a nor'easter would carry us into the Atlantic. For that matter the flimsy *kwedun* would buckle like a paper boat in any kind of chop. I cursed myself for not begging or stealing a compass at Annapolis. There was no sense in paddling blindly so we drifted through the daylight hours and half the night. Then a breeze came, warm, with the scent of vast forests, a sou'wester if I ever smelled one. But I waited for the stars, for a sight of the Dipper, before we took up our paddles. At last we made out the loom of the land and crept in till we could see and hear the break of the swell on the shore and, not liking it, held our distance.

The land looked innocent enough in the morning sunshine, a mass of pine forest coming down to a red-clay bank above the rocks. We coasted for a bit seeking a landmark. Crabtree had been up this shore with the Machias men who raided the St. John and burned Fort Frederick in '75, and before long he exclaimed and pointed ahead with his paddle. "There's Point Lepreau!"

I was for pushing east to the St. John. Crabtree could think of nothing but Machias and his Prue.

I said, "Every man of Machias that's worth his salt is on the St. John with Colonel Allan. Will you have it said that you went home to the women?"

He grinned, "Don't put sinful ideas in my head." But after a moment he pointed his paddle toward the east and grunted, "All right. St. John! Come on before I have time to regret it."

We were famished and at our rope's end when we sighted Partridge Island and swung in to the broad mouth of the St. John. A fine harbor and a noble river; there is nothing in the peninsula to compare with it. I have often marveled since at the single-mindedness of our Cape Cod fisherfolk, who chose to settle the rocky face of the Nova Scotia peninsula for its handiness to the Banks, ignoring the fertile shores of Fundy and leaving the rich St. John Valley to the Indians. Other New Englanders, less obsessed with codfish, had come later and settled around the Bay, and there was a considerable settlement which Crabtree called Maugerville, fifty miles up the great river. But the settlement at the mouth of it was a poor thing, a small scatter of houses and sheds on Portland Point. A flutter in the wind showed us the American striped flag flying over the charred ruins of Fort Frederick, and we could see a number of whaleboats drawn up on the shore.

There we found Captain Jabez West of Machias with a company of a hundred men, half of them refugees from Cumberland. They had arrested Hazen and White, the chief Tories of the place and had them under lock and key. Colonel Allan was up the river gathering a force of settlers from Maugerville and Indians from the big Malicete camp at Aukpaque, and reinforcements were expected from Machias, where Eddy was busy recruiting. Captain West billeted us in one of the Tory houses, and the women fed us with an ill grace and some astonishment, for we ate like the starved wolves we were. I was asleep the moment I got my head down and lay like a dead man till the next noon.

'Twas a comfort to know that John Allan commanded these forces on the St. John. I had a confidence in his cool Scotch head and in his ability to get American support that I had never felt with Eddy, but I was astonished to find the preparations so poorly advanced and said so, with the spleen which (as usual) found its way to my tongue. That earned me no friends. Dr. Clarke, late of Fort Lawrence, and Captain Tom Falconer of Cobequid were among the refugees from Cumberland, and they looked upon me with suspicion and spread their suspicion amongst the rest. The refugees were in a savage mood. Their homes and properties in Cumberland had been confiscated by the Crown and sold for beggarly sums to Tory bidders. Their women and children, driven out, had made their way perilously down the Bay in canoes and whaleboats and afoot through the woods all through the bitter winter and hungry spring. They were still coming, with tales of cruelty and hardship. There was no room in Cumberland now for anyone of rebel sympathies. No family with a son or father absent in the rebel ranks had any standing in the courts. Property could be taken on the unsupported word of any greedy informer. Any Tory could serve a warrant. Women of runaway rebels were abused and even beaten, and no one could lift a hand in their defense. Colonel Gorham had protested against these things but as usual took no action for good or ill. He was too absorbed in other things—his debts, which were notorious, and the division of his regiment. On instructions from Halifax, able Major Studholme had drawn the pick of the Royal Americans and was making them into a fighting force. Gorham was left with the dregs.

CHAPTER 41

Captain Helyer

ON THE LAST MORNING in June I wakened at cockcrow and sat up in my Tory bed to view the weather. The St. John mouth is a foggy hole in May and June, and from my small window I could see the gray mass stirring a little in the dawn wind. I lay back lazily. Crabtree was nearly dressed, sitting on the edge of his pallet latching his shoes. I knew what he was thinking. The month of June was gone—a month that he might have spent with his Prue—and nothing to show for it. Colonel

Allan was still up the river; Colonel Eddy was still at Machias. A good fighting month wasted. He walked over to the window and announced, "Fog's clearin'. Hello, there's a vessel off the point. And one —two more. See their topmasts. Hulls'll be clear in a minute. D'ye s'pose—by the Lord it must be—it's Eddy with the Massachusetts troops!"

I sprang out of bed at that and began flinging on my clothes and went to the window, still hauling up my breeches. The hulls were still vague—all but one. That one I knew, and the knowledge sickened me. So Halifax had moved first! I might have guessed it. General Massey was not the kind to let the June grass grow under his boots.

"It's a king's ship—the *Vulture*—the one that brought relief to Fort Cumberland!" I shouted, reaching for stockings and shoes.

Crabtree looked again, and as the mist opened, "Right! And there's H.M.S. *Mermaid*—I know her, damn her!—and another sloop—it's the *Hope!* A fleet, by the Lord!"

We ran out and scrambled to our posts, where the drums of the Machias company were already ruffling defiantly. The gutted barracks and charred palisades of Fort Frederick mocked us now. We took shelter behind rocks and houses near the shore and poured such a volley into the first boatload of armed seamen from the *Vulture* that they were glad to limp back with their dead and wounded. The *Mermaid* was getting a spring on her cable to bring the broadside to bear, and her cannon were not to be faced with muskets, so West ordered us to fall back to the high woods above the village. He had secured a retreat up the river by bringing his whaleboats over the famous reversing falls at high tide. We commanded the old Indian portage across the neck, and the boats of the men-o'-war could not cut off our retreat until the next tide. But at best we could only fight a delaying action. We could see boatload after boatload of marines landing and forming up along the foreshore like a wave of the red Fundy tide and farther down the nondescript uniforms of the Royal Highland Emigrants. We hung on, shooting viciously at their advanced parties and praying for a sight of Eddy and the force which Boston had promised or Colonel Allan with his Indians and the woodsmen of Maugerville. The marines and Highlanders seemed in no hurry to come at us. Some of our men began to shout at them, "Come on, ye lobsters, are ye afraid to get lost in the woods?" It looked as if they were, for they had force enough to beat us five times over, ay, more. There were hundreds of marines, collected at Halifax all spring by the busy Massey, and the Highlanders had done some successful recruiting in Newfoundland and appeared to be at full strength.

We were so busy watching and counting them that no one had eyes for the wooded flank to the east until an Indian, one of West's Passamaquoddies, came running and grunting "Greencoats!" That word meant one clear thing to me—Studholme and the Royal Americans from Fort Cumberland—Studholme who knew the St. John like a book. I cried that out to West, and as I yelled there was a familiar "Huzza!" in the woods below to our left and the flicker of bayonets amongst the trees. We turned and shot hard at them, but it would have been Cumberland all over again if West's forethought had not brought our boats above the falls and placed a guard on the portage. Our little force fell back, shooting from tree to tree, toward the boats and the line of retreat up the river.

I should have gone with them, I suppose. But the sight of the greenjackets was too much for me. I swung myself into the leafy mass of a big oak above the portage and waited, patient as a hunting cat, with a heavy charge of powder and two balls rammed into the old musket West had given me. It was hate, not courage. The war for me had boiled down to Captain Helyer and myself. Nothing else mattered. The Cause? The Cause was hopeless. The slow machinery of the British military mind had moved at last, recognizing its danger by the waters of Fundy. It would keep on moving now. These troops would crush all rebellion along the St. John, and after that Massey would not be content to stand athwart the road to Nova Scotia. His superiors would consider slowly in the British manner, and Massachusetts would have a chance to waken yet; but this affair already cast its shadow on Machias, which had risked everything in our Cause, and in another year that shadow would move on to the Penobscot.

The greencoats passed below my perch in small, hurrying groups. They had an air of discipline and purpose that I had not seen at Fort Cumberland. My finger twitched on the trigger more than once. 'Tis a queer thing to sit like that, unseen and unsuspected, and hold a man's life on your finger tip. I was tempted when Lieutenant Clinch, the Royals' adjutant, passed underneath. I could have dropped a twig upon his leather helmet. And he was followed by Studholme himself, the cool gray major with his keen sun-wrinkled face, ordering a party to proceed to the Indian camp by Marble Cove to get canoes for the pursuit.

I waited for one face, one set of shoulders, for the sound of one well-remembered voice. The stream of greenjackets dwindled to a trickle, then a few ones and twos, then stopped. A sickening disappointment. Evidently Helyer had been left behind at Fort Cumberland with the other undesirables.

Then he came. Alone. Bringing up the rear? There was no sign of others. He had been ordered to pick up any stragglers, no doubt. And there were none. Under the glazed peak of the round, black leather helmet his face was purple and glowering, and I guessed that Studholme, a discerning man, had put him on this minor duty for good reason. The charge up the wooded slopes had winded him, and the heat of the muggy June day was sweating the wine of Cumberland out him; the long idleness and self-indulgence there had padded his ribs and belly so that the green jacket threatened to burst its buttons and the thick flesh over his riding muscles bulged the tight white breeches from hip to knee. He came along slowly, cutting at the bushes sulkily with the drawn sword in his hand and looking like nothing so much as a parish bull. I cocked my hammer, and the sharp click halted him and turned his face upward as I knew it would. He stared wide-eyed at the gap in the oak leaves. He could not see enough to recognize in that shade; my face was snuggled against the gunstock, sighting along the barrel at the thick green chest. His eyes narrowed, glancing to right and left.

"Don't move!" I said. He was not twelve feet from the muzzle.

"Who are you?"

"I'll tell you that in good time."

"You're one of the rebels."

"Yes—don't move! There's a load of double-battle powder in this gun and two ounces of good lead."

"You can't escape if you shoot me. My regiment's ahead, and the Highlanders are moving up behind."

"Any more?" I taunted.

"The marines—and some of your countrymen, militiamen, under the new Indian agent—that's Michael Francklin."

"Ah!"

His eyes were desperate, but I saw no cowardice there. A bull is a courageous beast. He said persuasively, "You must have someone you want to see again. Your mother, perhaps, or a sweetheart—a wife—have you a wife?"

He was playing for time, of course, as he would have played a poor hand at whist, watching for a break in the trumps.

"No," said I. "Have you?"

"Yes."

"No doubt you love her very dearly."

"I do."

"And no one else?"

His eyes tried to pierce the green oak leaves. "That's my affair."

"I see. Don't move! I ask, Captain, because a man should know how many people he'll hit when he shoots. Where is this wife of yours?"

"In New York."

"So far? That's a gay place, New York."

A change came into his face. He said slowly, "I know who you are. You're the fellow who followed her to Cumberland and caused all the trouble. You're Strang! You're the fool who ruined her. . . ."

"And you're the one who played her false. That's why I'm going to kill you."

His eyes widened again. His lips twitched. Then he said rigidly, "Well, suppose you kill me. Suppose by some miracle you get away. You'll seek her out in New York as you did in Cumberland. But do you think she'd have a kind word for her husband's murderer? You know better."

"She'll never know. You'll be reported killed in battle. A soldier's death—more than you deserve."

"Ah! Then consider this, Strang—and I'm dead earnest now. What can you offer a high-spirited creature like Fear, who loves polite society and the fine things of this world? The clothes you stand in? Two chambers and a kitchen in some little provincial town where she'll be dead of boredom in a year or wishing herself dead? A bonnet once in five years and a pine seat in the meetinghouse? I've heard her speak of those things, Strang. I once heard her say the smell of codfish drove her away from home."

"Her father was a merchant."

"He dealt in codfish then. You say I played her false. I'd question your authority but let it go. Suppose I did. A man in good health's bound to make a fool of himself from time to time. But mark this, Strang—it was jealousy that drove my wife to what she did. Jealousy! She wanted to hurt me—because she loves me, always did and always will! Your bullets can't change that, Strang. She'd loathe you. She'd despise the very air you breathe. You know that."

He paused. Sweat was running down his florid face.

I said, "Is there anything more you wish to say before I kill you?"

"Yes. Consider Fear. Her family have cast her out. She's in New York dependent on the charity of an aunt, an empty, raddled, scheming creature you doubtless saw in Halifax two years ago. My death would leave her entirely at the woman's mercy."

"And if you live?"

"Studholme's sending me back to Fort Cumberland—he doesn't like me, that man. I've written begging Fear to come back to me. I love her and respect her—and always did. And she was true as steel to me, as you know well. I found out the truth about that night in South-waite's farmhouse, sweated it out of 'em after Fear had left me, after the trial and the scandal. A wife more honest never walked this earth. I appreciate that now. I want to make it up to her. And I can give her the life and position she needs for happiness, as no one else can. That's all."

'Twould have been so easy to kill him then. He stood so perfectly still. One slight pull on the trigger and King George would be rid of a bad officer and the world of a scoundrel.

I said harshly, "Get out of my sight!"

He hesitated and said stiffly, "You understand—I'm not begging for my life. I'm a gentleman, damme, and can die like one! But it's Fear's own life that matters to you and me. For her sake and that alone . . ."

"Oh, get out!"

He marched off, head high, shoulders square, as if on parade, and disappeared toward the river without once looking back.

CHAPTER 42

Retreat

I INTENDED, when I began to set down these memories of a troublous time, to record in detail my adventures upon the St. John in the summer of '77. They have interested my children and their children. But the hand that holds this quill has not the tireless quality of an old man's tongue, and the great and growing mass of foolscap marred by my crabbed scrawl begins to appall me with its size. And what was our fighting along the St. John but another chapter in a war of lost opportunities? It is the victories that count with posterity, and they leave no room for such mournful echoes as the failure of the Cause in the provinces of Canada.

History loves great battles, the tramp and color of armies, the thunder of the fleets. The struggle for Nova Scotia, the key to all Canada, was fought in a silent wilderness, in scattered and lonely settlements, on forest trails and rivers and along a thousand miles of well-nigh empty coast. It was waged by small bands of men in buckskins and homespun, poorly armed and worse supplied, against troops who were often as ragged as themselves but lacking nothing in the way of stores and arms and ammunition—and very much better led. The Cause in Nova Scotia was foredoomed by the failure of support from the other colonies and damned by their actual hostility when things went wrong; it had to reckon first and last with the genius of Michael Francklin, and always in its lonely battle it had to face, in a country everywhere open to the sea, the wide-reaching power of His Majesty's navy.

I have known the St. John River since, the beautiful inland waterway to Canada, have seen its rich banks populated by Tory exiles from the victorious States, have sailed my own trading vessels ninety miles upstream to the town they built and called Fredericton. But its beauty for me is tinged with bloody memories. The full story of that desperate retreat of ours must await another pen. The full tale will never be told, for the men who might have told it are moldering in forgotten graves in the forest beside the river or have eaten out their hearts in exile far from Nova Scotia. 'Tis a tale of bitter labor at paddles and oars, of days without food and nights without rest, of savage little battles in lonely clearings, of ambush for the pursuers and stealthy surprise for the pursued, of gallantry and treachery and desperation and revenge, all waged in the lovely summer sunshine and the hot, still nights and witnessed only by the dark, sad forest and the great stream flowing down from Canada. What I know let me write quickly and have done—how I found Crabtree lying in a thicket with a bullet in his foot, how we stole a canoe under the noses of the Highlanders at Indiantown and crept past the bivouacs of Studholme's Royal Americans one rainy midnight under the gloomy shadow of Eagle's Nest, and how we fell in with a party of fugitives, Machias men and Cumberlanders, and with them fought our way up the river.

Studholme pursued hotly. The Highlanders were fierce and eager after their long idleness at Halifax and Windsor, and the Royals had the disgrace of Cumberland to wipe away. As at Cumberland, so along the St. John they burned the lonely farms that sheltered us. Our own force was scattered. We fought out little battles in solitary groups. Powder was scarce, as always, and we grudged each shot that was not sure. Our handful of Passamaquoddies remained faithful, but the sly Malicetes along the way betrayed us again and again, as they would have betrayed the king's troops had the shoe been on the other foot. We and our enemies moved by night and fought by day. More than once Studholme's advance canoes passed us in the darkness on the broad river, especially amongst the islands, and we had deadly surprises in the day-dawns. Sometimes our rebel group found another, and for a time we had what seemed a force; but it dwindled with every red stab of musketry out of the darkness, and some took to the forest, where the Malicetes waylaid them for their empty guns and the few poor things in their pockets, and some, exhausted or wounded, had to be left by the river, where the soldiers bayoneted them or sent them down as prisoners, according to their whim. I know that some reached Halifax jail and lay in irons without trial as late as the spring of '78, and I know that some were tried for treason and that the stubborn Halifax juries refused to convict.

We had one hope—that Colonel Allan had managed to muster the men of Maugerville and the Malicetes of Aukpaque, whose chiefs Ambroise and Pierre Tommo had fought beside us at Fort Cumberland. But when we reached Maugerville there was no sign of Allan or his men. The people gave us food but refused to join our battle. They had been stout enough in our Cause the year before and had sent men to fight at Cumberland. But all was changed, and they told us why; sea marauders from New England, stealing up the river in sloops and whaleboats the previous fall and full of double talk about liberty and plunder, had soured them all to any further dealings with the Cause. They would have none of it now, saying sullenly that they wished only to be let alone—and a plague on king and Congress.

We pushed on grimly and rested a night, I remember, in three tumbledown huts, all that remained of the old French village of St. Anne's, where now stands the town of Fredericton. Many years afterward I saw stonemasons busy laying the foundation of Government House on the spot where I peeled a birch for bark to repair our canoe. We had outdistanced the troops and so rested our weary bones far into the next day. Late in the afternoon our outpost cried a warning, and we set off once more.

Our Passamaquoddies were unfamiliar with these Malicete hunting grounds and considered Aukpaque a long way off, but after a few miles we came upon it suddenly, the biggest Indian camp I ever saw, a town of bark huts and wigwams sprawled over the slope on the south side of the river, and as we paddled in cautiously a swarm of Malicetes, men, women, and children, poured down to the bank.

There was no welcome on their faces, only a savage and calculating curiosity. Through them a scatter of white men thrust their way to us, bearded, haggard, many wearing bloody bandages, the remnant of the "Army of the St. John." And suddenly the Indians parted, and John Allan came, tall and resolute in buckskins, his long hair loose about his shoulders, with the blaze of the sunset red behind him—a picture I shall never forget. All the weary story of the past two years was in his somber eyes: the fruitless journeys back and forth, from the General Court to the Congress, from the Congress to General Washington's headquarters, and back to Boston again; the endless promises and deceits, the fiasco at Fort Cumberland that ruined his sound plans, the unavailing protests against privateers raiding the Nova Scotia settlements, and closer to his heart the knowledge that Mary and her children, forbidden to leave Cumberland, were hostages for his every word and deed.

He came to me eagerly and wrung my hand, demanding news of his family, and his bearded jaw dropped when I confessed I had not seen them since November. But there was no time for talk of things past. We said the troops were at our tails and asked if the Malicetes would fight. There were enough of them to give Studholme a drubbing—enough to destroy his whole force, properly handled.

Allan drew us aside cautiously. In the shade of a big cedar with our sweaty and bearded tatterdemalions sitting, standing, or sprawled on the warm earth all about him, he confessed in a voice of despair that Ambroise and the greedy Pierre Tommo wanted a huge price for their warriors' services. "They treasure the wampum and letters from General Washington but they won't fight without a price in trade goods that those penny-pinching fellows in Boston refuse to pay."

"Suppose Halifax pays it?" I said. "Michael Francklin's had himself made Indian agent—and he's on the river now!"

Allan's eyes blazed. "If Halifax pays it the Malicetes will lay waste the whole of Maine east of the Penobscot. They want to be on the winning side. Eddy made a terrible mistake when he took Ambroise and that crafty devil Tommo to Fort Cumberland. They measure the Americans' chances by what they saw there."

"What are you going to do?" I asked.

"Make one last appeal to them before the soldiers get here."

I'll never forget the speech he made. I hadn't enough of the Malicete tongue to follow it word for word, but I knew those brown wolves were hearing the oratory of their lives. He played on their cupidity by promise of a bounty waiting for them at Machias, on their religious zeal by mention of the kindly French missionaries whom the redcoats had driven out, on their memories by reminding them how Monckton laid the valley waste in '55, on their fighting blood by tales of old Malicete triumphs going back into the dim past—naming the battlefields fluently. I remember the tall figure on the council rock, the strong voice ringing in the twilight hush, the sea of savage faces, and the glitter of their eyes. And I remember how, when he ceased, old Ambroise rose and pledged his people to Wachita's cause, and how Pierre Tommo sprang up like an angry cat and spat out that they should wait and see the color of Wachita's blankets first, and how the brown mob fell to snarling back and forth and fingering the hatchets and crooked knives at their belts.

In the end they divided. Four or five hundred men, women, and children came over to us with Ambroise. The rest chose to stay with Pierre Tommo and see what Michael Francklin had to offer. It was a triumph for us in a way. But with the Indians so divided we dared not offer battle at Aukpaque—a misfortune, for the wide stream was broken there by islands and capable of defense with musketry. Also the channels between the islands offered a chance of ambush by lurking flotillas of canoes, and we might have destroyed Studholme's tooeager soldiers and changed the course of history. We retreated up the river. A few miles past Aukpaque as you go upstream the river takes a sharp turn to the southwest, and at about ten miles there is a fine clearing on the south bank, made by the French in the old time. Many years after our affair the Indians removed from Aukpaque to this place, which the Tory settlers called Kings Clear. In the summer of '77 it was a grassy place dotted with old French cellars, the ancient seigneury of Villerenard, destroyed by Monckton's men. Here in high hopes we chose to fight. But in the morning our Malicetes murmured, pointing out how they were burdened by their women and children and short of ammunition and arms. They were greedy for the promised bounty at Machias and wanted to go there. Allan harangued them again, but his eloquence was lost. Ambroise and his people withdrew upstream to watch the battle, and we whites were left to fight it out alone—about fifty in all, all that remained of the "Army of the St. John."

The fight, our last stand on Nova Scotian soil, was hopeless, of course. We were too few, too harried, too ill-equipped to stand long against Studholme's picked Highlanders and Royals. Pierre Tommo, eager to claim the four hundred dollars offered for John Allan, dead or alive, guided Studholme's men to our position, and they came sweeping up the river in a fleet of canoes and assorted ships' boats.

From our cover we stung them defiantly, and they drew off a little and landed, while Tommo's warriors explored us. Then they came at us from all sides. We fought . . . but why go into that? It was all over at nightfall, when Allan and I and a handful of wounded crept across the river in three canoes and joined Ambroise and his silent people in the shadows of the north bank. Together we fled westward along the river as far as Meductic, and there took the old Indian warpath into Maine, by way of the Eel River and the Chiputneticook lakes. We turned off to the St. Croix and made our way through the Schoodic lakes to the Machias River portage and came to Machias on a hot evening in mid-August with our savage followers chanting loudly in anticipation of the promised feast, like the people of Israel out of the wilderness.

CHAPTER 43

The End of a Dream

I CANNOT SAY that the good people of Machias were glad to see our savage swarm. The Malicetes had played a bloody part in the old frontier wars, and nobody loved them in all Maine. Also they came expecting bounty, where there was none. Nor was there anything that Massachusetts had promised Allan in the way of troops and stores. Colonel Eddy was there with some recruits and a few stands of arms, that was all. We were so used to diappointments of this kind that one more made no difference, but I felt sorry for the Machias folk, who had taken us in and fed us and rummaged clothing to replace our lice-infested rags. From the first they had thrown themselves heart and soul into the fight for Nova Scotia, and I knew that His Majesty's armed forces, having driven us off the St. John, would not let the fighting season pass without a blow at them. We walked the stony street of the settlement or stood in the little fort, wondering which would reach us first—His Majesty or the tight-fisted arm of Massachusetts.

As usual it was His Majesty. The admiral on the Halifax station had prepared a descent on Machias as soon as word reached him of our defeat on the St. John, and Sir George Collier came with his heavy-metaled ships and his swarm of disciplined seamen and made a thorough job of it. I'll spare the details—they are in the history books. Suffice it to say that our Nova Scotia exiles fought shoulder to shoulder with the Machias men and the Malicetes played their part—a marvelous proof of Allan's hold on them, for no Indian likes long odds.

I thought bitterly, watching the red jets spurting from the gun ports of Collier's big *Rainbow*, that the powder he burned in a single broadside would have been enough, in our muskets, to change the tune when his parties ventured ashore.

And as we saw the fleet sail away in triumph, with the smoke of houses, sheds, and wharves rolling up black in the August sunshine, we offered our curses impartially to the vanishing topsails and to the invisible General Court.

War is pain. It is fear and horror; it is hunger and thirst and sweat and fatigue; it is lust and brutality, a weariness shot through with sudden gusts of strength. But mostly it is waiting, and that is the worst of all. I have been through two wars in my lifetime, and I know. You wait for an order, for a leader, for reinforcements, for arms or ammunition. Ashore, you wait for ships. Aboard ship, you wait upon something ashore. Or you wait for weather, for a password, for a river to fall or a tide to rise; often you must even wait for an enemy. But mostly you just wait. When I read a tale of high daring-do, with some dauntless hero rushing blithely from one clash of arms to another, I know that it is false. War is not like that. Nor is love as I have known it. There may be loves, I suppose, that come together at once and never part, like a pair of brooks in the hills that form one flowing river together. They must be beautiful but very dull. If a mere coming together is love, then my Hereford bull is in love with the heifer that Solomon Ives is just bringing through my gate as I write.

It seems to me that true love is mostly waiting, like true war. Love is eating your heart out for a look or a word or a pair of soft lips under yours; love is separation and longing and the queer, mocking emptiness under your ribs that no food can satisfy; love is the taste of a kiss that lingers when you are separate and afar, the echo of a word, the scent of coiled hair, the light step on the starlit road, the soft laugh in the dark. Love is the sweet ghost that comes to trouble a man in the still of the lonely night, the despair that drives a man from his kind like the sick stallion from the herd, and the hope that draws him back again over hills and rivers and seas. I could write a book about love—but not this book. This is a book about hate, the kind that puts brother from brother, that divides men and nations, and makes borders where there should be none. And hate is a waiting game also.

So we waited in the ruins of Machias for the next thing to happen. We had no notion what it might be. We were absorbed in our own affair. The news of Burgoyne's march from Canada seemed like a tale out of a book. In my ignorance I supposed the difficulties of that march greater than they were. Montreal seemed remote as the moon, and the notion that a force of pipe-clayed British and German regulars could make their way through the wilderness to the Hudson Valley made me smile. Even the fall of Ticonderoga, which appalled the Machias men, meant nothing to me.

I remember John Allan's finger on a rudely drawn map of the provinces, showing me how the states would be cut in twain and New England crushed like a nut if Howe marched up the Hudson to join Burgoyne coming down. That, he said, was why Massachusetts kept her eyes toward the north. I said grudgingly that if Massachusetts had exerted herself to drive His Majesty's handful out of Nova Scotia in '76, the British nutcrackers would lack a handle on the east, and Burgoyne would not have dared stir from the St. Lawrence if indeed he got to Canada at all.

The gloomy weeks went by. It was October before we heard the amazing tale of Saratoga. We went wild, capering up and down the stony street, firing guns and pistols—a sinful waste—and yelling our heads off. Our hopes shot up to the stars again. With Burgoyne taken and Canada left naked, the men of New England could turn their eyes down east. Massey, we knew from the Halifax committee, was unable to muster more than 1300 troops in the whole sprawling expanse of Nova Scotia. We cried that we would hoist the American flag over Halifax within a month, and Canada would fall like a last leaf in the winter wind. One flag, one people, and one continent! There was an anthem in those words, and we sang them in our hearts in those bright October days, when the hardwood leaves were one blazing banner on the hillsides, and the west wind was the cool strong breathing of the continent. Machias was like home to me. The river was about the size of ours, and the straggling homes along the bank, the woods coming down to the harbor shore, the clean smells of fish and salt and new-sawn lumber—all things made me think of home. But all of us thought of home in those hopeful days.

Most of our Cumberland exiles were gathered there—including Mary Allan, who had escaped with her children at last—and full of plans for the recovery of their confiscated homes. Even Colonel Jonathan Eddy, stalking up and down at the head of his recruits, gorgeous in blue and buff and sword and plume—for like Yankee Doodle he had stuck a feather in his hat—paused now and again to say some word of his farm by the Missaguash marshes and the prospects for spring plowing.

We were eager; we were in a fever to be on the move, and when young Crabtree, still limping from his wound, yelled into my open window that the long-awaited messenger had come from Boston, I ran all the way to Allan's quarters for the news. My head was full of Massachusetts troops, ships, and guns.

I strode in without the formality of a knock and found myself in the presence of Colonel Allan, tall and silent and grim as death, and the spy Aaron Trusdell, tired and dusty from the Boston Road and still smelling faintly of the fishing sloop which had brought him from Casco Bay. A letter, hastily opened and flung down, lay on the plain pine table with Aaron's hat.

"What is it?" I stammered. "What's the matter?"

Neither spoke for a time; then Allan turned to me and said with the deep Scotch burr that always crept into his voice when he was stirred, "Massachusetts has abandoned the expedition to Nova Scotia. I have orders"—stabbing an accusing finger at the paper on the table—"to disband all recruits and return what arms and stores we have received."

"For God's sake why? Why?"

Allan shrugged. "Now that Burgoyne's captured, Boston reckons itself safe."

I turned to the spy in a fury. "And the Congress?"

"The Congress," Aaron said ironically, "is absorbed in more important things."

I knew what he meant. I had heard the gossip in Machias. The Congress was busy knifing General Washington and every other man who placed the country before itself. But in my anger I burst out in a long tirade against them all, from Sam Adams to Washington, not forgetting Trusdell himself.

The spy heard me out with a stony face, but when I came to Washington he stopped me short. "Enough! You're a young man with a hot tongue, and hot tongues won't save America. What the Congress or the General Court of Massachusetts may have promised you Nova Scotia people is no concern of mine. I was sent into your province by General Washington himself, to see what I could see. I went from place to place. I talked with your committees in every town and settlement. I cautioned them to attempt nothing without word from Washington himself. To rise without support would only play into the British governor's hands. I made my report to the general, and you must know what he said—he wrote it down for any man to see. He refused any diversion of his stores and forces. And he was right! This war couldn't be won in Nova Scotia, but it could be lost in the Hudson Valley. That's the plain truth if you want it. But tell him yourself, Colonel—you saw General Washington himself on this very matter last winter!"

"Ay," said Allan heavily. "Who didn't I see on this very matter?" He talked like a man in a melancholy dream. "I left Boston late in November—on the same day, had I known it, that all was lost at Fort Cumberland. I went by horseback through the states. At Providence I called on Governor Cook. At Norwich, Governor Trumbull gave me a pass into the country. I crossed over the Hudson at Fishkill and after much wandering fell in with General Gates—who'd been an aide-de-camp in Halifax in the old days. He took me to Washington's headquarters. I dined with Washington on a Sunday, I remember, just three days before Christmas. He was kind; he was sympathetic; he astonished me with an intimate knowledge of the Whig sentiment in Nova Scotia. But he said we must wait. He would promise nothing. I left his headquarters on Christmas Day—the day before he crossed the Delaware to fall upon the British. I rode to Philadelphia, to Baltimore. I was received by the Congress. They gave me a colonel's commission. They made me Superintendent of the Eastern Indians. They recommended my Nova Scotia plan to the government of Massachusetts. But Massachusetts . . ." He gestured dumbly at the letter.

"What's wrong with those muttonheads in Boston?" I demanded. "Let's forget that most Nova Scotians are New England born— Yankees of the Yankees. Forget all sentiment. Can't they see that Nova Scotia in hostile hands is a pistol pointed at the heart of Massachusetts? Look at the map! All the old governors of New England saw that and struggled more than a hundred years to wrench it from the hand of France. Nova Scotia was bought and paid for with New England money and New England blood. Now the General Court's decided to let it go without burning a pinch of powder. Are they mad?"

"Just blind," Allan said.

I shoved my hands into my waistband and walked to the window, staring out on that desolate village which Boston had abandoned with the rest.

"What are you going to do, John?" I asked over my shoulder.

"My duty."

"What's that?"

"Try to save Maine. Michael Francklin's thrown himself into the river country, working to win the Malicetes, the Micmacs, the Passamaquoddies and Penobscots. I must do the same, for the sake of the frontier people."

There was a little choked cry from the doorway and a rush of skirts. Mary Allan flung herself into his arms. "Oh, John, no, no! You can't! You've done enough! We've all done enough! I can't stand any more! Oh, John, let's go with our poor friends from Cumberland . . . take up a piece of land somewhere away from all this fighting and misery . . . the New Hampshire grants . . . somewhere like that. John!" Her younger children, alarmed by her cries, ran in and clutched her, muffling their small weeping in her skirts. I moved toward the door.

Allan said, "Where are you going, David?"

"I don't know. Away from here, anyhow. Salem . . . Boston, maybe. Join the Continental army. A berth in one of the state warships, perhaps. Something. Anything."

He took my hand and wrung it in a long silence, and Mary gave me a quick, impulsive hug and put her tear-wet face against mine. Aaron Trusdell put a friendly hand on my shoulder, but I shrugged it off. He was a brave man and had played well his dangerous game in Nova Scotia but he worshiped his commander too thoroughly to have time for sentiment or to inspire any sentiment in me. I saw him as part of the miserable bog in which we had floundered all this time.

I never saw any of them again. But I was to hear of John Allan in the bitter months and years to come. Of his labors alone in the wilderness, matching wits with Michael Francklin, who played his own lonely part for the British. Of the incessant journeys by canoe and afoot; of hunger and suffering and danger always; of triumphant treaties with the savages, ruined by the failure of Boston to send the promised gifts; of his young sons held by the Indians for months as a pledge of his own good faith; of black failure, relieved again and again by Francklin's own difficulties with the jealous Council at Halifax. Someday that story must be written also. Alone, with no weapons but their own wits, the two men fought their strange duel up and down the St. John and amongst the lakes of eastern Maine until the war's end, when Francklin died, worn out by the struggle to save what's now New Brunswick for the British flag. During all that time the bemused Indians hovered up and down the warpath without once striking an effective blow for either side, a triumph for both men, all things considered, and what they both desired.

For saving eastern Maine the Congress long afterward gave Allan a grant in far Ohio. A slice of the moon! He chose to live in Maine—at Lubec, as near to his beloved Cumberland as he could get without setting foot on British soil—and there he was buried in the year of Trafalgar, as noble a patriot as ever breathed American air.

How many others from Nova Scotia broke their hearts in exile God only knows. There was an exodus that did not dry up till the peace of '83. The quill-driving, guinea-chinking officials of Halifax were too busy swindling the Tories who came, to count the Whigs who left. I only know that I met them everywhere in New England: poor, friendless, hopeless, subsisting on any labor they could find, rightly blaming both king and Congress for their troubles, but saving their blackest curses for the government of Massachusetts.

CHAPTER 44

In Valediction

O PURBLIND GENTLEMEN of Massachusetts! Doubtless you were estimable men, family men, God-fearing men, active and ingenious men, men much absorbed in business and in state. But somehow I see you always in one person, a plump and comfortable person of neat-powdered hair, stout shoes and respectable cloth, seated by a smart fire of dry maple in that dark Boston winter of '77 and with penknife clutched in slightly snuff-stained fingers, calmly paring a rind of cheese.

You told me—do you remember the ragged young man from Nova Scotia, O Man of Boston? You called him jocularly Blue Nose, that new cant nickname for the downeast Yankee folk—that Massachusetts was not Nova Scotia's keeper, that the war had cost a mint of money and now that it had rolled away to the south and west—"for which the Lord be praised"—now was the time to whittle expenses.

In a few short months, O Man of Boston, the British would move down into Maine. Even that would not alarm you for a time. But then you would raise the army and fleet that might have saved Nova

Scotia in '76—and squander them on the Penobscot in the bloody tragedy of '79.

You could not see the future then, of course. 'Twas the past you put behind you when you turned your back on me. You pared your cheese—remember?—and poised a shaving, greasy and yellow as gold, on your blade for a moment before popping it into your mouth. Daylight was drawing away from the frosty windows of your counting-house, and a sudden fall of coals in the hearth sent a ruddy glow over everything in the room. A cheerful glow, red as a winter sunset, red as a Fundy tide, ay, redder than that. Red as the blood of Phips' men, Ben Church's men, and the men of March, of Nicholson, of Pepperell, of tragic Colonel Noble—the tide of good New England blood that beat and broke upon the shores of Nova Scotia for a hundred years and finally conquered it and peopled it. Connecticut folk, Rhode Island folk, but mostly Massachusetts folk, flesh of your flesh and bone of your bone—these were the people you first abandoned and then loosed your dogs upon. No wonder our Indians were astonished. Not even a savage would do that.

Ay, you cast us off, and if dead men's bones could speak there would have risen from the graves of Nova Scotia such a shout of protest as would have rattled your smug Bostonian panes to shivers.

But fighting men sleep soundly in our Nova Scotia earth, in the green graves about Annapolis Fort, by the marshes of the Missaguash and Tantramar and the clay banks of the Petitcodiac, in the bleak barrens of Louisburg, in the pleasant Grand Pré orchards where once upon a time the French and Indians slaughtered Noble's men in the snow, in the outposts of Halifax, amongst the rocks of Canso, in the small, lonely mounds beside the Nova Scotia trails and rivers and lakes—wherever New Englanders fought and died to make a fourteenth province for their own. No voice can trouble you now, not even the voice of conscience. So be it.

CHAPTER 45

Exile

SEEKING LUKE was like hunting a needle in a haymow. 'Twould have been easy if he had stuck to Seth Harding, for our old townsman was a great man in New England now, and all Boston was talking about his capture of the Jamaica packet, the richest prize brought in that year. I met him in a tavern, where he told me Luke had left him months before. He offered me a berth in his ship, which I refused, as I refused the money he tried to force upon me, seeing my rags.

I thought I might find Luke in Plymouth, amongst our Massachusetts relatives, and went there, but none had seen him. Plymouth was like home, or perhaps I should say that our Liverpool was a little Plymouth set down in the wilds of Nova Scotia. All the familiar family names were there—Bartlett, Cobb, Slocombe, Thomas, West, Bradford, Doggett, Ford, Foster, Hunt, Kempton, Harlow, Morton—and I was passed eagerly from home to home and plied with questions about the Nova Scotia kinsfolk. Their sentiment seemed to be Whig without the wild ranting that I found so often in Massachusetts, and that, too, was like home. I think the Pilgrim blood contained more of the salt of tolerance than the Puritan. Otherwise how was it possible for stout John Thomas, graduate of Harvard and founder of the Old Colony Club, to remain openly and avowedly a Tory in their midst? I spent an evening at his home and found him tolerant in his opinions like the rest; the first Tory I had met that I liked. After the war he removed to our Liverpool and was an honored magistrate in our town and my good friend until the day he died.

Plymouth was a fine place, and I was pressed to stay on every side, but all this smelled to my high nose of charity, and I would have none.

I spent most of the winter in Boston, working for a little old woman who sold books in a lane off Tremont Street. She gave me a bed in her garret, and there I filled the evenings and the deathlike Bostonian Sundays with much poring over selections from her stock in trade. Ma'am Fitch encouraged me in this and pointed out things that I should read—not for the improvement of my mind at all, but because they were interesting in themselves. And so I acquired the love of books which has clung to me all my life; indeed, how much I owe to that quiet old woman's interest in me I cannot estimate. I know that she saved me from going mad in that black, hopeless winter and early spring of '78.

The people who came to her shop talked gloomily of the war. All the joy of Saratoga had vanished when the king's troops entered Philadelphia. The remnant of Washington's army was wintering in some miserable den called Valley Forge. But I noticed that many of these people consoled themselves and poor Mrs. Fitch with the notion that all the fighting would be done to the south and talked hopefully of a profit out of the war if it lasted long enough. Privateering was already so popular that it was difficult to find recruits for the Massachusetts Line. The smugness of Boston had enraged me; what sickened me was this rising note of greed in every voice. I wondered if all the patriots had died on Bunker Hill.

I was restless and unhappy. I had put Fear out of my mind by an effort of will, but she left an emptiness that gnawed like hunger. When the sun began to shine warm on the shop front and turned the sooty snow to black slush in the gutters, there was a growing itch in my feet. In April I bade farewell to my benefactress and shook the mud of Boston from my shoes. I had no notion where I was going but instinctively I turned my face toward Machias. It was good to be afoot again, even on the muddy Bay Road. The sun shone, and a salt whiff of the sea drifted up the hollow wherever the road crossed a stream. There was no lack of refreshment, for every few miles I met a merry party of seamen making for the girls of Boston. Each had his belongings done up in a handkerchief on a stick; each had his pockets full of paper currency, and every party carried a jug of Medford rum by a rope yarn slung through the handle. Ah, Salem was the place, they said, and recommended this captain and that, with a good deal of hilarious argument amongst themselves. Nothing like a Salem privateer for civil usage and quick profits! Was I a Cape Codder?—I talked like a damned Cape Codder. Nova Scotia! A Blue Nose, by Godfrey! They winked and nudged each other. If I was a Blue Nose, why, Cap'n Leach or Cap'n Simmons or Cap'n Carlton—those were the boys for me!

I sighted the steeple of Salem's First Church late in the afternoon. Gallows Hill and Blubber Hollow lay off to the left by North River, and the Mill Pond was placid under Castle Hill to my right. Then I was walking down the main street, sniffing the savory supper smells that drifted from every kitchen on the warm spring air. Thanks to good Mistress Fitch I had a stout pair of shoes on my feet, a pair of new leather breeches, and a gray linsey shirt, and because I had mentioned some notion of going to sea, she had got me a serviceable red nightcap and a blue jacket of good fear-nought stuff. In my pocket jingled five shillings, a noble gift; hard money was scarce in Boston in the spring of '78. These and the clothes were my wages for the weeks I had spent with her, a gross overpayment, for God knows I had done little but eat and read.

Salem was a big town and prosperous. Halifax was not a patch on it. The houses were mostly painted and had gardens in the back where shrubs and fruit trees were just budding out; the men and women were well clothed; the shops were busy, and there was an astonishing number of gentlemen ahorseback, not to mention people in chaises and top chairs and curricles and sulkies, rattling over the cobbles. Salem was a Whig town of the violent sort, though I was told that old Parson McGilchrist of St. Peter's Church continued to pray for the king. There were no better seamen in the world than these tough, unruly men of Marblehead and Salem; they had taken to privateering like ducks to water, and their ventures were financed and directed by as shrewd and energetic a group of merchants as could be found in North America. If I was to make my fortune at the expense of King George, as became a new citizen of Massachusetts, here was the place to do it.

I put up at a seamen's tavern down by Town House Cove. There were no privateers recruiting at the moment, but I found work unloading a vessel from the West Indies and so saved my precious shillings. The tavern loafers gave me ready advice on the matter of privateering. Some ships were better found than others, and captains were good or bad according to their manners and their luck. There would be plenty of choice. Thirty privateers were sailing out of this one town. Last year there had been six. Next year there would be fifty, a hundred—the figure mounted with the drinks. Prizes were being fitted for the trade as fast as guns could be got for them, and bigger ships were abuilding. The place was a roaring hive, and all the talk was of shares and prize money and hopeful prospects of a long war.

About the first of May I met a Nova Scotian, a fellow named Doane from Barrington. He was waiting for a berth in a big, new two-hundred-tonner built at Salisbury and expressly designed for privateering.

"There's two kinds o' privateers out o' Salem," he observed, regarding me with a sidelong eye. "There's the good-sized 'uns that reach far out—far as England, some of 'em—an' fetch home good-sized prizes or nothin'. An' there's the little jiggers an' schooners an' such, that never go further'n Quero Bank—but always come home with somethin'."

"That's an argument for the little 'uns," said I.

"Umph. I said they never go further'n the Banks."

"Well?"

"Where d'ye s'pose they get their stuff?"

"Well, where?"

He sniffed and spat. "They're holdin' a vendue o' prize goods sent in by a little schooner privateer, in that store up the street yonder. Go an' take a look."

The store was a fairly large one crowded with seamen and women of the poorer class, and the auctioneer's voice pealed forth from the open door. I wormed my way in. "Naow, folks!" the fellow howled, "the package goods and bar'lled goods is all bought in by the merchants, but here's a lot o' odds and ends that's got to be sold s'afternoon to clean up Cap'n Leach's last cruise to the east'ard." He waved a soiled hand toward the shelves at his back and a long counter piled with stuff. 'Twas a queer assortment. The stuff had a used look—herring nets, mackerel nets, codfish trawls with rusty hooks, a stack of short oars such as shore fishermen whittle for themselves out of ash, a pile of small sails whose canvas was weathered and worn thin, several pairs of sea boots waterproofed with fish oil. Had Cap'n Leach, that famous patriot, stooped to rob a few poor Newfoundland hookers in the Gulf?

But there were other things—scythes and reaping hooks, three or four wooden-staved churns of the sort the Lunenburgers make, a bale of dressed moose hides, eel spears, a number of neat, homemade rugs, a pair of steelyards, a pile of quilts fashioned with beautiful needlework even to my ignorant male eye, a wooden clock, a barrel of tallow candles. And along the shelves was ranged an ironmonger's nightmare of iron and copper kitchenware, china and pewter ware, a few bits of silver, and a good deal of tinware, mostly knives, forks, and spoons. Some good brass candlesticks and a silver teapot, a pewter inkwell with a sand caster of the same metal, tin lanterns and brass warming pans, and books of all sorts and conditions, including Tom Paine's *Common Sense*, well thumbed, a strange thing to see there. There were some chests and leather trunks, and the auctioneer rapped sharply on the lid of one with his gavel for attention. "Naow, friends" —he flung back the lid—"we'll start with these boxes o' mixed goods, to be sold with contents as they are."

The women crowded close, buzzing like flies in an attic window in October. Over their bent heads I could see female clothing of the common sort, jammed into the trunk all anyhow, and at the top a small looking glass, a sewing basket, and a pair of child's shoes very neatly sewn of caribou hide.

I turned away then. The air these chaffering people breathed was poisonous all of a sudden. But I knew what I wanted after all the weary months. I wanted to go home.

There was a little, dark rum shop in an alley off Town House Cove where the Nova Scotia smugglers came. I knew it from gossip at my lodgings, and Doane had told me that he went there sometimes for a word from home. Its windows were small and obscured with thick red curtains of dyed sailcloth, and when I entered and shut the door behind me I had to stand blinking for half a minute before my eyes could see an arm's length. I found myself in a dim room perhaps twelve feet by twelve, with a sanded floor and board walls covered with a thick ships' paint of Spanish brown. A couple of men in seamen's dress sat on kegs by the low counter, and behind it was a clutter of bottles and black leather drinking jacks on two or three shelves. On the counter itself sat a rum keg in chocks, with a spigot ready for business and at the side a cask or two of wine or perhaps only beer.

At the sound of my entry a fleshy woman in a frilled cap and blue cotton gown emerged from behind a curtain like a seventy-four out of a fog. Her face was swarthy and large, with a small parrot nose in the middle and a rich black mustache to the south of it, and from her ears hung a pair of pendants which looked like purple strawberries and turned out to be miniature grape bunches finely made of gold and lacquer work.

She and the men regarded me silently.

"Madame Tibbo?" said I.

"Yes?"

"A rum, please—and two for the gentlemen on the kegs. Ye'll join me, friends?"

They joined me. I mentioned the weather. 'Twas fine, they admitted curtly. I complimented Madame on her excellent rum—it really was—and she accepted the compliment with an unsmiling nod that set the grape bunches dancing. I ventured a hope that her health was good and drank a stiff swig to it gallantly. A nod, no more. The men sipped. The rum was of a smooth but potent Cuba sort which warms but does not burn the stomach and conceals its power in a mellow taste. I guessed that it had never seen a gauger's rod but aloud I discoursed upon the state of the codfishery, the season's prospects for sauce gardens, the view from Castle Hill—Heaven knows what not, though I carefully steered clear of the war and ignored the existence of the province over Fundy Bay. I paused from time to time for comment, but 'twas always the same—I did all the talking and most of the drinking, with my precious hard money placed on the counter and advanced toward Madame, coin by coin, like a one-sided game of chess. I ran out of conversation after a time and sat as glum as the others, slowly putting away drink after drink and getting as full as a tick. And all the while Madame Tibbo stood watchful behind her counter, a fat black-eyed image of suspicion.

I was never a diplomat, and all this beating about the bush irked me to the teeth, and at last the rum got the best of me.

"Friends," said I loudly, "I'm a plain fellow that likes plain talk and don't mind a short answer if it's to the point. I'm from Nova Scotia and want a passage home. Where'll I find it?"

Silence. 'Twas wonderful to see the seamen freeze, one with his jack just short of the parted lips, the other about to sound his conch in a large red handkerchief. But Madame came to life shrilly. Through the small parrot nose, in an *Acadien* accent that had lost nothing in twenty-three years of exile, she cried upon God to witness that she and all who came to her shop were good Whigs and patriots, who spat upon all foreigners—especially those good-for-nothing *Nouvelle-Ecossais*. Zut! I must be *dronk!*

I was, by that time. My head sang like a frog pond in springtime, and when I tried to say something witty and disarming my thick tongue refused to coil around the words. The two seamen seized my arms and half pulled, half lifted me toward the door, and of course I began to roar and throw them about, though they clung like leeches. I was making too much noise for Madame's liking. I had a glimpse of her drawing from some hiding place behind the counter a cudgel whose end was curiously padded with leather, and soon after that my head was a darkness filled with sparks. She struck me at least twice more, for I heard the blows dimly, as you hear the shut of a door from some far part of the house. I heard her saying, "Not outside, fools—up the alley farther," and that is all I remember except a clammy feeling of water or mud and the reek of rotten fish and other things.

CHAPTER 46

Nova-Damn-Scotia

I OPENED MY EYES in a small wooden box that was swaying dizzily in the dim light of a smoky lantern. I lay stupidly watching the curious behavior of a pair of greatcoats on the wall, the water in a glass decanter set in a rack beside the door, and the lantern itself, all moving to and fro in unison like figures in a dance. For music there was a familiar chorus of creakings and groanings and somewhere beyond all that the boom of the sea. I was aboard a vessel, then, and a small one by the feel of her. At the moment of this remarkable discovery the door opened, and a man came in, a small, wiry fellow of forty-five or so, with a brown hatchet face and a thin nose set like a putty knife between a pair of twinkling gray eyes. Water clung in beads to his thick, blue sea jacket and dripped from a pair of stout canvas trousers and home-tanned sea boots. He took off a tarpaulin hat to shake the water from it and revealed a queer head, bald from front to dome, with the long strands of side and back hair gathered into a little tarred pigtail no thicker than a bucket rope.

"Who are you?" I demanded. "What ship's this?"

He lifted his eyebrows, as if surprised to find that I could talk, and a ripple of wrinkles ran up his bare skull. "Name's Locke, Cephas Locke. As fer the vessel, now, that depends." He grinned and twitched his nose. "Depends, that does. If ye was one o' them who-are-ye-damn-ye captains o' His Majesty's navy, why, I'd say this here is the Nova Scotia coaster *Loyal Sam*, Barrin'ton to Annapolis, an' blowed off o' the home coast in a norther some days back. On t'other hand, if ye was master of a Salem privateer, say, or one o' the state ships, why, she's the *Liberty*, sloop, that's jist took a load o' 'scaped American prisoners from Yarmouth to Marblehead an' got papers to show for't. But if ye're a poor devil of a Blue Nose that wants to git home—which is what I think ye are—why, she's the *Two Friends*, out o' Ragged Island, that's jist run in a cargo o' good green cod, split an' slack-salted, to certain merchants o' Salem, an' now is homeward bound with a few bar'ls o' flour an' suchlike."

"Fish to Salem!"

"Why not? Patriots has got to eat, an' all the Salem fishermen's in privateers."

"How did I get here?"

He grinned again. "Drunk as a lord. And sick. Fact is, I was doin' some business with the aforesaid merchants in Madame's back parlor an' heard the whole thing. She took ye fer a spy from the Committee o' Safety or mebbe the Committee o' Correspondence."

I threw off the blanket and struggled out of the narrow berth, mother-naked, catching at a hook on the wall for support. My head was full of little stabbing knives now, but the chief discomfort was my ears, which ached and sang all the way back into my skull and gave a special throb at every step. My mouth was dry and tasted as bilge water smells. I wanted fresh air—the atmosphere of the little cuddy was that of a washhouse on a Monday morning.

The master of the *Two Friends* stopped me at the door. "Ye can't go out on deck like that, friend. 'Tain't decent."

"Who's to see?"

"Besides which it's a rough night with a cold westerly blowin'. Wait here whilst I git your clo'es. They stunk o' the alley ye laid in an' had to be wrung out with plenty o' soap an' water. They're dryin' on a line in the hold."

He whisked out of the door and after five or ten minutes came back with my breeches, shirt, stockings, and shoes. "Your jacket's a mite clammy, an' I left it to dry some more. Put the blanket round your shoulders if ye're bound to go on deck."

The wind was a breath of life, though my head ached faithfully with every step. The weather was clearing fast, with the westerly gale whipping black scud off the face of the stars. I saw the Dipper and the polar star and knew we must be making famous progress homeward. The vessel was what Salem folk call a Chebacco boat, a kind much favored around the corner of Cape Ann, a little two-master with no bowsprit, the foremast set right up in the eyes of her, and the mainmast raking aft. Under her two plain sails she bowled along sweetly in the dark.

Besides Cephas Locke, the crew seemed to consist of a man and a boy. The boy stood silent at the mainmast weather rigging. The man at the tiller was a lean old fellow, a Nantucketer by his speech, intent on his steering, with the wind blowing his loose gray locks about his head. The sea was black as ink, except where the bluff bow of the *Two Friends* shattered in it a hissing white blotch.

I felt better in the morning, though my ears still throbbed when I walked. I offered to spell the boy at the tiller. He refused, but Cephas Locke bade him give over to me. The weather had shifted again and was blowing what we call in Nova Scotia a smoky sou'wester, a strong, warm gale with fine rain and mist. A fair-enough wind for home, but the thick scud made it dangerous for rounding Cape Sable if the weather held. All that day we drove before it, with the boy perched in the foremast rigging and Cephas humming psalm tunes through his nose and the Nantucketer vowing that this weather would be the death of us if it did not clear.

"It screens us from the king's ships anyway," I suggested to Cephas.

He shook his head. "They'd not bother with so poor a prize." But his voice was uneasy.

At dark the Nantucketer told me curtly to turn in, and I did, glad enough, for my head had begun to ache again dismally. I started up once in the night, hearing a stir on deck and what seemed to be the feet of a child, or children, running about. I decided I was dreaming and dropped back into slumber.

Much later I wakened again, with the full awakeness that sets every nerve twitching and forbids a man to lie abed. The candle in the lantern had guttered out and the close air of the cuddy stank of its greasy death. The small window glasses were gray with daylight. I pulled on my clothes, and as I opened the door the sound of breakers startled me into a cold sweat. The weather was still blowing thick, and Cephas had doused his mainsail and sat hunched at the tiller staring fiercely into the smother ahead. The little vessel bowled along at a great rate under its foresail. I could see the boy aloft and the Nantucketer clutching the foremast stays.

"Come on the coast a mite quicker'n I figgered on," Cephas grunted. "Couldn't git a smell o' the land with this wind. Fust thing I knowed we was amongst the islands." I could feel my scalp prickling. The islands of Cape Sable had wrecked more ships and drowned more men than any other danger on our long and rocky coast.

"Why don't ye haul your wind?" I shouted.

For answer he pointed a long finger to starboard, and my staring eyes made out a low point smothered in breaking surf. But it was the white flutter of gulls that scared me. The gulls in those parts roost about the main shore until the turn of tide and then go winging out in yelling, white squadrons to the low points and reefs of the islands, ready for the ebb harvest. So we were caught on a lee shore and in the ebb of the mighty Fundy tide, which rushes through the islands like a mill race. The point vanished, but soon another showed, with another white flock of gulls, and to leeward I could hear a steady, dull boom of surf.

"D'ye know where we are?" I screamed at Cephas.

He nodded calmly. "Made out Green Island back there a way."

"Where are ye heading, man?"

"Into the Hawk."

I sat down then, not trusting my legs. From Father, from Mark, from all our Liverpool seamen I had heard evil tales of that twisting and dangerous passage between Hawk Point and Cape Sable Island. A bad-enough place in clear weather, with a good wind and tide. In this . . . !

The boy aloft and the Nantucketer stood immovable as figureheads, staring into the drizzle ahead. The little Chebacco boat seemed to have a terrific speed. I marveled at the hardihood of these smugglers, taking such chances rather than face the ships of His Majesty's fleet— or the swarming American privateers.

Cape Sable Island remained invisible, but Cephas, watching the compass in the box before him and calculating by the easing of wind and sea how far we had run inside the shelter of the island's long westerly arm, shifted his tiller confidently. The surf sounds on either hand came and went like the voices of passers-by in a dark street, and Cephas nodded now and again as if in greeting. At last they fell away, and we got the full blast of the westerly weather again. The boy came down the rigging, and the Nantucketer sauntered aft. 'Twas full daylight now, and their eyes looked weary, but there was no sign of excitement in their wet, brown faces. I guessed that the *Two Friends* ran the Hawk Passage quite often and with good reason.

Cephas motioned me to the tiller. "Keep her no'theast by east for a spell, friend, whilst I git some breakfast and the others catch a nap. Keep an eye to port, and ye may see Cape Negro if the weather opens."

He and the Nantucketer hoisted the mainsail before diving into the cuddy, and presently I caught a whiff of wood smoke from the stovepipe.

The weather held thick. But the wind fell fast, and after two hours the sails were flapping dismally in the wet.

Cephas sniffed. "We'll git a slant from the nor'west afore long."

"That'll clear the weather," I suggested.

"Humph! An' give us a hard thrash to wind'ard, gittin' in home."

In another hour we heard sounds in the fog ahead. Gulls, thought I. They sounded like men, but the big black-backed gulls we call preachers always sound like men at a distance. They came nearer. They came into sight and they were men right enough, as wild and rough a crew as I ever saw. There were twenty of them, bearded and sunburned and shaggy-haired, and their craft was a battered old whaleboat of the kind we call shaving mills because, I suppose, they look as if they'd been whittled out with knives. Their single sail was furled, and they were walking the boat along with their long ash oars when they saw us. They made for the *Two Friends* at once, and Cephas gave a peculiar double rap on the cuddy door.

Out came the Nantucketer armed with a pistol and a whaling harpoon with the shaft sawn off at six feet, a nasty weapon in a boarding scrimmage. He passed the pistol to Cephas, and Cephas laid it on the deck.

"They're too many fer us," he said out of the side of his mouth. "Let me do the talkin'." The man at the whaleboat's steering oar, a big black-bearded fellow in ragged and greasy homespuns, laid his craft alongside expertly, and they swarmed aboard. They were armed with a queer collection of weapons—I saw one old bell-mouthed blunderbuss that must have seen service in King Philip's War—and besides muskets they had one or two pistols and a number of rusty cutlasses and steel tomahawks. The sole armament of their craft was a small swivel gun mounted at the bow. She was entirely open from stem to stern, and I guessed that they hovered close to the coast and spent their nights by a fire ashore.

"What vessel is this, now?" asked Black Beard, pleasant enough. They were all pleasant, grinning all over their greasy faces, trying the fastenings of the hatch cover, and peering down into the cuddy.

Cephas put on the uneasy whine of a countryman beset by footpads in an alley. "Sloop *Liberty*, Salem to Ragged Island, arter takin' home some patriots as got wrecked on Nova Scotia in the Congress brig-o'-war *Cabot*. I got papers to show fer it, friend"—he fished inside his shirt eagerly and produced several folded and well-thumbed sheets —"there's a letter from Cap'n Olney o' the *Cabot*, an' here's a paper from Cap'n Harriden o' the Massachusetts brig *Tyrannicide*"—he pronounced it Tyrant-side—"that took part in the same action, ag'in the British frigate *Milford* . . . an' this here is a pass from the Committee o' Safety at Salem . . . an' . . ."

Black Beard snatched the papers out of his hand and studied them, a matter of some difficulty, for he held one upside down and studied that the hardest.

One of his crew, a youngster not more than fifteen, with the dark, cunning face of a mischievous ape, had picked up Cephas' pistol and made a pretense of examining it—with the muzzle pointed at my chest. Another ragamuffin walked over to the Nantucketer and held out his hand for the harpoon. He hefted the weapon as if to test its balance, and then flung it expertly into the sea.

Black Beard looked up, and his big hands tore the papers across and across and flung the scraps into Cephas' face.

"Papers!" he said coolly. "All you smugglers got papers. Besides, we're from Conne'ticut, and what's your damned Salem committee to us? Breakin' the embargo, you are, don't deny it. It's ag'in the laws an' regulations o' Congress an' the state o' Conne'ticut, an' I claim this vessel lawful prize. What's in the hold?"

"Nawthin'," whined Cephas, "'cept a couple bar'ls o' flour an' suchlike to keep our fam'lies from starvin' till the summer crops."

The ragged men were already taking off the battens, and in a moment they whipped off the canvas and then the hatch. They looked down and whistled. Black Beard walked over and took a look.

"Well! Well!" He put back his head and laughed, and the teeth shone white in his bearded mouth. Everybody laughed. 'Twas a most humorous company. Even Cephas smiled—a sickly smile like the morning sun on a tombstone.

Said Black Beard, "Who's them people? Don't tell me—I know. Tories, ain't they? Smugglin' 'em off to Nova-damn-Scotia, ain't ye? An' their menfolk still fightin' for the British tyrant, like as not! Nice little business you got! Rebels one way, Tories t'other. Reckon ye make a pretty penny off 'em too. Where's the money?"

Cephas broke into a sweat, but the whine was gone from his voice and the half-witted smile from his lean face. "Listen, friend, I take no money from these people. American prisoners on the run from Hal'fax have no money to pay. No more have the Tory refugees so far as my acquaintance goes. Them women an' children in the hold was bound from New York to Hal'fax when a privateer overhauled their vessel an' took her into Salem. There they was, turned ashore in a strange town that don't love Tory folk an' told to git out o' the place any way they could—an' the quicker the better. I took pity on 'em an' offered 'em passage. They've got nawthin' but what they stand in. No more have I, barrin' them two bar'ls o' flour an' the bar'l o' molasses an' the half bar'l o' beef ye see down there."

"A likely yarn," scoffed Black Beard. "Search the cuddy, boys!" Three grinning fellows went below, nothing loath, and found nothing but Cephas' boy, hiding under a berth. They pitched him on deck, neck and crop, and came forth reporting failure.

"She's a queer little thing," observed Black Beard, running an eye over the rigging and gear, "but she'll serve us very nice. Shift over the swivel an' stuff, boys."

"What are ye goin' to do?" asked Cephas anxiously.

"Why now," replied Black Beard cheerfully, "we're agoin' to make a trade, you an' me. Our vessel for your'n—an' I'll give ye the passengers to boot. That there shavin' mill's as neat to handle as anything y'ever see. Ye'll have to keep bailin', that's all, for she leaks a mite.

Otherwise she's as well found a craft as ever come out o' the Coakset River, an' that's sayin' a heap. Call them people up."

Cephas went to the hatch and called down in a low voice, and in a few moments a woman came up a ladder of some kind, clutching a child in one arm. Two boys of eight or ten followed and stood by her, holding her skirts. Another woman appeared, middle-aged and more commonly dressed, a servant perhaps, carrying a baby in a shawl, and then a pale young woman in a well-cut, blue traveling gown and jacket, very bedraggled and looking as if the air of the hold and the motion of the *Two Friends* had made her seasick to the point of death. Altogether there were nine women and twenty-one children of all ages. They stood in a tight group by the hatch, with bloodless faces, watching that wild, grinning crew.

"That all?" grunted Black Beard.

"One more," the Nantucket man said. "She stayed below to pass up the little ones."

All eyes were on the gaping little hatch of the *Two Friends*, and there was a silence. We made a dramatic company in that moment: the Tory women in their rumpled clothes, the wide-eyed children, Cephas and his boy, the tall old Nantucketer who looked like a bearded prophet out of the Scriptures, the ragged, wild men of the whaleboat. And there were the white walls of fog that shut us in and swirled slowly, thinning and swelling again, and there was the smell of the sea that is the very breath of our Nova Scotia and the voices of sea birds crying in the mist and the smooth green swell that lifted and gently lowered the whaleboat and the sloop and set them nudging coyly at each other; the blue wisp from the stovepipe, and the empty slatting of the sails. Suddenly I knew who would come through that dark opening. I can't explain. It came upon me simply and naturally, as the sunrise comes upon a man facing east in the last deep dark of the night.

When Fear stepped out upon the deck of the *Two Friends* it was like the fulfillment of a promise.

But there was no promise in the look she gave me. Only a flicker of recognition and then a blankness, as if a curtain had been drawn. And she turned a slow, contemptuous gaze upon those Connecticut picaroons that set them shuffling and glancing sheepishly at one another and stepping to the side to spit noisily in the sea—a form of bravado I have noticed more than once in human animals confronted by a courageous mind. None of us spoke. There was nothing to say. The Nantucketer jumped down into the whaleboat, and we passed down the women and children to him and followed ourselves. Black Beard and his men watched us take up a pair of oars and crawl away northward into the mist. I think they expected some sort of outburst at the last. One child whimpered, that was all.

And Cephas muttered, with a last look at the *Two Friends* over his shoulder, "There goes all I had in the world."

The boat was in a filthy state and leaked near the bow from some recent scrape amongst the rocks, but we took turns at bailing, and she was tolerable for the short journey that remained. The nearest point of habitation was Port Roseway, where a great multitude of Tory refugees afterward founded the city of Shelburne, but that meant a hard luff against the rising offshore wind, with danger of increasing the leak; so we made straight for Cephas' home at Ragged Island, twenty or thirty miles to the northward. It took us the rest of the day and part of the night, even with a stiff wind in the patched and weatherworn sail. In all that time there was little talk in the boat. Cephas and the Nantucketer were graven images. The youngsters chattered and squirmed on the thwarts, but toward dusk even they fell silent, huddling close against those desolate women whose pale, set faces stared so emptily over the darkening sea. I was aft, bailing sometimes, at other times tending the sheets or taking a spell at the steering oar. Fear sat on a forward thwart with a child asleep in her lap. I looked at her many times, and once or twice our eyes met. But that was all. No word passed. The expression in her eyes puzzled and haunted me, but she must have read the bitterness in mine. I had guessed why she was returning to Nova Scotia, and the knowledge filled my mouth with salt and ashes.

When at last we stumbled up a boat slip of peeled poles slippery with fish gurry and wakened the settlement of Ragged Island with much thumping on doors and windows, we were greeted sullenly by people who took us for rebel privateersmen on another raid. The village had been robbed bare. No one had been spared, not even the great man of the place, Colonel MacNutt, an outspoken Whig who had urged open rebellion in Nova Scotia against the king and in time past had given American privateersmen every assistance in his power. He had spent his life and fortune in extravagant schemes for settlement in Nova Scotia and was content to take his portion on this lonely stretch of coast. Now everything was gone, even his prized books and silver spoons. We should have felt sorry for him but we were a sorry lot ourselves, and the tale of Ragged Island was the tale of every lonely settlement on the south shore.

CHAPTER 47

Blown-by-the-Winds

I SLEPT with the Nantucket man on the kitchen floor of Cephas' home and was early astir seeking some kind of craft in which to make my way to Liverpool. All the Ragged Island boats had been taken or destroyed except those that happened to be out fishing on the Roseway Bank and had not yet returned. The refugees decided to wait for a chance in a coaster to Halifax. I wandered along the island shore a little way and came upon an old canoe abandoned by Micmacs on one of their coastal migrations and set to work patching it with scraps of sail canvas and daubing the seams with tar. In the midst of my labors I looked up and saw Fear standing on the salt-bitten turf above, with the morning wind blowing the green gown about her legs and whipping strands of chestnut hair out of the great shining knot at the back of her head.

"Let me go with you, David," she said. Marriage and sorrow, or perhaps only maturity, had deepened her voice. It was low and rich and liquid as brook water.

"I'm just going home," I said woodenly.

"Will you take me that far, David?"

"The canoe's a poor thing—you see how rotten it is. I'll have to hug the shore the whole way and haul up whenever there's a bit of sea. It may take a week if the weather's bad—living like an Indian in the edge of the woods."

With something of her old spirit she returned, "If you can do that I can. I'm no china shepherdess, David. I've paddled a canoe before this—and two paddles are better than one."

That was simple truth, so I muttered reluctantly, "All right."

It gave me a twinge of dour humor to think what a scandal it would have made in peaceful times, this departure of a young married gentlewoman with a ragged adventurer like me. It made no stir in that mournful village, except that some of the refugees looked at the canoe and begged Fear not to go for fear of drowning. The people gave us some broken ship biscuit and salt herrings out of their poor store, and a fisherman let me have a bear skin off his chamber floor for bedding. The MacNutts pressed one of the few remaining blankets on Fear before they would let her go and poured on me such a torrent of advice about sea marks and such that my head buzzed. They came down to the shore to see us off, and the Nantucketer bade them all go down on their knees while he prayed a safe voyage for us. They were singing a psalm as we set off, and the wind brought it out to us in broken snatches as we drew away.

With a man at the bow paddle I could have made Liverpool in a day. 'Twas not above forty miles, even following the shore of the bigger bays, and an offshore wind kept the sea down handsomely, though it blew a dangerous blast down every lonely inlet as we steered across the mouth of it. I watched Fear's slim, straight back as she swung her paddle through the hours and in the afternoon I noticed a faint droop to her shoulders. We were then about to pass the mouth of Port Joli, an uninhabited creek running seven or eight miles back into the land. I swung the canoe's bow into the northwest wind, and we crept inside.

Port Joli is a lovely place where our Indians go to hunt wild geese in the fall; white sands and blue water and miles of clam flats when the tide is out, all sheltered by ridges of tall pine and spruce, with little clear springs trickling down to the sea. Fear cried out in pleasure as we drew in to a wooded nook on the western side, and when I eased the flimsy craft in to the sand she sprang out and ran up to a patch where the shade of the pines fell across the flat and dropped on her knees, scooping up fine sand and letting it run through her fingers like a child. The morning's labor in sun and wind had brought a flush to her pale cheeks. She called over her shoulder to me, "A beautiful place for dinner, David. Do hurry! I could eat a herring raw."

I picked up the herrings and the little bag of biscuit, together with a small iron pot I had found in the stern sheets of Black Beard's shaving mill, and carried them to the head of the beach, where a spring ran out between granite boulders and made a dark, wet splotch on the bone-white sand. Some dead pine stubs and an armful of driftwood made a fine blaze after a few strikes of my tinderbox, and we ate that prison fare and washed it down with spring water as if they were cakes and ale. 'Twas pleasant there, lying on the warm sand in the sunshine, with the wind bending the pine tops and not a breath below. The headlands wavered in the mirage thrown up by the hot sands, and between them the sea was a low blue wall, and high above us a lone gull flashed white in the sunshine. Some dunes across the inlet gleamed like snow; I could see the dead tops of smothered trees and thinking of the endless war between the sand and the forest I murmured, "The Indians call this place Pemsuk. That means 'Blown-by-the-winds.'"

"Like our people in Nova Scotia," Fear said, unhappily, and we were silent.

Then she said, "I like the French name better. *Joli* means pretty, doesn't it?"

"Pretty, yes. Not much 'Port' about it, though. When the tide goes out there's nothing but clam flats."

"This reminds me of the shore frolics when we were children. How long ago that seems!"

I was tempted to snort that it was only four years since the last of them. What would she say, I wondered, if I reminded her of the strawberry frolic which had so modified my own life and so little affected hers? But that was gnawing at dead bones. She had wearied of the gay life with Aunt Shaddock amongst the Tories of New York and was returning contritely home. All my thoughts came back to that, somehow.

I sat up and announced, "We'll be getting along. We can make Port Mouton by dark and get shelter for the night. One or two fishermen live there."

She did not stir. She was lying in an attitude both indolent and graceful with one leg thrown over the other and resting her cheek on one outstretched arm. Her eyes were closed. She said in a small voice, "I can't paddle any more today, David. My hands are sore."

"That was to be expected," I said harshly. "But remember—you wanted to come. Get into the canoe. I'll do the paddling."

"Besides," she said, "I'm tired. I could sit up another hour in that tippy old canoe and I won't. Go on, if you want. Leave me here. I don't care."

There she lay, looking greatly righteous and put-upon, and what was a man to do? I walked down to the canoe and back, scuffing the sand gloomily, and she sat up, nursing her knees and watching me.

"Perhaps you'll tell me," said I wrathfully, "what we'll eat for supper—since our going must wait your pleasure."

With an energy surprising in a tired woman she sprang up and ran around the wooded point. The outgoing tide had bared a long spit where fragments of clamshell gleamed whitely in the sun, but a broad salt stream still flowed between it and our shore. I did not stir, but presently something caught my eye, and I perceived the green gown, the black bodice, and the clocked white stockings fluttering gaily in the wind like banners, hung on the gaunt spikes of an old pine windfall on the point. Then I saw her wading toward the spit, undressed to a flimsy shift and a richly laced petticoat which she lifted higher and higher as the water deepened. I swore and ran down the sand, knowing the strength of the ebb current in these shallow creeks and expecting to see her swept off her feet any moment.

By now the water was well up her thighs, and the flow must have been sucking hard at the sand under her feet, but she went on resolutely with the long smooth legs emerging and shining like wet marble in the sunshine. She looked back then and saw me and promptly dropped the petticoat. It clung to her wet legs like a thin tops'l caught aback in a rainstorm. She began to dig with a stick, squaw-fashion. I determined not to lift a hand to help her in this caprice and to show my contempt I walked over and sat on the dead pine where her garments fluttered and ribbons and garters streamed—it looked like a fallen Maypole.

The tide ebbed fast. When the muddy heap of clams was big enough to suit her she caught up the laced edge of the petticoat with one hand and threw the whole mess into the bight of it and crossed the sandy gully between the spit and the shore through water barely ankle-deep. She dropped the clams at my feet and looked with a comical dismay at the great black splotch on her petticoat.

"You're acting like a child," said I angrily.

"And you," she answered tartly, "are talking like a man."

"I am a man. And you've no right to go taking off your clothes and disporting yourself before me in this fashion. 'Tisn't decent!"

"Now you're talking like Mrs. Mawdsley. The trouble with you, David, is that you come of a long line of pious Cape Cod deacons with a taste for rum and scalps. They thought a sense of humor was something invented by the devil and they believed a woman was a necessary but indecent object to be hidden in dark corners like a chamber pot. Don't deny it! Have I outraged your modesty? La, sir, who do you think stripped your duds off and bathed you and got some life into you aboard the *Two Friends*? Who washed the smell of Salem out of your clothes and dried and mended 'em?"

"Not you?" I stammered, and felt myself blushing like a fool.

"None other. Now—crawl away and hide your manly shame. I'm going to rinse my linen and bathe myself in the pool over there."

I retreated with more haste than dignity. But she was wrong about my sense of humor. I found myself chuckling as I reached the smoking embers of the fire and I lay back and laughed at myself till the tears came.

We baked the clams Indian-fashion, first digging a pit in the sand and covering its floor with hot stones from the fire, then dropping in a layer of wet kelp, a layer of clams, kelp again, clams again, and so on, covering the whole with sand to shut in the steam. They were food for a king. We ate them all, and I said with all malice, "A pity your hands are so sore—you might have dug more."

For answer she thrust out her palms before me. They were red as fire, with a swollen ridge along the base of the slender fingers; the paddle blisters there and at the finger joints had softened in the water and broken at her clam digging, and the fold between thumb and forefinger was as raw as a slice of beef.

I was shot with remorse. "I thought you were just being lazy," I blurted out.

"You had a right to think that, David," she answered gravely. "I always wanted the easy way of things, didn't I?"

"You wanted the things you'd been taught to want. Who's to blame?"

The sun was going down, and there was a coolness in the air, with long mares'-tails blowing up the evening sky fanwise from the southeast in a manner that spoke an ill wind for the morrow. I gathered several armfuls of driftwood for the night's fire and took a clamshell and went into the woods to collect some salve for her hands. The thin gum in the bark blisters of the young fir is our sovereign remedy for cuts and smarts of all kinds, and Fear put out her hands meekly while I spread it over her hurts.

"I must have a piece of your petticoat to bind over the stuff and keep out the sand and air," I pronounced solemnly, like Parson Cheever discussing a grave disease.

"My good laced New York petticoat?" she cried indignantly. "No sir!"

"Your shift, then."

"I'll need my shift, sir. But there's . . . something. Wait here."

She walked to the fallen pine where her washing hung nearly dry and came back with some cambric torn into strips. I bound her hands with selected pieces and discovered a drawstring, just the thing to tie the stuff in place.

She stuck up her hands before her and surveyed them comically. "La, sir, you're too thorough. How shall I do anything for myself?"

Said I in the same spirit, "If old Cheever could be preacher and schoolmaster and surgeon to our whole town, surely a broken-down rebel soldier could be your maidservant, ma'am."

Her eyebrows went up, and the imp was in the cider eyes. "You'll spoil me, David."

I scooped a hollow in the sand to give her easy lying and showed her how to roll herself in the blanket. I threw down my bearskin at the other side of the fire. No air was stirring, but a high drift of cloud from the southeast covered the stars. The driftwood burned green and blue and red, and with the lift and fall of its flames the pine trees advanced and retreated like a night watch of giants. The tide lapped softly over the flats as it came in, soothing as my mother's songs when I was young, and after the long day I should have slept well. But I dozed and waked all through the night, and each time I woke I stared across the embers of the fire expecting to see Fear gone, as she had vanished so often in my dreams. Her face was hidden, but the fire glow marked the long, sweet curve of waist and hip and thigh as if in reassurance.

CHAPTER 48

In Which There Is a Bundle

FEAR STOOD in the yellow flare of the sunrise with her blanket about her shoulders, gazing seaward. A chill wind blew up the inlet, and I could hear the distant boom of a rising sea outside. The tide was just on the flow, like a salt river brimming its banks and about to creep over the flats toward the shore. Different winds make different sounds in trees, and there is nothing more dismal than the swish of a rising southeaster in the tops of seashore pines. That is the cold, wet sea wind of our Nova Scotia, never so bleak as in spring, when the sun has promised better things; the wind that puts the green in our grass and the blue in our noses; the wind that scatters the fishermen on the Banks and makes our coast from Cape Breton to Cape Sable one long lee shore, the graveyard of ships and men.

"We'll do no canoeing this day," I observed glumly. I remembered suddenly that we had no breakfast—nor dinner—and the tide was on the mend already, and the flats would not be dry again till nearly nightfall. I caught up a stick and ran out on the flat and fell to digging furiously for clams. Fear came to me barefooted, with the green gown rucked above her knees.

"You can't dig with those hands," I growled, feeling in a hole for an elusive clam.

"Go and put your other clothes on—they must be dry now. And stay where you belong." I am not at my best humor in the morning.

I got enough for one good meal before the water made digging impossible and I was glad to get ashore. The ebb tide in a sandy harbor in May is a pleasant thing, where the water has lain several hours on the warm flats, but the flow comes straight from the Atlantic and its touch is the touch of ice.

I carried the canoe into the bushes lest a gust of the sea wind lift and damage it and I built a fireplace of stones and, facing it, a rude bivouac of fir branches big enough to shelter two people lying fairly close. Such shelters are a delusion in a southeaster; they blow down, or the rain comes in. But we were screened from the wind pretty well by the trees about our small cove, and when our brushwood roof began to leak I thought of the bearskin and slung it over the top, weighting both sides with stones. There was not room to sit up, so we lay there all the day. From time to time I crawled out into the wet and piled more driftwood on the fire to keep it alive. We talked a little—very little. Our very nearness—her face was not more than fifteen inches from mine—put a clamp on our tongues. In the late afternoon the downpour eased. Drops from the tall pines pattered drearily on the sodden skin overhead. Outside, looking past our outstretched feet and the reeking fire, I could see a cold drizzle blowing in from the sea. We had eaten nothing since breakfast. I had saved our small store of clams for a hot meal at evening, to help us face the chill of the long night, and after much blowing on the fire and hunting for bits of dry wood under the overhang of the bank, I got the pot to boil. Fear had her blanket wrapped about her. We lay on our elbows and ate, flicking the shells outside. I am fond of clams but I do not recommend them for steady fare, even when boiled in sea water for the savor of the salt. They made a warmth in the stomach for a time, and that was all.

By dark the miserable chill was back again, to the marrow of my bones, and I started to crawl outside. Fear started up and cried out like a lonely child, "Where are you going? Don't leave me, David!"

"I'm just going to walk along the beach awhile," I said, "to thaw my blood."

"You'll only get wet," she said crossly. "There's room in this blanket for both of us. Now do be sensible. . . ."

"No!"

"Will you stop acting like a Cape Cod deacon, David Strang? It doesn't become a soldier." She added mischievously, "I'm told that billeting and bundling go together in the rebel army."

I said nothing.

"You've bundled before this, David—don't tell me you haven't!"

Silence.

"Besides, it's not like bundling with some greasy woodsman's daughter, for I'm clean and I don't snore. And . . . and . . ."—a plaintive note—". . . I'm just as cold as you are."

"You don't understand," said I stiffly.

"But I do!" Then, scornfully, "You're afraid!"

That nettled me. I dropped down beside her.

Bundling is an uncomfortable business. In the course of my wanderings I had been obliged to bundle a number of times, usually with the child or children of the house, sometimes with men, once or twice with women—one of them a crone of sixty who made a prodigious noise in her sleep. The warmth of two bodies close in a blanket is not to be despised when bedding is scarce and the weather cold. But you must lie in each other's arms, and there lies discomfort also, despite the rhymes of our country wits and the ranting of the preachers. In the first hour there is warmth and the blessed ease after the long day's march, and if you can get to sleep then, all is well. But as the night grows there comes a cramp in the bones from long lying in one position, and the arms begin to prickle and pain from shoulder to finger tips, and from then on it is one long wish for daylight. With a stranger for whom you care nothing, it is ordeal enough. With Fear in my arms, with Fear's soft breathing on my neck, so near and yet so very far, and the vision of Captain Jack between us, telling me again what he had told me on the St. John—"She'd loathe you. She'd despise the very air you breathe . . . a more honest wife never walked this earth"—with all these things the night was torment. I tried to count my blessings as the Roman folk count their beads. I was done with war and the life of a hunted beast. I was going home. I was healthy and young and full of wise plans for my future. And it was Maytime when the sea and the streams and the very air are filled with new life or old life returning. I had never been so near to happiness. But that was the devil of it.

The southeaster blew itself out in the course of that weary night, and when morning came there was an air down the inlet from the west, with a promise of fine weather. I carried the canoe down to the water, and Fear followed me in silence, like a dutiful squaw, with the blanket about her shoulders and the little iron pot in her hand. I said,

"There's something I want to tell you, Fear, before we go. I've been a pig. After all you did for me . . ."

"No!" she cried, turning her face away.

"It's got to be said. I loved you; I was mad about you; and when you married Helyer I was like a sulky boy stamping the pantry floor because the pasty jar's out of reach. I was still the sulky boy when you appeared in that Halifax court. You trod on your good name . . . position . . . everything . . . just to save my life . . . which wasn't worth it."

"Please don't talk like that, David."

"It wasn't!" I insisted. "And I hated you for it. I'd seen myself as a martyr to the Cause and gloried in it, and you spoiled it—you and Uniacke. But I want you to know that when I saw those people abusing you outside I—I suddenly realized all you'd sacrificed for me. I wanted to rush over and drive that cowardly scum away—I wanted to grovel at your feet. . . ."

"Don't!"

"But I was ill, and Father took me away."

"I know." She looked at me. "Are you still the sulky boy, David?" I stared toward the sea. "I'll always be the sulky boy."

A silence. Then, "David, have you wondered why I came back to Nova Scotia?"

As if I'd thought of anything else since I saw her aboard the *Two Friends!* I yapped out like a kicked cur, "You're going back to him . . . because you're still in love with him and can't live without him! You're going to humiliate yourself before all those purring cats at Fort Cumberland . . . ask his forgiveness . . . as if he had anything to forgive . . . and be the fond and dutiful wife . . . because he's charming when he wants to be, and that's enough. . . ."

I bit off the rush of words then, seeing the tears in her eyes. I mumbled, "I'm sorry," and motioned her to get into the canoe.

She was fumbling in the breast of her gown with her bandaged fingers and brought forth a folded paper with a broken seal—a letter of some kind.

"David, when we're in the canoe . . . when we're out on the water . . . I want you to read this. Not till then. Will you promise?"

I nodded indifferently and took it. I kept her paddle in the stern with me, lest she try to use it and so chafe her hands again. When we were nearing the entrance she called over her shoulder, "Read the letter now, please."

It was dated in October of last year and addressed to Mrs. Anne Shaddock at New York.

Fort Cumberland, Nova Scotia.

Dear Madam,

I address these lines in the belief that you know the whereabouts of Mrs. John Helyer, your niece, and in the hope that you will convey to her as delicately as possible the news of her husband's death. In view of the unfortunate contretemps which resulted in Mrs. Helyer leaving Fort Cumberland I feel bound to give you the facts and let you decide how much or little she should know.

It was an affair of honour. Captain Helyer was called out by a commissary named Fanning upon a matter involving Mrs. Fanning's name. They went with their seconds and the regimental surgeon to a secluded spot in the marshes. The affair was conducted in the usual manner, and when the two men turned to fire, Fanning cried some remark about Helyer's fear having left him, and Captain Helyer in an unaccountable rage fired hurriedly and missed. The man Fanning then shot him dead.

I may say, Madam, that I have striven to stop the incessant dueling at this post, but the long idleness in a lonely garrison seems to breed it as the marshes breed mosquitoes. I have secured the dismissal of the commissary, who left with his wife today. I regret to add that Captain Helyer's personal property is all held here by writs for debt. Please convey my utmost sympathy to Mrs. Helyer, for whom I have the greatest sympathy and respect, and believe me to be, Madam,

Your Obedt. Servt.
Joseph Gorham, *Lt. Col.*
Royal Fencible American Regiment.

CHAPTER 49

Home

THAT WAS a silent journey from Port Joli. Fear sat in the canoe's bow staring straight ahead, her long hair blowing about her face, a figurehead in green. All I could see was the slender back, and I read sorrow in every line of it.

The letter lay at my feet where I had dropped it, with Gorham's scrawl staring up at me like a churchyard epitaph. The sea had dropped to a steady green swell. The wind was fair; nevertheless under my one paddle we seemed to crawl the twenty-odd miles along the coast to

Liverpool. As we crossed the broad mouth of Port Mouton Bay I could see the topmasts of two schooners anchored inside Spectacle Island and guessed them to be American privateers. All the sea marks were familiar now. White Point's curving sand, Black Point's dark rock face and gloomy woods, the low reefs of Gull Island white with birds drowsing in the sunshine, the steep brown banks of Western Head with their high woods, and at last the bristling spruces and firs of Peleg Coffin's Island guarding the entrance to our narrow Liverpool Bay.

We crept up the calm water lying blue between the steep, dark-wooded ridges, and as we passed Dipper Creek I saw Fear gaze toward the scene of the strawberry frolic. I looked that way, too, but what I saw there put away all thought of strawberries. A big wreck lay on the reefs inshore, a foreign-looking hull, a Frenchman's build if I knew anything of ships. She had gone clean over on her starboard side and was showing half her coppering, with her three masts and a raffle of spars and cordage and rags of canvas reaching over the ledges to the very edge of the woods. A man-o'-war by her gun ports, and the victim of some desperate fight, for her visible side was marred by many white-splintered shot holes, and two of her gun ports were actually blown into one. The gilded lettering on her high stern spelled *Duc de Choiseul*. I was mystified. Was France at war with Britain? There had been no word of it in Boston, which always had the first intelligence from Europe.

Fear looked long at it as we passed, and I admired the line of brow and tilted nose, the fresh lips, and the rounded chin, against the green woods of Great Hill.

She shivered and broke her long silence. "War! Will there never be an end of it?" In that passionate cry of hers was all the sorrow of all the women in the world.

I beached the canoe on Battery Point, to spare Fear the staring eyes on the town wharves. The little cleared knoll was bare, the two old cannon gone, and the grass green where they had stood. We walked together through the rows of fish flakes to the beaten path which becomes our town street as you saunter westward.

I stopped there and asked, "Where do you plan to stay, Fear?"

"With one of my friends—Judy Freeman, I think. Why?"

'Twas on the tip of my tongue to ask how soon she would take ship for Halifax and her father's home. Instead I blurted emptily, "I think you'd better go on alone. If you're seen coming out of nowhere with me there'll be gossip."

She threw up her brown head and looked me straight in the eyes. "Is that all you have to say to me, David?"

All, good God! I wanted to go down on my knees and beg her not to leave me, now or ever. But all I could think about was the sadness in her eyes and that bald letter of Gorham's which she kept at her breast, as if in self-punishment. His blundering description of the duel must have stabbed her to the heart—and she kept it there, turning the knife in the wound, seeing herself responsible for Helyer's death. Besides, what could I offer her now? I was penniless. I hadn't even a trade now that shipping was ruined. My home? I knew what my father thought of her.

Time! There must be time for her to put that letter from her breast, and with it all that was past; time for me to settle myself and make some sort of home to receive her when—and if—she gave me Yes. God knew what would happen in the meantime. In these days a man could only work and fight—and hope.

"That's all," said I miserably.

She turned her face away and uttered a cold little "Good-by, David."

I stood drearily watching her walk up the road and disappear amongst the houses.

My meeting with my mother I shall not describe. That was written in tears so very long ago that ink seems a poor substitute now.

My father greeted me grimly with some quip about a fatted calf. He seemed shrunken and old—he spent most of his time in his chair now—but his tongue had lost none of its edge. He asked no word of my past year's adventure but he knew of the fighting along the St. John and must have guessed the rest.

I bathed my lean self in the old half-puncheon in the wood shed, filled with buckets of hot water from the kitchen, and with a cup of soft soap at my elbow. And I shaved my hairy jaws and put on clean stockings and shirt and a pair of decent smallclothes from the chest in my chamber. They smelled of the sweet fern which my good mother had kept in little packets in the bottom of the chest, and she must have aired them and returned them neatly folded many a time since I fled from the *Senegal's* men. When I came downstairs she sat me in a kitchen chair and undid my pigtail and trimmed my hair with the shears, as she had done for us all since we were youngsters. And while she clipped and combed she talked happily.

"Mark and Joanna—they've another little one now—are living in a small house your father built for them near the tan-yard brook. They're coming for supper. It'll be so nice to have you all together again. Except poor John."

"What about Luke?" I blurted like a fool.

Calmly she said, "Luke's here, David. His vessel's at Port Mouton, and he's walking through the woods to have supper with us. He'll be surprised."

"No more than I," I said truthfully. Luke had been gone so long without word of any kind that I thought him dead. Privateering was a chancy trade.

Mother prattled on, "We've had such excitement lately. A few days back we heard a lot of gunfire in the harbor mouth, and in came a big French ship with His Majesty's frigate *Blonde* right behind, fighting hammer and tongs. The Frenchman got the worst of it and hauled down his colors just as he struck the reefs."

"I saw the wreck," I said.

"And what do you think she was, David? A French man-o'-war, mind you, sailing under merchant colors. From Nantes, your father says, with rebel colors in her flag locker, and a letter from Silas Deane—that's the Congress agent in France—addressed to somebody named Morris who's a member of the Congress. The *Blonde's* captain billeted the prisoners all over town, and some of them were real French nobility; Monsoor Heraud, Captain Pettier, Lieutenant Baudier, the Chevalier de Sucay—I can't remember half the names. Captain Milligan of the *Blonde* sent food from the wreck to feed them while he removed the best of the cargo; then he took them all off to Halifax. He told Colonel Perkins to salvage anything that was left. But that's not half of it, David. As soon as the frigate was gone, in came a pair of Massachusetts privateers, the *Lizard* and *Washington*. They were very polite. Captain Preston of the *Washington* sent a flag ashore and asked Colonel Perkins to come on board, and Simeon went. They told him our people must hand over everything they'd got from the wreck because it was the property of the United States. Colonel Perkins handed over everything he'd got and—would you believe it?—wrote out a claim on the Congress for salvage. Your father was *so* angry—called Simeon a pious old hypocrite and goodness knows what else. The rest of our people wouldn't give up the stuff they'd salvaged, and the privateersmen came ashore in the night and broke into houses and stores and stole everything they could lay their hands on, whether it belonged to the French ship or not. That's the first time the Americans have ever bothered our town. I don't know what got into them."

"Why not?" I snorted. "They've been raising hell everywhere else on the coast."

"Don't you swear in front of me, David Strang!"—giving me a sharp rap over the head with the shears—"Your father says they haven't bothered Liverpool because it's the biggest town in the province after Halifax and too big a mouthful to chew. But I say it's because we're all one folk—Yankees as we say—and people don't steal from their own relations. Besides, they're decent, godly men, not savages. Why, there's scarce a Sabbath goes by that some of their privateersmen don't walk through the woods from Port Mouton just to sit in our meeting-house and hear the Word."

"And see what ships are in the harbor!"

"David, that's—that's blasphemy!" She laid the shears aside and nudged me to get off the stool.

"Just common sense," I insisted, and thought of Thomas Paine. "Privateering's a business, like any other, and can be made to pay mighty well, judging by what I saw in Salem. I think myself it's time our own people got into the trade. Everything else has been ruined."

"Nonsense!" said my mother crisply. "Where would they get cannon and such things?"

She turned to her kitchen tasks with the air of a woman who has settled an idle argument with one unconquerable fact.

"King George would supply 'em ready enough."

She turned and looked at me curiously. "What do you mean, David?"

"I mean there's two sides to Fundy Bay, and it's a poor game that two can't play."

"David Strang, what on earth's come over you?"

"I've grown up," I said soberly.

CHAPTER 50

The Home-coming of Luke

WHEN MARK CAME, big and brown and smiling, we fell upon each other wildly as we always did. And I kissed Joanna so soundly as to make her blush and run to help my mother with the supper things. Then Luke appeared, walking up the path from the wharf. Evidently he had decided to come by boat from Port Mouton. There was a stranger with him, and my mother, peering from the kitchen window, made a little mouth of disappointment. "I'd hoped just for ourselves, but the Lord's will be done. Lay another plate, Joanna."

I threw open the kitchen door eagerly. I'd not seen Luke since the night he showed me the king's sign manual on his back. He was wearing a pair of wide seaman's slops cut off at half-mast and exposing a lean length of woolen shank running down to big, pewter-buckled shoes; but the rest of him was very fine, a clean white shirt and stock, a blue coat with brass buttons and fashionable tails, a trifle too tight for his wide shoulders, and a cocked hat sitting back on the club of his pigtail. His face was brown, not quite so wolfish as I'd seen it last, but hard enough.

"What! Davy?" he sang out and strode ahead to me, seizing my shoulders and giving me a shake. "Ah, Davy boy, it's good to see you again!"

The stranger was a gaunt man in broadcloth and gray stockings and wearing a wide-brimmed blue hat with a single cock at the back. His large sleepy-lidded eyes were green, the rich, still green of a stagnant pool, and as expressionless. He talked in a nasal Salem drawl and had the manner of Marblehead.

"Cap'n Sparhawk," Luke announced, and off came the blue hat with a flourish, and the green eyes flickered lazily from one to another as we murmured our greetings.

Old Molly was minding house for Joanna, but François came with his little bright-eyed squaw and sat beside me at table with his lame arm hanging and the useless hand tucked into his jacket pocket. The women bustled and the kitchen was full of savory smells, and presently in the familiar hungry silence we bowed our heads to Father's grace. 'Twas a good meal and we did it justice, though appetite outran performance in my case. I think hard living and short commons shrink a man's stomach.

Eating was ever a serious affair at our house, and the talk was thin, though my mother was bursting with eager questions, and we all had yarns to spin. When at last we pushed our chairs back, and Mother put on the table some sticks of smuggled Virginia twist and half a dozen new clays and turned to hurry the dishwashing so she could hear the talk, Captain Sparhawk spoke up.

"Cap'n Strang, sir, I'm much obleeged to you and Ma'am for this repast and the privilege o' sittin' here with ye. Kep' thinkin' to myself all through, Jonathan, rub your eyes or ye'll think ye're to home. That's a fact. Home! The sailor's comfort and the traveler's delight. I ain't a sentimental man, sir, but while I set here eatin' in your midst there come a lump to my throat so big I could scarcely swaller. Fact! If I was an envious man—which I thank God I am not, and I say it reverent —why, I'd be downright covetous, that I would. Here you are, sir, with a fine fam'ly about you, a good stout house and barn, a hayloft tight ag'in' the weather, a wharf o' good red-pine spiles and rock ballast, a store for the fish-and-lumber trade—all set down by a good-sized river at tidewater, handy the Banks, and a vargin forest behind. What more could a man ask? What, I say?"

"Well, what?" my father said.

"Peace, sir—peace to enj'y it!"

"We have peace, after a fashion."

"That ye have, sir, and may it long continue. There's few towns on the seaboard o' this continent that ain't heard the horrid clash of arms and seed the blood o' their noble sons awettin' the dust in the cause o' Liberty. Ye're privileged, sir, blest if ye ain't. I jine with ye in thanks to the Lord for't. And that's what I've come to talk to ye about."

Captain Sparhawk glanced behind him at the silent women. "It's a matter fer men, sir—all friendly-like, y'understand. Would ye mind?"

I heard my mother's indignant sniff. Father gave her a single imperious nod, and she gathered up Joanna and the Indian woman and swept out of the kitchen, closing the door with a slam to speak her mind. François brought a coal from the fire to light our pipes and went from one to another holding the glowing knot in the tongs.

"And now, Cap'n," resumed Sparhawk, "a dram all round, if I might be so bold. Nothin' like a dram to keep things pleasantlike."

"Business first and a clear head, and drinking afterward," my father said.

"Ah! A good moral that, and you young men take note of it."

Captain Sparhawk sat across the table from me, with Mark between him and my father in the big chair at the table's head. Luke was on my right and François at the left. We were all leaning elbows on the board and sucking at the dry new clays, with the blue eddies rising and hanging above the table like a tester over a bed.

The Salem man blew out a long jet and announced, "Ye're an old soger, Cap'n, and a man of affairs, so I'll not beat about the bush with ye. I am master o' the privateer *Lizard*, in Congress service and now lyin' at Port Matoon jist around the corner to the west'ard. I might say the privateer *Washin'ton's* in comp'ny. Now, t'other day there was some unpleasantness concernin' stuff taken out o' the French wreck in your harbor."

Father raised his shaggy brows as a frigate raises her gun ports for a broadside. "You mean your men came ashore under cover o' night and broke into the houses and stores, contrary to law and order, ay, and contrary to all agreement."

"That there cargo," said Captain Sparhawk in an injured tone, "was consigned from France to the Congress o' the United States. I—uh—represent the consignees."

"Then they've picked a scoundrel for an agent! Besides, this talk of ownership's a quibble. Any Salem sea lawyer knows that lawful-prize goods belong to the captor, to dispose as he sees fit. The British captain told us to salvage what he'd left—and that's exactly what we did. Not for King George, I may say, but for ourselves. The goods were ours by right of law—and you took 'em at night, by violence and threat, breaking and entering—half the crimes in the calendar."

The privateersman turned and spat over his shoulder into the hearth. "We're talkin' in circles, Cap'n Strang, and time's short. I'll give it to ye straight. It's come to my knowledge that ye got a lot o' stuff off o' the *Duck de Shozzu*. I dunno what 'tis but I suspect it's clothin'—seein' you're in the storekeepin' line. I call upon ye to deliver them goods to me tonight—or the town'll suffer the consequences."

"What consequences? Privateers have already stolen half our vessels!"

"They could take the rest, Father," Luke said sharply. "They could plunder the town itself, ay, and burn it, come to that. There's twenty sail o' privateers atween here an' the Cape—an' ye know what's happened up an' down the shore."

"I know," Father murmured, and I felt my neck hair stiffen. His mood was never so savage as when his voice was low. "I don't doubt ye could burn the town over our heads, you and your thievin' friends. There's enough o' ye. But we'd make it a right lively burnin', we would, Cap'n Sparhawk. 'Cause we ain't helpless any more. The 'goods' I took out o' the wreck was nigh two hundred stand o' new French muskets with powder and ball and plenty o' spare flints. Funny how that English frigate captain overlooked 'em, wasn't it? All tucked up nice and dry in the half deck, too. Could it be, d'ye s'pose, that he left 'em there apurpose for us?"

Sparhawk fixed him with one poisonous green eye. "What d'ye mean?"

"Meaning that a time has come when American persecution's a

damned sight worse than the king's! Meaning that we're men and will fight like men if we're pushed too hard too long. Meaning that if we fire a shot—one shot, mark ye!—at a rebel flag, the governor'll send us cannon, stores, anything we want. 'Cause that's what he's been waiting for, all these months. Liverpool's the strongest Whig town on the whole south shore, and every other Yankee settlement's held its hand whilst we made up our minds."

"We're all Americans," intoned Captain Sparhawk piously. " 'Behold how good an' how pleasant it is for brethren to dwell together in unity'—from the Psalms, that is."

"Umph! Glad to see you Salem folk still read the Scriptures, anyhow. There's a bit in Proverbs that says, 'A brother offended is harder to be won than a strong city.' Keep that in mind, friend."

"Listen, Father!" Luke said urgently. "Ye've got to figure this out like a sensible man. D'ye realize what it means—this French ship? It means France has recognized the independence o' the American colonies. Means France'll join the war in a few months. Means England'll be fightin' for her life afore the summer's out. She'll have to call the fleet home. Take away the fleet and what's left? A few reg'-ments o' redcoats firin' muskets into a continent! Tell ye, Father, it means the end o' King George's rule in America. And Nova Scotia, yes, and all Canada, has got to go the way o' the rest. Don't ye see that?"

"All I see," Father said stubbornly, "is you're asking me to give up, under threat o' violence, goods that belong to our people by right o' salvage."

"Make your ch'ice," Captain Sparhawk said, sprawling in his chair. "It's king or Congress—no three ways about it. Them that ain't fer us is ag'in' us."

"It goes deeper'n king or Congress," said my father slowly. "It comes down to law and order at the last. What I see is law and order on the one hand—bad law in lots o' ways, law that's administered wrong—but law for all that, something ye can depend on, put your faith in, something ye can build a business on; and on t'other hand nothing but a Congress that nobody minds, and Committees o' Safety and Sons o' Liberty and Patriots and Friends of America in every town and village, all making laws o' their own, and not one knowing or caring what t'other's doing. Someday maybe the Congress'll get the upper hand o' the king's troops. Afore that, though, they'll have to get the upper hand o' your Committees o' Safety and the rest. Then ye'll find yourselves paying taxes and tidewaiters' fees and import duties and all t'other things ye think ye've scuppered forever—and buying tea from John Hancock, say, at John Hancock's price. Then maybe there'll be law and order south o' Fundy Bay, and maybe the left hand'll know what the right's doing. But I ain't chucking my hat over the moon on the chance o' 'maybe.' It's today that matters now. To-day ye call yourself a privateer in Congress service. Where's your com-mission, eh? Where's your letter o' marque from the Congress? Ye've got none! No more than fifty other sea thieves out o' New England ports that's ravaging our coast! Salem's fattening on stolen goods; so's twenty other towns across the mouth o' Fundy. D'ye mean to tell me the Congress—or General Washington, say—approves or even knows o' the thieves swarming across Fundy Bay in whaleboats, shallops, jig-gers—anything that'll float—and laying in our lonely bays and cricks for the first unsuspecting trader or fisherman? In a week they've got a ship and a gun here and a swivel there and away they go, flying the American flag, robbing and destroying as it suits 'em, sending a boat into every defenseless settlement and demanding anything they want. Ye can't tell *me!* I've had to deal with your kind, talk polite to 'em, give 'em what they wanted these past two years—men that I'd ha' kicked off my wharf in ordinary times. I knew more'n one of 'em from my old days in New England—a lot o' wharf rats and jailbirds turned pirate in the name o' Liberty. Well, if that's liberty ye can have it and be damned!"

"Then ye won't give up the guns?" drawled Captain Sparhawk.

"Not while I can hold a gun myself," my father said.

The Salem man arose, and Luke stood up with him, and my father cried out, "Luke!" in a queer voice, an appeal that shocked me, for I suddenly realized how old and broken he was and what the past two years had done to him.

Sparhawk said easily, "Luke's along o' me in the *Lizard*, with several other smart lads from your town"—and turning to Mark and me— "What about it, lads? Better a stroke fer liberty, with prize money into the bargain, than stayin' to home to be pressed into the tyrant's ships on poor pay and wuss vittles and a bosun's mate lacin' your back if ye 'much as say Boo!"

Mark shook his big head fiercely, as if to shake off temptation, and the brass earrings danced.

"Davy!" Luke appealed to me. "You'll go. You're for liberty!"

My mouth was dry. Thickly I said, "I'm done with fighting for a word, Luke. I'm for myself—and Mark and Father and all the rest of us who want to live in some kind of peace on this coast. I'm for fighting whoever interferes with us, whether it's king or Congress or only a bloody Salem pirate flying the Congress colors."

"The blood be on your own heads then," pronounced Captain Sparhawk from the kitchen door.

"Get out!" my father said.

The door slammed behind them, and in the kitchen silence, above the tick of the wooden clock and the whisper of dying coals in the hearth, we heard the sounds of a boat pulling away from our wharf and dropping down the river.

My father sat staring down the empty table.

"Mark, you're here?"

"Yes sir."

"Davy?"

"Yes, Father?"

"Those privateers are planning to plunder the town. Some o' their men come overland to drink at Pratt's and talk too much. Sparhawk just wanted to make sure we didn't raise a fuss."

"Well, can we?" Mark said bluntly. "You were bamming about those French guns!"

"Some," admitted Father with a grim little smile. "They got back most o' the guns we salvaged—scared Simeon Perkins into giving 'em up and flattered his greed by accepting his claim on the Congress for salvage money. Simeon ain't content to sit on the fence; he wants a foot on the ground, both sides."

"Then we're helpless still," I muttered.

"No, Davy. When the privateers moved in to Port Mouton 'twas too close for comfort, for all their promises to leave us alone. So I got up a petition to Halifax asking for arms to defend ourselves. I didn't expect anything from it, tell ye the truth, but some weeks back a government schooner came in and landed fifty or sixty muskets, with flints, powder, and ball. They're in the haymow now—old things from the French war and captured rebel muskets and suchlike, but fixed up by the garrison armorers and good enough. 'Tell you, I couldn't believe my eyes. Somebody who knows what's going on has been whispering in the governor's ear; Arbuthnot wouldn't ha' done it on his own hook."

I said nothing. I could almost hear the voice of Michael Francklin.

Chapter 51

The Breaking Point

THAT WAS AN UNEASY NIGHT. I was for rousing a guard of men to sit on Battery Point all night and watch the channel, but Father said coolly, "They won't come tonight. They reckon we'll stand guard tonight and get ourselves nice and tired for tomorrow night or the next after. Maybe Sparhawk was bamming too. Maybe they won't come at all. It never pays to worry yourself too much about what the other's going to do—'specially when you've got a living to earn. The chief thing is to know what you're going to do yourself if the worst comes to the worst."

So we went to bed, and nothing happened. The town's chimneys smoked so peacefully in the morning sunshine that Captain Sparhawk seemed like an unpleasant dream. It was alewife time. The silvery fish were thronging at the Falls, and most of our townsmen went up the river on the morning tide with their boats and gondolas laden with empty barrels. Mark and I planned to go next day and were busy coopering Father's old fish casks and repairing the smokehouse when someone came running, all out of breath, and gasping, "Cap'n Strang! Cap'n Strang!"

It was Colonel Perkins, hatless, with sweat dripping from his little owl beak and his stockings all down about his calves. We had carried Father in his chair to a sunny spot on the riverbank where he could oversee our labors. He started up and sank down painfully, shouting, "Well? Well?"

"Privateers! Coming up the harbor!"

"In broad daylight?" demanded Mark, astonished.

"I was down to the wreck, Captain . . . in my big shallop . . . trying to salvage the pig-iron ballast . . . for His Majesty, you understand . . . two rebel privateers . . . big schooners . . . the same that robbed my store the other night . . . dear, oh dear, oh dear . . . what'll we do, Captain Strang? What'll we do?"

"Fight!" my father snapped.

"But most of the men are upriver at the alewife dipping. . . ."

"I'll send my Injun for 'em; he can run like a deer. You go and rouse out what militiamen ye can find."

Off went Simeon as fast as his small, worried legs could travel.

"Mark, fetch those muskets out o' the haymow! David, hitch the oxen to the wagon and take the bells off their necks. We'll make no more noise than we can help."

"What's your plan?" I asked.

"They're big schooners and sit deep. Tide as it is, they'll have to anchor outside the bar and send in their men with boats. There's a West Indy schooner in the stream, half discharged, but too fat a prize to miss. They'll tow her out over the bar first and make sure of her. By that time we'll have some men at the Point. It's an easy musket shot to mid-channel, and we'll have their damned boats where we want 'em."

"Calculatin' devil, ain't ye?" Mark said admiringly.

"I learned my trade in a hellish school. No disrespectful names! And, damme, stop wasting time!"

By the time we had traveled the length of the town with the wagon-load of muskets, the kegs of powder and balls, a keg of cartridges, my father sitting atop the boxes of flints, with his chair slung on behind, the privateersmen had got the West India vessel over the bar and anchored her. Two of their boats had returned past the Point for another prize. The *Washington* and *Lizard* were anchored mighty close to the Point, with their guns run out and their decks crowded with armed men. From their gaffs a pair of new striped ensigns fluttered and gleamed in the sun. There had never been earthworks on Battery Point, despite its name, nothing but the two old cannon which the suspicious governor had removed to Halifax.

The Point lay like a green finger pointing across the bar channel to Sandy Cove, and its knuckle was a low mound covered with stumps and bushes and boulders. The Widow Dexter's little gambrel-roofed tavern stood under the shoulder of it, where the ferry went across to Sandy Cove, and in the tavern yard we found Colonel Perkins with about twenty men. Simeon was a comical mixture of pious courage and shaking timidity, but for once in his life I think the courage had the better part.

Behind us the town looked peaceful still beside the river, and we could see the two Salem boats, full of armed men, busy towing Captain Bradford's sloop toward the bar. The breeze was baffling and in any case too light to sail her out. They were laboring hard at their oars.

Men were coming on the run through the fish lots from the town, in hot and breathless twos and threes, and Mark and I passed each a musket and a hatful of cartridges. Colonel Perkins watched us uneasily.

He was hoping that a show of force would drive the privateers off, and the savage note in all our voices troubled him. Our townsmen had been tried too long; that was the trouble; the fanatic spirit of their Pilgrim forebears had welled up in them, but the Pilgrim patience was gone. It seemed to me that if the approaching boats had been a press gang from one of His Majesty's ships they would have said the same things in the same way, with the same hard hands on the musket stocks.

Obed Cannell arrived panting, with young Abner at his elbow, mutely reaching up for guns. I knelt in the wagon looking down on them and said curtly, "D'ye know what this means? We're going to fight those people."

"And may God forgive us!" Obed said, holding out a hand. I passed the muskets down. Then came Ephraim Dean, the most ardent of our Whigs, still pale from his imprisonment at Halifax. I told him what I'd told Obed, and he answered sharply, "They took my schooner into Salem two weeks back and kicked me ashore to get home any way I could. Give me a gun."

The voice of Parson Cheever came to us sharply. He was cold sober for a wonder. "The Philistines be upon thee!" He pointed with the musket in his bony hands. The towing boats were closing in to the Point and the anchored privateers beyond. Under their jerky efforts the towline rose taut as a fiddlestring, flung a shower of glittering drops, drooped and dipped a long bight into the harbor again.

In the shade of the tavern yard our men were busy fixing flints and loading and priming their muskets, and Simeon had sent Joseph Freeman with ten fishermen to man a swivel gun on the wharf below.

"Looks like the trouble's come to a head," my father told the militiamen hoarsely. "But it may be we can yet work 'em out without bloodshed. Let me do the talking, Simeon. My boys'll carry me down to the shore where I can hail 'em close. The rest o' ye creep amongst the rocks and stumps, Injun-fashion. Be where ye can shoot, but don't let 'em see how few we are. There's all o' two hundred men in those vessels."

By this time we were fifty or sixty, a most unmilitary company in homespun and work-stained leather breeches, some in shoes and some in moccasins, some with hats, some in fishermen's red nightcaps, some bareheaded, and all sorts from boys to white-haired men. A few veterans of the French war had their old crossbelts and cartridge boxes, the leather all dry and cracked with the years, and Colonel Perkins had a sword, though I could not imagine him swinging it at anything bigger than a dandelion in his garden path. Not even our guns were uniform, what with the French ones from the wreck, still coated with grease as they came from the arms chests, and the arms from Halifax, a queer, mixed lot, the odds and ends of the armorers' shop, and few bearing the king's broad arrow on the butt. Most of them, I guessed, were taken from captured rebel ships. But not all, for when I unwrapped a gun for myself I looked upon a miracle that shook me to the heels. 'Twas the gun of Louisburg, which I had left in the picket line at Fort Cumberland! I took it up with a strange feeling of destiny, as if my path had been laid down for me in the beginning of the world. My hands shook as I fixed a new flint and loaded it, as they had shaken that distant morning on the bog with François and Peter Dekatha.

Mark and I picked up Father in his chair and carried him down to the tip of the Point, Mark growling, "Are ye mad, Father? Ye'll make a mark as easy as a pumpkin on a post!"

"Is your blood so thin, then?" Father snapped. "Take shelter if ye want. They'd not listen to Simeon but they will to me."

His wonderful voice boomed over the narrow water to the straining boats.

"Ahoy!"

Above and behind I could hear small scufflings as our men wriggled into position for shooting.

"Ahoy!" answered the steersman of the second boat. It was Sparhawk himself.

The oarsmen paused and the bight of the tow rope sank into the water. The captured sloop crept toward them under its own way for a little.

"Sparhawk!" my father roared. "Tell your thieving friends to give over towing that vessel and get out o' this harbor, quick!"

Sparhawk ignored this. His voice came clearly, "Give way ag'in, boys."

"Sparhawk! I warn ye if ye don't give over we mean to stop ye!"

"You an' who else, Cap'n Strang?" There was mockery in the Salem voice. The oars were dipping again.

"The town militia, sir. Stop, I say!"

"Keep rowin', boys," came Sparhawk's voice, assured and amused. To us he called, "Wouldn't fire on your own countrymen, now would ye, Cap'n Strang? On your feller Americans? Why, there's some o' your town lads in this very boat! Not you, Cap'n. You go on home, an' take the militia with ye afore they git hurt." He turned and hailed across the bar, "*Lizard*, ahoy!"

The nearer of the anchored schooners answered with a cheer and a ruffle of drums. She lay not half a cable's length from the tip of the Point, with her guns trained on it and the wooden target of the lower town beyond.

"Fire a shot," cried Sparhawk, "an' we'll blast ye off o' that p'int like hens off a roost an' give your town a dose o' iron fer good measure! Go home, ye herrin' chokers! Home, ye Blue Noses! Home an' mind your business or by thunder ye'll suffer fer it—or my name ain't Jonathan!"

"Mark!" Father said coldly.

"Sir?"

"The steersman o' the leading boat. D'ye see him?"

Mark stared. "Oh, my God, Father, no! No!"

"It must be that man, for when he falls the leading boat'll lose its helm, foul t'other, and put both at our mercy. They'll see reason then. And if we purchase reason at the cost o' one man's blood, let it be blood o' mine. I owe that to these people who ha' trusted me."

"No!"

"Davy!"

"Yes, Father?"

"The steersman o' the leading boat. Aim well, son. That man and no other."

That man was Luke. There was no mistaking him, standing at the stern and urging on his rowers, not seventy yards away and drawing abreast.

Father said to me in the cold, low voice, "Those are dead men all if ye delay. Our fellows'll shoot in a moment, regardless—and will ye let it be said that a stranger killed him? This is a matter between us Strangs!"

"Backs into it now, boys!" Sparhawk's voice from the second boat. "They daresn't fire! Pull! Pull! Another cable's length an' she's over the bar. *Lizard*, there! *Lizard* ahoy! Give us a tune!"

From the *Lizard's* deck came the rattle of a drum and the thin tweet of a fife. The tune was "Yankee Doodle," and I heard Father suck in a sharp breath as if he had been stabbed. To that tune twenty years before he had marched with his rangers against the walls of Louisburg, fighting for the king. 'Twas a jaunty thing, born nobody knew where, that had a way of picking up the feet when they were tired with the march and the musket heavy on the shoulder. The words were nonsense. "Yengees"—that was the way the Mohawks pronounced "English." But now somehow it betokened a separate race.

All the story of the revolution was summed up in the change of meaning in a word. And there was blood in that change and sweat and sorrow and all the pully-haul of ideals and greeds and passions that now convulsed the continent and no man yet understood.

My father's eyes were fixed above and beyond the boats, as if he saw there nothing but his twin gods Law and Order, accusing and demanding. The oars rose and fell together; the captured sloop moved slowly toward us and the bar, like fate itself, and the drum and the fife played bravely, and the privateersmen lifted their voices in a defiant chant:

> *"Yankee Doodle went to town*
> *Aridin' on a pony,*
> *He stuck a feather . . ."*

"Now, Davy!" my father said. I put up the gun of Louisburg and sighted along its lean brown barrel at Luke's chest.

"Make it sure, my son. We owe that to his mother—and to him."

I squeezed the trigger, and there followed the familiar downfall of hammer, the sparkle of flint on steel, the flash of the pan, and then the jump and bang of the long gun spouting smoke into the sunshine. I thanked God reverently for the smoke. It spared me the sight of him toppling into the channel, and later, when Abner Cannell saw the wet stains on my powder-smudged cheeks, I knuckled my eyes and loudly damned the burnt saltpeter for smarting them so. There was a dead silence after the shot, and the leading boat came to a stop in a tangle of oars, as Father had foreseen. But he had not reckoned with the man in the boat behind. Sparhawk was no fool. He had seen the curious heads and pointing muskets of Simeon's militiamen and quickly slipped his tow and struck out with all his oarsmen's strength for the cover of the *Lizard's* guns. At that moment someone behind us fired, then another, and in a moment my father's wild cursing was drowned in a ragged volley that seemed to spurt from every stump and boulder on the Point. The smoke came rolling down to us, and Mark and I swung up Father in his chair and stumbled off with him to shelter. He railed at us for cowards and beat our heads with frenzied fists all the way to the rocks. There we could see dimly Bradford's sloop safely aground inside the bar and Sparhawk's boat fairly walking across the water on its oars. But the leading boat was gone, and in its place was a raffle of floating oars and wet black heads, with the water all about them jumping up in little bright jets.

"The schooners!" my father roared, and his voice cracked. "Fire on the schooners, fools!" As if to confirm his judgment there came now a shocking broadside from the anchored privateers and a whir and tearing in the scanty trees and bushes like a flight of woodcock flushed from cover, a voice crying out in pain amongst the rocks, a sound of hail on the roofs and walls of the tavern and the houses and sheds beyond, shingles flying and falling in the silence afterward like brittle autumn leaves. In that silence we reloaded and began to fire at the vague shapes of the vessels in the smoke. The privateers thundered back at us with every cannon, swivel, and musket they could bring to bear. We ducked at the shrieking blasts of grape, though most went far over our heads, and we fired and fired, till the gun barrels blistered the touch, and the shimmer of hot air over them ruined the aim. Voices arose—Father's, Simeon's, Sergeant Major Tinkham's—calling on the men to save their powder for the work to come. For it seemed certain that the Salem men, no cowards, would drop down past Ballast Cove to land their whole force and storm the town. But the ordered path of our destiny lay in other ways, and two more years of war were to pass before our town saw fighting in its streets.

The privateers chose to lie at their anchors within musket shot and hammer it out with us, ship against shore. A wasteful burning of good powder on both sides, for our muskets could not hurt the ships, though our lead must have made the splinters fly, and their four-pounders could not dislodge determined men well hidden amongst rocks and stumps. We had the weather advantage. A waft of air down the river blew the privateers' cannon smoke back in their faces and sent our own smoke down to them. Our supply of cartridges was spent, and men and boys were dodging back to the wagon in the tavern yard and fetching powder and balls all thrown into a hat together and tearing up their shirts for wadding. The men from the Falls had arrived and with them a rabble of whooping Micmacs; and what with the thunder of cannon and the fusillade jumping from every part of the Point and the Salem men cheering and ours yelling back, and the Indians adding their high dog yapping to the din, the world seemed ready to split apart.

We had set Father in his chair between two great rocks, where he could peer out as if through a loophole, while Mark and I fired over the tops. I was aware of small sounds behind me and once I saw Parson Cheever there, pointing a musket into the smoke and snapping a worthless flint again and again and calling on the Lord to make him fruitful. I put my hand behind me for the powder horn, and my fingers closed on a cartridge, freshly made, by the feel of the paper. I accepted it as a man accepts the rain from heaven and tore the end in my teeth, primed my pan, poured the rest of the powder down the hot barrel, and rammed ball and paper down after it. In a moment I was groping again, and there was another cartridge at my hand. I looked around then and saw Fear and my mother down on their knees, with an apron spread on the ground and a little black heap of powder, a packet of cartridge paper, and a scatter of lead balls upon it. Their nimble fingers were making cartridges like magic.

Fear looked up, and, "Where did you learn that?" I cried.

Her eyes were very wide; she cried up to me defiantly, "At Fort Cumberland!"

I threw back my head and laughed at the mad world. I noticed then a flutter of bunting going up the flagstaff by the tavern, where in time of peace the fishermen of the Point hoisted pennants to signal ships inbound. The Widow Dexter was hoisting a faded and much-creased British union. Very strange it looked there. We had never flown a flag in our town until then, and the sight of it filled me with rage. I had hated the flag of Britain ever since I saw it flapping from the *Senegal's* gaff, day after gloomy day in the winter of '75, and I had damned it for King George's handkerchief as I watched it flying on Fort Cumberland. I started toward the tavern, to tell the silly woman to take it down, and Father caught my passing wrist in a grip of iron.

"Let go!" I screamed at him. "We're fighting for ourselves, not England or its king!"

"Stop being a fool!" he snarled. "It's done! The flag's up! By God, it must go on flying now if we have to hold it up with our hands! No surrender—now or ever. 'King or Congress, no three ways about it'— that's what he said, the Salem man—under my own roof, damme! So be it, then! Look there!"

The smoke had opened for a moment and the sun was shining on the *Lizard's* ensign.

"That's the Congress flag?"

"Yes, yes—but——"

He jerked a finger at the Widow Dexter's bunting. "Then this is ours, if one and one make two!"

Ay, the British flag was ours, by the simplest rule of arithmetic, and all this gunpowder was blowing us apart from the America we had known. What the outcome would be not one of us could guess, though we knew the deep sources of American strength and saw the weakness of the king's in the very presence of these privateers, attacking our town in broad daylight under the nose of the Halifax admiral.

The utter and final separation of the thirteen colonies from the old country seemed fantastic still, and the separation of Nova Scotia from New England was like cutting an arm from a living body, an outrage to humanity and common sense. We were to learn bloodily in the time to come. My father had foreseen that today's events in our town would prove a sign and portent for the hitherto neutral Yankees of the whole south shore. But none of us saw the five long years of fratricide ahead, with New England craft increasing their raids on every part of our coast and a fleet of Nova Scotiamen—one of them under my own command—taking a savage price from the other side of Fundy's mouth.

Nor could we measure the war's aftermath, the astonishing flood of Tories banished from the thirteen colonies and their influence on our own province and the vast empty country to the west. They brought a standard of life and education that we had not known—and needed. But they brought also what we did not need, a black hatred of the victorious states that has not died in my time and will not in the time of my children's children if statesmen are not wise.

For me the separation was one of regret that deepened as the war-time rancor faded. For me as for many another, New England remains the home of our fathers, the natural center of our trade and our learning, the region to which we belong by all the rules of sentiment and geography; while England remains afar, a country we have never seen and know not, though we have seen our children with shining faces sing "God Save the King."

The loyalist exiles from the thirteen colonies have swelled our towns and villages and carved the new province of New Brunswick out of Nova Scotia's sprawling bulk and peopled the great rich country of Ontario, and their children have married ours and turned their faces west where in the old days we looked south.

Someday we shall make a nation in this northern wilderness where now is only a scatter of poor British colonies. What form it will take I cannot see, but one thing I know—that nation will rule itself. For out of our struggle here by the sea has emerged a notion of self-government that cannot die and will not be denied while there's a Blue Nose man to fight for it with tongue or pen—or fist, come to that.

We have journeyed some way along that road, and amongst many things I have seen my old friend and fellow rebel Richard Uniacke return in triumph to represent our county of Queens in the provincial assembly, become attorney general of Nova Scotia, and finally a member of the Council itself.

Ay, and I have burned the midnight candles with him, talking of these very things, in his mansion at Mount Uniacke, where we halted on our way to prison so very long ago.

CHAPTER 52

To Other Arms

THE FIGHT—if such a sorry burning of powder could be called a fight —came to an abrupt end when the *Lizard* and *Washington* cut their cables and hoisted their bullet-riddled sails. They took the Bermuda sloop with them, and as they began to move Captain Sparhawk's voice came faint but defiant against the warm breeze off the land. "We'll be back!"—a promise kept.

I jumped on a boulder and cried down the wind to him, "We'll be waiting!" And that promise was kept also. Not without heart searching, for there remained many in our town who clung to neutral notions and reproached us for shedding New England blood, and pious Colonel Perkins was to try many another compromise before he and they gave in to destiny at last.

The affair had seemed both long and short. I put it at an hour or more, and some said two or three, and Abednego Tappitt the town half-wit was fond of telling afterward how we "fit like Satan's devils from dark to dark." But the Widow Dexter, sitting calmly in her sanded parlor and regarding the clock, declared it took no more than three quarters of an hour from first to last.

The privateers fired a parting blast of ball and grape into the fishermen's huts at Herring Cove as they went out, and we marched several miles along the harbor shore in case they fancied a landing farther down. But they held on to sea, and that was the last we saw of them for weeks.

"They've got a bellyful!" said Tinkham, the militia sergeant major.

My father turned on him roughly. "None o' that! They're hard men yonder and they'll want hard pay for this day's work; depend on't. We must make a proper earthwork on the Point and send to Halifax for cannon and ammunition. From this time on we must keep a watch on the harbor mouth, and every man must keep his musket handy and his powder dry."

And, "Mark!"

"Sir?"

"Bring up the wagon and take me home. Your mother's there by now, I reckon. Silly woman! No business here! No business here!"

I muttered, "Luke . . . does she . . . ?"

The eyes he turned to me were hard as flint. "No. He went in the privateer. Let it go at that. Mind!"

I nodded dumbly, watching the wagon jolt away, wondering how long Mother could remain ignorant of a thing the whole town knew. I wonder still. I only know that she never again mentioned Luke's name in my presence, all the days she lived.

I felt like Cain. In a shuddering spasm of wretchedness I turned to seek Fear, instinctively, as a hurt dog seeks the shade. Nothing was more natural. Preachers never understand why love and war go hand in hand, why in time of horror and bloodshed a man should turn to a woman, and not to Heaven, for comfort and release. Heaven is too far and much too bodiless at such a moment; that is why the good God put woman in the world and made her what she is. In her, seeking forgetfulness, a man can find his soul again. I know that now. But I was not thinking of my soul when I ran shouting Fear's name that morning. I knew only that I must find her quickly or go mad. Only she could save me from this black and shaking terror of myself. If I could let my mind fill with the love of her, see only her, feel only her, know only her, if I could surrender myself utterly to her, then the nightmare must remain outside. And if she loved me—if she loved me the world was right and good and sweet, and so long as she loved me nothing evil could ever touch it.

Fear! Fear! She was not amongst the anxious women standing silent in the tavern yard. I took the path through the fish lots. Suddenly, miraculously, there she was, sitting on Tinkham's kitchen doorstep; rather, my mother sat on the step, and Fear was on her knees beside her with the bright brown head buried in the lap where I had taken all my troubles as a boy.

A cannon ball had pierced the shingled house wall, and Tinkham's youngsters were fingering the splintered hole and chattering curiously.

My ears still sang with the shooting, and I shouted loudly, as the deaf do.

"Mother! Mother, is she hurt?"—flinging down my gun and running.

The brown head did not move. My mother gave me a grave little smile and said quietly, "Just wrought-up, poor lamb. She'll feel better when she's had her cry out. Are you all right, David?"

"Yes. Father and Mark have gone home."

"So shall we, by and by. Do you feel like walking now, my dear?"

Fear lifted her head and nodded. She did not look at me. They stood up together, clinging to each other as if I did not exist. I was in no mood to be ignored like that. I dragged Fear into my arms, crushing and kissing her desperately and crying that I could wait no more and would wait no more, that she belonged to me and no one could ever take her from me, that nothing stood between us but a letter, a ghost, a loyalty to a sentiment that was dead—Heaven knows what magnificent nonsense I babbled there. Fear submitted meekly to all this. It was my mother who brought me to my senses, speaking sharply as if to an hysterical child.

"Stop shouting!" she said tartly. "The girl will have something to say on that, I think. She's told me something of herself and you— and if I were her I wouldn't say Aye or No without a decent offer of marriage. Look at yourself, David Strang—acting like a drunken Indian. In front of these children too!"

But there was pity in her eyes and understanding, and it was a mother pleading for her son who turned to Fear and said very gently, "Do you think you could be his wife, my dear? Now? Without waiting any more? He needs you so very much. Don't hold the girl so, David! She can't breathe. Now, my dear."

Fear said not a word. She simply lifted her head from my breast and looked at me. In her eyes was the courage that always belied her name and the promise of heaven and earth, of all that a lover could ask. A word would have spoiled that moment. I put my thirsty lips to hers and drank.

"Hmmm!" interrupted my prim mother at last. "There's Justice Hunt's house just up the road."

Justice Hunt, his gray locks powder-stained and awry, was just putting his musket back on the caribou horns over his mantel. He was full of the day's affair and its consequences and was a little testy when we insisted on a matter so trifling as marriage. Nevertheless he turned a pair of quizzical blue eyes on Fear and said baldly, "Heard ye'd married a British officer to Halifax."

Without a word she produced Gorham's letter. He had to call Ma'am Hunt for his spectacles and read the thing slowly, mouthing the words—I wanted to kick him, old as he was, but Fear stood all the while with her eyes on mine, and all her strong and sensitive heart was in them. The ceremony was short enough to suit me—the old man gabbled it through impatiently—and when it was done my mother declared, "There ought to be a ring. No woman's a wife without one."

Fear's fingers were bare; even the bandages were gone, for the magical balsam had done its work. But Justice Hunt surprisingly rose to the occasion. Formerly he had done some trucking with the Indians at the Falls and rummaged in a chest of trade gewgaws and found a small brass ring that fitted her finger neatly. (I got her a gold one later on, out of a prize I took in Block Island Sound, but she would have none of it and wore the brass one all the years until she died.)

The day was far gone now, and bright-eyed Ma'am Hunt insisted on our staying to supper, fussing over Fear, and exclaiming, "A bride in my house, well, well! And very nice, too, after all this fighting and foolishness!"

When supper was finished it was candlelighting time, and a silence fell upon us. I was wondering where I should take my bride, knowing what my father would say. I had a notion to ask Ma'am Hunt if we could stay the night, but my mother settled that. She stood up, brushing out her skirts.

"And now, my dears—home!" It was a command.

Wordless, we walked through the town together. The winding street had never seemed so long, but at last we turned in the path to the familiar door.

"Give me that letter," said my mother briskly, "and wait here a few minutes."

I felt my darling trembling and slipped my arm about her waist. We waited an age. At last I said roughly, "Enough! Let's go in and face him down and have done with it. We've our own life to live, and the devil with his opinions!"

We entered the kitchen together and found my father in his chair at the table. Mother stood at his shoulder regarding us calmly. A pair of candles burned on the long board. Joanna had got his supper and gone, and someone—Mark, I suppose—had fetched him a jug of rum from the cellar. His thin face was flushed with drink, and I drew Fear back in the doorway defensively.

Resolutely Mother said, "Matthew, this is our new daughter, David's wife."

He turned his head slowly and gave my girl the full blaze of his fierce old eyes, looking her up and down as if she were a heifer come to market.

At last he growled, "Umph! Takes after her mother. A good build, long in the leg and full in the bodice. No Bingay there! Ha! A slim run and a good sheer's best—women or ships. Think ye can take the itch out o' his feet?"

"I'll try," my darling said bravely, and smiled a little, though her eyes were wet.

"Umph! David!"

"Yes sir?"

"Take her to bed!"

I needed no candle to light me along the dark hall to the familiar stair and I paused at its foot, out of sentiment, to kiss my sweetheart where Mark had kissed Joanna long ago. From the lighted rectangle of the kitchen doorway came my mother's voice, chiding Father for his brusqueness, and I heard him burst out, "Peace, woman, peace! The girl knows what I mean. She'll breed good sons and keep a bit between his teeth . . . what he needs . . . and he'll not mind the curb so long as the taste is sweet . . . eh, lass? . . . Did I? . . . Did I, ever?"

My chamber window was full open to the warm May night, and there was a sliver of new moon over the dark pine wood to the west, like a slim, naked woman reclining and waiting her lover. Small frogs were piping a chorus in the swamp by the tan-yard brook, and owls were hooting in the pines, and below the house was a lapping of water where the river met the tide and the splash of a salmon leaping for joy at the first taste of sweet water from the hills. On the side of the low town ridge I knew the wild pear was in blossom again and the slender white birches putting on their leaves, and the alders were heavy with catkins; and the sheep laurel in its fashion had opened its fiery flowers before the leaves, so great was its haste to be blooming. And there were dandelion and buttercup like a scatter of gold coins in the pastures, and slender violets cool in the shade of the brookside, ay, and wild strawberry flowering white on the harbor slopes.

There was a scent and stir of these things in the darkness and a smell of plowed earth from our small fields and the faint, rich reek of burned brushwood which always spells spring to my nostrils. And there was the familiar smell of the room, the mingled smell of paint and homemade soap and clean bed linen freshly aired, and new and strange and delightful there, the scent of my love's own hair on my shoulder, of her unsteady breathing, and the subtle and charming woman fragrance that a man breathes in through his pores.

This was where I belonged, in my father's house, whose timbers had grown in the woods of Massachusetts and come with him in the ship in the beginning. Scornfully—because the first settlers expected Indian trouble and clamored for land hard by the sea—my father had built it here in the northern outskirt, at the very edge of the forest, whence the broad river flowed with its mysterious whisper of menace. A symbol then and a symbol now for all of us, sound of beam and stout of post and rafter, all doweled together like the timbers of a ship, secure against all winds and weathers, and built upon the rock spine of the country itself.

Here a man could find security, so long as he kept his head high and his fists hard. And between these walls if nowhere else he could have peace—the peace that a man finds in the arms of his love, easing his taut nerves in her supple warmth, drawing strength from her eager yielding as lean rivers lie in our green Nova Scotia valleys, drawing strength from the round loveliness of the hills.

The house of the Strangs, which had been full and was now so empty, would be filled with young voices again. There would be sons, as my father prophesied. They would be tall and hard of hand and voice, granting friendship sparingly but giving with it a loyalty unshakeable and ready to fight, suffer, endure anything for the sake of it. They would be a little hard with their women, but passionate in their tender moments, and women would endure the ice for the sake of the fire. But our sons would never give themselves wholly to anything but this rocky homeland on the sea's edge, where life is a struggle that demands a man's utmost and will take no less, where beauty alone is bountiful, and only death comes easily; where courage springs from the eternal rock like the clear singing rivers, like the deep-rooted forest itself.